"YOU'RE BEAUTIFUL."

Voicing the thought came hard to him—he was unaccustomed to expressing such sentiments.

"I am?" she asked in barely more than a whisper. Her eyes were riveted on his face and he felt her breath fan his hand.

Yes, she was. The delicate planes of her face offered him a dozen places he wanted to kiss. Her long lashes, dark and lush, framed her eyes and made them offer promises he knew she could not keep. He wanted to skim his hands along her breasts and feel their fullness against his palms. He longed to tuck her in his arms.

But he could say none of those things. And those desires were only a daydream. He let his fingertips rise to graze her flushed cheek and run along the edge of her jaw. He just wanted to touch something soft in a life marked by coarseness.

"Kyla." He pressed his forehead against hers. "Kyla, may I kiss you?"

Desperate Hearts

Alexis Harrington

A TOPAZ BOOK

TOPAZ
Published by the Penguin Group
Penguin Books USA Inc., 375 Hudson Street
New York, New York 10014, U.S.A.
Penguin Books Ltd, 27 Wrights Lane,
London W8 5TZ, England
Penguin Books Australia Ltd, Ringwood,
Victoria, Australia
Penguin Books Canada Ltd, 10 Alcorn Avenue,
Toronto, Ontario, Canada M4V 3B2
Penguin Books (N.Z.) Ltd, 182–190 Wairau Road,
Auckland 10, New Zealand

Penguin Books Ltd, Registered Offices:
Harmondsworth, Middlesex, England

First published by Topaz, an imprint of Dutton Signet,
a division of Penguin Books USA Inc.

First Printing, December, 1996
10 9 8 7 6 5 4 3 2 1

 REGISTERED TRADEMARK—MARCA REGISTRADA

Printed in the United States of America

BOOKS ARE AVAILABLE AT QUANTITY DISCOUNTS WHEN USED TO PROMOTE
PRODUCTS OR SERVICES. FOR INFORMATION PLEASE WRITE TO PREMIUM MAR-
KETING DIVISION, PENGUIN BOOKS USA INC., 375 HUDSON STREET, NEW YORK,
NEW YORK 10014

*For being my tireless cheering section
thanks to Janet Brayson, Susan Crose,
and Marg Vajdos.*

*For the inspiration,
thanks to Don Henley, Glenn Frey,
and most especially to
Alex McArthur and Suzy Amis.*

Prologue

❦

Blakely, Oregon
September, 1895

"Apparently Mrs. Bailey wasn't interested in your offer to, shall we say, comfort her in her bereavement? How ungrateful of her." Luke Jory leaned back in his swivel chair, his long-fingered hands steepled in front of his chest as he considered the man standing before him. "She must be more discerning than I gave her credit for."

Tom Hardesty stood on the other side of the desk in the rancher's office. He shifted from one foot to the other, working hard to formulate an answer. He resisted the impulse to cover his face where a three-inch-long knife cut was finally beginning to heal. Several stitches had been required to close the wound that ran from his temple nearly to his jaw. An ugly scar was bound to be the result.

"Well, Hardesty, what's your explanation?"

He felt as though he were a boy being called to task

by the schoolmaster. Beneath his feet lay a thick blue carpet. Expensive furniture filled the room. Jory liked his comforts, and he had a cultured tone and a high-falutin' way of talking. Even when he didn't shout, that attitude, combined with his dark, piercing eyes, could make a man feel like a skewered pig turning on a spit. When he did raise his voice, and that was often enough, the sound made Hardesty think of the gates of hell opening. But it didn't do to show him fear. No sir. Jory could home in on fear like a hungry wolf smelled blood.

"The woman left at least a month ago." It galled Hardesty to admit it. "Word is that she's run off to find Jace Rankin."

Jory sat up straight again, tight lines forming on either side of his mouth. He brought his fist down on the desktop. "Yes, I know that! Damn it, Hardesty, we have a nice operation going here in the region, and it's finally running smoothly. If you've jeopardized it because you think more often with your lust than your brain, I will personally see that you pay. The last thing I need or want is someone like Rankin poking around here. You told me the woman wouldn't be a problem. Do you know which way she went?"

Hardesty felt his neck grow hot. "Rankin's in Silver City. I got a wire from a couple of our men who spotted him there. If we've got him, she shouldn't be far behind. I'll teach her not to run off again."

"I want Rankin stopped—I don't give a tinker's damn what you do with the woman." Jory stared pointedly at the scar on Hardesty's face. "Or what she does to you. That's *your* business, and I don't want it interfering with mine. Report back to me when you know something worthwhile. I expect that to be soon." He turned the swivel chair away from Hardesty and looked out the window, effectively dismissing him.

Tom Hardesty left Luke Jory's office, burning with anger and humiliation. That Bailey bitch had been making a fool out of him for years, but nothing—not even her knife blade ripping down his face—could douse the fire she lit in his blood. That long hair and creamy skin . . . the very thought of her stirred him up until he couldn't think straight.

Furious that the Bailey woman had slipped away from him, he mounted his horse and wheeled it around. But, he recalled, the two men in Silver City had instructions to bring her back. And when she returned . . .

He had mastered her once, and he would do it again. This time, she wouldn't forget who was in charge.

Chapter One

Silver City, Idaho
September, 1895

"Better get the sheriff, Noah," Chester Sparks called to a youngster on the other side of the street. "A mean-looking cuss has someone cornered in my saloon and he don't seem to be interested in a card game."

The boy took off running, and Chester and his customers lingered on the sidewalk, curious and pop-eyed, peeking gingerly over the swinging doors that opened into the barroom of the Magnolia Saloon. Just moments earlier they'd stampeded out through those doors, beers and cards abandoned, when a man Chester originally mistook for a youth walked in and leveled his rifle on a drifter holding a poker hand.

All they could see was the back of the man's head and most of that was hidden by his wide-brimmed hat and the turned-up collar of his duster. Chester had a bad feeling about this. As rowdy and wild as this town had been over the years, and with all the fights and shootings that had occurred, nobody had ever been killed in *his* place.

That might be about to change.

In the Magnolia Saloon, Jace Rankin stared down at the saddle tramp sitting at a table by the stove. The man's silver hatband gleamed like tiny mirrors in the shaft of afternoon sun that cut through the side window. A pile of money was heaped in front of him and he held a fan of cards in one hand. The other hand, Rankin figured, rested on the grip of his gun, hidden by the terrified saloon girl who sat immobilized on his knee. She wore only a camisole and drawers, and a flimsy shawl. Her upturned face was ghastly pale under her powder and rouge. Rankin pressed his mouth into a tight line as he struggled with cold fury.

"Get moving, honey," Rankin instructed the girl. She leapt to her feet and hurried toward the doors, her backless shoes flapping.

Rankin held his attention on the gambler, appraising his winnings. "Let's see if your luck will hold, Clark. You put both hands on the table where I can see them and maybe I won't have to shoot you."

Offering him an arrogant smirk, Sawyer Clark dropped the cards while keeping his eyes fixed on the barrel of the Henry rifle aimed at his forehead. Slowly, he rested his hands on the scratched tabletop.

"I see you know my name," Clark said, "but who are you, *boy*?"

Rankin felt his blood rise at the insult, although he'd heard variations of it often enough. Because of his size and youthful face, people often supposed him to be a lot younger than his thirty years. But he had a certain reputation, justly earned, that made some people nervous and balanced the scales. He paused a beat before answering the man's question.

"Jace Rankin."

For the first time, Clark let his attention stray from the rifle to the face of the man holding it.

Rankin saw the man's throat work as he swallowed, and he felt an instant of satisfaction as Clark's bravado slipped away from him like a wet bar of soap. "So? What do you want? I don't have a price on my head." Clark grinned suddenly. "Before the law figures out I was involved, I'm gone."

"Not this time. I'll kill you first."

The grin faded. "What's your complaint, Rankin? You got nothing on me."

"I see you like the ladies," he replied, referring to the saloon girl who had scampered away.

"What of it?"

"Think back a few years. Remember a pretty young blonde in Salem, a blacksmith's wife? Celia McGuire?"

Clark shrugged negligently. "Can't say as I do. I've known a lot of women in a lot of towns. I never bothered with piddling details like whether they were married." A chuckle rolled out of him. "Did her husband hire you to find me?"

Rankin drew a slow breath, working to keep his finger easy on the trigger. "This isn't about some barroom scrape, Clark, or a jilted husband. She's the woman you bragged about killing while you sat in that poker game a couple of months ago in Burns. You strangled her for laughing at you, you said. Remember now?"

"So?"

Rankin gently touched the rifle's cool muzzle to a spot just above the bridge of Clark's nose. "Celia McGuire was my sister."

Comprehension flooded Clark's expression and sweat popped out on his forehead. "You can't prove nothing."

Rankin smiled. "Oh, but I can. It doesn't matter anyway. I could shoot you right now and save everyone a lot of time and trouble. This old Henry wouldn't leave much of your head," he said, leaning into the weapon. "And I could walk away from your bleeding carcass without a twinge. But we're going to do this right. The sheriff will be along any minute and I've got witnesses willing to testify, Clark. Riled witnesses. You shouldn't cheat at cards—it can come back on you."

The remnants of Clark's smug expression contorted into a malevolent glower. "I ain't going to jail over some lousy hay roll, not for a minute. She had it coming—she sure as hell don't laugh at anyone now." In the blink of an eye the drifter overturned the table and reached for the revolver strapped to his right hip.

Rankin jumped back, avoiding the shower of cards and beer. Time and events slowed to a crawl and became slightly distorted. Even Clark's actions seemed sluggish, as though he were moving through winter-cold molasses, giving Rankin plenty of time to take aim and pull the Henry's trigger—

* * *

"Leave the bottle."

"Yessir, Mr. Rankin." The skinny, nervous bartender who had introduced himself as Chester Sparks polished a tumbler on his apron. He set it next to the whiskey bottle he had delivered to the back table, then hovered solicitously. "Is there anything else you want?"

Rankin eyed the nosy group that loitered in a semi-circle behind Sparks. They maintained a safe distance, but they were gawking just the same.

"Yeah—to be left alone." With slow, deliberate movements, he laid the Henry across the table. The rifle seemed especially heavy.

The action had the desired effect. Chester looked at the long, polished barrel and flinched. He took two good paces backward. After all, the bartender had seen him kill a man with that weapon just an hour earlier, and right here in his own saloon. Even the old man playing the piano froze, choking off the peppy melody of "Camptown Races" in mid "do-dah."

Chester turned and herded off the spectators. "You boys heard Mr. Rankin. Let him be now. We've had enough excitement around here today."

The men shuffled to the bar with backward glances, murmuring among themselves. Rankin stared them down in order to hurry their progress. A couple of drunks at a corner table stared at him as if he were the most interesting thing on the face of the earth. Their curiosity felt different from that of the others, but no less annoying. He watched them until they looked away, then he lowered his gaze to the bottle in front of him and breathed a deep sigh.

Nearly seven years after his sister's murder, Jace Rankin had finally found the man who had killed her. The sheriff, after talking to him and the other witnesses of today's events, was satisfied, and the matter was considered closed. Now Sawyer Clark lay stretched out in the undertaker's back room with a bullet in his chest.

For a long time Rankin had believed that Celia's husband, Travis McGuire, had strangled her. McGuire had even served five years of a life sentence for the crime. That was what being in love got a man. But when his accuser, in a deathbed confession, admitted to false testimony McGuire was freed.

It had been hard for Rankin to grasp McGuire's guilt—they'd been good friends. But once he had, it was even harder for him to let go of it.

He shrugged out of his duster and hunched over the table, hooking his boot heel on the chair rung. He made no move to pour a drink from the bottle Sparks had left him.

He ought to be celebrating. He had expected to celebrate. His vendetta had sent him looking for Travis first, then Clark. The search had taken him all over the Northwest. It had ended today, when he faced Clark in this dark, smoky saloon. After having eaten up so much of his life, it was now finally behind him.

So why didn't he feel better about it? It didn't bother him the slightest bit that he'd killed Clark. He'd assumed that might happen, depending on the circumstances. Without a second thought he'd killed other men, men with black hearts and no consciences. But this evening he felt a strange emptiness.

He had thought he would buy a saloon girl for the entire night, maybe get good and drunk. Well, he supposed he could get started on that. He let his hand drift down the side of the whiskey bottle. A stiff drink might do the trick—and shut off the questions bumping around in his head.

Tomorrow he'd cross into Oregon and head for Misfortune. He owed it to Travis to let him know that Celia's killer, the man he had spent five years in jail for, was dead. Then . . . what?

As if he could see the future in its clear amber depths, he studied the full shot glass on the table. He supposed he would go back to the job he'd been doing for ten years, the one that had earned him a reputation that generally made men think twice about crossing him. He had craved their nervous respect to make up for those years when no one had respected him at all.

But winter was coming again. It got damned cold up here, and every year seemed colder than the last. He hunched forward, with his elbows on the table and the shot glass between them. Maybe this year he'd go to California or Arizona—there were just as many wanted posters down there, and the weather was kinder. The more he thought about it, the more it appealed. He had nothing holding him here now—no kin, no friends, no grudges left to satisfy.

Just then, a drove of loud, braying miners burst into the saloon to disturb the funereal hush that hung over the waning autumn afternoon. They whooped and hollered like cowboys just in from three months on the trail, and they smelled a hundred times worse.

Rankin looked up, irritated. He couldn't even sit

here and drink in peace. And with their arrival he felt a subtle shift in the tension in the barroom.

Six or seven strong, the miners brought with them a cloud of dust and dragged along a scrawny kid Rankin figured was no older than fifteen or sixteen. Strung out in a line along the gouged pine bar, the rowdies ordered whiskey and beer.

"Come on, sonny," the loudest of them directed, "we'd better give you a *real* drink and wean you off that sody water you were pullin' at outside." The miner's coarse, bearded face bore a scar that looked to be a souvenir of a knife fight.

"I don't want any," the boy snarled, trying to twist away. "Let me go, you stinkin', shovel-pushin' ox, and give me back my gun!" The kid's words sounded tough, but his voice thinned out to a soprano twang, betraying his fear. His hat was knocked off in the tussle, revealing a head of fire-colored hair that grazed the tops of his thin shoulders. Rankin took note of the empty holster on the kid's right thigh.

"You mean this gun?" Scar-Face dangled a blue-barreled revolver in front of the boy's face. "You're pretty young to be carryin' a weapon like this. You'll have to prove you're a man to earn it back. What's your name, boy?"

"None of your damned business." The youngster pulled harder against the grip that Scar-Face had on the back of his collar, but he couldn't break away.

Unseen at his corner table, Rankin leaned back in his chair and watched the proceedings. He saw ice-cold terror in the kid's eyes as a whiskey glass was forced to his mouth. His only choice was to drink or drown. The boy coughed and sputtered, trying to catch his breath. The rest of the miners roared in amusement, and one clapped him on the back, nearly knocking him off his feet.

Bullies, Rankin thought. He hated bullies. As a kid he'd had more than his share of misery from them. He unhooked his boot heel and sat up.

"Let me go, you mangy bastard!" The youngster struggled like a wet cat.

"By God, you're a smart-mouthed little snot, aintcha," one of the other miners remarked with a booming laugh. "Full of piss and vinegar. Must be that red hair that gives you so much sass."

Behind the bar, Chester Sparks cleared his throat. "Clem, maybe you ought to let the boy go. I'd like to finish the day without any more fuss."

"You just stick to sellin' your beer, Sparks, and there won't *be* any fuss," the scar-faced Clem warned, pointing his finger in Chester's face. "We found this young'un hangin' around outside, all curiouslike. We aim to oblige him and show him what a man does in a saloon."

"I told you I was waitin' for someone," the kid protested. Clem tightened his hold on the back of the boy's shirt and shook him the way a dog would a rag doll.

"Hell, if you want to stick with that story, son, that's fine. We was all greenhorns once ourselves. Time you learned about life. Here, have another drink." Clem grabbed the whiskey bottle from the bar, sloshed another shot into the youngster's glass, and repeated the force feeding. Half the liquor dribbled down the front of the kid's shirt.

"Now, let's see if one of Chester's girls don't have time to make you a man proper. You're such a little spud, she'll probably let you dip for honey cheap. Anyway, it ain't good for a man not to get a leg across a gal now and then."

Clem scanned the barroom and spotted a saloon girl. "Gracie! Hey, Gracie! Look what we brung you!"

Rankin recognized the long-limbed painted female who had occupied Sawyer Clark's lap earlier. Seeing the youngster, she disentangled herself from her chair and sashayed over.

"Hi there, boys. Where'd you get this little rabbit?"

"You got a few minutes for him, don't you, Gracie?"

"Well, sure. I like 'em young. They're more polite. And they're quick." She flipped her shawl over her shoulder and surveyed her prospective customer. "This one looks a mite scared, but we'll get along just fine." She took his hand to pull him along.

The boy renewed his efforts to get away, kicking over a spittoon in the process. But the miners only laughed again and pushed him toward the stairs. Gracie stopped to take his face between her hands, and leaned in to kiss him.

This had gone far enough, in Rankin's opinion. Disgusted, he scanned the saloon. While the customers in the Magnolia watched with ardent interest, no one appeared inclined to break this up. The two drunks who had been watching him from the corner looked on with guarded interest but didn't move. Damned cowards, all of them. Obviously, Clem and his gang were just fearsome enough to keep the men in this place from defending a scared, unarmed kid. When the miners passed Rankin's table, he pushed back his chair and stood.

"Let the boy go."

Gracie turned toward Rankin and uttered a squeak. She looked at the boy again, as if really seeing him for the first time. She dropped his hand and backed away.

Clem pushed his battered hat farther down on his big, square head. "You'd best mind your own bidness, stranger. We're just having some fun with the little feller."

Rankin considered the youth. His face was the color of chalk. "He doesn't appear to be having fun. Find someone closer to your own size to push around."

Clem looked him up and down. A sour, knowing grin split his scarred face, revealing rotten teeth. "I guess that wouldn't be you, either, would it, runt?"

Like the wind sighing around the corners of a house, a quiet, wordless moan rolled through the spectators. At the surrounding tables, Rankin was aware of people rising and inching toward the door before profound silence blanketed the saloon. Sawyer Clark's smirk flashed through his mind.

He stepped closer, staring unblinkingly into the miner's ugly face. Clem didn't blink either.

Rankin heard Chester clear his throat again, harshly, as though he had a quail egg stuck in it. "Clem, this here is Jace Rankin—you know, the *bounty hunter*. He killed a man in here today."

Rankin felt all eyes focus on him, though his own gaze remained fixed on the miner.

"I ain't scairt of no son-of-a-bitchin' bounty hunter," Clem declared, but his eyelids twitched.

"You should be," Rankin whispered, and smiled slightly. Before the slow-moving Clem could react, he drew his revolver and nudged the miner's bearded chin with its point.

It took all of Rankin's willpower to keep from backing up; the miner's breath smelled as bad as an outhouse in July. From the corner of his eye he saw one of the other miners reaching for a long blade at his belt.

"If your friend doesn't let go of the hilt of his knife, you'll lose what's left of your bottom teeth when I blow off your jaw. I think Chester here will tell you that I mean it."

Chester nodded emphatically.

"Now let the boy go."

The color seemed to drain from Clem's face. "Well ... who gives a damn about this wet-tailed little pup, anyway?" He turned the boy loose with a hard push. "Get the hell out of here and go back to your mama."

"His gun?" Rankin reminded him.

Clem nodded impatiently at one of his cronies, who handed the boy his revolver. The kid grabbed it and scrambled to pick up his hat.

Rankin stepped back and holstered his own gun. "I hope you *gentlemen* won't be giving Chester any more trouble." He glanced at the bartender, who watched him with wide eyes and a frozen expression. "He's had a bad day."

"Come on, Clem," one of them mumbled. "This place ain't no fun anymore."

"No, it sure ain't," Clem groused, scratching his chin where the gunpoint had pressed. "Let's go down to the China Doll. They don't let kids hang around there to pester people." As a group, they turned and shuffled through the swinging doors.

Following them to the door, Rankin watched until they were far down the street, then he walked back to the bar. Cutting a wide path around him, the customers finally returned to their chairs.

The boy breathed a long, shaky sigh. His eyes were red with choked-back tears. He dropped his head and brushed at them impatiently. "Thanks," he mumbled to Rankin. Then with more vigor, "But I wasn't scared! I coulda handled them."

Rankin stared pointedly at the wet liquor stain on the boy's shirt, a memento of his ability to "handle" the miners. He didn't bother with a reply, but stepped around the slime from the capsized spittoon and brushed past him.

He reached into his pocket and flipped a silver dollar to Chester Sparks before walking back to the table to retrieve his duster, his rifle, and the bottle of whiskey.

"Y-you already paid me for the whiskey, Mr. Rankin." Chester held out the dollar as Rankin walked past the bar.

"Keep it. I'm going to the hotel. Your place attracts too much trouble to suit me."

Rankin stepped out into the lengthening shadows on the sidewalk and lit a cheroot. The sun had dropped behind the Owyhee Mountains but the street was still busy with mules, wagons, teamsters, and miners, all headed, it seemed, to the saloons and sporting houses here on Jordan Street. He leaned against an upright, scanning the shadows around him and the faces of approaching riders. Looking right and left was something he did partly out of habit—a bounty hunter was always a target for someone's revenge. And partly because he felt directionless tonight. He wasn't sure which way to turn. Right now, he was certain only that he wanted a clean bed and a quiet room. He headed down the sidewalk toward the hotel. So much for celebrating.

"Hey, Mr. Rankin, wait up!"

Looking over his shoulder, he saw the same pest he'd just left behind in the Magnolia. The boy's tangle with the miners apparently hadn't taught him to leave well enough alone. Rankin didn't stop.

The boy jogged up alongside him in the street, leading a good-looking dun. "Hey, wait a minute!"

Out here in the twilight, it was even more obvious that there wasn't much to the kid. He had bones like a bird and no muscle to speak of—even Gracie might have bested him. His clothes hung on him, and beneath the dirt his face was smooth as a cue ball. Hell, his voice had barely even changed. He looked like he had probably always been the butt of harassment and torment from older, bigger kids.

Rankin could empathize with that.

"Shouldn't you quit while you're ahead, kid?" Rankin grumbled. He glanced ahead at the hotel in the distance, where yellow lamplight gleamed from the windows, and he kept walking. The boy trotted to keep up with the pace Rankin set.

"My *name* is Kyle Springer. And I've got business with you. You're the reason I was waitin' outside the

Magnolia in the first place. I've been lookin' for you for more than a month."

Oh, damn it, Rankin thought, consumed with bitter weariness. He'd probably just saved the kid's skinny neck so that he could challenge him to a draw here in the street.

It didn't happen often, but once in a while some hot-head got a yen for the kind of reputation that outgun-ning Jace Rankin would bring. And this one was just a drip of a boy, with pale skin and a few freckles to go with that red hair. Well, he had to hand it to him—the kid might not have common sense, or the brawn to make up for its lack, but he had grit.

"Yeah? What do you want with me, *Kyle*?" He went along with the steps of this dance, but he knew where it was headed.

"I want to hire you to kill a man." The young voice was cold, flat—devoid of anger or any other emotion. His eyes matched his tone.

Rankin stopped in his tracks and glared at him. That sure as hell wasn't what he'd been expecting. He tossed away the cheroot. "Not interested." He turned and walked on.

"I can pay you," Kyle called after him. "Isn't that what you want?" He could hear Kyle's steps and the horse's on the hard-packed dirt as they trotted along behind him.

Rankin had his standards, and his anger flared at the insulting question. "You'd better get your facts straight, kid. I'm a bounty hunter, not a hired gun." He sidestepped a mule skinner who came staggering out of a noisy saloon.

"You've killed men. Everybody knows that, and I saw you shoot that drifter today. I saw it through the window."

Rankin's hand tightened on the Henry. "If you were watching, then you saw it was self-defense. It always has been self-defense. Anyway, I guess you don't know why I was after Clark."

"It don't matter to me. Some people need killin'."

Rankin stopped again and faced the kid. His curiosity got the best of him. "Like who?"

As if a grim memory cut across his mind, Kyle let his gaze drift to the mountains that embraced Silver City. The horse whickered and nudged his shoulder. Catching his balance, the boy wiped his nose on his shirt cuff, then tucked his hair behind his ears.

"His name's Tom Hardesty. He murdered a man over in Blakely, Oregon, and stole a ranch there that rightfully belongs to me."

"What makes it yours?"

A sharp autumn wind rushed down the street. Keeping one fist clamped on the horse's reins, Kyle hunched his thin shoulders and shivered. "My pa left it to me. But Tom—he's one of Luke Jory's bootlicks. Jory heads up the Vigilance Union. He arranged for Tom and the Union to come and force me off the ranch so's Tom could take it."

Rankin hadn't been to Blakely in several years; vigilantes there were news to him. "So? Tell the sheriff."

The boy hitched up the waist of his jeans with his free hand, then absently stroked the dun's nose. "I did tell the sheriff, but it didn't do no good. The Vigilance Union *owns* Blakely. They can make the law do whatever they want. They're just a bunch of lyin', thievin' bastards who murder men so they can steal their cattle and land. There's been a lot of that goin' on. That's why I set out to find you. The Vigilance Union has to be wiped out."

Rankin had never been a defender of widows and orphans, and he wasn't about to take up the chore now. "Forget it. Too messy. I'm only interested in bounties. And this isn't my fight." He looked up and saw that he'd stopped in front of the undertaker's dark windows. "Besides, I've got business to take care of in Misfortune, and that's where I'm headed in the morning. You get on your horse, go back to Blakely, and try to stay out of trouble. Those miners could've carved you up for dinner back there."

A tinge of desperation crept into Kyle's voice. "I got no place to go *to*, not in Blakely, not anywhere. If you won't help, I'll find someone who ain't afraid to. Or I'll do the job myself." He rested his hand on the butt of the revolver in his holster. "I swear to God I will."

"Yeah? Have you ever shot anybody?"

A sigh and downcast eyes were Kyle's answer.

Rankin nodded. "It doesn't make you feel better, and it doesn't mean you're a man. Besides you'd probably get yourself killed for your trouble."

"Well, I gotta *try*, at least!" Kyle curled a hand over the dun's bridle. "I got nothing left to lose, anyway."

Rankin stared at the boy in the gathering darkness. He was too young to feel that way, but Rankin understood it. There seemed to be a number of things about this kid that he understood. And one or two that he didn't. But he had a lot of stubborn courage despite his wispy build.

That brought memories back to Rankin of a boyhood spent first running from bullies, then eventually standing up to them and taking the inevitable beatings that resulted. The worst ones had come from his stepfather, until the day he strapped on a gun and threatened to pull the trigger.

And now, after thirty years of a hard life, he faced another cold winter and another youth who reminded him of all those beatings. Maybe it was something in the kid's eyes. Later he'd probably kick himself, but he asked, "Can you prove that Hardesty killed anyone?"

"I saw him do it," Kyle answered, shivering again. He leaned against his dun's shoulder for a moment.

Rankin shrugged. "I don't give a damn about politics and I'm no do-good, so I'm not about to tangle with vigilantes. And I won't take this job to kill Hardesty. I'll see to it that he's delivered to the law in another town to stand trial." Seeing that Kyle was about to object, he cut him off. "Believe me, that's a sight more trouble than just shooting him—but it's the only way I'll do this. I have to go to Misfortune first, though. Are you still interested?"

"But it won't help to get rid of Hardesty if Luke Jory and them damned vigilantes are still around. They ain't gonna leave me in peace."

"That's my offer. Are you interested or not?"

The kid looked disappointed. "Yeah," he grumped. "I guess."

"How much are you planning to pay?

Kyle stared at him dead on. "I'm not sayin' how much I've got."

"And I'm not asking. The bounties I go after usually start at about five hundred dollars."

"F-five?" Kyle stammered.

"But I'm willing to help you out for half of that. Two fifty."

"Well . . ."

"Damn, kid, you don't think I'm going to do this for free—"

"No!" The horse sidestepped nervously. "I'm gonna pay you, but I ain't got the money with me."

"Where is it?"

"It's in a strongbox, buried in a secret place."

"Let me guess—I'll bet this 'secret place' is at the ranch."

Kyle hunched his shoulders and nodded.

Figuring he already knew the answer, Rankin had to ask anyway, "Have you got *any* money with you?"

Kyle wiped his nose on his sleeve again and glanced at his scuffed boots. "Yeah, seventy-eight cents."

"Have you got a place to bed down tonight?"

"I've been sleepin'—out—" He gestured over his shoulder in the general direction of the scrubby hills outside of town.

Rankin shook his head—this was getting worse by the second. The kid probably didn't have one penny more than seventy-eight cents anywhere, and there were too many things about this situation that bothered him. He sure as hell didn't want to take on the job of nursemaiding this weaner. It was hard for him to imagine how the kid had even gotten this far from

Blakely. He knew he should walk away from this situation right now.

But he didn't.

Instead, he dug into the pocket of his jeans and pulled out two silver dollars. "Here," he said and tossed the coins to Kyle, who scrambled to catch them with one hand. "Take your horse to the livery, then get a room at the hotel. If you still want my help, be out front at daybreak."

Kyle gave him an even stare, and a moment of silence passed. Finally he looked at the money, then closed his fingers around it. "I'll pay you back," he insisted, "just as soon as I can get to the strongbox." He turned, hauled himself up into the dun's saddle, and headed toward the livery down the street.

Rankin regarded the lift of the youth's chin—proud, defiant, foolhardy. The kid had guts, if nothing else. And he had to admire that.

The boy who had introduced himself as Kyle Springer closed the door to his hotel room and turned the key.

He threw his hat and the poke carrying his belongings on the mattress, then fished through his pockets for a match to light the plain bedside lamp. Purple dusky shadows gave way to the bright kerosene flame, and he looked around to see what Jace Rankin's dollar had bought. It ate at him that he'd had to take money from the bounty hunter. Kyle usually paid his own way or did without, and if he weren't so dead-dog tired, he'd have refused. But his struggles, first with the miners, then with Rankin, had drained the sap right out of him.

It wasn't the best room in the place—faded green paint clung to chipped walls and the shabby jumble of furniture sported threadbare upholstery. But the iron bed looked clean and inviting, and it beat the hell out of spending another night in the open. The earth was like granite, and the cold made his hands ache. These past few mornings he had awakened to a hard chill and frosted landscapes.

Bouncing once on the mattress, Kyle decided that the springs wouldn't screech enough to wake him. At any rate, he was so weary he imagined he wouldn't move once he closed his eyes. He stood and unbuckled his gunbelt, slinging it over the bedpost where it would be close at hand.

After pulling the shades on the two windows, he walked to the cloudy mirror hanging over the washstand and stared at his reflection, taking in the lank, uneven hair and dirty face. He knew he was lucky, that he played his role so convincingly no one ever questioned his identity, but sometimes he got tired of this masquerade. The bad grammar was becoming a habit. So was the swearing. And graceless acts like belching and using his sleeve for a handkerchief were almost second nature.

But they worked. For a moment, though, he had thought the saloon girl Gracie had caught on to him just as Rankin intervened. Her look of surprise—naw, he was probably imagining things.

Hell, he had even fooled Jace Rankin, a man who

had a reputation for seeing through people as if they were panes of glass. But he didn't suspect the truth.

Still watching the reflection, he unbuttoned his shirt and long underwear with hands that shook with fatigue and strain. Beneath the thin shirt was a length of fabric, wrapped in tight circles around his ribs. He removed the safety pins, releasing the constricting pressure.

And Kyle Springer, the boy, was transformed into Kyla Springer, an ample-breasted, twenty-four-year-old female whose nipples felt as if they'd just been unbuttoned from her backbone. An ache spread over her chest as circulation surged into her compressed flesh.

The binding prevented her from taking a decently deep breath, but it also prevented the world from seeing the curves that would put her in far more peril than she had experienced at the Magnolia Saloon. Certainly that had been frightening enough. It had taken every bit of bravado she could muster, false and real, to maintain Kyle's angry hostility, and to keep his voice deeper than her own. Traveling as a boy for safety might have its drawbacks—it hadn't saved her from humiliation—but not nearly as many as would traveling as a woman. Her life might depend on her disguise, and she did everything she could to protect it. She even made sure she carried nothing with her that might give her away; no sweet soap, no silver-backed mirror or hairbrush, no feminine trappings of any kind. Not that she owned many.

Kyla sucked air into her lungs and scratched her rib cage where the fabric had pressed red grooves in her skin. After pouring water into the washbowl, she went to retrieve a piece of plain soap from her gear. What she really wanted to do was pull off her clothes and crawl into bed. But she'd had to abandon enough of the things that made her a woman—washing wouldn't be one of them.

Yes, she was tired, but nudging aside that fatigue was grim triumph. She had finally caught up with Rankin. After a month on the road, following rumors and news that he had been someplace but had left the night before or two days earlier, she finally tracked him to Silver City. After that, it was easy. Word of Jace Rankin's presence in town buzzed through the streets like St. Elmo's Fire.

That he had rescued her from certain disaster at the Magnolia Saloon did not make it easier for her to like him. In fact, much as she needed his help, she didn't like him at all. There was something despicable about a man who made his living by hunting his own kind.

Kyla knew her attitude was hypocritical. After all, wasn't that why she had hired him, for his reputation? But her situation was different; Tom Hardesty had stolen more from her than she could count, more than she could ever replace. Her personal vendetta against him had nothing to do with bounties or rewards.

Rankin might have said he wouldn't shoot Hardesty, but he had the look of a cold-blooded killer if ever she'd seen it. His face was young, but she saw it in his eyes—ice blue eyes as old as the grave. She'd find a way to change his mind by the time they got to Blakely. She had to.

She looked up at her reflection again. Some people needed killing.

Tom Hardesty was one of them.

Chapter Two

❧

Kyla stamped her feet and burrowed deeper into her saddlecoat. She had been standing here in front of the hotel for fifteen minutes, and she was getting cold. Streaks of pink and gold lighted the eastern sky but there was no warmth in the sunrise. She could see her own breath, and her horse's, too.

Across the street, a shopkeeper came out to sweep the walk in front of his hardware store. A few doors down, the bakery windows opened. Wood smoke from breakfast stoves drifted on the air. The town was just beginning to stir. But not so much that it made enough noise to drown out the heartbeat of Silver City's mines. In the dawn quiet, Kyla heard the distant muffled roar of powder blasts coming from the mines, and the dull racket of the stamp mills pounding ore into gravel.

Juniper, her sturdy dun gelding, pulled against his reins restlessly. She glanced at the hotel doors again. Where was Rankin? she wondered. He had told her to be here at sunup, but he was nowhere to be seen. She took out her pocket watch again. It was after seven, and now she'd been waiting for twenty minutes. What if he'd forgotten? Or worse, what if he'd changed his mind?

Tying Juniper to the hitching rail, she flopped down on the hotel steps and pulled a cold biscuit from her coat pocket to nibble.

It vexed her that Rankin was bossing this arrangement, and that they had to travel first to Misfortune. In fact, everything about Rankin vexed her. Almost as much as he terrified her. Only her hatred for Tom Hardesty had given her the courage to cross miles of open, desolate prairie to seek Rankin out.

Last night, he had even invaded her dreams. She'd seen him again as he'd looked when he'd outstared Clem, the scar-faced miner. So coldly confident was the expression in his eyes, so menacing was his deadly quiet voice that it wasn't until later that she remembered the miner had been much heavier and at least a head taller than him. Rankin seemed enormous, as though he towered over all of them. Kyla had lurched to wakefulness, the bedsprings screeching and her heart thundering in her chest with fear. It had been only a dream, but not far from the truth.

Kyla envied that, the ability to kindle fear in an enemy. She could have used it over the years . . . especially that night—

Just then the doors behind her opened, and she swung around to find Jace Rankin standing there. Jumping to her feet, she paused on the bottom step, her breakfast clamped in her hand. Their eyes met and he stared down at her as if trying to place her. He gripped his rifle, but let his hat hang by its bonnet strings and rest against his shoulder blades. Without that wide-brimmed hat hiding half of his face, he seemed a bit less fearsome. *Only* a bit.

It was an interesting face, she conceded. It held a strange mix of youth and hardened age beyond measure. Actually, if she were forced to describe him honestly, she would have to admit that he was sort of, well, attractive. That vexed her, too. She put the biscuit back in her pocket.

It struck her again that he was not a big man, certainly not as big as his reputation made her expect. But his size didn't matter. He was very intimidating— and very dangerous. Even given his present state.

In her opinion, he looked like he had spent the night working his way to the bottom of a whiskey bottle, probably with the help of a saloon girl. Kyla knew his type—he only wanted one thing from a woman, making her doubly grateful for her disguise. His eyes reminded her of the American flag she'd seen fluttering over the Silver City courthouse: red, white, and blue. But mostly red.

He gazed at her until her identity obviously registered. "Oh, shit . . . yeah," he muttered, half turning away from her. "Kelly Springer—" He rubbed his face with his gloved hand. A day's growth of beard shadowed his jaw.

"Kyle," she corrected, keeping her voice low. He wasn't going to back out now, was he? He'd already agreed to help her. Briefly she clenched her back teeth. It was a nervous habit she had developed in the last year or so. Sometimes she woke up with a headache from grinding her teeth in her sleep. "We made a deal, Mr. Rankin," she reminded him, using Kyle's tough persona to hide her fear of him. "Two hundred and fifty dollars. I'm ridin' with you to Misfortune, then we're goin' together to Blakely."

The sun inched its way up over the rim of the Owyhees, and Rankin squinted against the knife-sharp brightness spearing his aching head. Damn, he'd almost forgotten about this kid with his blood grudge.

After he and the boy parted, he had bought a room and a bath upstairs. He sat in the tub, drinking and thinking. It was a bad mix. A man ought to do one or the other, not both. And the more he drank, the more his thoughts drifted to the blank emptiness that seemed to form his future. It was as if finding Sawyer Clark and killing him had closed not just a chapter in his life, but the whole goddamned book. And this hangover didn't make things any clearer. From one of the mines in the west, the deep rumble of a powder explosion shook the planking under his boots. It reverberated through his legs and up his spine, further torturing his skull.

He glanced at the kid again, who watched him silently with eyes that seemed to miss nothing. At least he'd washed the dirt off his face. Now he looked like any other farm boy his age. Skinny, a few freckles. A little on the delicate side, especially in the face. But something else about him seemed off kilter and Rankin could not put his finger on just what that was. Maybe it was the sensitive curve of his mouth, or the way he tended to bite his bottom lip.

Oh, hell, he thought, he *had* agreed to help him. It wasn't syrupy benevolence that made him decide to let the kid tag along. After Misfortune, he just didn't have anything better to do. Gently, to avoid jostling his head, he put on his hat.

"Right, kid—Kyle. We've got a deal. I'll get my horse."

The boy gave a short nod and jumped down to untie his own gelding.

Rankin descended the steps and started off toward the livery. He turned suddenly and walked back to the dun's side. "But let's get a couple of things straight. I'm used to working alone and traveling alone. So if you can't keep up, that's your problem. I expect you to pull your own weight, and do as you're told. If the going gets hard, I don't want to hear any bellyaching. And if you *ever* get the notion to point that gun at me," he continued softly, indicating the kid's revolver, "well, let's just say that I'll turn it into the biggest regret of your life."

Kyle's expression was stony. "Okay, Mr. Rankin."

"And while we're at it, lay off that 'Mr. Rankin' stuff. You might as well call me Jace."

Kyle glared at him, then spit in the dusty street. "Jace."

The terrain was rough and craggy, and the going slow as they picked their way down through the mountains. But Jace set a steady pace that allowed no dawdling. A lot of the time they rode single file, with Jace ahead of Kyla. That was fine with her—at least she didn't have those cold eyes boring into her back.

Hours passed with nothing to look at but the rump of Jace's horse and passing tumbleweeds, punctuated by scrubby sagebrush or an occasional sudden chasm. Overhead the sky was deep blue, that particular shade seen only in autumn; now and then a hawk would cross the face of the sun and cast a shadow on the dust.

They were too far apart to talk, and even if they hadn't been, Kyla didn't know what she would say to the man. Nothing about him encouraged conversation. He was everything his reputation claimed: cold, detached, intimidating. He rode far ahead, never looking back to see if she followed, and by his manner he made it plain that Kyle Springer was not much more than a nuisance to be tolerated.

At any rate, ever conscious of preserving her disguise, she was doubly glad to be out of his range of vision. And it was just as well that they didn't talk much; subduing her feminine voice was the hardest part of being Kyle, although she knew she didn't sound too girlish. As they descended from the mountains and the sun climbed, so did the temperature. She took off her coat, confident of her binding. Her only inconvenience was finding scrub tall and dense enough to let her attend to personal needs in seclusion.

"You're pretty damned shy for someone who talks as big as you do. You don't own anything I haven't seen before," Jace groused impatiently after she returned from a long walk to a sage thicket. His eyes shone like shards of blue ice.

"Then you ain't missin' nothin', are you," she said curtly, putting her foot in her stirrup. She hoisted herself into the saddle. "Sometimes a man likes his privacy."

Jace snorted. "Yeah, right." He was already on his horse, and Kyla supposed he probably would have left her if she hadn't come back when she did.

By the time they reached more level ground, they had crossed into Oregon and most of the day was gone. Jace reined in his horse next to a spindly ponderosa pine and waited until Kyla caught up to him. He'd taken off his duster and rolled his shirt sleeves up to his elbows. She was surprised to see that what she'd mistaken for the bulk of a coat across his shoulders was really muscle. She hadn't noticed last night, given the circumstances.

He pointed to a sheltered place against a canyon wall and pulled out his rifle. "We'll make camp over there. I'm going to get something for dinner. You get the fire started—I hope you can cook."

She chafed at the greenhorn role he had put her in. She gestured at her Winchester in its scabbard. "I can shoot game as good as any other man," she said, pushing out her chin a little. "You don't have to treat me like I'm helpless, like some—some *girl.*"

Jace lifted his brows, shifting his hat. "We had an agreement—you were going to do as you're told. So now you can get dinner *and* start the fire. I don't mind at all."

Caught in the snare of her own boasting, she bit her tongue. She knew she couldn't complain about the double work; if she did, he might refuse to help her with Hardesty, and like it or not, she needed him.

"I saw a rabbit back there a quarter mile or so." She turned Juniper and took off across the field.

Jace watched the boy trot away, and then climbed

down to unsaddle and water his own horse at the flat, slow-moving creek that ran through the canyon. Hunger made his stomach rumble and he searched through his saddle bags for a piece of dried beef to fill the void until the boy returned with that rabbit—*if* he returned. Instead he found a leather pouch filled with silver dollars, the coins that he had made as much a part of his reputation as the Henry. They were heavy, and certainly not as convenient as his gold coins. But he liked their weight, and fancied the way they felt in his hand. He couldn't eat them, though, and he found no jerky in the saddle bags.

Using the saddle as a headrest, he stretched out on his bedroll and tipped his hat over his eyes. He'd just have to wait for Kyle to come back.

He breathed a long sigh. He was finally rid of his headache, but it felt good to lie down for a while. It had been one hell of a long day. The ground wasn't as soft as the hotel bed had been, but he had spent years on the trail—he was used to it. It just wasn't as easy anymore.

He peered at the lengthening shadows through the slit under his hat brim. Damn, he was really getting hungry. He probably should have insisted on going after the rabbit himself. It might be midnight before the kid came back with something to eat, if the coyotes didn't get him first.

He wondered again how he'd let himself get talked into helping Kyle. Even now he could hardly believe it. Jace had made it a point to avoid most people. Every lick of good sense he owned seemed to have flown away when he met that defiant red-haired kid.

But he might change his mind yet. If the boy took one step out of line or became too much of a pest, Jace would simply call off their deal.

He was an odd one, that was a fact, Jace thought as he crossed his ankles. Kyle was angry and tough, but other things about him still felt out of step. The kid had a bad habit of biting his lower lip in tight situations. It didn't just give away his uncertainty, it had a sissy look about it. Somebody ought to teach him to develop a better poker face.

And that story about the ranch—if it was true, how did a boy his age expect to run the place by himself? Even if he had a little money and could afford to hire help, no one would take orders from a green kid. He would be lucky if the hands didn't steal him blind.

That part was none of his business, he reminded himself. The boy wanted his help and he had the money to pay. Probably. Well, maybe. But that was all. Jace let his shoulders relax against the bedroll—he might as well get comfortable. He knew he was in for a long wait and his stomach was starting to rumble again. He'd give him an hour. If he wasn't back by then he'd go get his own damned rabbit.

Just then, the distant crack of a gunshot brought him upright. He listened intently for other shots but there were none. Instead he heard the sound of hoofbeats just before Kyle trotted back through the brush, holding a rabbit by its ears.

"I'll be damned—" Jace muttered to himself.

Kyle gave him a brief look but said nothing. Jace leaned against his saddle again, crossed his arms over his chest, and considered the boy. He wore that determined, mule-headed expression again. He had to give the kid his due—he had gotten the animal, and without much fuss. Kyle swung down from his gelding, and within minutes had a fire started. He worked quickly and quietly, and soon the rabbit was dressed and spitted over the flames.

Kyle squatted by the fire, tending the roasting meat, saying nothing. Jace glanced at the boy's small hands.

"Where'd you learn to hunt and cook?" he asked, plucking a rabbit-laden skewer from the fire.

Kyle shrugged and took a skewer for himself. The meat was hot and he blew on it before taking a bite. "It ain't so unusual. I wasn't raised in some fancy city house, y'know." He dragged the back of his hand across a dribble of hot grease on his chin.

Jace bit off a hunk of the tough meat. "I never would've thought that," he observed wryly. "How old are you, anyway?"

"Old enough." His voice cracked.

"It's a secret?"

"No, it ain't a secret, but what do you care?"

Jace took another bite. "I don't give a damn, kid. But usually women are the only ones who are touchy about their ages."

Kyle looked away. "I just don't like answerin' a lot of questions. I told you what you need to know."

"Not by half. I need to know enough to make sure I don't walk into a trap and get my head blown off. Tell me again how Hardesty got this ranch you say is yours."

"I ain't just sayin' it. It's the truth." He threw a bone into the fire and wiped his hands on his pants legs.

"Fine, tell me about it anyway. I don't want to get to Blakely and be . . . surprised. I hate surprises." Jace listened carefully while Kyle repeated the story he had told him the first time, no more and no less.

"Who did Hardesty kill?"

Jace heard him sigh. "He was my—he worked at the ranch as foreman. After he was dead, the rest of the hands scattered. I can't blame them." He threw another bone into the fire. "I tried to hold Hardesty off, but I couldn't do it by myself. He had the Vigilance Union behind him."

"How long has your father been gone?" Jace extracted a cheroot from his saddlebag.

"He died almost two years ago."

"Any sisters? Brothers?"

Kyle glanced up at him sharply. "No!"

Silence fell for a moment then, interrupted only by the soft snapping of the fire and the call of a peregrine as it crossed the darkening sky.

"Hardesty's soul is festering and rotten, and he must pay," Kyle concluded, his voice cold and flat, just as it had been yesterday.

Jace nodded but said nothing. There had to be more to it. He knew the boy was withholding something, and that the part he was hiding was vital. He would keep an eye on him; that was the best way to discover whatever secret he kept.

In his experience, most people betrayed themselves eventually.

Kyla glanced at Jace Rankin across the dying fire. He lay with his head on his saddle again and his rifle in a loose grip. He *looked* like he was asleep, but she suspected that the snap of a twig would bring him instantly to his feet.

She wrapped herself up tightly in her bedroll and looked at the stars overhead. In the distance, a coyote howled at the sliver of cold white moon riding the western horizon.

This wasn't the life she had imagined for herself: banished from her home, dressed in a boy's dirty clothes, running around the countryside with a bounty hunter she disliked and feared, hoping to convince him to kill a man, while a white-hot coal of anger and vengeance burned within her night and day—

She had seen none of this coming. When Kyla imagined her life, in her mind's eye she had finally thrown away all of her boy's clothes. Sometimes she pictured being married to a strong man, one who would be her equal in wits and will. A man who would honor her independence, but whose heart was noble and whose touch was tender. There weren't too many men around who would have found that an interesting partnership. Hank had been almost like that . . . but not quite.

And now? She turned her head to look at Jace again, the stubble-shadowed jaws, the rifle in his hand. Even asleep he was forbidding. She had been scared and lonely sleeping in the open by herself in the month it took her to find him. But now she felt even more vulnerable. At least when she'd been alone, the chances were slim that her true gender would be detected. Tonight, she'd nearly given herself away at least three times. And oh, when he had made that remark about women and their reluctance to discuss ages, she was certain that he had found her out. And if he did?

But no. She was safe. She had practiced posing as a boy, in varying degrees, since her girlhood. As long as she was careful, no one would ever know the truth.

They were on the road again early the next morning. Jace was stiff from sleeping on the ground. It was cold. A layer of frost covered everything, and mist drifted over the valley, making the sun look like a watery white ball on the horizon.

He wasn't in the best of moods. After all the commotion in Silver City, he'd forgotten to buy coffee before they left town. Hot coffee on a morning like this wasn't too much to ask for, but he had none.

And he still had Kyle tagging along behind him. He could hear the dun's hooves back there, clopping on the summer-baked earth. Jace never looked over his shoulder to check on him. It was his job to keep up. He supposed he couldn't gripe too much. The kid was a rugged, capable traveler, and he was doing his share without complaint.

But Jace wasn't used to having someone around all the time. Despite the vast expanse of empty land around them, he felt crowded, as if he needed to shrug off an unwelcome hand on his shoulder.

He didn't like people much, and trusted them even less. Often enough they appeared to wear one face, then proved to have another. Years of chasing wanted men had taught him that. Some of those men, when they'd wanted to, were able to fool people into believing they were just one step down from choir-boys. But their true faces were usually those of bank robbers, cattle rustlers, and murderers.

Women were another story altogether, but he'd avoided personal entanglements with them, too. The risk of losing everything—heart, mind, and self—was too great. He'd never had time for them beyond a saloon girl now and then. Anyway, not too many women were likely to beat a path to a man who earned his living bounty hunting.

He heard Kyle sneeze behind him. At least the boy didn't talk his ear off. But he made Jace uncomfortable, riding back there, and watching his every move. Why the hell had he decided to let him follow along, anyway? He nudged his horse to quicken its gait. He was supposed to go to Misfortune to talk to Travis, not provide traveling company for this silent, sullen boy with a peck of trouble. Well, he'd made a mistake, but not one that couldn't be corrected.

Cord was the next town up ahead. They'd reach it come afternoon, and he could buy coffee there. It might also be the perfect place to unload one angry kid.

When Jace and Kyla reached the tiny town of Cord, dark clouds were stacking up against the foothills of the Cedar Mountains. After two days of seeing no buildings or other humans, from the distance Cord looked almost like civilization to Kyla. But as they drew closer she saw that most of its few weathered buildings were abandoned. The town had the look of a community on its last legs. In fact, the only two busi-nesses that remained were the same ones usually established first in a new town: the general store and the saloon. The street was dusty, and tumbleweeds had blown to a rest in some of the empty horse troughs; plainly, no horse had drunk from them in a long time.

Kyla saw only one other person on the street, a trail-dirty man heading out of the saloon. He paused to stare at them through narrowed eyes as they passed, his hand resting on the batwing doors. Something about him was ominously familiar to Kyla, but she didn't know why. The look he gave them was malevolent, but Jace didn't favor him with even a glance.

Jace led them to the general store and dismounted from his bay. Securing the reins to a wobbly hitching rail, he looked up and down the street. Kyla remained in her saddle. She longed to get down and look around in the store, but she was too tired to fight with him if he were to bark at her. Actually, he didn't bark—half the time she had to lean in to hear him when he spoke. It was one of his unnerving characteristics. However, although he'd been no more taciturn than usual, she'd sensed his sour mood.

"There sure isn't much left of this place." The remark was made more to himself than to Kyla. Then he glanced up at her with speculative eyes, and she thought she saw an odd expression of disappointment, as though he'd hoped for more here. It made a funny chill run through her.

"Well, come on if you want," he said finally, turning toward the store. "I'm not going another morning without coffee."

She jumped down and followed him across the

rotted plank sidewalk, mindful of the holes. When they walked into the store, Kyla noticed the poorly stocked shelves and the lack of warm, inviting scents that floated through most general stores.

While Jace ordered coffee from the clerk, she idled at the glass display case. Her eyes fell upon a pair of real tortoise shell combs that lay on a scrap of yellowing lace, and an unexpected surge of regret tightened her throat. She'd worn combs like that when her hair hung to her waist. When she'd finally had the chance to grow it out, she had thought it was her best feature, her long, thick hair. That was before she stood at a mirror a month ago, with tears in her eyes and a razor in her shaking hand, and resolutely hacked off the blazing badge of her femininity. Now it was hideous, a jagged-edged mop. She wondered if she'd ever get the chance to wear it long again. Not as long as Tom Hardesty lived, she vowed silently, her fist clenched against her chest.

When she looked up, she saw that Jace was studying her, the same speculative expression in those ice blue eyes. Realizing that her interest in the combs might seem odd, she hastily moved on to examine a crosscut saw hanging on the wall.

Jace watched the boy a minute longer, then turned back to the clerk. "Could you use some extra help around here?" he asked, keeping his voice down. "Maybe give that boy over there a job if I left him here in town?"

The clerk snorted and gestured at the nearly empty shelves. "Hell, even a blind man could see I don't need any help. You're joking, right, mister?"

Jace stared at him, but said nothing.

He swallowed hard under the scrutiny. "Uh, no, I don't suppose you are. Well, Cord hasn't got much left to it beyond the saloon and this place. It's folding up like a spavined horse."

Jace nodded. Despite his wish to be rid of Kyle, the boy didn't deserve to be left in a town like this. Misfortune wasn't in much better shape than Cord, but maybe Travis could give him work in the blacksmith shop when they got there. It might put some bulk on the kid's bones. He glanced over his shoulder and saw him studying the peppermint sticks in the jar on the counter. At least he'd quit eyeing those women's geegaws in the display case.

"Hey, Rankin."

Without seeing who the voice belonged to, Jace recognized its tone. Even if he hadn't, the expression on the shop clerk's face told him plenty. The man's eyes darted between Jace and the speaker behind him, and he looked suddenly chalky, as if a gun were pointed at him. He backed up until he bumped into the empty shelves lining the wall. Jace felt Kyle tense next to him, too.

Jace pivoted slowly, tucking the front edge of his duster behind his holster as he turned. He recognized the skinny young saddle tramp he'd seen when they rode in—he was one of the two men who'd sat at the corner table in the Magnolia Saloon, obviously conferring about Jace. It wasn't easy to forget someone so ugly. His pale eyes bulged like a frog's and what remained of his teeth were ocher-colored and overlapped one another behind a pair of lips that made

Jace think of calves' liver. His stained buckskins looked as if they'd been on his back since the first day he put them on. He was unsteady on his feet, and the smell of sweat and pop skull whiskey radiated from him in waves.

And Jace had read the shopkeeper's fear like a newspaper—the weasely little bastard did have a gun pulled, but it was trained on Jace's own chest.

"You've been following me. Who the hell are you?" Jace inquired.

"Name's Hobie McIntyre, not like it's your business."

Jace looked him up and down. "Well, McIntyre, it's my business now. Where's your partner?"

"Lem's around, don't you worry 'bout that."

"I guess nobody taught you it isn't polite to point a gun at a man's back. If you learn it from me, it's going to be a hard lesson."

As soon as he said the words, the other customers in the store—two men—looked up and dropped the coil of rope they'd been measuring, beating a hasty retreat. Only Kyle stayed put, frozen in place like a rabbit with a hawk circling overhead.

The stranger didn't lower his gun. "Damn, if this ain't my lucky day—Jace Rankin. I knew it was you as soon as I seen you ride by. Where's the Bailey woman? I know she found you in Silver City. A saloon girl told me."

Jace felt every nerve in his body snap to attention. He had no clue what the man was talking about, but with that gun pointed at him he chose his words carefully. "I don't know anything about a woman, mister, but I can promise you that you'll be sorry you ever walked in here."

"No, I won't. I heard all about you and her at the Magnolia Saloon. They say she's a real looker, all nice curves and fire-colored hair. Now, there's folks lookin' for her, and I aim to know where you got her."

Jace's senses, focused sharply on all the details around him, suddenly and completely fixed on the business of survival. Though he didn't take his eyes off the man in front of him, in the periphery of his vision he saw the grime-smudged windows, the festoons of cobwebs in the rafters, a rag doll on the shelf. He smelled the coffee behind him, the trail dust on his own clothes. A cool, detached calm came over him, the same deliberate control that he'd learned long ago. Hotheads made mistakes; sometimes they landed in the undertaker's backroom.

"Do you see a woman here? You'll just end up with a bullet in your head," he warned again, more pointedly this time. "Go sleep it off, and you'll wake up to live another day." He could usually outstare almost any man and scare the pee out of him, but it wasn't working with this saddle bum. Christ, not much was worse than a drunk with a gun. Any kind of wild shot was likely to fly.

He felt Kyle still holding his ground, but he couldn't risk sparing him even one glance or a word to tell him to move. Damn-fool kid—didn't he have the wits to stay back? Jace had enough to worry about without that boy getting in his way.

"Whatsa matter, Rankin? You scared? Prob'ly no tougher than him." McIntyre snorted and gestured at

Kyle, then his red eyes narrowed. "Say—now I remember. A boy—Gracie said she was dressed like—"

Kyle gasped as McIntyre turned suddenly in his direction and advanced on him. That was exactly the opening Jace had been looking for. He leveled his revolver on him. But with familiar dream-slow movement, he saw Kyle whip out his gun and aim at the drunk. The man grinned evilly and kept coming. A brief confusion of close gunfire exploded in the tiny store, combined with the ping of ricochets and broken glass. Through the smoke Jace saw McIntyre go down. Jace could not tell who had shot him. He might have, or it could have been the boy.

When the air began to clear, McIntyre lay howling and swearing on the floor. He gripped his shattered, bleeding right hand.

"You son of a bitch! Look what you did to me!" he yelped, adding to the chaos.

The racket scraped Jace's nerves. He kicked McIntyre's boot. "Shut up that goddamned caterwauling!"

Jace whirled and saw that Kyle was down, too. He sat slumped against the rough counter, his face white, and his eyes blank and staring. He still gripped his gun with tight fingers but he didn't move. Jace dropped to a crouch next to him and grabbed his shoulder. He looked dead.

"Kid! Damn it to hell, kid, why didn't you get out of the way?" he demanded.

Slowly, the boy turned his head to look at him. "My name is *Kyle*," he muttered.

Relieved, Jace almost laughed. "Where are you hit?"

"My arm, I think." He looked down his left

shoulder at his upper arm where a bullet ripped his coat. "It's burning like fire." His eyes drifted closed for a moment, and a sheen of sweat broke out on his thin face.

Jace considered the sleeve that was growing soaked with blood and shook his head. "Where's the doc in this town?" he shouted to the shop clerk.

From the depths behind the counter, the clerk replied, "We don't have one anymore. He got killed in a card game last year." His voice shook so much, Jace had trouble understanding him.

He made a noise of impatient disgust. He thoroughly regretted ever stopping in this place. It seemed like his mistakes were compounding by the day. "It figures. All right, then," he said, and hauled Kyle to his feet. "I'll see to this."

He put an arm around the boy's waist to keep him upright, and was struck again by how slight he was.

"I can walk," Kyle protested, and pulled away. Swaying, he rested against the wall and cradled his injured arm at the elbow.

Jace leaned over to look behind the counter. "Come out of there—it's all over," he snapped at the clerk. Even Kyle had more guts than he did. "I want some bandages, and a bottle of whiskey."

The store had no bandages, but the rattled clerk produced a package of a dozen new linen handkerchiefs and a dusty bottle of expensive rye that had obviously been in stock for years.

While Jace tied up Kyle's arm with a temporary bandage, McIntyre finally stopped yowling long enough to regain his feet.

"You'll pay for this, you bastard!" he vowed as he staggered out the door.

Jace wanted to get out of Cord just in case Lem lost interest in the proceedings at the saloon and decided to come looking for his partner.

"Can you ride?" he asked Kyle. He didn't like the kid's pasty color.

The boy nodded. "Let's get the hell out of here."

"Right."

They left town at a gallop, but when no one followed they slowed to a trot.

Jace broke with their established custom and rode next to Kyla. She could feel his eyes on her but she couldn't turn to look at him. She was too drowsy and exhausted—it took all of her concentration to stay in her saddle. The landscape of endless beige dotted with scrub zoomed in and out of focus, and the horizon bounced around as if it were not attached to the earth. Juniper's gait made her arm throb; it felt like a thousand hot knives were stabbing it. She was chilled everywhere else, though, and beginning to tremble with the cold. If she'd had tears, she wouldn't be able to stop them. But she had none.

Jace said if they were lucky, she had only a flesh wound, that the bullet had plowed a deep furrow in her arm but had not lodged. That way, he told her, he wouldn't have to dig the lead out with a knife.

Shot. She'd been shot. She considered it with numb surprise that would probably sharpen after the shock wore off. Seldom in her life had she known such fear as when that filthy, louse-ridden McIntyre pointed his gun at her. Now she recalled seeing him at the Magnolia Saloon two days before. Surely it was only the worst possible luck that had brought him and his partner to Cord.

That Jory or Hardesty would send men to capture her was something she had not once considered. No one knew where she had gone except for a few of the Midnighters. Now she had been tracked all the way to Silver City—God, this was a hundred times worse than she'd thought.

So Gracie *had* realized Kyla's true gender during that incident at the Magnolia. Oh, damnation, she thought. Who else would the woman tell?

During the confrontation at the general store, she'd seen the bounty hunter's face under the brim of his hat—icy, controlled. He never raised his voice. The universal respect and fear he roused in people made her wonder why anyone would dare cross him. Drunk or sober, McIntyre had to have been a complete fool to challenge Jace Rankin.

And *she* had challenged McIntyre, so who was the bigger fool? But the reaction that made her draw on him had been purely instinctive. She didn't know why she hadn't done the wise thing and hidden in the corner, instead of staying close to the danger and Rankin. But it required far too much energy to figure out now. She remembered the feel of Jace's arm around her when he pulled her up from the floor. For a second, it was almost comfortable to lean against him. But even in her shock she'd known she couldn't give in to it. She didn't want to be touched, and Kyle wouldn't permit such mollycoddling. And anyway, she didn't like Jace.

"How are you holding up?" she heard him ask.

She glanced at him and shivered hard enough to make her teeth chatter. "I—I'm okay. B-but it's so cold."

He swore, as if she'd said something wrong.

Jace knew Kyle was not okay. He was cold and sleepy—he could see that in the kid's face, hear it in his voice. He had to get him to a warm fire and check his arm. The hankies he'd wrapped around him in Cord were only makeshift. He hoped the bullet hadn't gone in too deep—he'd dug out his share of lead but never from a kid.

Added to that, the clouds that had rolled into the sky earlier were now producing a fine, soaking drizzle. He twisted in his saddle and peered through the gray veil, searching the broken limestone formations for a sheltered place.

"We've got to get out of this rain. It'll be dark soon and I don't want to be riding around after sundown."

He led them along a creek until they came to a spot under a rocky overhang that was dry and out of the weather.

Jace dismounted, then stood at Kyle's foot. He looked bad, Jace thought, still sickly white and a little disoriented. But maybe a sip of whiskey and something to eat would put the color back in his face. He sure as hell hoped so, anyway. Beneath his open coat lapels, the boy looked as blood-soaked as a soldier wounded on a battlefield.

"Can you get down by yourself?"

Kyle nodded but for a moment he didn't move. Then with obvious effort, he slowly swung a leg over his dun. Just about the time it cleared the pommel, his eyes rolled back and he fell into Jace's arms.

Jace carried him to the wall under the overhang and opened his coat. Jesus, his shirt was so red, he must have been hit someplace else. Who could tell in the confusion of gunfire and their flight from Cord? The kid himself was probably too stunned to realize the extent of his injuries, and Jace hadn't had time to look.

He yanked off his gloves. Without hesitation he grasped the front of Kyle's blue shirt and ripped it open. Beneath, he encountered blood-stained binding that was working loose. Baffled, he sat back on his heels and pushed up his hat. God, he was nursing broken ribs, too?

No. Something was wrong. Something—

Pulling out his long-bladed hunting knife, he grabbed the bunched binding in one hand and cut it open with a single slice. He stared down in stunned disbelief at full, rounded breasts that were definitely not a boy's.

"I'll be goddamned—"

He quickly brushed a hand between the kid's legs and felt nothing there but rounded female warmth. His body responded to hers so swiftly, with such intensity, he felt hot and a little breathless.

Of all the possibilities that had crossed Jace's mind when he considered the puzzle of Kyle, that he— she—was a woman had never occurred to him. And a woman she certainly was, no mere girl. The soft mouth, the delicate planes of her face, her light bones—sure, they all looked out of place on a boy, but on a woman they were very desirable. The freed binding revealed not just a bosom, but the very decided curve of her waist, and skin that looked as smooth and pale as cream. She was beautiful beneath her disguise. And now more trouble than she was before.

So this was the big secret, huh? This was the reason he felt twitchy around her. How could he have missed something that now seemed so obvious? He must be slipping.

Satisfied that only her arm was wounded, with a cold, escalating fury he jerked together the edges of her shirt. He stared at the slack face and he pulled his mouth into a tight line. Now, instead of being saddled with a grudge-bearing boy he thought he knew a little about, he had a gunshot woman he knew nothing about. Except that someone was chasing her, and now him too.

She wouldn't be his problem for long, though, he resolved. Not for long.

Chapter Three

Chased by terrifying images, Kyla fought her way back to consciousness. Tom Hardesty, horned and hoofed like a demon, pursuing her with a staff that split open her arm with fire ... Hank, awash in his own blood, struggling for breath to tell her about a bounty hunter with a killer's reputation ... a pair of ice blue eyes that fascinated her as much as they frightened her.

She didn't know where she was, but she heard the soft, faraway sound of a woman weeping. Firelight flickered against her closed eyelids and the whisper of falling rain penetrated her confusion. And whiskey, she thought she smelled whiskey. It was strong, as if it were right under her nose. Beyond that was the scent of brewing coffee. She took a deep breath and the nightmare visions receded. But her arm, that pain was very real.

When she opened her eyes, she saw the blurry form of a man looming directly over her in the darkness. He was wiping her face with something white. Gasping, she wrestled to escape while reaching for her gun. She found that not only was it missing, but her gun belt was gone, too. Her heart pounded behind her breastbone. Further, she was bundled in blankets and stretched out like a mummy next to the small fire.

"So you're finally awake."

She recognized Jace Rankin, his long dark hair and pale eyes that gleamed in the firelight. The veil over her memory began to lift. He sat back against the rock wall next to her and crossed his ankles.

Gingerly, she touched a hand to her arm and couldn't suppress a moan. Her shirtsleeve was missing, torn off at the shoulder, and the skin on her arm was hot to the touch, even through the bandage.

"I cleaned up your wound with the whiskey and put a new bandage on it. You're going to have a scar."

She moved her hand from her arm to her wet eyes and face.

"You were crying," he added, and tossed a handkerchief at her. His tone was flat, the expression on his face, a cold blank.

She gripped the hankie in her fist. "Where's my gun?" she demanded in Kyle's voice. She struggled to sit up, a task she found surprisingly difficult with only one arm to balance on.

Jace held up the gun in its holster. "Right here. Along with some of your . . . underwear."

Kyla recognized the fabric that made up her binding. It was bloodstained and looked as though he'd cut it off her. She gaped at it in heart-stopping horror. Groping around under the blanket, she felt her shirt-clad ribs without the constricting wraps. No wonder she could breathe so easily.

He held the very heart of her disguise in his outstretched hand. She felt vulnerable, exposed. Her armor, the shield she showed to the world and carried before her—the persona of Kyle Springer—was lost to her. And to take it away from her, that meant he'd seen her down to her bare skin. God, how long had she been unconscious? And what else had happened during that time?

"How dare you?" she demanded, clutching the blanket to her, terrified, indignant. "What gave you the right—"

He smiled slightly and threw the rags into the flames. "So there *is* a woman under there. Anytime someone puts me in the line of fire I have the right. I opened your shirt to see if you were shot more than once, and found your—surprise." Then he added with cold dryness, "But I told you the other day that you don't have anything I haven't already seen. And anyway, unwilling women have never interested me, in case you were worried." He narrowed his icy eyes as he raked her with a contemptuous glare. "Who are you?"

Dizziness washed over her and she leaned sideways against the wall. This was all horrible, just horrible. She felt him staring at her while he waited for an answer. "Kyla Springer. Well, Kyla Springer Bailey."

"So now it's *Kyla*, huh? You lied to me, lady. I hate being lied to even more than I hate surprises."

He rose and she recoiled from him. Who knew what form his fury would take? Her arm ached with a tremendous fiery throb. She winced but did her best to ignore the pain. She could have far more trouble with Rankin than with her wound, and she needed to stay alert.

His movements were swift and fluid, almost graceful. But he only leaned over the fire to pour a cup of broth from a small pot in which he'd boiled a piece of dried beef. He handed a blue enameled cup to her, then got himself a cup of coffee and sat down again.

She released her breath. "I'm the one who got shot, you know. Not you. Besides, how far would I have gotten traveling alone as a woman?"

He acknowledged the question with a lift of his brow and an assessing gaze that seemed to take casual measure of her through her clothes. "Not very far with those men looking for you. Of course, now they're also dogging me, thanks to you. What else have you lied about?"

"Nothing! Everything I told you was true. I didn't know anyone was chasing me." She held the cup to her mouth with a hand that shook so badly she was in danger of scalding herself.

Firelight and shadow played over his face, making his youthful features look even more sinister. "Big bad men came and took your ranch?"

If she had felt better, if she were stronger, she would have challenged this man and his sarcasm, fearsome though he was. "Yes! And Hank Bailey sent me to look for you."

He frowned at her. "Hank Bailey—how do you know him?"

She looked at him dead on. "He was my husband.

Just over a month ago, Tom Hardesty shot him in cold blood. Then with Luke Jory's help, he forced me off our ranch." Her words were blunt and direct, and a look of surprise skittered across his face. It was the best way she could think of to deal with Jace. He was not a weak man and he seemed not to tolerate weakness in anyone else. But she put her hand to her eyes for a moment. The memory was so terrible—she hadn't loved Hank, but she'd liked him and respected him, and the guilt she felt over his death had not diminished one bit.

Jace stared at the woman. This was stunning news. Hank Bailey, dead? He'd known him for a long time, although he'd lost track of him in the last couple of years. He was a tough son of a bitch, an ex-Texas Ranger who had come north and taken up bounty hunting. He had no patience with the scummy people that bounty hunting tended to churn up, and was inclined to take advantage of the "dead" option on the wanted posters. Now and then their paths had crossed, and on a rainy night or two they'd tipped a few beers and traded stories. Hank wasn't the kind of man to be overcome with a nesting instinct to get married and take up ranching. He liked the ladies, all right, but mostly the saloon girl variety. Now this plain, tough-talking female with chopped-off hair and boy's clothes claimed to have been married to him? None of it figured. He tossed a twig into the fire.

"A lot of people have heard of Hank Bailey, and he damn sure wasn't married the last time I saw him. How do I know you aren't making this up, too?"

The woman turned from her cramped position to

rest her back against the rocky wall, her face hidden in shadow. She was silent for a moment before she spoke. "I'm not making it up. You heard McIntyre yourself. He referred to the Bailey woman. Hank and I were married six months ago. Why on earth would I put myself in the position to be chased and shot at, if it were a lie?"

Her voice was rich and smoky—Jace had never heard anything quite like it. But it was definitely a female voice. And she chose her words more carefully than she had when "Kyle" was talking.

"How do I know? Maybe you stole something, or ran away from somewhere. Bailey isn't an unusual name."

"I'm telling you the truth," she said, "and I'm taking a big chance in doing it."

That was small comfort, he thought grimly. "How did Hank get killed?"

The wind picked up and she pulled the blanket closer around her, mindful of her arm. "He was the leader of the Midnighters. They're a group of Blakely citizens who are trying to get rid of the Vigilance Union. Hardesty shot him down like a dog, point-blank in the chest just outside the barn. I saw it all. That's the way Luke Jory operates—if he wants something he'll just take it. Tom Hardesty is his right-hand toady, so he can do the same with Jory's help." She drew a deep breath. "Hank died later than night." Her voice faded away, and she closed her eyes for a moment.

The story sounded plausible enough, although it was still hard for Jace to picture the man he remembered married to this woman. Her femaleness—femininity wouldn't be the right term in this case—was more apparent now that she spoke with her own voice, throaty though it was. And of course, he'd seen the physical evidence—but beyond her small face and big eyes, it was hard to tell what Kyla, the woman, looked like. He could well imagine it, though.

Apparently his thoughts showed on his face, because she added, "I wasn't born looking like this, you know. I tried to stay at the ranch, but it became impossible for me to live there alone. After Hank died the other two hands were frightened off, and Hardesty deviled me day and night. He told me he'd be moving into the ranch house. I was more than welcome to stay—if I, well, cooperated. One night he broke down the kitchen door. He was drunk and—and I slashed his face with a paring knife." She shivered again and reached up to close her shirt collar. "I think he's probably as mad about that as anything else—Hardesty fancies himself to be a ladies' man. That night, I cut off my hair, put on boys' clothes, and set out before daybreak to find you."

He took a big swallow of the coffee. "When were you planning to tell me that you're not a boy?"

She shrugged her good shoulder. "I don't know—maybe later if I felt like I could trust you. So probably not at all."

The barb was not lost on him but he ignored it. Something about this still didn't figure. He leaned toward her. "Who is Tom Hardesty to you? Why did he want your ranch? Why not someone else's?"

Her gaze slid away from his. "No others would do.

He's coveted that land for years. When my father married Aggie Hardesty after my mother died, she brought her son, Tom, with her. All of my kin are dead now. Tom and I are the only ones left. He's my— stepbrother, I guess." She said this last with special distaste and bitterness. "He was gone for a few years, and I thought I'd seen the last of him. A year ago, he came back. Like a bad penny."

"Stepbrother? And you wanted to hire me to kill him?" This situation was getting worse and worse with every fragment of information she revealed. Jace shook his head. "Oh, no, no. I'm not getting involved in some family squabble over land ownership. You need a lawyer, not me. Our deal is off, lady."

"Damn it," she cursed, sounding more like Kyle again, "my name is *not* 'kid,' and it isn't 'lady'! And this has nothing to do with land rights or a family squabble. Tom Hardesty is not my family. This is about murder and thievery. I don't need a lawyer or a nursemaid. I need someone who can help me get my home back. Hank sent me to find you because he said you were that man. He said maybe you've had a change of heart since the Bluebird Saloon. I suppose he could have been wrong."

Jace stiffened and he felt his face heat. The Bluebird Saloon—God, he had very nearly put that night out of his head. Five years had passed since then, and he'd finally stopped thinking about it, dreaming about it. He'd almost forgotten that woman who had begged him to help her and her little girl. Didn't want to get involved, he'd told her. . . .

"What did he tell you about that?" he demanded,

wary now. He would not have expected Hank to turn gossipy like an old lady. And Kyla Springer Bailey made him *very* uncomfortable. She knew things that he did not, and things that she shouldn't. He was unaccustomed to having so little control over a situation.

"Nothing. He didn't tell me the story. He just said that you let someone down."

Jace frowned. Huh, yeah, he had let someone down. The results had been disastrous. And even from his grave, Hank was reminding him of it. He let his gaze drift over Kyla again. Maybe she was his chance to finally make things right.

There was a lot more about all of this that he wanted to know, but he couldn't question her anymore tonight. She had had a really lousy day, one that would have been hard for a man. But for a woman, trying to maintain a disguise while confronting a drunk in a gunfight and getting shot—Jace had to admit again that she had a lot of grit. A hell of a lot, considering the events that had led to this afternoon.

Right now, though, she was too tired and in too much pain to keep talking. In fact, he was worn out himself.

"Drink that broth and get some rest," he said shortly. "If Hardesty has his people following us, we'll have to backtrack a little before we ride to Misfortune. I want to get an early start." He stood up to open his bedroll on the other side of the fire.

"Does that mean that you're going to help me?" she asked, tipping her face up at him.

"Looks like it."

"That's not much of an answer. How do I know you

won't change your mind? You could probably hand me over to Hardesty and make more money than I can pay you."

He frowned at her. "Not everything is about money."

"Every man has his price—sometimes it's too high."

"I guess you'll just have to take my word for it. I'll help you."

She eyed him. "For sure?"

The hope and fatigue in her voice committed him to see this through. Although he still thought it was probably a bad decision, he was in for the long ride. He considered her eyes—blue-green, they were like turquoise, even in the firelight.

"Yeah, for sure."

The night was an endless, rainy darkness of pain and worry. Kyla's sleep was fitful and shallow, despite her exhaustion. Oh, to be back in her own bed, clean, warm, and safe with the nightmares behind her. Instead she was unwashed and cold, wounded, sleeping in the damp.

Hardesty had to pay, she vowed darkly—for this, for Hank, for every filthy innuendo and sly look, for making her feel dirty. He might not have pulled the trigger himself this time, but he was just as guilty as McIntyre. That worthless saddle bum would not have shot her if Tom hadn't sent him to find her.

During the dragging hours her arm throbbed, and she woke often with her jaws clenched. Whenever she opened her eyes she saw Jace Rankin across the fire from her. He lay in the red light of the embers, his head propped on his saddle, looking the same as the night before, with the Henry next to him. He appeared to sleep with the maddening ease of a man who had no worries and no regrets. The stubble of his beard grew heavier each day, making him seem all the more threatening.

Her masquerade had given her strength, courage, and freedom—it was easier to move around in this wild, unforgiving country as a male. But now Jace knew the truth, at least most of it, and he could easily take whatever he wanted from her. If he decided to do that, could she fight him off? No, not even on her best day. He far outmatched her strength with his lean, quick body, and danger radiated from him. He could claim disinterest in unwilling women, but she had no particular reason to believe him.

She pulled her blankets more tightly around herself, and with some effort rolled over. In the process she snapped a stick under her boot.

Jace flew out of his bedroll and crouching on one knee, pointed the Henry at her. His expression was as fixed and flat as a snake's. She froze, her breath caught on the thundering heartbeat in her chest and her eyes on the barrel of the rifle. Her mouth formed a silent scream as she waited for the sound of a shot.

He stared at her in the dim firelight as if getting his bearings, then lowered the rifle. "Damn," he muttered. "Sorry. I thought I heard a gun being cocked. Are you all right?"

Her breath returned and the stricture of her throat relaxed. "All right? You almost shot me again!"

He shrugged. "I wouldn't have. I saw you didn't

have your gun." He lay down again and settled into his blanket. "Go back to sleep." In a moment, she heard his breathing smooth out to a regular rhythm.

Oh God, she wished she were far away from here, and away from this terrible, dangerous man. Tears slid down her temples, though she told herself they would do no good.

Theirs wasn't much of a partnership, she reflected. He didn't trust her . . . she didn't trust him. Despite his halfhearted agreement to help her, he could give away her true identity anytime he got tired of having her around.

Yet at the same time she felt a conflicting sense of security just knowing he was there. He intimidated her, but he scared almost everyone else as well. Reconciled to that, she dozed the last couple of hours before daybreak.

When she woke again, the sun was on its way up the eastern sky and Jace was gone from his place near the fire. It had stopped raining but the air was damp and chill, and moisture clung to everything beyond the shelter of the overhang. As uncomfortable as her hard bed was, Kyla was loath to leave her blankets. Next to her, she found her gun in its holster. Apparently, Jace had decided to trust her enough to return her weapon.

Over by the flat, narrow creek she saw him already saddling their horses. He stood with his back to her, a silhouette against the slate-colored sky, and she watched him, the way he smoothed the silky equine manes, his strong hands surprisingly gentle on their bridles, the way his own dark hair brushed his shoulders. He bent to tighten Juniper's cinch strap, and his shirt stretched over his shoulders and lean waist. There was nothing hesitant or awkward in his movements. He had a powerful, easy grace. It was easy to forget that there were taller men; he had a very imposing presence, an intangible something that made him seem far bigger than he actually was. She supposed some women found him attractive. Luckily, experience had made her immune.

He turned suddenly, as if feeling her eyes on him. "There's coffee if you want it, and a couple of biscuits. But get out of your bedroll and eat quick—we've got to move out of here." He came back to the fire and rolled up his own blankets.

Kyla worked her way to a sitting position. Upright, she realized how terrible she felt—stiff and slightly ill with a queasy headache, a lot like that time years ago when she'd gotten into her father's corn liquor. Her injured arm was as heavy as lead. She glanced down at the bandage and found that it was still clean and white. At least the wound hadn't begun bleeding again.

She lifted her head and looked around at the gray dawn. Spending the day on horseback was going to be misery. With considerable effort she managed to strap on her gun belt. She was forced to use her left hand to do it, though, and it frightened her how much it hurt. It meant her arm would be of little use until it healed, perhaps weeks from now. In the meantime, she was left vulnerable in perilous circumstances. At least she could still fire her revolver.

From the corner of her eye, she noticed Jace

watching her fumble with the buckle. That blue gaze felt like it penetrated her clothes with icy heat. He moved closer and dropped to a crouch.

"Sorry if I scared you last night. How's the arm?" His tone was a bit gruff; obviously she was more of a liability to him than ever.

She pulled back, protective of her injury and wary of him, too. "It hurts like hell. I swear I'll get even with Hardesty when I get the chance. He doesn't deserve to stand trial. This is his fault. *All of it.*" Including last night, she thought. She heard the bitterness in her own voice.

He studied her a moment longer and then shrugged. "Yeah, it probably is his fault. But right now we're going to Misfortune. If we're being followed, it'll be a good way to throw them off. Misfortune is the last stop to nowhere." He gestured at her bandage. "You're going to need a sling. Have you got a bandanna in your gear?"

She shook her head.

He took off his own neckerchief and tied its two ends together, then handed it to her. "Use this."

Hesitating, she finally struggled into the sling. It smelled like him, like horses and leather; that wasn't totally unpleasant, she conceded. But she wished she had her binding back. Every time she moved, she felt her shirt brush against her unbound breasts, reminding her that her true identity was fully revealed. It didn't matter, she remembered wearily. Even if she had fabric to wrap around herself, she wouldn't be able to do it without using both hands. What could she do, ask for Jace's help? She swallowed the bubble of hysterical laughter that swelled in her chest at the idea. Just getting her gun belt buckled had been hard enough.

While she choked down a dry biscuit and a few sips of coffee, Jace packed up her blankets and put them on Juniper. At least he was a bit less hostile and suspicious than he had been last night.

In another minute, with a well-placed hand on her buttocks he boosted her onto her gelding's back, nearly pushing her over the other side. She bristled at the intimate contact of his warm hand. But mounting a horse without the use of her left arm was almost impossible, and her helplessness nettled her. Finally the feat was accomplished and Jace swung into his own saddle. Gathering his reins, he turned to her.

"This thing with Hardesty, it isn't going to be easy. Before we start it, is there anything else I should know? Just to keep us from getting killed?"

She hesitated to mention the problem that had occurred to her during one of the endless hours last night. But she had to tell him if he was going to help her. "I think McIntyre figured out that I'm not a boy."

Jace gazed at the bright horizon through narrowed eyes. "Shit." His chuckle was sharp and humorless, and he wheeled his horse around. "Then we'd better ride."

Jace led them on a circuitous journey through the foothills of the Cedar Mountains. They doubled back so often that Kyla, though she'd been watching the sun for reference, was thoroughly confused. Traveling fast, they recrossed their own tracks through rocky canyons and traversed streambeds; he even made her trade mounts with him a couple of times to alter the hoofprints the horses made. Once or twice, she suspected that they might be lost, but a glance at his set face quelled her doubts. He knew exactly what he was doing.

The weather, though, was not obliging. Clearing briefly, it finally settled into a steady gray downpour, and Kyla lost her point of reference. As the hours passed, she tried hard to maintain the tough hardiness that Jace had come to expect. But she was cold and miserable, and by afternoon, when he finally pointed them toward Misfortune, her energy started to drain away. Yet she dared not let it show—she couldn't let anything get in the way of traveling back to Blakely.

To stay alert—and on her horse—she forced herself to think about her ultimate intent: to see Tom Hardesty dead. Jace Rankin was her means to that end. She had to make him understand the urgent necessity of her goal. She drew up alongside him.

"How long do you think we'll need to be in Misfortune?" she asked.

"As long as it takes to finish my business." His tone reminded her that he did not like being questioned.

Her brows locked at his flip answer. "Well, how long will that be? I want that damned Hardesty off my property."

He turned to regard her, and despite her weariness once again she studied his good looks. They couldn't be considered classic—his eyes were far too intense. And the jaded cynicism lurking in their ice blue depths made him seem unapproachable. She could have kicked herself for even noticing, but his hand-someness was fascinating, like a dark star that glinted in the night sky.

"You're sure in a hurry to get shot at again. I'm not," he went on. "Besides, Hardesty doesn't sound like he's going anyplace. He'll be in Blakely when we get there."

His cavalier attitude clashed with her growing headache. "I just want to settle this. Jail isn't bad enough for what he did." She stopped just short of saying she wanted to see Hardesty dead.

"Look—we're going to do it my way or not at all. I need to make certain we've lost his hired guns. I don't want to be caught between them and the vigilantes."

Kyla understood the strategy, but only vaguely. Pain and her hate blurred the details. "Didn't anyone ever make you mad enough that you just wanted to get even?"

He kept his eyes on the rain-shortened horizon and his jaw tightened. "Once."

Once. Jace gripped his reins. Yeah, it had happened to him. A cold, dark vengeance had blotted out every other thought he'd had, and his focus narrowed down to one purpose—to exact revenge. He'd traced his best friend all over the territory, and he would have shot him without thinking twice about it. At least not until it was too late. When Travis had convinced him of his innocence, he had continued with single-minded deter-mination until he found Sawyer Clark and killed him.

And so what? His sister Celia was still dead. Avenging her hadn't changed that. He was simply left with that same bitter emptiness he'd felt since the afternoon in Silver City. He wished to God he could shake it.

But this woman, with her spirit and courage, who seemed to be more wild mare than human female, did not know what lay in store for her. And maybe she should.

"I'm not in the habit of giving advice," he said. "People usually do what they want, anyway. But ... whatever grudge you bear against Hardesty, nothing will be different, not if he sits in jail till kingdom come. Not even if I were to kill him. It wouldn't bring back Hank." He gestured at her head. "Your hair wouldn't grow out overnight."

A frown creased Kyla's pale face and she leaned forward in her saddle, allowing the soft roundness of her bosom to press against her shirt. From this angle, her sling didn't conceal her chest very well. Instantly, the memory of her smooth breasts and small waist sprang to his mind.

When he realized he was staring, he forced himself to look away. He knew that he should have nothing to do with this female—so why did she crowd his thoughts to the point of distraction? A naked woman was nothing new to him, but he thought about this one and the beauty she hid under her clothes a lot more than he wanted to.

"What are you saying, that he should go on about his life as if he's done nothing?" she demanded. "He murdered Hank. And all the times he let my father down—quitting school, gambling, getting drunk, stealing money—all those times he pushed me into corners and grabbed at me and—and—" She choked and a red stain crept over her face. She turned her head away and rain dripped from the brim of her hat. "Are you saying none of that matters?"

Jace glanced at her sharply, but she stared straight ahead and refused to meet his eyes. "No, I'm not saying that," he replied.

She'd let slip another fragment of the information he knew she was keeping back. Maybe there was a reason that "Kyle" was so convincing; the role might not be new for her. Maybe Hardesty was guilty of more than killing Hank and taking her ranch. He felt a surge of anger boil up in him. The more he heard about the man, the more he disliked him.

"This isn't the first time you've dressed as a boy, is it?"

"That's none of your damned business," she retorted with a harder edge. Her turquoise eyes glinted like glass. "I don't have to explain myself."

Jesus, but she was prickly. She had a chip on her shoulder the size of an anvil and she was always daring him to push it off. He'd never known a woman so exasperating. Or so challenging.

He tried again, searching for words that didn't feel so awkward to speak aloud. "I'm just saying that hate can eat a person up, until sometimes there's nothing left. When Hardesty is locked away, you'll still have to live your life." He'd heard this same warning a year ago. He hadn't listened, either.

"I ain't about to start lovin' my enemy, so that sermon would be wasted on me," she said, lapsing fully into Kyle's voice before falling silent. The way she surrounded herself with the personality sent a shiver down Jace's back. She used it like a spiny shield to hold the world at bay. How had Hank managed to find the woman behind it?

As the miles passed and she maintained her silence, Jace noticed that she was really beginning to look poorly. The blood seemed to fade from her face, as if her fiery hair had pulled out all the color. She hadn't complained about her arm, but he knew it must hurt. Hell, his own shoulder still ached in rainy weather like this, and nearly a year had gone by since he was shot. Plus he'd had a doctor to see to him and a place to rest until he could get back on his feet. A spark of empathy stirred in him; she'd had only some makeshift medicine on the run, and was spending her days in her saddle. Maybe old Doc Sherwood could look at her when they reached Misfortune.

Travis's wife, Chloe, might be able to help her find some decent clothes so she could feel like a woman for a change. At least while they were in Misfortune. He cast a sidelong glance at her and caught himself wondering what she'd look like if she were cleaned up and her true prettiness allowed to shine through.

Nope, nope—just stop right there, he told himself irritably. He felt a grudging respect for her, and that was enough. This was just business. She was Hank Bailey's widow, a wild little hellion who'd hired him to do a job. He'd collect two hundred and fifty dollars—if he was lucky. He still wasn't convinced any money existed.

Finding a dry place to camp that evening proved difficult, but by the time sunset gave a final blaze to the horizon, Jace had shot a rabbit for dinner, and she had the fire going.

Despite Kyla's determination, privately she feared that she was not doing very well. The pain in her arm was unrelenting, enough to bring tears to her eyes. She felt hot and cold and more tired than she had ever been in her life. Dizziness rolled over her in sickening waves. Of all the rotten luck, she railed to herself. At a time when she needed her wits and her strength, this had to happen.

Across the campfire Jace chewed on a roasted rabbit leg. Her own appetite had diminished to almost nothing. Beyond that small circle of light, darkness crowded in around them, concealing everything, making her feel as if they were the last two people on earth. Feeling his gaze on her, she found it to be a frightening thought.

She took just one bite from the piece of rabbit on her plate. It was all she could choke down.

"You'd better eat," Jace said, breaking the silence. "If you don't you'll wear out faster than shoes with cardboard soles."

She shook her head, the tin plate forgotten on her lap. "I'm not hungry."

He regarded her, then rose and walked over to her. When he stretched out a hand toward her injured arm, she flinched and pulled back. "What are you doin'?" she demanded.

"Damn it, don't be so jumpy," he said. "I'm just going to check your bandage."

She scooted back. "It's fine. I don't need your—"

Just then, the call of a bird sounded from the

blackness around them. It came from everywhere and nowhere. Jace put up a hand to silence her as he listened intently to the repeated call. She reached for her gun, but he stopped her hand and frowned. His hand on hers was warm and firm. And frightening. But she didn't move.

Then in a perfect echo, he mimicked the sound back to the prairie. A big grin lighted his expression when the sound was repeated. It was the first time Kyla had really seen him smile—it transformed his youthful face and she stared in amazement. It caught her notice in a way that his dark frown did not.

"I may come to your fire, Jace Rankin?" a low voice now asked. It filled the darkness as the bird call had.

"Yes, come on, Many Braids. There's rabbit and coffee for you."

Kyla drew a startled breath when a very tall, slender Indian swept quietly through the sagebrush directly in front of her. He seemed to materialize out of the night. She didn't know if he had a horse or if he had simply walked in from the prairie, but he was a giant of a man, the biggest she'd ever seen.

Under a battered old J. B. Stetson, he wore his ebony hair in four neat braids that hung down his chest, two on each side. His clothes were a combination of buckskin pants, knee-high fringed moccasins, and what looked like an army officer's coat without the gold buttons or epaulets. Beneath the jacket he wore a calico shirt, the kind distributed on the reservations.

She didn't mean to stare, but he was a formidable, imposing man, straight as a yew tree, and with blade-sharp mahogany features that made it impossible for her to determine his age. He could have been thirty, he could have been sixty.

Kyla hadn't seen many Indians since the army forced them onto reservations years earlier. She watched him with fascination, but mostly with fear.

Jace and the Indian shook hands solemnly. The contrast between their heights was striking, but the man would have dwarfed anyone who stood next to him. "It's been a long time, Many Braids. What are you doing out here, especially in this weather?"

The man shrugged. "This land no longer belongs to the People, but sometimes I yearn to rest my eyes upon it."

Jace turned to Kyla. "This is Many Braids. He's a Nez Percé medicine man, and an old friend of mine."

Hiding behind Kyle's bravado, she nodded at him and wiped her mouth on her sleeve. "My name's Kyle Springer."

With limber dignity he dropped to sit cross-legged next to the fire. He studied her with black, unwavering eyes. Light from the flames turned his face deep copper. Kyla forced herself to stare back, but his gaze felt as though it flicked over her heart and soul, looking for secrets.

"You are the woman I have heard about," he said finally. "Men are looking for you."

She set her jaw to hide her suddenly pounding heart, aghast at his prompt recognition of her gender. Her bulky coat and the sling hid her breasts, so she knew her shape hadn't given her away. And she wasn't about to own up to it. "I ain't no woman," she retorted with a scowl.

"It is a very good disguise. A brave one. But you are a woman." He spoke with simple finality. "My people would call you Winter Moon, because you change your appearance and show different faces."

Seeing her reaction, Jace tipped her another quick grin. "You might as well give it up, Kyla. Many Braids knows more about nature and people than any man I've ever met. You can't fool him. I should have had him with me when I met you." He gave the Indian a cup of coffee.

Kyla pressed her lips into a tight line and moved the plate from her lap. The medicine man unnerved her. How much could he divine? What else did he know? She had posed as a boy many times, and no one had ever seen through her masquerade. Now in the course of only a few days, two people had figured it out. She felt even more vulnerable than before. She was wounded and tired, and had nowhere to hide.

Jace's voice broke in on her thoughts. "Kyla was married to Hank Bailey. We're looking for the man who murdered him." To her distress, he went on to tell Many Braids about the Vigilance Union and Hardesty taking her ranch. Kyla flashed him a cold look. Why on earth didn't he just take out an advertisement in the newspaper and tell the whole world?

Many Braids nodded, making the beads on his braids click softly. "I know of these men. Their hearts are dark."

Jace handed him a joint of roast rabbit and sat down. After giving him a chance to eat, Jace asked, "What have you heard in the last few days? Do you know if we're being followed?"

"There were two men outside of Cord—one of them shot you," Many Braids replied, looking at Kyle. "They chased you till the sun was gone, Jace Rankin, but you are cunning like the coyote. Even I had trouble finding you. And those men were lazy and gave up easily. They would rather drink whiskey than work." He stood, unfurling his tall body as smoothly as he'd folded it to sit. "It is a good thing for you."

"Why?" Kyla asked suddenly, worried that some other danger lurked ahead or behind.

Many Braids considered her again, looking down at her from his full height. "You are injured and will need time to heal before you meet your enemies again."

She had the uneasy feeling that the shrewd old medicine man could see into her thoughts with no trouble at all. But that was ridiculous, she told herself. It was an act, just as she pretended to be Kyle.

"You don't need to go back out into this weather, Many Braids. Share the fire tonight," Jace said.

Kyla shot him a wide-eyed, silent objection but he ignored her. That was the last thing she wanted, to have this big Indian here all night, scrutinizing her.

"No, but thank you, Jace Ranking, for the food." Many Braids turned to her then. "The men you rush to meet are much more dangerous than I am, Winter Moon." She felt her face get hot. "I will find you when you need my help. It will be soon."

With that final cryptic remark, he faded back into the brush.

"What did he mean by that?" Kyla asked, her voice

fading to a rough croak. The night had grown cold and she fought another shiver.

Jace tossed away the remains of his coffee and stowed the tin cup in his gear. "It's hard to say. Many Braids pretty much roams free and tends to show up where he's least expected." He began laying out his bedroll next to the fire.

"Aren't you afr—I mean, can you trust him?"

He stopped what he was doing and looked at her. His eyes were like pale agates. "As much as I can any man. You're one to talk about trust. Up until yesterday, I thought you were a boy."

"I told you why I did that," she snapped, her brows rushing together. Even now she was conscious of rounding her shoulders and pulling in her chest.

The corner of his mouth turned down. "Well, I've never let Many Braids worry me. But then, I've never had anything to hide."

Kyla doubted that. Everyone had something to hide.

Chapter Four

Tom Hardesty sat at the kitchen table at the Springer ranch and watched Mayella Cathcart finish putting together his supper. He appraised her straight back and soft fullness. She wasn't a bad-looking little thing, he decided. Not bad at all, considering that she was just fifteen years old. Hell, fifteen could be called a woman in his book and anywhere else in the world. Girls that age got married and had babies. She wasn't quite finished growing yet, but a lot of promise was packed into the sweet curves that were beginning to emerge. And like icing on a cake, she had big brown eyes and long, corn-silk hair that brushed her waist. Yessir, she was a pleasing young woman.

She turned from the stove and brought his plate to the table. "I hope you like it, Mr. Hardesty," she said, a bit timid. He liked that. She treated him with proper respect, not like that fire-haired she-devil who tormented his dreams and most of his waking moments.

"Say, there, Mayella, where's your dish? You aren't

going to make me eat alone, are you?" He teased her mildly—no point in spooking her just yet.

He felt her eyes flick over his face, treading lightly on the healing wound the she-devil had carved. Anger at Kyla rumbled in him again, then settled down.

Mayella colored a little, and she glanced over her shoulder at the yard beyond the kitchen screen door. "M-my pa will be coming for me any minute now. He said I was only to cook for you, Mr. Hardesty, and then I have to come home and do my own chores."

He pushed out a chair invitingly. "Aw, come on, Mayella," he coaxed. "I know he wouldn't expect you to go hungry. The least I can do is offer you some of the supper you cooked." He leaned over the plate and inhaled deeply the aroma of steak and fried potatoes. "It smells too good to pass up."

So did she, he thought, with her faint, innocent scent of vanilla. It gave him an abrupt, fierce appetite for more than just food.

She looked toward the yard again. "No, really, my ma would wear me out if she knew I ate with—if I don't have supper with the family. I'll just wash up these dishes in the sink while I'm waiting for Pa."

"Well, maybe tomorrow night, then," he pressed, and smiled at her. A nervous half smile crossed her mouth, then she sidled around the table and went back to the sink.

Being a well-placed member of the Vigilance Union had its advantages, Tom reflected as he cut into the steak. His housekeeping predicament, for example. When he had explained it in just the right way to Abel Cathcart, the man had obligingly agreed to send

Mayella over to cook for him. Oh, he'd been reluctant at first. He'd squirmed around and said it wasn't proper for a young unmarried girl to be alone in a man's house. During the conversation that took place over Abel's fence, Tom conveniently recalled that Luke Jory was assessing a little charge on all the ranchers in the area. The money would ensure that no mysterious midnight cattle rustling would occur. Abel hadn't yet paid, had he?

Mayella's services suddenly became available.

And the girl did a good job. She had even put some wildflowers on his table, the last ones of the year. He stared at the flare of her hips under her plain gingham dress and felt a familiar heat build.

Mayella might not be the one he hungered for, he thought. But she'd do just fine till Kyla Bailey was where she belonged—in his bed and under his thumb.

"We'll make Misfortune by this afternoon."

Walking the few steps to the stream, Kyla nodded without turning to look at Jace. His voice came from behind her as he poured hot coffee. She recognized its scent and the sound of the enameled pot clanking against the rocks of the fire pit. A blue jay on a nearby outcropping squawked as if to complain about the noise.

She lifted her head and scanned the sky. At least it had stopped raining sometime before dawn. Now thin sunlight filtered through the clouds and mist trailed along the ground as it began to dry out.

The horses were already saddled but they were getting a later start than they had the last couple of mornings. Maybe Many Braids's information about McIntyre and Lem had convinced him that they were safe for the moment. It was silly of her to think that perhaps Jace was trying to make it easier for her. He was a hard man, a coldhearted killer, who was not inclined to make things easy for anyone. She glanced back over her shoulder and saw him polishing the barrel of his rifle with an old piece of flannel and long, slow strokes. The blue-gray metal gleamed dully in the morning light.

"I'd think a man in your line of work would want a newer rifle, like a Winchester," she commented, searching her pants pocket for a handkerchief. "That thing must be thirty years old."

"And it works just fine. I trust this Henry—it's never let me down." He caressed the rifle as if it were a lover. "That's more than I can say for a lot of people I've known," he added.

Kyla frowned. There was something wrong with that kind of reasoning, but she wasn't up to analyzing it. Crouching on the gravel next to the stream, she dipped the hankie into the icy water and washed her face. Her hand shook and her cheeks were so hot she almost expected to hear the wet fabric sizzle on her skin. She must have a fever, she thought, but there was nothing to do except press on to Misfortune. She had come too far to give in to an injury.

Leaning over to dunk her washcloth again, she avoided looking at her reflection. The water was clear and slow-moving, and made a perfect mirror. Kyla had never thought of herself as a vain woman, but if she looked as bad as she felt, she didn't want to know.

She hadn't bathed in a tub since escaping from Blakely. She had been able to wash her clothes a few times, but they were old and thin when she first put them on. Except for the night in the hotel, she had camped in the open for more than a month. To sleep in a real bed, or even in a barn, out of the wet and cold, might perk her up. She hoped so, anyway—she had no more use of her arm this morning than she had had for the last two days.

"Come and get a biscuit," Jace said from his seat by the fire. "You didn't eat anything last night, and if you get weak you won't be able to keep up."

Tired and worried, the admonition only gave voice to her own fears. "Just get us to Blakely. I'll keep up all right."

Rising unsteadily, she walked back to the fire on legs that felt as if they ended just below her knees. It was a frightening sensation but she did her best to ignore it. Tucking the wrung-out handkerchief into her gear, she looked at her gun belt lying next to her bedroll. When she picked it up; the leather was cold and hard in her hand, and it seemed so heavy this morning. How on earth would she buckle that thing again? It would be a monumental task, and she didn't know what to do.

She was determined not to show Jace the weakness he was waiting for. It wasn't only pride that drove her—a moment of defenselessness, of being unprepared, could be a person's undoing. No one knew that better than she did.

She looked at the top of his head where the sun picked out deep red highlights in his dark hair. He looked up, too, and for an instant the gun belt in her hand was forgotten. She stood engrossed by ice blue eyes, by the strong jaw, by a wide mouth that was neither thin nor full. The odd flutter in her stomach had nothing to do with hunger or fever—she could not identify it, but it unnerved her.

Now that he knew her true gender, everything felt changed between them. He didn't act differently, but she saw a powerful awareness in his gaze that had not been there before.

Quickly she turned her eyes and tried to flap the buckle end of the gun belt around her hips. It clanked against her body, probably leaving a bruise every time it struck.

Jace watched the struggle, faintly amused. With her arm in the sling, she made him think of a goose trying to take off with one wing tied. Hot color filled her face and she panted with the effort. Laying aside the rifle he put on his hat and rose from his place by the fire.

"You're going to beat yourself to death before you get that gun strapped on." He seized the belt in midswing. "Hold that other end."

"I can manage—" she said stiffly, trying to step back.

He gripped the buckle, preventing her escape. "You'll *manage* to stand there for the rest of the morning and still not have this belt on."

She smelled of wood smoke and sage. Not exactly like a typical woman rinsed with rose or lavender water. But given the circumstances, the scents suited her. At any rate, she was hardly a typical woman.

Before she could pull away again, he shot out a hand to grip her waist. It was a mistake. Through the fabric of her thin shirt he felt an unexpected supple warmth against his fingers. If her appearance belied her gender, her softness did not. Thinking of the ample curves that swelled under her clothes, he didn't have to work hard to imagine the potential beauty hidden beneath them.

The reminder brought him up sharply. Glancing at her flushed face he saw panic in her turquoise eyes, and she jerked away.

"Quit pawin' me like that!" she snapped in Kyle's voice.

He released her, feeling as though his thoughts were stamped on his face for her to see. "Jesus Christ," he barked back, "I'm not pawing you. But how the hell am I supposed get this damned thing buckled if you keep moving away?"

"I don't like to be touched!"

"That must have made marriage hard." Hell, women didn't usually work *that* hard to get away from him, he thought, feeling a bit insulted. He narrowed his eyes as he considered her. "I told you I'm not interested in unwilling females, Kyla. But if you were the one I wanted, I'd make you feel too good to tell me no."

"Yeah, right." She glared at him and pressed her mouth into a thin line.

"Come on," he said gruffly, "let's get going."

She held still long enough for him to cinch the leather around her slender hips, but he felt her edginess. Hell, he even felt his own tension, a gathering tightness in his groin. It didn't matter how many times his head told his body that this was business, and that his craving to touch her, to hold her, was just wrong-headed. His head didn't have much say in this.

"Do you even know how to fire this thing?" he asked, needing to interrupt the awkward silence. A woman wearing a gun certainly wasn't unheard of in the West. But he didn't come across it every day, either.

"Well enough to shoot McIntyre in the hand," she replied smugly and turned to roll up her bedding.

Jace's brows flew up and he resettled his hat. "You think *you're* the one who shot him?"

"Yes, I do." Her back was to him and he tried to avoid looking at her rounded hips, but failed.

He didn't know whether to laugh or get mad. She was challenging him again. "Well, think again, Kyla."

She faced him and he thought she sighed. "Shall we go?" She still looked unnaturally flushed and the spark in her eyes had faded to a funny glazed look.

He stopped himself from gripping her shoulder. "Are you all right?"

"I'm fine. If . . . if you could just give me a hand up." She reached to grip the pommel and put her left foot in the stirrup. But when she pulled herself up, she didn't swing her leg over the saddle. Instead she hovered there as if suspended, swaying drunkenly on horse's flank, her foot wedged in the stirrup while the dun danced sideways.

"Whoa, steady Juniper," Jace called to the gelding, bounding alongside, worried that Kyla would fall. He threw out his hands, and she tumbled backward into unconsciousness and into his grip. Her battered hat fell off and wheeled into the stream, carried on a stiff breeze.

He lowered her to the ground and clamped his hand under his arm to pull off a glove. When he touched her small face, the heat he felt there scared him.

"God, girl, you're burning up." But the words were lost on her—she didn't stir. He picked her up and carried her to the edge of the creek to splash a little water on her fevered face. Her lashes formed dark crescents on her red cheeks. She remained limp in his arms. He could feel the heat of her fever even through her clothes.

She hadn't admitted how sick she was. She wouldn't let him look at her wound, and he had only guessed that she might not be doing very well.

He held her limp body closer and looked around, gnawing worry filling his chest. If desolation was a place, this was it. Surrounded for miles by scrub and yellow-grassed emptiness, this was nowhere to be stranded with a sick woman. The nights were already cold, and the days were losing their warmth, too.

Damn it, he should have asked Many Braids to tend her arm when he'd had the chance. The old medicine man might have been able to clean it up better than Jace had. Kyla would have squawked like a wet hen; now he worried that she might not regain consciousness.

They had to get to Misfortune, to Doc Sherwood. He had originally estimated that they'd be there by this afternoon. That was before this happened.

After tying Juniper to his own pommel, he lifted Kyla to his saddle. He held a hand on her to balance her there until he could jump up behind her. Then he settled her against him, with her warm back pressed to his chest.

A feeling of protectiveness came over him, a feeling as reluctant as it was surprising. He was startled by the unexpected pleasure of this human contact. Tentatively, he rested his chin on the top of her head and felt the softness of her butchered hair.

What little he knew about this woman suggested that her wounds ran deeper than the one on her arm. He shook his head. He'd spent most of his life avoiding entanglements with people, especially with women; he wanted to keep things just the way they were.

He had no idea why fate had made her his responsibility—his life hadn't prepared him for this. He had drifted for years, doing as he chose and answering to no one. But he had no choice except to see this through.

He would need help, though.

Pointing their ragged little band north, they headed toward Misfortune and one of the few friends he had in the world.

"Hang on, we're almost there."

"You'll like Chloe McGuire. She's got a lot of grit, just like you."

"Doc Sherwood will have you patched up and on your feet in no time."

As the miles passed, Jace talked to encourage himself as much as Kyla. Whether she heard him or not he didn't know. She had not stirred even once in all these hours. Only an occasional whimper escaped her.

Darkness was closing in when he turned the last

bend in the road and saw Travis McGuire's black-smith shop up ahead. Kyla, still unconscious, lay against him in his arms.

The last time he'd ridden up to this white farm-house, a year ago, he'd arrived with the single-minded intention of killing Travis. He had been blindly certain that his best friend and sister's widower, was respon-sible for her murder. Thank God he had come to his senses and they'd made their peace.

But now as they approached, something seemed wrong here. The house was dark, even in the kitchen, and no telltale wisp of smoke rose from the chimney over the shop. The gate to the backyard swung lazily on the cold twilight wind, banging against the fence when a strong gust came up. Curtains still draped the windows but a feeling of abandonment hung over the whole place.

What the hell was going on? he wondered. He slid down from the saddle and brought Kyla with him. Carrying her up to the front porch, he laid her on the swing to knock on the door.

"Travis!" he yelled, pounding his fist on the frame of the screen door.

There was no response.

He glanced at Kyla, lifeless and pale now, slumped on the porch swing like a full-size rag doll. He could not take her any farther. Night was coming on, and the last few days had been hard enough for her. She needed shelter, and to have her arm tended. They had to stay here, whether or not they were invited. If Travis and Chloe didn't like that, they could take it up with him later. The decision made, he pulled open the screen door and turned the doorknob.

The dusky light revealed a front parlor with only a few pieces of furniture. He returned to the porch and picked up Kyla. She felt so small. Her head lolled against his arm and he carried her inside to a dark green settee.

Confident that she would stay put, he left her to check the other rooms, baffled by the emptiness. It was the same in the kitchen—the stove was still there, but the cupboards were empty of all the food and most of the dishes. The kitchen table remained but one chair was gone. It was as if they'd taken sudden flight, grabbing what they could carry as they left.

He looked out the windows at the coming night. He had brought Kyla here hoping for the help of friends, but it looked like they were on their own. He had to go for Doc Sherwood, and they would need food, even if he had to buy something from the saloon. Doc would know where Travis and Chloe had gone.

He strode back to the parlor and pushed Kyla more firmly against the back of the settee.

Crouching next to her, he studied her slack face and said, "Now, listen, I'm going for the doc, but I'll be back as soon as I can, before you even notice I'm gone." She mumbled incoherently, but her eyes remained closed and she gave no indication of understanding him. "You stay here, okay?" he added, feeling a little foolish.

He lighted an oil lamp that still stood on a table by the settee, then with a final look at her, walked to the door and pulled it closed behind him.

The fast ride down Misfortune's one street proved to Jace that there was even less of the old mining town than there had been a year ago. A couple of the boarded-up buildings were beginning to lean on their foundations. Dark windows bracketed the length of the street. The whole place looked as if a good wind gust would carry it all away, leaving nothing but its memory. Only DeGroot's Mercantile and the Twilight Star Saloon remained in business.

When he came abreast of the abandoned Rose and Garter, a picture flashed through his mind of a hushed September afternoon, and the battle that he and Travis had waged on the second floor for the life of Chloe Maitland. When it was over, Jace had a bullet in his shoulder, and Chloe's kidnapper was dead, shot twice in the heart by Travis. Despite the bitterness that had stood between them, Travis had saved his life, and Jace returned the favor by leaving Misfortune and taking his grudge with him.

At the opposite end of town, Jace spotted Doc Sherwood's house. Its windows were as dark as the others.

"Goddamn it to hell!" he swore viciously. A piece of paper nailed to the front door fluttered in the chill wind that moaned down the corridor of abandoned buildings. He dismounted and took the porch stairs in two leaps to read a weather-bleached note that said Dr. Miles Sherwood had passed away last spring. . . .

So be it, then, Jace decided grimly, crumpling the paper in his gloved fist. He didn't know why the job had fallen to him, of all people. But it was up to him to take care of Kyla Springer Bailey.

* * *

"All right, all right, I'm coming! Keep your britches on and stop that pounding."

The long shade covering the door of DeGroot's Mercantile flew up, and Jace stared at the balding, bespectacled man who gaped at him from the other side of the glass. A napkin was tucked into the collar of his shirt and behind him, a light shown from the living quarters in back of the store.

Several seconds passed before Albert DeGroot tore his astonished gaze away to fumble with the lock and open the door. The familiar scents of coffee, cured meat, and spices rolled over Jace, along with the smell of an evening meal.

"Jace Rankin, I'll be danged! If this ain't a surprise! It's been a long time since you were through these parts—why I b'lieve it's been a year or better. It was after that sorry day at the Rose and Garter. I was just now setting down to supper. The missus and I usually eat about this time of—"

"I need to buy some things," Jace interrupted, pushing his way into the store. He'd forgotten how yappy the man was.

Albert glanced down at the Henry in Rankin's hand. "Well, uh, sure, sure!" He yanked the napkin from his shirtfront and hurried behind the counter to light a lamp.

Jace fired off a list that included bandages, canned food, coffee, and another bottle of whiskey.

"I only have moonshine from the Grover sisters," Albert reported, holding up a mason jar full of honey-colored liquid. "We don't get hardly any whiskey shipments through here anymore."

"It'll do," Jace countered.

"What brings you to Misfortune this time, Mr. Rankin?" He glanced over his shoulder and shot Jace an eager, confidential look. "Hunting a bank robber? Maybe a killer? 'Course I have my hands full with this store, but I always thought my true calling was to be a lawman of some kind."

Jace stifled the urge to laugh. He'd encountered this attitude more times than he could remember: men with safe, boring lives who postured before their shaving mirrors, pretending to face make-believe outlaws. Men who rarely even handled firearms and imagined that being a bounty hunter was exciting.

He had never thought of it as exciting, except for those times when someone like Hobie McIntyre pointed a gun at him, holding his life on the point of a moment. That wasn't the type of excitement he wanted—the kind that triggered his survival instinct and left his insides churning for hours afterward. But he couldn't let the pressure show—he had to keep it hidden. That kind of life could tell on a man eventually.

He walked over to a stack of boys' clothing and rummaged through them until he found a small pair of jeans and a blue shirt. If Kyla had to dress as a boy, she might as well have clothes that weren't bloody or gunshot. He threw them on the pine counter. "Put these on the bill, too."

Albert peered over the tops of his spectacles at the denims, his wispy brows raised. "Those pants ain't going to fit you."

Jace stared at him and made no response. Nervously, Albert whisked them into the pile of other merchandise.

"This town has changed plenty since you were last here," he said, moving from shelf to shelf to fill the order. "It's gotten nigh on to impossible to keep this store. If it weren't for the farmers—"

"Where are Travis and Chloe McGuire?" Jace asked.

As if the question signaled a pause for conversation, Albert stopped and rested his elbows on the counter. "They moved to Baker City. Let's see . . . they left in June, a few weeks after old Doc Sherwood died. That McGuire feller made a big gold strike up in the hills here. He and Chloe wanted to go somewheres more lively, I guess. Can't say as I blame them." He shook his head and chuckled. "The old-time prospectors around here, Lordy, they were mad enough to chew horseshoe nails. Who'd have guessed some outsider would come in here and dig up a fortune, considering the rest of 'em have been scratchin' around up there since—"

God, the man was a lunkhead, Jace thought irritably. He had no sense of urgency, no hint that he was getting on Jace's nerves. He leaned close until his face was mere inches from Albert's. "I'm in a hurry," he said softly, letting impatience slide into his tone.

Albert lurched upright. "Oh, sure, right away." He grabbed a sack of sugar. "Did you say you were here to visit McGuire?"

"No, I didn't say. What about the house? Who owns it?"

"Well, I guess they still do. McGuire paid off the mortgage and it ain't like there was someone around here begging to buy it. He wouldn't tell what they planned to do in Baker City. It was always so blamed hard to get information out of that feller." Albert shrugged. "They just took what they could carry away in a wagon, happy as two peas in a pod, and left the rest. They could sure afford to buy whatever they needed when they got there. That was a real step up for Chloe, I'll tell you. She scraped along for years after her father died. You know that's how she and that McGuire feller came to meet. Looking for a black-smith, she was and he . . ."

The man prattled on, but his voice faded to a drone in the back of Jace's mind. That was good news about the house, and it explained why some of the furniture was still there. They wouldn't mind, then, if he and Kyla had to stay there for a while.

He glanced out the window—full darkness had fallen. He needed to get back to her. She was burning with fever and hadn't eaten for two days. He inhaled the aroma of food again—

"You said you were just sitting down for dinner?"

Albert waved a hand affably. "Oh, well now, don't you worry about that. It'll keep for a few min—"

"What are you having?"

"Mrs. DeGroot makes the best chicken stew in eastern—"

"I'll take that, too." He plucked a crock from a pyramid of jars on display. "Put it in here. I'll pay you for the jar and the stew."

"But that's our—I mean—our supper—"

Worry and fatigue exhausted his patience. Jace pulled five silver dollars out of his pocket and began flipping them at the astounded shopkeeper, one at a time. Five dollars was more than any meal was worth.

Albert scrambled to catch the coins, but a couple of them bounced off his chest and rolled across the floor.

Jace reached across the counter and gently grasped Albert by his shirtfront. He pulled him close, and murmured, "Now you shut up a minute and listen to me. I've got a sick boy to look after and I don't have time to think about how we're going to eat. I'll buy this stew from you, and I'll pay your wife good money to cook and bring the food to the McGuire house every day until we leave." He released him and tossed the last dollar to him. "Have we got a deal?"

Albert, speechless for once, could only nod.

"Good. Then I'll take that stew now."

The shopkeeper gripped the crock in an unsteady hand and disappeared into the back for a moment. A moment of heated murmured discussion followed, punctuated by the sound of an indignant female voice. At last Albert reappeared with the jar, redolent and steaming with stew, and placed it in the box containing his other purchases.

"Mrs. DeGroot said she'd be happy to do your cooking, Mr. Rankin," he said, his smile wobbly on his now-ashen face.

Jace nodded and paid for the merchandise. "I'll expect her tomorrow morning, then."

Hoisting the box, he turned and walked out the door. He glanced back once and through the window saw Albert DeGroot scuttling around on his hands and knees picking up the silver dollars.

Maybe Kyla was right, he pondered as he untied his horse. Maybe every man did have his price.

Chapter Five

❧

"Leave me alone!" Kyla thrashed and kicked on the bed, scowling at Jace as if he were a murderer, her eyes wild and unseeing. Her boot heel connected hard with his arm and he scowled back.

"Ow! Damn it, Kyla, hold still!" he snapped, tired and frustrated.

Where did she find the energy to fight like this, sick as she was? Some private demon chased her through her delirium, he was certain of that, making his job too hard.

After he'd put the horses away in the shop, he carried her upstairs to this bedroom, grateful to find a bedstead here, as well as one in the small adjoining room. The mattress was bare, but it beat sleeping on the ground in the rain. In the hall he had found a battered chest of drawers that contained threadbare linens, including patched towels and sheets, all worn as thin as tissue paper. How to make the bed with her on it was a chore he would think about later.

Right now, he was trying to undress her, and

having no luck. The best he'd been able to do was get her out of her coat and pull off one boot. He reached for the other one.

"Don't you dare touch me again, Tom!" she warned. Her husky voice was full of anger and fear. "I swear I'll get Pa's shotgun and blow your goddamned head off!"

Hardesty, again, he thought, adding another black mark to the man's name in his mind.

"I'm not Hardesty, Kyla!" he shouted back, trying to make her see reason. "I'm Jace!"

He jammed his hand through his hair. This was ridiculous, they were getting nowhere. He stood with the boot in his hand, wondering how to proceed. Her struggling had caused the wound on her arm to begin to bleed again, and it had to be tended. But she fought like a wild mare every time she felt his touch.

Wild mare.

An idea came to him. This was an area he knew something about; he had gentled his share of horses. A quiet voice and a light touch sometimes worked wonders. Maybe the technique would work with Kyla, too. He pulled a spindle-backed chair close to the bed and sat down.

"Kyla, girl, listen now," he said, keeping his voice low and soothing. He leaned close. "You're safe. No one is going to hurt you. We're in Misfortune, in the McGuires' house. Travis and Chloe moved away, but they won't mind if we use the place. We're going to rest here for a while, till you're better."

Her face was still flushed and damp. Checking for fever, he touched her forehead. She jerked away. If anything, she felt hotter than before. For a lucid instant, her eyes locked with his and he saw her terror. He had no idea if she understood what he was saying, or was just responding to the sound.

He hurried on, trying to quell her fear. "We've done some hard traveling lately, and that shoot-out in Cord really put a kink in our rope. Your arm is starting to fester and we need to take care of it."

Her eyes drifted shut, and a small frown lodged between her brows and stayed there. She turned her head from side to side, but she was quieter, mumbling now and then.

Carefully, Jace put his hand over hers where it rested on the blue-striped mattress tick. She didn't pull away. It was hot, too, and surprisingly soft considering "Kyle's" roughneck appearance. Her fingers were long and slender, their smoothness a remnant of the woman who remained hidden. It felt nice to lay his palm over her hand, he admitted to himself. Nicer than he wanted.

She stopped fussing.

He broke the contact. Leaving the chair, he paced to the end of the bed.

"Well—we've got to change your clothes. There are no two ways about it." He kept his voice down, but his tone became businesslike. He'd never felt as awkward as he did now. A flush crept up his neck and heated his face.

He had undressed women in his time, slowly and quickly, depending on the urgency of the moment, with no hesitation or fumbling. But this was the damnedest situation he had ever found himself in. It had nothing to do with pleasure. If it had, at least he'd know what to do. But he was Kyla's doctor by default and that seemed to make things more difficult instead of easier.

For a moment he considered going to the general store to bring DeGroot's wife back here to help. He rubbed his stubbled chin. No, that wouldn't work. She was probably as nosy and annoying as her husband. And anyway, he had to protect Kyla's true identity. Eventually, Hardesty's men were going to come after them again. Whether it was Hobie McIntyre or someone else, the fewer who knew about her the better.

Like it or not, he was the man for this job.

"I made a deal with the owner of the general store to have his wife to cook for us," he continued conversationally. "After all, you won't be up to shooting any rabbits for a few days. But I didn't tell anyone who you are or why we came here."

Kyla settled down, stilled by his words. He grasped her ankle and pulled off her other boot, dropping it on the floor.

He knew that sitting her up to take off her shirt would be impossible; she would start fighting him again. There was only one thing to do. He reached for the long-bladed hunting knife at his waist. It would be tricky, but the blade was sharp and he was fast—

"I got you a new shirt at the dry-goods store." He stretched the thin fabric tight and zipped the knife along the buttons. A few of them shot to the floor with a faint clicking sound.

Her mumbling grew softer.

Another quick slice or two and the shirt was in ribbons. Kyla seemed to be none the wiser but he had no such advantage. Again her slender waist and soft, rounded breasts were laid bare before him. And he felt like an egg-sucking weasel for looking. In truth, though, he was only a man. Impatiently, he grabbed the pillowcase from the end of the bed and threw it over her chest and shoulders.

Getting her pants off proved to be much simpler than he expected. She lay quietly as tears leaked from the outer corners of her closed eyes.

Suddenly he noticed that her russet hair was the only spot of color on the bed—the rest of her was as pale as the sheet he covered her with. In fact, she seemed to have slipped farther away from him and this room, as if she'd given up.

For the first time, Jace really began to worry.

Was this what it felt like to die?

Perhaps, Kyla thought, and it wasn't so bad. The pain in her arm faded, and the little that remained didn't seem to matter now. She floated in a safe, untroubled place where she felt light and free. Oddly, she sometimes seemed to be looking down upon herself as she lay covered to her collarbones with a clean white sheet. Her bare wounded arm was wrapped in clean white bandages. A lot of activity was going on around her, and it was all so crisply detailed, so clear. The smell of hot candle wax and travel dust. The feel of the mattress under her body. The long shadows that arched up the walls. Wind rustling in the trees outside.

She saw it all, felt it, smelled it. And yet she was not part of it.

No, dying wasn't unbearable, but it seemed sad to her that she would leave this world in a strange room, with only strangers to watch.

There was Jace Rankin. Hunched in a chair next to her, he sat with his elbows on his knees and watched her intently in the wavering candlelight. He massaged his forehead and pushed his long hair back so that it rested behind his shoulders. She was wary of his presence. But she was comforted, too, as if she had known him for a long time. Or was meant to know him now. His eyes were piercing blue, burning like low flames in his haggard, beard-shadowed face. He looked as if he hadn't slept in days.

Without surprise, she saw Many Braids on her other side. She felt no fear of him now. He chanted in a low, lulling tone while he whisked a fan of feathers over her, head to foot. Now and then he stooped from his incredible height to sprinkle a few grains of pungent-smelling powder on her head and each shoulder. Every time he performed this ritual, she was pulled back into her body, pulled back into the searing agony of her pain.

She was tired—it was too hard to decide what to do. It would be easier to float away again, to drift on to a place where her parents and others who had once loved her now waited, and even beckoned to her.

There was her mother, sweet-faced and smiling, with her arms open to her.

"Mama!" she called, joy and tears making her throat tight. Oh, it was Mother—she had missed her so much.

Kyla wanted to run to her, to be held in her arms again, to hide her face in her neck, and inhale her scent of honeysuckle. She hadn't known such comfort, such loving security since the winter night her mother died. It was very tempting to offer herself up to it now. Love was so utterly lacking in her life, so completely lost to her.

To drift to love and safety, where Tom Hardesty would never trouble her again . . .

But something kept her tethered to the earth and stopped her from reaching for familiar, outstretched hands. Some reason that eluded her and waited in a mist ahead of her.

"You stand with one foot in each world," Many Braids told her. "You must decide which you will choose."

Yes, she must decide if it was worth the struggle to go on, if the thing that bound her to the living was worth finding. Kyla gazed down at the fragile body on the bed, her arm and her heart ravaged. Perhaps it wasn't worth it at all.

Jace looked at her. His expression was pale and blank, but disbelief colored his words. He sat forward. "You're too young and strong to die. Too stubborn."

He gripped her hand where it lay on the mattress. She didn't mind now—in fact, it was comforting. He spoke to her, and his voice was louder, almost angry. "Kyla, are you going to let that son of a bitch Tom Hardesty do this to you? Are you going to let him win?"

She pulled against the energy that was dragging her

back toward the bed. No, no, it didn't matter now if Hardesty "won." That all seemed trivial now, all of it.

But once more, that nameless elusive thing called to her from the mist, drawing her closer. Revenge?

"We still have work to do here," he went on. "Things aren't settled up between you and me."

Her arm throbbed, and her body grew heavy again, as though flatirons were tied to her limbs. Many Braids's chanting echoed in her head and ricocheted off the shadows in the corners.

"Kyla." She felt Jace's voice in her heart.

Chanting.

The bounty hunter's words.

Ice blue eyes.

The sharp-smelling powder.

The room whirled at a dizzying speed. Colors, voices, textures, and scents all clashed together in a mix that took Kyla's breath. She plunged deeper and deeper until nothing but night and darkness engulfed her and covered her like a wave.

Nothing but empty, dark silence.

It was bright now. Kyla could hear someone breathing. It was not loud or labored. More like the deep, quiet breaths of a sleeper.

Leather and horses. She smelled them close by.

Barely conscious, she turned her head toward the sound but her eyes were slow to open. And it was so harshly light. It flooded her face and painted the insides of her lids brilliant red.

Dreams, there had been so many dreams, wild and frightening.

Finally she opened her eyes just enough to see Jace, asleep next to her on top of the bed she had dreamed about. The shaft of light that touched her face fell upon his well-formed torso. He lay on his side, sheltering her with his body. His hand rested on her uninjured arm as if to protect her. Even in slumber he looked exhausted.

Dream or not, she was content to find him there. Kyla let her drugged sleep overtake her again.

"Guess where I got this," Albert DeGroot said and held up a silver dollar for Sheriff Fred Winslow's inspection.

Fred was much more interested in the display of plug tobacco on the counter. He made a face at the scanty selection. "Albert, how come you don't get that Lorillar chaw anymore? That was a lot better than any of this stuff. These just anger up my insides something awful."

"Hang it, Fred, don't bother with that now. Look at this dollar." He held it a little higher.

Ever since Misfortune's newspaper went bust a few years earlier, Albert had considered it his solemn duty to dispense news to anyone who stopped by his store with a mind to listen. He wasn't much for telling a man something straight off, though. He liked to drag it out for the best possible effect. Today he looked as if holding back was going to give him the fantods.

Fred looked at the coin. "Well, it's just a dollar."

"It ain't—I got it from Jace Rankin right here at this counter. *Last night.*"

The sheriff's hand froze on the tobacco and he

stared at the silver dollar. It gleamed like an evil eye in a shaft of morning sunlight. "Jace Rankin? Here?"

The shopkeeper put the coin on the counter and crossed his arms over his chest, looking very pleased with Fred's reaction. "Yes, indeedy. He's squatting in Chloe's old house and paying Mildred to bring him his meals. Says he's got a sick boy he's taking care of."

"Jace Rankin," Fred moaned to himself, feeling his dyspepsia kick up. That bounty hunter caused a helluva ruckus the last time he was in Misfortune, and Fred was getting too old and too fat to deal with big ruckuses. Why would Rankin come back here? There was no reason for anyone to come here anymore, but by God, that didn't stop the parade of strangers traipsing through this dying little town. And in Fred's mind, two people in one year constituted a parade. "Didn't he settle his score with that McGuire feller?"

Albert drummed his index finger on the coin. "This don't have anything to do with McGuire. I think Rankin is here for another reason altogether. Maybe he's hiding out. Maybe that story about a sick boy is something he just made up."

"Oh, bushwa, Albert. Who'd chase *him*?"

"Well, there's one way to find out." Albert peered at him over the tops of spectacles. "You're the sheriff here. You could go ask. After all, he's trespassing."

Fred shook his head and took one step backward. "No, sir. Not in my opinion, he ain't. Anyways, I'm more than willing to look the other way. We'll just wait and see if something happens."

* * *

Insistent knocking brought Jace out of his doze. Automatically he reached for his gun before he realized someone was pounding on the door downstairs.

He glanced at Kyla. She still slept—and he knew it was only sleep, not unconsciousness. Her fever had finally broken just before dawn.

The knocking continued. God, it was probably that nosy Mildred DeGroot. Now that this crisis was finally over, he might be able to do some of the cooking and be rid of her once and for all. She had delivered the meals they had agreed on, but her personality grated on his nerves like sandpaper on a sunburn.

He sat up on the edge of the mattress. His back creaked and his knee joints popped. All the hours and days spent in the spindle-back chair had stiffened him like an old piece of leather. He'd finally decided to lie down for a couple of hours but his muscles were still tight. He jammed his shirttails into his jeans and headed for the hallway in his stocking feet.

When he got downstairs, he saw Mrs. DeGroot's bulky shape through the lace curtain on the front-door window. She had opened the screen door and leaned close to the glass to peer in.

He knew her curiosity itched at her like woolen underwear. Over the last four days, she'd asked all kinds of questions about him, and "the boy," and tried every way possible to wangle an invitation into the house. Jace managed to deflect her prying with flinty looks and by simply not answering. But she would not give up.

He heard her turn the knob. Crossing the parlor in long, swift strides, he yanked open the door.

She jumped back a good three feet, no small trick for a woman of her girth. Her multiple chins quivered slightly, and with her hand on her chest, she stared at him with an expression of mild horror.

"Mr. Rankin! Land sakes, you gave me a start. I—I thought maybe you left. I came by earlier and no one answered."

Jace conceded that *might* be possible. The last couple of nights had been a stretch of hell on earth and he was worn out. Glancing past Mrs. DeGroot he could see that the day was well past its midpoint.

"Is the boy any better?" She tried to see around his shoulder into the house. "I'd be happy to come up and have a look. What folks are left around here have come to rely on me for their doctoring since Miles Sherwood passed away."

She babbled as much as her husband did. How either of them got a word in was beyond him. He had to work to keep from closing the door in her face.

"The boy will be fine, and I imagine he'll be hungry."

She dragged her gaze from his face and gestured at a basket sitting on the porch swing. "Well ... good, good. I have more beef broth for him, just like you wanted, and fried ham and potatoes for you."

He took the wicker basket and fished around in his pocket for a dollar. The food smelled good, and tired or not, now that he knew Kyla would live he felt his appetite stirring again.

Mildred snatched the coin from his hand as

smoothly as a pickpocket. Given the lack of residents in Misfortune, she was probably making more money cooking for him than Albert could drum up at his store. "Is he sick with something catching? I don't recall that you said what ails the boy." She peered at him again.

"I'm glad to hear that your memory works, Mrs. DeGroot. Thanks for the food." He shut the door and went to the kitchen on legs that felt like lead.

Kyla woke as soon as Jace left the room. She lay on her back and let her eyes roam over her surroundings. Everything seemed familiar but only in a dreamlike way. This room had belonged to a woman, she thought. The flowered paper on the walls, the lace curtains at the windows—no man would have chosen them. Maybe they had finally reached Jace's friends in Misfortune, and this room belonged to the woman named Chloe.

As consciousness settled on her she became aware of two things: her arm felt much better, and she didn't have a stitch on under the sheet that covered her.

Just a heartbeat ago she would have been furious, outraged. Now she was too weak to do more than note the multitude of questions that spun through her mind. She knew she had been ill; she had a vague memory of a fever yesterday on the trail. After that, everything was a blank.

The faintest scent of sachet reached her. She pressed the sheet to her nose and smelled lavender. She'd had a room like this once. There had been a bit of lace and needlework, flowers and ribbons. She had been ladylike and feminine. But it had been a lifetime ago, and it had only lasted a brief time.

What was happening to her here and now was the most important thing she had to think about. And the man who had the answers was on his way to this room. She could hear his footsteps beyond the door. She pulled the sheet up to her chin.

Their eyes locked as soon as he came in, and he smiled almost jubilantly.

"You're awake. Welcome back," he said.

"Back?" Her voice croaked from disuse and she cleared her throat. "I didn't go anywhere."

Jace sat in the chair next to the bed, and Kyla pulled the sheet closer still.

"Yeah, you did. You've been unconscious since we got here to Misfortune four days ago."

"Four days?" she echoed, dumbfounded. She had lost whole days and had no memory of them? No sense of their passing? It was stunning.

"And then night before last you ..." He faltered, and looked away, seeming to take great interest in a loose thread on the mattress.

Apprehension swept over her. "I what?"

He glanced up. "Well, you almost died. For hours I wasn't sure if you'd make it or not."

Trying to assimilate what he was telling her, she said, "Many Braids ... I saw Many Braids. Did you send for him? Is he still here?"

He gave her an indulgent look. "We haven't seen him since the night by the campfire."

"Yes, yes he was here." She knew what she saw. "He had feathers and herbs, and he chanted over me.

He said I had one foot in each world. I remember that now."

"You've been pretty sick—a person's brain can play funny tricks when a fever gets that high."

Kyla lifted her brows. She couldn't have imagined that, or dragged out some old memory to be relived as new in a hallucination. The medicine man performed rites she had never seen before, had no knowledge of.

"What do you know about him?" she asked.

"Well, he's a pretty amazing man. He was a venerated elder of his tribe and a great warrior, too, before the surrender with Chief Joseph. He knows more about herbs and medicines than most white man's doctors. Sometimes I've even thought he knows a little magic. That is, if I believed in that stuff." He leaned forward and put his elbows on his knees, letting his hands dangle between them. "But he hasn't been here. I'll tell you, though, I would have felt a little better that night if he had been with us."

It didn't make any sense but ... if Jace said the medicine man hadn't been here, it *must* have been just the two of them. It was a very odd sensation, though, remembering a dream as clearly as a waking moment.

Suddenly she realized how bad he looked—exhausted, unshaven. His eyes had the same dull, bloodshot appearance they had that morning she met him outside the hotel in Silver City. He obviously hadn't slept much, or eaten either, for quite a while.

Kyla had not liked Jace from the moment she met him. He was a killer, a hard, intimidating man who seemed to have no heart. Some of that was still true. Now, though, she was forced to see him in another light. He had saved her life. He had sat by her for days and taken care of her. She did not remember that. She simply knew it was true.

He could have left her anywhere along the way, at some farmhouse, or with a family here in town. But he hadn't.

"What about Hardesty's men? Won't they find us here if we stay in town too long?"

"I don't think so. We backtracked and sidetracked enough to throw them off. No one comes to Misfortune, anyway. Cord was on a main road. This place isn't. Besides, I'm keeping an eye out for them."

"Where is this?" she asked, gesturing at the room. If they were staying with his friends, why hadn't he mentioned them?

He told her then about Travis and Chloe going to Baker City, and about Mildred DeGroot cooking for them.

So, they were alone together in this house? That, too, would have terrified her last week. Now, after everything that had happened, it seemed a little less daunting.

Getting well was more important. She knew she needed rest and care. She was willing to allow that she would get both. An astounding thing happened in this room today, something nearly as astounding as the story he had just told her.

Kyla Springer Bailey began to trust Jace Rankin.

She slept a lot over the next couple of days. Sometimes the disturbing dreams came back, but she never wondered where Jace was—he was always nearby.

He brought her broth and pablum, which she crabbed about but ate anyway. She let him take care of her wound; his touch was surprisingly light and gentle. The acute pain was almost gone now, and the wound had finally begun to heal properly.

After a search of the house turned up no women's clothes, Jace gave her one of his shirts to wear because its tails were long, reaching to her knees. Like his bandanna, it smelled of him—leather and soap and horses. But it was still a pretty skimpy garment and Kyla felt trapped by her lack of suitable attire. She wasn't ready to put on her own clothes, but couldn't very well get out of bed if all she had to wear was a man's shirt.

Trust or no, Kyla never lost sight of the fact that Jace Rankin was a man and, she observed, a full-blooded one. And as she improved, she became more and more aware of it, in a way that she had not been before.

That fact was made very clear to her one morning when she woke and rolled over to see Jace shaving at a mirror in the little room that adjoined hers. She knew he slept there, just steps away from her own bed, but she had been too weak and tired to give it much thought.

Fascinated, she studied him through the open doorway. He wore no shirt and his bare back was turned to her. A strange breathless flutter rippled through her when she looked at the planes and shadows of his shoulder blades. The muscles in his right arm and shoulder flexed ever so slightly as he plied the razor. The light scraping sound made goose bumps rise on her scalp and arms. When he tipped his head back to shave under his chin, his dark hair, wet from washing, dripped water down the column of his spine into the waist of his jeans. Her gaze drifted lower, down narrow hips to his legs and back again.

Jace cleared his throat, bringing her out of her reverie. Hastily she averted her eyes and sat up on the edge of the bed away from his door. Her face grew warm, but this time not from fever.

No man had made her blush before. Although she had not fully submerged into Kyle's persona until recently, Kyla had hidden behind a tomboy's demeanor and clothes for most of her young womanhood. It wasn't that she hadn't liked being a girl, but Hardesty had robbed her of the freedom to be one. And in trying to fend him off, she had kept all men away from her.

Hank had been different. He'd taken her as she was, hurts and all, and made her his wife despite her straightforward opinions and need for independence. He knew that their marriage would be in name only. And she had not loved him the way a woman was supposed to love her husband. He had told her he would wait until she was ready, until the time was right. The time never came. But now the man in the other room intrigued her, despite her entrenched fears.

Without thinking, she put her hand to her hair. She had managed to take enough sponge baths to stay fresh, but her hair was another story. Days of being confined to bed had turned it into an itchy, snarled mat. She tried to comb it out with her fingers, but it was useless.

"I think we can fix that."

She jumped at the sound of Jace's voice and spun to face him. He stood in the doorway, still without a shirt, and she didn't know where to look. His jeans hung low and snug on his hips. Her immediate impression was of a man slender but powerfully built. Of a flat belly and muscled flanks that led up to a wide chest. Of old eyes in a young face. Then her gaze darted to his left shoulder where a shiny pink scar marred an otherwise rugged torso. It appeared to be just recently healed.

"Fix what?" Her words sounded impossibly high and skittish to her own ears.

"Your hair—" Jace began, then followed her gaze and glanced down at the old injury. "Oh, yeah," he said, sounding a bit self-conscious. "That's a souvenir from my last visit to this town. I got into a scuffle over a lady's honor."

"You were shot?"

He shrugged and leaned against the doorjamb. "It was a little more complicated than dealing with a bunch of rowdy miners who just wanted to contribute to a young boy's corruption." He smiled ruefully. "You'd think I'd have learned my lesson by the time I got to the Magnolia Saloon."

"Does it still hurt?" she asked quietly, wondering not only how long her pain would last, but his, too.

"Sometimes. Especially when the weather changes." He looked at her evenly. "You'll have a scar, Kyla, there's no getting around it. But your arm will heal."

She turned her head. "Oh, I know. I don't care how it looks. No one will ever see it, anyway."

A moment of uncomfortable silence fell between them.

"About your hair," he said finally.

"I'd love to wash it, but it would be pretty awkward with—"

"I'll do it."

She stared at him, astonished. Her first impulse was to refuse. It seemed too close, too personal, a touch that reached beyond the scope of bandaging her arm. She knew that her illness had forced him to the intimate task of undressing her, and she cringed at the thought, but that had been an emergency.

She wavered, though. There *was* a piece of soap in her gear, and a comb. The prospect of clean hair was too tempting to refuse. And a few moments later she found herself standing over the kitchen sink wearing a sling, his shirt, and her longjohns, while his strong hands massaged lather into her hair. They bumped hips and thighs, and his left arm crossed between her shoulders. Tense at first, she began to relax as her dislike of being touched retreated for the moment. In fact, the experience was both soothing and stirring. A little sigh of contentment escaped with her breath.

What an incredible turn this had taken: Jace Rankin, dangerous bounty hunter, a man with a killer's reputation, was washing her hair.

Jace's thoughts were running along the same path. Of all the jobs he'd done in his life, being a nursemaid was a new one for him. Never mind that it felt kind of nice, his hands in her sudsy hair, or that the back of her neck was remarkably smooth and pale, a place that begged a kiss—

"Ouch!" Kyla's smoky-voiced protest bounced up from the bottom of the sink. "Don't scrub so hard."

"Sorry," he muttered, easing up on her scalp. He kept telling himself that under ordinary circumstances this woman, tough and delicate, was not one he would look at twice. That it would be the biggest mistake he could make to entertain the ideas that had been stealing through his mind. Hell, she was Hank's widow and Hank's body was barely cold.

But the battle he had waged against her death had changed his viewpoint. People left their lives behind every hour of every day, and he'd been present to see a few of them go. Yet he'd never had the feeling he had that night when he realized that she was so close to death. Helpless. Angry. Even cheated somehow.

"Actually, you're pretty good at this," she commented, bringing his attention back to his task.

"Great," he quipped, "maybe I should give up bounty hunting and go to work in a barbershop."

Her shoulders jumped when she giggled briefly. He'd made her laugh, he marveled. It was as though he'd discovered a small, rare treasure. He had never heard her laugh. He tried again.

"Oh, so you think I couldn't do it? Can't you picture me stropping my hunting knife to scrape the scruff off some leather-hided old bullwhacker? Hell, they'd stand in line for a block just to be shaved by a famous bounty hunter."

"They probably would. And I could tell them I was your first customer," she teased, laughing again, and he joined her. That felt kind of nice, too.

He rinsed her hair with clear water that had been

warmed in the teakettle. Then he rubbed her head with a thin towel he'd found in the chest upstairs. "Sit over here by the stove." He pulled a chair close to the heat and handed her the comb.

Settling in the chair, she started working out the tangles, which were considerable in her thick hair. "This feels so much better."

He surveyed the jagged edges that began to emerge as she forced the comb through. Gesturing at the water-darkened mahogany mass, he said, "You know, I'll bet I *could* straighten that up. I found a funny-looking pair of scissors around here the other day."

A look of grave doubt crossed her small features, and her hand stilled. "Oh, I don't know—"

"Yeah, sure, I can do it. Well, I couldn't make it any worse than it is now."

She dropped her gaze to her lap, then after a pause looked up again with a defiant expression. "I wasn't tryin' to be pretty, y'know, so you can just forget about that. I'm supposed to be Kyle Springer."

Jace was beginning to realize that anytime she felt threatened, or criticized, or hurt, she retreated behind Kyle for protection.

"Kyle Springer can have an even haircut, can't he?" he asked more kindly.

She nodded slightly. "Yes, I guess so . . ."

"All right, then." He retrieved the scissors from the parlor and stood behind her to inspect the damage she'd done. "Have you ever seen scissors like this?" He held them out for her to see. "What could a person cut with these little short blades. They're like a toy."

She reached for them with a tentative hand. "No,"

she said finally, her voice growing softer. "They aren't a toy. They're embroidery scissors. They're used to cut thread so the blades don't need to be long. My mother had a pair like this." She gripped them briefly before handing them back.

"Well, they're hair-cutting scissors now. What did you use to do this the first time? An ax?"

"No, a razor. I was in a hurry the night I did it. In a hurry to get away from Hardesty. I was afraid he'd kill me after I slashed his face."

Jace came around to stand in front of her while he trimmed the sides of her hair.

She sat just low enough in the chair that he was forced to lean forward and look into her face as he worked. He was suddenly very aware of her, the turquoise eyes, the smell of her washed hair, the light scent of sage that clung to her even now. And with her hair combed back he realized that her face was more than pretty. He glanced down at her mouth, full and close, and knew he wouldn't have to lean in much closer to touch it with his own. . . .

She looked up at him. "I'm hoping I'll get to grow it back someday. You won't cut it too short, will you?"

The plaintive question went straight to his heart. "No, we're just going to trim it up." He wanted to know what had happened to this woman, why she'd given up the person she really was. Keeping his eyes on his work and his face screwed up with the effort of this unfamiliar task, he said casually, "I think you've practiced being Kyle for a long time."

She sighed slightly. "Sort of."

"Because of Tom Hardesty?" He combed the wet

hair that just brushed her collarbone and trimmed off a tendril that hung by itself.

Snip.

"Partly."

Snip.

"Pestered you a lot, did he?"

"I thought that dressing like a tomboy would keep him away."

"You're pretty convincing—it must have worked."

Snip snip.

Reaching out, she stopped his hand holding the scissors and stared straight ahead into his shirtfront. She took two deep breaths, then spoke with a flat, hard voice.

"It didn't. He raped me in the barn last fall."

Chapter Six

"What the hell do you mean you lost her?" Tom Hardesty was working up to a fine white-hot rage. "You were in the same goddamned room with her, and Rankin, too!"

Hobie McIntyre faced him on the back porch at the Springer ranch house. His red, shifting eyes betrayed his uneasiness. "But like I said, I didn't know it was her straight off. Not until just afore the shootin' started." He held up his right hand to prove his point. It was wrapped in a dirty bandanna.

"You said you could find her, and that's what I'm paying you to do."

"But she was wearin' a disguise—she looked like a draggle-tailed plowboy, not the way you talked about her. And she had on a hat." That last, apparently, was to explain everything.

"I showed you her picture before you left, McIntyre. And I told you she might be wearin' men's clothes. What more did you need?"

"Mebbe you mentioned them boys' duds, but you

got all hot and bothered talkin' about what a fine-lookin' woman she is. So round and soft and pleasin', *inside and out*, I b'lieve you said. And with a long red mane and smooth skin. I figgered her to look like her pitcher 'cept with pants, so that's what I was lookin' for. I wasn't lookin' for no short-haired hellcat who spits and curses and can fire a gun. Shee-it, I didn't see nothin' about her that was worth gettin' hard for, much less cut up with a knife"—he gestured at the scar on Tom's face—"or shot in the hand." He took off his battered hat and beat it against his thigh to shake out the dust. "Why, I bet she can even piss standin' up."

Tom grabbed McIntyre by the front of his shirt and slammed him against an upright. "I didn't ask for your opinion, and I'm not paying for it. If she and Rankin are in the eastern section, why did you come back here? Why aren't you looking for them?"

"Their trail just dried up after that," he protested. "Me and Lem, we searched for days. I thought they'd be easy to find, with her hurt and all, but Rankin's too slippery."

Tom released him. "Hurt—what happened to her?"

"I dunno, exactly," McIntyre hedged. "There was a lot of shots fired. She shot at me, I fired a couple of times, Ranking was shootin'."

"Is she dead? Is that why you aren't looking for her?" he demanded.

McIntyre shook his head. "No, no! She just got winged somehow."

So, now she would have a scar, too, Tom thought with satisfaction. He wished he could have been the one to inflict it. "You get back out there and you find them again. If you don't, you'd better not come back here or I'll shoot you myself. I might just do that anyway if you're still here in five minutes. I want her here and I want Rankin dead. Do whatever it takes, use as many men as you need. Now get out of here before I change my mind about using you for target practice." He gave McIntyre a push off the porch to get him started, then spun on his heel and thundered back into the kitchen.

At the stove, Mayella jumped and stared at him with wide eyes. She looked like she must have heard all the shouting outside. Well, good, he thought. He didn't want anyone, not *anyone* to think that Tom Hardesty was a man to be trifled with. Not for one damned minute.

"Y-your supper is almost ready, Mr. Hardesty," she said, a spoon in her hand.

He didn't want to eat. He wanted to smash his fist through something. That proud bitch was still out there because Hobie McIntyre had just walked away from her! It was really Kyla's fault, though. If she hadn't run off, if she'd done as she was told—

The fury raging in him needed a release, the kind that he'd found with Kyla squirming under him that night in the barn. She'd fought like a wildcat, but in the end he'd overpowered her, humbled her. He wished she was here now, by God. He would have her on her knees and teach her a lesson in respect she wouldn't forget.

She wasn't here, though, damn it. She was off

running around the countryside with that bastard Jace Rankin.

He glanced at the girl at the stove.

But Mayella was here . . . soft, timid Mayella.

He smiled and took two steps toward her. "I'm not hungry for supper, Mayella. I'm hankering for a taste of something else."

She backed up, shaking her head, alert as a doe. "N-now, Mr. Hardesty, this stew is all there is." She knew what he wanted. He could see it in her wide eyes, hear it in her quavering voice. Her fear both annoyed him and aroused him. He shot out a hand and grabbed her by the back of the neck. She shrieked and pulled against his grip, stiff with terror, her hands in two fists pressed side by side to the base of her throat.

"Come on now, Mayella," he crooned, smiling again. He could feel sweat popping out on his scalp and down his back. "You're supposed to help out when you're here. There's no woman around to do the little things a man needs."

Her eyes were huge and her whole body shook. "I—I'm only here to cook and c-clean. Th-that's all. My pa is coming—"

"Abel won't be here for another half hour. And tonight we're going to do something besides cook and clean." Suddenly, he pulled her to him and pressed a hard kiss on her mouth, muffling her protest. He could feel her lips mashed against her teeth, and he ran his tongue over them trying to loosen her up. Groping for her small, firm breast, he pinched her nipple.

She broke free then, screaming, and ran toward the

open door. But he was too fast for her. Grabbing the back of her dress he jerked her back. The light fabric gave way and tore open to reveal her plain white camisole and a hint of bare skin. The sight of it was like kerosene on Tom's open fire.

Gripping her arm, he yanked her out of the way and kicked the door shut. "Don't you make me mad, Mayella, honey," he warned, grinning and breathing hard. "And you don't need to bother with yelling— there's no one to hear you for miles around."

"P-please, Mr. Hardesty, let me go," she begged in a whisper choked with sobs. "I want to go h-home."

"You'll go home," he said, reaching for his belt buckle, "when you're finished—"

"Hardesty had been gone for three years, and I hoped gone for good. I even let my hair grow long, and sometimes I wore dresses, especially after Pa died . . . But then Hardesty came back to Blakely. As soon as he realized Pa wasn't around, he started riding out to the ranch and trying to run things, acting like it was his right."

Kyla kept her eyes on the worn tabletop and spoke into the cup of coffee that Jace had put in front of her. He sat on the other side of the table; she could feel his gaze resting on the top of her wet, bowed head. A slash of sunlight cut a path between them.

"I was sitting up that night in the barn with a mare that was ready to foal. When he walked in, I had a sense of—doom, I guess. There was no one around. Hank and the others were in the bunkhouse on the far side of the yard. His eyes had a wild look. Even though he pretended to be nice at first, I knew better. A skunk can't change its stripes."

Kyla paused. Talking about this was like reliving it. But not talking about it was almost worse. Only Hank knew what had happened that night, and he was dead now. Maybe if Jace understood how cruel and depraved Hardesty was, he would be willing to kill him instead of taking him to jail.

When she continued, her voice shook with the words. "I did everything I could to get away, but it was no use. He was so much bigger than me, so full of lust and hate, I couldn't stop him. It wasn't like he just—well—" she faltered and glanced up at Jace before plunging her gaze to the coffee again. "He didn't just—want me. He wanted to *break* me, I guess."

He had nearly succeeded, too. She could still smell him, still feel his weight crushing her into the straw. All of it, every detail, was burned into her memory as if it had happened just last night. Her hands were tight fists in her lap, and hot tears scorched her eyes. She brushed at them angrily.

She had washed and then washed again until her skin was raw—she lost count of the number of baths she took. None of them helped; she still felt dirty, contaminated. Nothing took away the humiliation and pain. She didn't sleep, she didn't eat, she didn't work. She could barely leave the house.

And it was *her* dirty little secret. She told no one what had happened, or why she crept around like a stricken animal, jumping at every noise, refusing to go to the barn to seen the new filly. How could she talk about it? And to whom? But Hank was suspicious, and when at last she admitted what had happened, he strapped on his revolver to gun down Hardesty. Kyla stopped him, though, believing at the time that killing her rapist would be a breach of basic humanity.

She took a sip of the now-cold coffee, and finally looked up at Jace. She could see the muscles working in his jaw. "I have regretted that every day since. I should have let Hank go after him. Then he said that short of killing him, if I were married I'd have some kind of legal protection for me and my land, especially with Luke Jory and the Vigilance Union running things. Tom Hardesty is just the kind of man Jory would like. I knew Hank was right, so we got married. And if we hadn't he'd still be alive. I might as well have pointed the gun at Hank's chest myself and pulled the trigger."

Imagining the scene in the barn—this small, scrappy woman overpowered by that son of a bitch Hardesty—Jace felt a familiar icy knot form in his stomach. He'd known men like that; he'd hunted men like that.

He studied Kyla. Her eyes were as flat and hard as the colored stone they resembled. "You know you aren't responsible for Hank's murder. Nobody made him marry you—he wanted to."

She laced her fingers together on the table and clenched them until her knuckles turned white. "I've told myself that, but the truth of the matter is that being my husband got him killed. When I married Hank, I gave Tom a reason to shoot him: I made sure that he would never be able to claim half the ranch as his. And Hank got nothing from me for himself. What should have been his was stolen by Hardesty, and I couldn't let him—couldn't bear— He married me for *nothing*." This last came out in a hoarse, angry whisper.

Her meaning was clear enough. Frightened, trying to recover from a brutal assault, faced with a marriage of convenience—he understood why she shied away from being touched. But she didn't need to shoulder the guilt for Hank's murder.

"Wait a minute," he said. "Didn't you tell me that Hank led that group—the Moonlighters, the Moonshiners?"

"The Midnighters."

"Right. Isn't it possible that if the Midnighters were a real threat to the vigilantes they would've wanted Hank out of the way?"

Her head came up at this suggestion, as if she were drowning and he had thrown her a rope. "Well, maybe."

"Sure, no maybe about it. One of the best ways to weaken or even destroy a group is to take away its leader."

"I guess that could be true, couldn't it?"

He leaned back in his chair and crossed his arms over his chest. "Hell, yes, it could."

She looked almost relieved. "I've relived that afternoon every single night in my dreams. It has always seemed like my fault." Then her face clouded over again. "No—Tom killed Hank because of me."

"You said that Hardesty pestered you for years—why didn't your old man do something about it?" he asked, sipping his own coffee.

She glanced at the floor again. "I never told him. It wasn't something I could talk about."

He put the cup down and put his elbows on the table. "God, girl, why not? If I were your father, I would have taken that mean son of a bitch out to the barn and strapped him until he learned some respect and decency."

Shaking her head, she kept her eyes lowered. "No. It wouldn't have done any good to say anything."

"Why?"

Kyla didn't answer. She only shook her head again.

Jace considered everything she'd told him and came to a single conclusion. Tom Hardesty had taken too much from her, all of it important—her freedom to be a woman, her right to choose the man she would give her virginity to, her husband, her home and security, and very nearly her life. Hell, he may have even intimidated her father. She was right. Jail *wasn't* bad enough for someone like him. The ghost of a pale, frightened woman in the Bluebird Saloon rose in his mind.

"What do you want me to do, Kyla?" he asked finally, already knowing what her answer would be.

She looked at him dead on. "I want you to make him to pay."

He let his gaze rest on her set face. She had told him that more than once since they met in Silver City. But this time there was no mistaking her implication—he could not assume that she meant anything else.

He nodded, once. "All right. I'll do it."

* * *

Revenge.

The promise of revenge, it turned out, was powerful medicine. Over the next couple of days, Kyla's
memory of Many Braids chanting over her became
more intangible. It had seemed so real, but maybe Jace
was right: her fevered mind had provided her with an
elaborate hallucination. She knew now that it must
have been her need for retaliation that had brought
her back from the brink of death.

Now her strength flowed back into her. When she
looked in the mirror, she saw a face with healthier color.
The purplish circles under her eyes were fading. And
thanks to Chloe McGuire's embroidery scissors, even
her hair looked a little better.

Mrs. DeGroot continued to bring their food to them,
but Kyla always made sure she was upstairs before
Jace opened the door to the woman. He said that she
had done everything short of walking in unan-
nounced, so piqued was her curiosity, and Kyla did
not want the woman to see her. Misfortune might be
off the regular wagon roads and trails, but they were
not out of danger. Tom Hardesty would keep looking
for her, and she knew that Jace was right: the fewer
who knew the truth of her identity the better.

More than anything else, though, Kyla didn't feel
quite so alone in the world now. Jace grasped the core
of her anger. He had an idea of the depth of her loss
and violation, at least enough to understand her
grudge.

Her partnership with him was an unlikely one, she
admitted to herself. They were not friends, but they
had more than just a business agreement. He had

saved her life. Although he was probably one of the most dangerous men in the territory, she didn't fear him as much as before, and that was a relief.

Now and then she wondered about the man behind the notoriety. He never talked about himself, so aside from his name and reputation, he was a mystery to her. Nothing seemed to matter to him, nothing much moved him from his cool detachment. She knew the reason for the shell around her own heart. But his?

He revealed part of the answer on the afternoon following her haircut. She still wore her sling, but now she was well enough to dress in her new clothes and spend the whole day downstairs in the chilly kitchen. The shirt he'd bought her was too big, but it hid her curves better than her old one had. The day was cold, hinting at a hard winter to come. After Jace threw some firewood into the stove, they sat at the kitchen table, and she watched him clean and oil the Henry.

He carefully polished every bit of the blued barrel, almost lovingly, Kyla thought. His shirtsleeves were rolled back to his elbows, revealing strong forearms dusted with dark hair. He had nice hands, she noted, strong hands, broad and deep-shadowed across the knuckles, with long, dexterous fingers. The smell of gun grease wafted through the kitchen.

"I've never seen a man so particular about his weapons," she remarked, tucking her feet up on the chair seat. "I still think you'd want something newer, like a Winchester or a Remington."

He kept his eyes on the rifle. "This Henry and I go back a long way. It's gotten me out of a number of scrapes." He turned the flannel polishing cloth.

"Besides, a man doesn't trade a wife for a new model, why should he do it with his guns?"

What a peculiar comparison, she thought. Was it possible that a man like Jace Rankin was married? Vague disappointment nudged her. "I guess your wife is glad to know that."

His face registered mild horror. "*I'm* not married. I've drifted too long to settle down." He screwed the brass cap back on the grease tube. He looked up at her and Kyla felt a wave of heat roll through her. Those blue eyes . . . He added, "Anyway, this isn't the kind of work that lets a man come home at sundown for a home-cooked dinner with the family, you know."

"No, I suppose not." Oddly relieved, she felt sorry for him, too. Being alone in the world was too hard; she'd had a healthy taste of it herself. She rolled a cleaning rod to his side of the table. "How did you get started in bounty hunting?"

He tipped a look at her, but kept to his polishing. "You're full of questions this afternoon, aren't you?"

She hitched one shoulder. "I was just wondering. After all, I don't imagine that many boys tell themselves, 'I want to be a bounty hunter when I grow up.' They'll say a sheriff, maybe, or a marshall. Or they'll follow in their father's footsteps on family farms or businesses."

"I wasn't about to do that," he muttered, a shadow of profound bitterness coloring his words. "I wanted to get away from my old man." After a pause he added, "And I guess I wanted a reputation that would make people think twice before they crossed me."

"Well, you've got that," Kyla said, curious about the

reason for that desire but afraid to ask. "I've envied it a little. Sometimes I wished that I could make people fear me just by walking down the street."

The flannel square froze a moment under his hand, then continued on. "It was all right. For a while, anyway."

Idly, she picked up the gun grease and turned it between her fingers. "No one is afraid of Kyle, but at least he gives me more independence than I have as a woman. It's easier to fade into the background as a boy."

He eyed her shrewdly. "Be careful you don't lose your true self to the disguise. It's a dangerous game you're playing."

She sighed and pushed the tube away. "I didn't want to look like this but Pa—Oh, men can't begin to understand what it's like to be at the mercy of anyone who's bigger."

He glanced up. "You don't think so, huh?" The expression on his handsome face made her blink. His eyes reflected the jaded experience of an old man's lifetime. "I know all about it."

"You do?"

He held up the rifle barrel and peered down its length. "When I was young, taller kids always wanted to push me around. There are people who can't resist tormenting someone smaller. I got the shit beat out of me more than a few times. I was an easy target for them." His words trailed off to a mumble. "When I finally strapped on a gun belt, it didn't matter that they were bigger."

That was a revelation. Jace Rankin seemed like the

kind of man who had brimmed with self-confidence and authority even in childhood. Who would want to tangle with him? Kyla shook her head. "Children can be so cruel."

"My stepfather wasn't any better. In fact, he was worse."

Kyla sat up in her chair. "God, why? How?"

"It was a long time ago, now. I don't think about it anymore."

She pressed on. "Your stepfather beat you? Just because you were shor—because you weren't tall?"

He stood up suddenly, startling her with the abrupt anger that flashed in his ice blue gaze. "You're asking too many questions that are none of your goddamned business," he snapped and leaned toward her. Towering over her like that, he seemed enormous. It was like hearing a wolf snarl, warning her that she had come too close. A surge of fear flooded her, and her heart clenched in her chest. Then in a cooler tone, he continued tightly, "I'm going out to check the horses. If anyone knocks on the door, don't answer it. Just go upstairs." He pounded out the back door and down the steps, the Henry resting against his strong shoulder.

Drawing a shaky breath, she went to the window and touched her hand to the cold glass, watching as he crossed the yard to the shop. He scanned the area once, his head up as if he sniffed the very air for danger.

Unwittingly, Kyla had touched a raw nerve in him that made him rear. It was as though a door to his soul opened just briefly, giving her a glimpse of some private hell before it slammed shut again. Now she felt that she knew even less about him than before. But then a new suspicion rose in her mind.

Maybe it wasn't courage that made Jace seem so brave.

Maybe it was fear.

In the chill musty gloom of the blacksmith shop, Jace leaned against a rough post and jammed a hand through his hair. From her roost in the corner, a cranky hen glared at him with malevolent beady eyes and squawked to shoo him away from her babies. The puffs of yellow down cheeped along excitedly, adding to the racket.

"Oh, shut up!" he ordered, and took one menacing step toward the hen, bringing his boot down hard on the packed earth floor. "I don't need your opinion." The squawking subsided, but the dirty looks did not.

Flopping on a nearby stool, he released a breath and leaned his rifle against the rough-sawn wall. He'd had to get out of the house before he said more than he intended.

After all these years, he had thought the raging bitterness to be long dead, the hatred dulled to indifference. Yet it had come boiling to the surface, there in the kitchen, prompted by Kyla's questions. They were innocent enough but he should have stopped her sooner. And with less bite, he supposed, thinking of the way she had flinched. But years ago he had made it a point to avoid thinking about his youth and the events that ultimately led him to his place in life. In the process, he had learned to shut off nearly all of his emotions, and that suited him just fine.

If Lyle Upton were alive, he would probably be pleased about it, too. Jace regretted that. It meant Lyle had succeeded. At least he'd stopped himself from telling Kyla about him.

So—she envied his ability to arouse fear in people on sight? It was a skill that he'd cultivated and honed to an art, thanks to Lyle. He couldn't deny its usefulness. But he had begun to realize its drawbacks, too.

He glanced around the abandoned shop, and his eyes touched briefly on its cold forge and dry water trough. The smell of rust and old metal were strong here. Of all places to seek refuge, he thought, appreciating the irony. He felt uneasy in any blacksmith shop—they all reminded him of his stepfather.

He never spoke of the man, but in the kitchen he had been about to blab his whole sorry tale to Kyla, like some whining crybaby. The words had formed so quickly, so easily. Maybe because he'd felt comfortable sitting at the table with her, incredible as it was to believe.

He found himself inexplicably drawn to her—she prowled his thoughts and dreams. He supposed it might be because he admired her courage; not every woman could do what she had done. And beneath her thorny surface he detected a rose, a core of simple goodness that attracted him like a fire on a cold night. Basic decency was not something he encountered very often.

He liked talking to her; that was a true rarity for him. Few of the people he dealt with had much to say that he wanted to hear. But a man could get tired of the sound of his own voice in his head.

He'd spent a lot of time over the years listening to himself think. Listening to the rain. Listening to the wind wear down the rocks. They were the sounds of being alone. Kyla's smoky sweet voice was a welcome change.

Then there were those other things about her, womanly things: the way she smelled, like new-cut grass, those big turquoise eyes, the soft curves of her that were no longer stifled by her clothes. Her boy's rigging now seemed like flimsy camouflage, and he wondered how he'd ever been fooled.

Jace wasn't used to this. For him, women had never been more than an hour or a night that he'd paid for. Simple physical satisfaction was all he wanted, the illusion of tenderness. It had been good enough.

But now, with only a few feet and a thin wall separating their beds, at night he could hear Kyla's sheets rustle, and he lay awake with the image of her fevered naked body imprinted on his mind. Just now, in the cool kitchen her nipples had pressed against her shirt, catching his attention. Lately he had found himself imagining what she would feel like in his arms, what her lips would taste like, how soft she was to the touch. . . .

And he could just stop imagining right now, he concluded. He pushed himself to his feet and crossed the floor to collect the horses' feed bags. On the way, he paused to look at the chicks pecking at tiny rocks embedded in the dirt. He could tell Kyla, and on good authority, that a life spent sealed off from human contact was a bleak one. But he knew the last thing she would want was another man getting close to her, regardless of his intentions. Jace wasn't even sure what his intentions might be. He looked up, and through the shop's side door, he saw her at the kitchen window, a solitary figure watching the open prairie beyond the house. He dropped his gaze to the chicks again.

Maybe he wanted to prove to her that a man's touch didn't always inflict harm, that it could soothe and comfort. That it could be as tender as she needed it to be.

Maybe he even wanted to prove it to himself.

God, what the hell was he thinking, anyway? He strode to the sack of oats leaning against a stall and scooped the grains into the two feed bags. He was no one's savior. He didn't have anything to give to another person, and right now just getting them to Blakely was as far ahead as he could see. He glanced back at the dark, cold forge.

The trouble was, if he would not look back, and couldn't envision a future, what was left?

"*Fred*, are you listening to me? Put down that blamed whittling and pay attention. I tell you, something funny is going on over at the Maitland house."

Sighing, Fred Winslow dragged his boots from the desk and tossed his knife aside. Mildred DeGroot's corseted bulk cast a shadow over his work anyway. The afternoon had been peaceful enough until she showed up in his office with some complaint that he was trying hard to shrug off.

"Oh, now, Millie," he began, trying a placating tone. "We don't know anything of the kind."

"You sure won't find out from here, whittling your life away. You're still the sheriff here in Misfortune, even if there's no one to put in the jail."

And that was exactly the way Fred liked it, nice and quiet. A month had passed before the excitement died down after the shoot-out last year with that McGuire feller and Jace Rankin. Besides that incident, Misfortune was a good place for a sheriff to work. He didn't want any trouble, and stirring up the bounty hunter was the surest way to find it. It had taken two helpings of bicarbonate to settle his stomach after Albert told him that the man was back in town.

Gathering up an old newspaper full of wood shavings, he rolled his chair to the corner stove and threw them inside. "Well, what in blue blazes do you expect me to do? Arrest him?" The very thought made Fred's dyspepsia rumble to life. "Chloe isn't here anymore to complain about Rankin using her house, so there's no one to file trespassing charges. Anyways, he's kind of a friend of hers and that McGuire feller she married. She probably wouldn't care." No one in town had gotten past calling Chloe's husband anything more personal than "that McGuire feller."

"I'm not talking about trespassing. Jace Rankin says he's taking care of a sick boy in that house, and I haven't seen hide nor hair of the young'un in all the times I've been over there. He won't let me have a look at him, and everyone around here knows I can doctor almost as good as old Miles Sherwood, God rest him. For all we know that boy could be dead. Maybe he even murdered him!"

"Murdered him! Oh, now, Millie," he repeated. Why couldn't she and Albert leave things be?

"Have you seen those cold blue eyes. He looks like a killer to me."

Oh, Lordy-Lord this was getting worse by the minute. The last thing Fred wanted to do was leave this office and confront a blue-eyed killer. But Millie looked pretty threatening herself. He dithered.

She drew herself to her full five-foot height. "Fred Winslow, you get up out of that chair and come with me to Chloe's house. We're still paying your salary here, and I guess I know what's what. I know something is wrong over there. And you're going to find out what it is."

"Aw, Millie—" he groaned and pulled himself to his feet with foot-dragging reluctance. He suspected that if he didn't move fast enough to suit her, she'd have him by the ear. "You don't need to come along."

"Oh, yes I do. It's your duty to protect the citizens of Misfortune, and I'm going to make sure you do it. So stop your bellyaching, Fred," she demanded, marching him to the office door.

Thinking of the salty-tasting bicarbonate, the sheriff figured his bellyache was just beginning.

Chapter Seven

Jace lingered at the corral fence until dusk fell. Now and then Kyla went to the kitchen window to seek him out. He stood there for a long time, apparently deep in thought, his arms resting on one of the rails. A brisk wind cut across the yellow plain, borne down from the surrounding hills that were frosted with early snow. It whipped his long hair and flattened his tan shirt against his lean body, but he seemed unaffected by the chill.

Her earlier alarm gave way to guilt blended with anger as she stared at his back. Who did he think he was, barking at her like that? She had only asked a couple of questions, and he blew up as if she'd accused him of stealing from a church collection plate. He had demanded a lot more information from her, and she had provided it without as much fuss. It was cold out there; she could feel it seeping through the glass. But if he wanted to stay at the fence and sulk, so be it.

Then, as if feeling her gaze on him, he turned and

looked up. Their eyes connected for just an instant, but the electric intensity that flashed between them stopped Kyla's breath in her throat. The wind caught the open edges of his shirt, revealing the sturdy wall of his chest. Was it anger she saw in his face? Regret? No . . . she sensed a yearning so powerful, a hunger so fierce—was it from him or within herself?—she backed away from the window, her hand at her throat.

It wasn't fear that shivered through her, at least not the kind of fear that Tom Hardesty roused. This was different. It was the same sensation that she'd felt the other morning while she watched him shave. One that spoke to the woman in her that she kept hidden from the world. The woman that no man—not Hardesty, not Hank—had ever reached.

She closed her shirt collar and peered at him from around the edge of the window frame. He had turned and was walking back to the shop. His movements were fluid and deliberate, his stride long and loose-jointed. When he was out of sight, she leaned against the wall, slightly breathless and flushed.

Jace Rankin probably did not hear the word "no" very often, she supposed. And suddenly, she could understand why.

A few minutes later, Kyla was struggling to put more firewood into the stove when she heard the door open behind her. A piece of cedar in her hand, she whirled and found Jace there. He carried the smell of cold, fresh air on his clothes.

She regarded him with her brows raised but said nothing. She didn't expect an apology, but she wasn't going to be the first one to speak either.

Apparently he realized that. "I didn't mean to, you know—earlier—" he said, stumbling awkwardly around his words. Reaching carefully into his shirt, he pulled out a ball of squirming yellow fluff that he presented to her on the flat of his hand. "Well, I thought you might like to see this."

A chick peeped at her and flapped the tiny buds of its wings.

"Oh, the sweet little thing!" she exclaimed, caught off guard. Dropping the wood, she took the bird from him and cradled it in her palm, laughing delightedly. "Where did you find him?"

He smiled, too, almost self-consciously. "An old biddy has a nest in the corner of the shop with five or six chicks." He chuckled. "I risked my neck getting this one—she wasn't too happy about me kidnapping him."

"I love newborn animals," she said and touched the bird to her cheek, smiling again at the feel of its soft down. "My favorite time of year at the ranch is when the calves and colts are born. They wobble around knock-kneed, trying to get their bearings. Then when they get a little older, it's fun to see them romping around the range."

"I grew up in town," he said. "If chickens ever roosted in my old man's shop, he would have set the dog after them."

"Back home, there's beauty to every season. The green hills in spring that turn golden in summer, the poplars along the river turning color in October. The clean white blanket of the first snowfall." She closed her eyes for a second, and a shadow of melancholy made her voice quiver slightly. She missed the place so much. "I can see it all so clearly. I can even remember the smell of the first fire of autumn in the fireplace. I'd be lighting it about now." She opened her eyes, and heat rose in her cheeks. "I guess it sounds kind of dull and mushy to you."

"No, it sounds nice. Homey," he admitted. He didn't smile exactly, but she saw one in his eyes.

"Ranch life is all I've ever known. I was probably no more than six or seven years old the first time my father perched me in front of him on his horse—I rode around with him all morning." She sighed and her grin faded. "That was before Aggie came with Tom . . ."

He nodded and moved closer to her while they studied the chick, close enough that his chest touched her shoulder. She pulled away at first, recoiling automatically. But then cautiously, tentatively, she let her shoulder brush him again. His heat penetrated their shirts and she felt the warmth as if there were no fabric between them.

Why, why, why was she drawn to him? she wondered with annoyance. She didn't want to have anything to do with *any* man; she just wanted to see justice served and to get her home back. There was no room in her plans for anyone else, and certainly not a man like Jace. Yes he was handsome, in a way that she'd never encountered before—with those unnerving eyes that made her feel as if he could see into her soul. But that wasn't enough to explain why she listened for his footsteps in this house, or what had pulled her to the window again and again while he lingered at the corral.

He was known for his reputation, menacing and fearless, but behind that reputation lurked a man with self-doubts and regrets. It was easy to respect his tough indifference—his very attitude demanded it—and just as easy to dislike him for it. But his uncertainty, she feared that most; it was what could touch her heart.

Jace knew he should do something, anything, besides hang around here with Kyla. She didn't shy from his touch against her shoulder—he wasn't sure if that was good or bad. He had brought her the chick as a roundabout apology for snapping at her, but the sweetness it brought out in her made him stay. Except for her clothes and hair, all traces of the boy Kyle were absent. Maybe a stranger would be fooled, but he wasn't. He saw what he believed was her true self: a tender, feminine woman.

Slowly she looked up at him. Though the kitchen had grown dusky with the fading light, he saw the fear in her turquoise eyes. But he also saw longing, perhaps for a touch that soothed and comforted.

Oddly, he felt as uncertain as he sensed she was. The tip of her tongue appeared when nervously she wet her soft coral lips. Putting a finger under her chin he tipped her face up to his. There was a world of hurt and courage in that face.

"Kyla . . ."

A kiss. Maybe a kiss would redeem them both. Was it possible—could it be that simple? Would it fill the emptiness he sometimes felt and temper her bitterness? Touching only her chin, Jace slowly lowered his head to hers. She smelled of sage and new fabric and some other faint undefinable scent that was all her own. He heard the slight catch of her breath and her eyes fluttered closed as his mouth hovered just above hers. He grazed the corner of her lips, lightly, easily. She was softer than he had dreamed. His pulse pounded in his ears; he heard nothing but his own breathing mingled with hers. Sweetness, God, the sweetness—

Then the kitchen door burst open.

"Merciful heavens!"

Kyla jumped back, gasping in utter surprise at the strange voice. Jace broke away with a violent start. In a purely reflexive action, he pulled his revolver before he drew another breath and trained it on Mildred DeGroot where she stood in the open back doorway. Her hands were at her throat in horror. The man he remembered to be Misfortune's sheriff hovered just behind her.

Swearing under his breath, Jace lowered the gun and pushed Kyla behind him. The chick in her hand peeped like an alarm clock, adding to the confusion.

"Lady, you nearly got a bullet between the eyes," he said to Mildred, his voice like a whip. That fact seemed to make no impression on the woman, however.

"Fred, do you see, do you see?" Mildred sputtered like a landed wide-mouth bass, and her chins quivered in indignation. "I told you something was going on but, but I never thought he and that boy—that boy and him—kissing! Merciful heavens!"

Mildred DeGroot was too thick-skulled to sense danger. If she had been a man her bad judgment would have gotten her killed years before, Jace swore silently.

Kyla looked up at Jace's granite profile, and she was glad to be standing behind him and not in front of his gun.

Fred Winslow, pale as whitewash, shouldered his way past Mildred. Jace lifted the revolver again and held it out the full length of his arm. It was astounding how fast he moved.

"N-now, Mr. Rankin, ain't no call for weapons here."

"I'm waiting to hear the reason why you two broke in here uninvited, Winslow." He didn't raise his voice. His low, deadly tone chilled the blood in Kyla's veins.

Winslow swallowed and swallowed but no words came out of his mouth.

Coolly deliberate, Jace cocked the gun.

"Jace, no!" Kyla shrieked. God, he wouldn't really shoot the man, she thought in a panic.

Winslow cowered and ducked as if he had fired.

"Why, it's a *girl*," Mildred marveled. She stared at Kyla with obvious fascination, but without a hint of embarrassment or self-consciousness.

Kyla cursed the position she was in. Once again her disguise had been exposed, and she could do nothing about it, due to the compromising position they had been caught in. Much as she wanted to, she could not very well insist that she was Kyle Springer, fifteen-year-old farm boy. She must have lost her mind to let Jace Rankin kiss her. Well, it wasn't really a kiss. But it would have turned into one. She could barely stand to be touched—how had she succumbed to the brush of his lips against hers? Was she so easily swayed with a dumb peace offering like a chick? Her moment of insanity might have endangered her life. At the very least, it was an embarrassing situation.

"I'm still waiting, Winslow," Jace said, maintaining his aim.

A gleam of perspiration shone on the sheriff's jowly face. He stared at the point of Jace's revolver, transfixed like a deer caught in kerosene lamplight. When he finally spoke, he sounded breathless. "Uh, we—that is me and Millie—well, mostly Millie, we were worried that something funny was going on here . . ."

"Funny?" Jace repeated and took a step forward.

"Well, she was worried because she had never seen the boy and thought maybe he had, uh, passed away—" Winslow gave Mildred a withering glance, then hurried on. "B-but I see we made a mistake. Sorry to have troubled you. Come on, Millie." He turned and prodded Mildred with his forearm. She stood fast.

Jace holstered his revolver, but his expression remained as dark and fearsome as a storm sky.

"Well, Mr. Rankin," Mildred said with a prim, knowing tone, eyeing Kyla up and down. "I didn't know you were keeping a *woman* here. If I had, I wouldn't have bothered Fred."

Kyla gritted her back teeth and made a fist inside her sling. "Now just you wait a minute—" she began, automatically dropping back into Kyle's voice, outraged at the insinuation. God, what a horrible woman!

Jace took another step toward the sheriff and Mildred DeGroot. And another. Kyla felt his fury rolling off him like waves of heat, but he maintained the same icy control that both frightened and awed people. He leaned over Mildred so that his face was just inches from hers.

"You don't know *anything*, lady. And you'd better plan to keep it that way if anyone comes to Misfortune asking questions about me or her." He tilted his head back slightly in Kyla's direction but did not use her name. "Because if you talk, if you say one word about either of us, I'll know. Believe me, I'll know. Now you both get the hell out of here and don't let me see your face again. Ever." The color drained out of Mildred's pudgy cheeks; apparently she finally realized the raw danger that stood before her. Jace shifted his gaze to Fred Winslow; the sheriff looked like a man who'd seen his life pass before his eyes. "Sheriff, the same goes for you."

Jace took yet another step forward, practically pushing them both out to the back porch. "And the next time you get the itch to meddle in someone else's business, remember that this was the day your curiosity almost got you killed."

He closed the door behind them then stood there, gripping the knob for a moment, as if fighting the urge to yank it out of the wood. There was a stumbling confusion of hurried footsteps on the stairs that faded away, then was followed by profound silence. Finally he turned to Kyla. His face was set and blank.

"I hope you're up to traveling because we've got to get out of here. Now, tonight. I don't trust either of them. I tried to put the fear of God in them, but as soon as the scare wears off, they'll tell everyone within a hundred miles about us. Even if Many Braids was right about Hardesty's men giving up the chase to get drunk, I don't think we're finished with them, and word has a way of getting around." He picked up his rifle. "Those busybodies will be watching every move we make, but they won't be expecting us to leave tonight. Do you need help to get your gear together?"

Shaken to the point of trembling, she said, "No, I— I'll be ready in a minute."

"Good. We still have the advantage, and I want to keep it that way. We're going to Baker City." He brushed past her, still tense with anger,

"Baker City?" Vexation overrode her fear, and she couldn't hide it. They had already lost so much time to her illness, she chafed at the idea of losing more.

"That was part of our deal. I have to talk to McGuire first—I owe it to him. Since he's not in Misfortune, we're going to Baker City." He turned and walked through the parlor to go upstairs.

She looked down at the chick gripped loosely in her hand. God, this wasn't the life she wanted—not this. She didn't want to be a regular participant in armed showdowns, she didn't want to live on the run. She just wanted to go home. It seemed like a lifetime since she'd last seen the ranch. And now he was telling her that she would have to wait even longer.

A sense of weariness came over her at the thought of leaving this half-furnished house to sleep on the trail again. But it was just as well that they were leaving the vague intimacy of this place. She must not lose sight of her goal, or let anything interfere.

Like that kiss—it was a stupid, reckless moment

that made her drop her guard. It seemed more dream-like than real. At least it might if dreams drew such vivid details as the rasp of beard stubble against her chin, or the smell of leather and soap, or the soft heat of breath ruffling her eyelashes. But it hadn't been humiliating or disgusting, like Tom Hardesty's slob-bering invasion of her mouth and ears. This had been almost . . . sweet. And for a frightening instant, she'd wanted to rest her head against Jace's shoulder and feel his arms around her.

One thing was certain: it wouldn't happen again. Ever.

She turned for the door to return the bird to its mother.

Full night blanketed the land by the time Jace and Kyla left the house in Misfortune to set out on the north road toward Baker City. Their saddlebags were loaded with the provisions he had bought at DeGroot's the night they arrived.

"It's a damn good thing I went there first," he mut-tered, taking a quick look around before leading his horse out of the shop. "If I had to talk to that fool now, I'd probably punch his face in."

The stiff breeze that had blown all day now had a decidedly sharp edge, and Kyla shifted Jace's duster on her shoulders. She hadn't wanted to take it from him. Although his attitude toward her had not wavered from the uneasy truce they'd reached when he had agreed to help her, his offer seemed, well, too chivalrous, too personal now. After all, she was sure he wouldn't have given his duster to Kyle. But her own coat had been ruined when she was shot, and the night was cold. So she accepted. Jace wore a heavy wool shirt and seemed indifferent to the chill.

Kyla wanted their relationship to return to what it had been before they came here—focused solely on their original business. And that was to get Tom Hardesty. No matter what Jace said, revenge had brought her this far. It would carry her through.

"All right, come on. Let's ride," he said, as if reading her thoughts.

She heard his saddle creak under his weight as he climbed into it. Pulling her arm out of her sling, she pushed her hat down on her head and mounted Juniper. Her arm was still tender, but well on its way to being healed.

The dark road was full of mystery, and silver-edged, patchy clouds drifted over the face of the moon. It appeared just often enough to give her a glimpse of Jace, but she could see little except the dark silhouette of him and his broad-brimmed hat.

When they had traveled a couple of miles, Jace pulled up and brought his horse around. "This is far enough for tonight. We'll find a place to camp and get something to eat."

He tried to read Kyla's expression, but it was too dark. She hadn't spoken more than a few words to him since that stupid kiss. And when she did talk, her words were cold and clipped. He felt awkward and guilty, as if he ought to apologize to her—*twice in one day*—and he didn't like that at all.

Making camp in the dark was not easy. There were no sheltering canyon walls nearby—the terrain was mostly flat for miles around. But they found a couple of shoulder-high boulders that provided a windbreak. Kyla managed to get a small fire going and heat a can of beans and some coffee while he unsaddled their horses.

When he sat down by the fire, she handed him a plate and a piece of bread. She would not meet his eyes but instead glanced at the clearing sky overhead. The silence was broken only by the wind in the grass and their forks scraping on the tin plates.

Jace had spent years with just the sound of his own heartbeat for company and it had never bothered him. He wasn't much for talking, and even less for listening. But he wanted to hear Kyla's voice, throaty and full. He wanted to know what she was thinking.

"How's your arm?" he asked, gesturing at it with his fork. It was a reasonable question, he told himself. She had almost died from that wound.

She continued to push the food around on her dish without looking up. "All right. I'm takin' off the sling tomorrow."

"Sure you're ready for that?"

"I don't like having only one hand—it throws off my pistol aim. And who knows when I might need to defend myself?" Her words were flat and to the point.

Jace felt heat fill his face, and he was glad that it didn't show in the firelight. "Are you saying that I can't protect you?"

Looking up, she scowled at him. "I ain't sayin' anything of the kind," Kyla retorted. "Anyway, I don't need protectin'. I can take care of myself. I've been doin' it a long time."

"Then what burr got under your saddle?" he asked. She might dress like a boy and talk like one, but he knew the sound of a woman's coldness.

"I ain't got a burr under my saddle."

He tossed his plate down. "The hell you don't. Whenever you get mad, you hide behind Kyle. And ever since the DeGroot woman caught us in the kitchen you've been all pinched up, like you sucked on a lemon." If she was mad, she could just tell him so.

Miffed by the comparison, Kyla lifted her nose a bit. "Kyle" had become such a habit, such comfortable armor, she didn't realize she was using him often enough to be noticeable. "Maybe I've been pinched up ever since you told me we *still* have to go to Baker City. I don't see why you can't talk to McGuire after we take care of Hardesty. What could be so important that he can't wait?"

Jace reached toward her suddenly, and Kyla pulled back, startled, still wary of him and fearful that she'd overstepped her bounds. Was he going kiss her again? Throttle her?

Instead he gripped one lapel of the duster that she still wore and withdrew a cheroot and a match from the inside pocket. His knuckles brushed the front of her shoulder with a surprising heat that raised goose bumps on her arms. Scraping his thumbnail across the sulphur match head, he lit it, keeping his ice blue gaze locked on her. She resisted the panicky urge to fidget under this scrutiny, but it wasn't easy. The end of the cheroot gleamed a hot, ember red and he exhaled a long stream of fragrant smoke.

Finally he said, "I have some news to give him—

something he's been waiting a long time to hear. And I owe it to him to deliver it." He spoke quietly as he often did, but his expression was pensive, and she felt the dead seriousness that weighted his words.

"Does it have anything to do with that drifter you shot in Silver City?" She'd heard fragments of gossip outside the Magnolia Saloon that afternoon, something about Jace's sister—

"Yeah," he replied and pulled on the slender cigar again. Then he took a sip of coffee and told her about the five years Travis had spent in prison for his wife's murder.

Firelight flickered over his handsome angular face. "My old man had me convinced that Travis killed my sister. He had everyone convinced, including the sheriff. God, I should have known better." He shook his head. "He was a blackhearted bastard. But he panicked on his deathbed, and admitted that he'd lied about Travis." He leaned against one of the boulders and crossed his ankles. "It had been hard enough to believe him in the first place—my best friend had killed my sister? And now he was telling me that he'd made all of it up. I couldn't accept it. When I finally knew it was true, I hit the trail to chase down Celia's real killer—not just for her, but for Travis, too. It took me a year to find Sawyer Clark, but I finally did. Maybe you understand now why I have to go to Baker City before I can help you?"

From the distant hills a wolf's howl rode on the wind, and Kyla shivered. Yes, she understood. What she didn't grasp was the meanness of Jace's stepfather. She hesitated to ask about him again. He'd gotten angry this afternoon when she had questioned him. As it turned out, though, he didn't need much more prodding to continue.

"Why would your stepfather lie about his own son-in-law? Is he a bad person?"

"No. In fact Travis and I were a lot alike once. Except he's tall." A short, bitter laugh escaped him. "I think Lyle enjoyed turning me against one of the few friends I had. I guess it stuck in the old man's craw that I got to five-foot-six and stopped growing. He was a blacksmith, a big shaggy bear of a man, and he made sure everyone knew that he hadn't fathered me. When I was a boy, I thought the loggers' stories about Paul Bunyan were really about him. He stood a good head higher than me. I was never sure if he thought it was fun to beat me with his belt, or if he intended to make a man out of his runt stepson. It got worse after my mother died."

Kyla blurted, "That's horrible! You couldn't help your height, any more than you could help"—she groped around for a comparison—"the color of your . . . eyes." Those eyes.

He smiled again, an oddly flat smile that she had seen him use on people who had exhausted his patience but didn't realize it. "He thought I was too puny to make it in the world. I know a couple of times he paid bullies to pick fights with me."

"Oh, Jace," she said, her voice low with regret.

Lifting his hat, he pushed a hand through his hair and shrugged, as if neither this nor anything else mattered much. "It made me strong. And I learned to fight back. Wolverines aren't very big, but they're vicious, fearless—they'll take on any enemy, no matter what size, including a human. And only a fool would forget that one can crush a man's leg in its jaws. I wanted a reputation like that, like a wolverine. I had to prove to the old man that he was wrong about me, that I wasn't a scared, puny runt. That's why I became a bounty hunter."

Kyla put aside her own plate. "It doesn't sound like you had much choice." Then she added, more to herself, "But why weren't we good enough for being ourselves?" Why hadn't her father been content with a daughter? Why had he been so eager for a son that he believed Tom could do no wrong?

Jace drew on the cheroot and took another sip of coffee. "What bothers me is that as much as I hated him for what he did, in a way he won. He did make me tough, but sometimes . . ." He swallowed and his voice trailed away.

"Sometimes?"

He gazed across the rangeland, glazed now in moonlight, and sighed slightly. "I guess I feel like I lost part of who I really was." He turned to look at her, and the wistfulness she saw in his eyes unsettled her. "That's what could happen to you. And it would be a pity, Kyla."

Jace didn't sleep much that night. He figured they were safe from Hardesty's men but just the same, it would be a hell of a thing to wake up and find the end of a gun barrel jammed between his eyes. So he only catnapped. The rest of the time, thoughts of Kyla Springer Bailey bumped around in his head. He felt useful somehow standing watch over her, even though she claimed she didn't need protecting.

He couldn't believe he had told her all that stuff about Lyle Upton. Hardly anyone knew about that; he sure never talked about it. Somehow, though, once he got started it was hard to stop. But he hadn't told her everything.

How could he talk about a twelve-year-old boy who had run from a pack of bullies who looked more to him like huge, ravening wolves? A twelve-year-old was almost a man—men didn't turn tail on a fight, no matter what. They stood their ground. That's what his stepfather had said.

Jace couldn't tell her that same boy, heart nearly bursting with terror, had hidden under a soap crate behind the general store, trying to stifle his panting, mopping his tears and his bleeding nose on his sleeve, angry and ashamed, but scared to death that he would be discovered.

Nobody knew about that. But Kyla had listened to the part he had revealed, and she didn't seem to think any less of him for it. He was beginning to think of them as kindred spirits, two desperate hearts alone in the world. Wearing only brave faces even when they wished they could hide. Something she had said nagged at the back of his memory, something about not being good enough as they were. . . .

He glanced at her bundled in her blankets on the other side of the fire. She looked sweet and tempting at the same time. It was a chilly night, and he wished he had the right to join their bedrolls. To put his arms around her and cradle her head against his chest. To finish that kiss he had started and begin to woo her back into her womanhood.

He sat up straighter, searching for a more comfortable place on the boulder to lean against. God, she gave him all kinds of damn-fool ideas. Now and then when he lay between sleep and wakefulness, he found himself envisioning the ranch she had described so vividly. If the idea had once crossed his mind that she wanted the place back just to spite Tom Hardesty, she had proved him wrong. She loved that land, and her devotion was plain to see. Maybe even catching.

It might be nice to sit on a porch swing at sundown with a glass of whiskey on his knee and this flame-haired woman next to him. To watch those colts she talked about romping across a newly green pasture. To sleep under the same roof every night, and wake up in the same bed with her in his arms.

Disgusted, he tossed a twig into the fire. Who the hell did he think he was, anyway? A regular, anonymous man who could simply decide to alter his life and take up with this woman? That was a joke. He was Jace Rankin, a bounty hunter, a man who was respected, but also hated and feared, thanks to the reputation that he had cultivated for himself. He couldn't just *change* that, the way he changed his shirt. This was the life he'd chosen for himself all those years ago. Like it or not, he was stuck with it now.

He let his gaze rest on Kyla again. Why did he think she would even want him? She had gone through hell to get to this point in time, and she didn't have much to show for it except bitterness and a bullet wound.

She wasn't likely to want a man who had to look over his shoulder every time he went to the outhouse.

Besides, he'd seen what love could do to a man. He'd watched his own sister truss up Travis McGuire like a Thanksgiving turkey—he had lost not only his heart but his sense of self.

Love was for fools. And Jace Rankin was no fool.

Chapter Eight

"We can be in Baker City this afternoon if we push it," Jace said, reining in to survey the terrain and the horizon.

The morning dawned crisp and clear blue, and after a quick breakfast he had them packed up and on an old wagon road to Baker City. It wound through the hilly yellow landscape, which was peppered here and there with abandoned mining operations and piles of tailings. Now their horses picked their way down the road that ran alongside the Powder River.

After hearing why it was so important that he talk to Travis McGuire, Kyla had accepted the detour to Baker City. She could spare a day or two for a man who had given up five years of his life for a crime he didn't commit. "We won't have to spend the night in the open?"

Jace's gaze skimmed the brow of the surrounding hills, ever watchful. She thought it must be exhausting to always be on guard, to always worry about what, or who, waited around the next bend, the next corner, the next day.

"No, we'll stay at the hotel. Tired of living like an outlaw?" he asked and gave her an amused smile.

"I'm feeling like one these days," she admitted with a sigh, "getting chased, getting shot, hiding out." Even her disguise was beginning to grate, elbowed by her growing desire to be feminine again.

If she felt like an outlaw, Jace resembled one. His jaws were shadowed with two days of dark stubble. With the beard and his hat brim hiding most of his face, he looked as sinister as any desperado she could imagine, and ten times more attractive. Now and then she caught the glint of his eyes—they were like cat's eyes, huge and blue. And just as with a cat, there was no telling what he was thinking.

They rode hard for most of the day, stopping only to rest and water the horses. Lunch was a hunk of dried beef wrapped in a slice of bread, eaten in the saddle. Kyla's arm was much stronger than she had expected; even without the sling her discomfort was minimal. But sitting around for two weeks in Misfortune had taken the traveler out of her, and in the afternoon her strength began to wilt. As the sun grew warm, she shed the duster and eventually became so drowsy she wished she could rest her head on Juniper's neck while he followed Jace's lead.

When they reached the busy streets of Baker City, though, the sun angled low and golden over the town, and Kyla felt revived by the bustle. It was the busiest place she'd seen since Silver City. Traffic of all kinds filled the dusty main street—freight wagons and teamsters maneuvered around horses, riders, and pedestrians. Cowboys, apparently in from fall roundup, tied their mounts to the hitching rails outside the saloons. It was more activity than she'd like on a regular basis, but the change was nice.

Jace led them to a dry-goods store and jumped down from his horse. "I'll be back in a minute. I'm just going to find out where the McGuires are living."

She watched him disappear into the store, following the line of his shoulders as he went. A funny kind of restlessness, a longing, came over her again, tired as she was. She couldn't put her finger on what it was, exactly—not hunger, not thirst. It wasn't even homesickness or her desire for revenge. But she had felt it several times during the last few weeks.

Stiffly, Kyla climbed out of her saddle, still favoring her arm, and tied Juniper to the hitching rail. She stepped up to the sidewalk, her boots reverberating on the boards. With her hands on her hips, she stretched her back, first to the right and then the left, and glanced around, hoping Jace wouldn't be inside too long.

"Make way, sonny," a woman said as she approached from behind with her children in tow.

"'Scuse me, ma'am," Kyla replied, jumping out of the way. She felt her face grow hot with embarrassment.

She had fooled these casual observers, just as she fooled everyone else. Nearly everyone else. At least the woman and children on the sidewalk took no particular note of her. And across the street, the men lingering outside the saloon didn't look familiar to her, or seem to pay her any mind. She simply blended in, and that was her aim. But suddenly she wished she could yell out loud, *I'm not a boy, I'm a woman!*

Maybe Jace would just get her a room at the hotel and visit the McGuires on his own. After all, if she met them who would she be? Kyle Springer, or Kyla Springer Bailey? Would she speak with Kyle's bad grammar and hold her fork like a shovel? Or would she be able to admit to her true identity, the one that drifted farther away from her each day?

The couple of times that Jace had warned her against that danger, there was nothing she could do except shrug it off. But now, in the shop's window, she saw her reflection. It was as if she were seeing herself for the first time, and her feeling of safety and courage faltered. Her shoulders were hunched and she had jammed her hands into her pants pockets, something Kyle would do. Her battered hat was pulled down tight on her head and she was wearing her binding again, made from strips of sheets she'd found in the house in Misfortune. The short hair, the straight shape and boy's clothes—was this really what she had become? This?

Looking beyond her own image, her eyes rose to a dress displayed in the shop window. There was nothing remarkable about it, but she stared at it longingly, as though it were the loveliest creation she'd ever seen. Made of forest green cotton, the full skirt was gathered to a point at the waist, and the three-quarter length sleeves were trimmed with two rows of long ruffles. The square neckline was cut for afternoon or evening wear and trimmed with smaller ruffles that matched the sleeves. A pair of high-button black kid boots stood next to it, along with a bag and a parasol.

Kyla didn't even realize that she'd pressed her gloved hands flat to the plate glass until a customer appeared on the other side of the window with the shopkeeper. The woman pointed at the dress and he took it out of the display.

"Oh," she moaned in a whisper, unaccountably disappointed. For just an instant, she put her hand to her hair. Her throat worked and her vision blurred with tears. She turned toward the wall, worried that someone would see Kyle's red eyes. Damn it, what was wrong with her? Getting shot, losing her home, seeing Hank die, those were things to cry over, not this.

Inside the shop, Jace had just asked about McGuire's blacksmith shop when he saw Kyla through the glass.

She gazed up at the dress and followed it with her eyes as it was taken out of the window. Her forlorn expression twisted his heart, and he wanted to look away. She made him think of a young girl watching a beautiful doll, one that she knew she could never have.

Jace shook his head. Jesus, but he was getting soppy and sentimental—the old man must be turning over in his grave. The idea gave him grim satisfaction. When he walked outside, he found Kyla brushing Juniper's mane with firm, determined strokes. She pulled the brush through the horsehair and smoothed her hand over it again and again, until it looked as silky as a woman's long hair. Maybe as silky as her own had been. . . .

Pushing aside the notion, he bounded down the

steps and untied his horse. "All right, let's go. We'll get rooms at the hotel, then I'll go talk to Travis."

She nodded shortly and put the brush back in her saddlebag. Then with one wistful backward glance at the shop window, she untied Juniper and hoisted herself onto his back.

"I didn't care about that old dress, anyway," she muttered.

BLACKSMITH AND LIVERY
T. MCGUIRE, PROP.

Jace paused in the street and considered the tall letters on the wall before him. The building was new, the paint bright. Around the foundation there was still a bit of sawdust left from its construction. Taking a deep breath, he walked toward the doorway where he lingered for a moment while his eyes adjusted to the dimness. Inside, the timbers were pale and clean, and a scent of new wood was strong enough to drift above the acrid smell of hot iron. Metal striking metal echoed off the walls.

The place didn't seem ominous. Jace didn't get that knot in his stomach that most blacksmith shops gave him. Instead, he had a sense of a man's accomplishment and hard work, a feeling of permanence.

A man wearing jeans and a long leather apron stood at the forge pumping the bellows while a chunk of iron he held in the coals turned white-hot. His back was turned to Jace but his tall leanness and stance were familiar.

"I'll be with you in a minute," he called over his shoulder.

Jace smiled. Travis McGuire would have made a good tracker or a good bounty hunter. He had managed to elude Jace for months while he searched for him last year. He didn't know any other man who was as aware of the moment and his surroundings as Travis was. It seemed as if he had eyes in the back of his head. Only Many Braids and Jace himself surpassed him in his skills. His single weakness, as Jace remembered, was his temper.

"How did you know I was standing here?" he asked.

"I heard your . . ." Travis let the sentence hang. His head came up slowly, and he turned to face him. He held the tongs like a weapon, with the red, glowing crescent of metal still clutched in its jaws. He looked stunned, wary, before his expression smoothed out behind a blank mask and gray eyes that lightened to almost silver.

"I heard your spurs. I didn't expect to see you again, Jace. What are you doing here?"

Jace took a couple of steps forward, mindful of the tongs. He could understand the man's mistrust, but he hadn't expected it. "I went to Misfortune to find you. Albert DeGroot said you moved up here."

Travis nodded slightly. "So you found me. What do you want?"

"To talk to you about Celia."

With two tense strides, Travis moved closer. "We said whatever was left to say about her a year ago. She's been dead a long time, and I put it behind me. I didn't kill her and I don't know who did."

"But I do know. He was a saddle bum named Sawyer Clark."

Travis blinked and lowered the tongs as though they were suddenly too heavy. He swallowed hard, but his voice had a strangled sound. "You're positive? Really positive?"

Jace nodded. "Yeah. He admitted it to me, and to a bunch of witnesses."

"Where is he?" His tone was dark and bitter. Jace thought that he looked ready to throw off the leather apron and strap on his gun to go after Clark.

"He's dead."

The color drained out of Travis's face. "You're sure?" he repeated. "Did you kill him?"

"Yes." Jace recounted the events leading up to the afternoon in the Magnolia Saloon—Clark's arrogant bragging and the brief gunfire that erupted. "I saw his body stretched out at the undertaker's."

Breathing a heavy sigh, Travis sank down on an upended nail keg by the door and sat hunched with his elbows on his knees. "God, after all those years in prison . . . all the nightmares . . . it's finally over," he said, his gaze fixed on the new planking between his boots. "I'm finally free." He was silent a long moment, then he looked up at Jace again. Pulling off his heavy gloves, he put out his hand. "Thanks, Jace, for letting me know."

They shook hands. "It took me a year to find him, but I did it." He gave him a rueful smile. "You didn't know what to think when you saw me, did you? I figured that coming here was the least I could do after, well, you know, everything. I'm sorry about it all. Lyle was a mean bastard."

"Yeah. He was," Travis agreed. "I don't know if he ever really gave a damn about anything or anyone except Celia. But you and I, we go back a long way." He glanced at the floor again. "You were the closest friend I ever had. I loved you like a brother."

Jace shifted from one foot to the other. Marriage and time must have mellowed Travis McGuire, he thought. Certainly he looked more content, as if he finally had found his place in the world after a lifetime of drifting. But even more striking was his openness. "I never should have let the old man convince me that you murdered Celia. We were friends a lot longer than we were enemies."

Travis shrugged. "But it's over. Even *you* will have to put this behind you and go on with your life. What do you think you'll do now?"

Jace turned over a crate and sat down across from Travis while he pondered the question. It was one that had crept into his thoughts every night since he shot Clark. What would he do now?

"I'm headed to Blakely with a woman I met in Silver City. She needs help with some trouble over there." And after that—what? a voice in his head asked.

"A woman, huh?" Travis lifted his brows and a smile crossed his features.

Jace shook his head. "Don't go getting any notions. Kyla isn't your typical female." *That* was an understatement. "She's a little rough around the edges."

Travis rested his head against an upright behind him. "I don't recall that you ever let any woman get too close, typical or not. What kind of trouble is she in?"

"It's a complicated story, but there are some men looking for her and it's best that they don't find her." Knowing he could trust Travis to keep it quiet, briefly he explained Kyla's predicament. He left out the details of her true grudge against Hardesty; he figured that was her business, and it was told to him in confidence. "We'll be heading for Blakely at first light, but I told her I had to stop here first." Jace lifted his hat and resettled it with a slight sigh. "We've had a hell of a trip so far."

Travis crossed his ankle over his knee. "So you're the one being chased this time? It's a lousy feeling, isn't it?"

Jace's head came up sharply at the comment, but the man's face registered no malice. "Yeah, well, it isn't just my own back I have to watch. But Kyla is pretty tough—brave, too. Kind of like your wife would be if she wore pants and a Colt rig."

Travis chuckled. "You ought to come by for dinner tonight. Chloe would be happy to see you."

Jace's laugh was flat. "Oh, yeah, I'll bet." Nobody was ever glad to see a bounty hunter.

"Sure she would be. After all, you took the bullet that was meant for me that day in Misfortune."

"I imagine she probably thought I got what I deserved for tracking you down," he muttered.

"No, come on to dinner, and bring this wildcat Kyla. It sounds like she might enjoy the company of another woman for a change."

Jace mulled it over. For Kyla . . . "All right, we'll be there."

Kyla lay across the white iron bed in her hotel room, wandering in and out of sleep. Her healing arm still produced a dull ache and she had pushed a pillow beneath it. Through the open window the muted sounds of wagons, braying mules, and general traffic drifted up from the street.

After a quick wash in the tub at the end of the hall, she was forced to put on her jeans and shirt again, since those were the only clothes she had. The simple luxury of being able to soak in a warm tub seemed so long past, she wondered if she'd ever know it again. As it was, her bath had been hurried and furtive, but at least she was clean.

As she dozed, the street noise faded and the sweeping grasslands of the ranch drifted past the inside of her closed eyelids. From the porch she saw a March sky at sunset, with huge dark clouds erupting on a delicately blue horizon, shot with bright arrows of the last daylight. Rain was coming. She smelled it. And she could see the vapor of her own breath; it would be a cold night. But inside the house it was cozy, with a good blaze in the fireplace. Inside the house he waited for her—a man with a tender touch that kindled a fire in her, too, when he held her. A man, lean and muscled, who smelled like leather and horses, with eyes the same color as the pale blue sky. In the house . . . she had only to go to him. In his arms she found strength and desire, and her troubles melted away under the flame that pulsed through her body. In his arms . . . in their bed . . .

Kyla came awake with a jolt, making the bedsprings squeak. She shot up to her elbow, her heart thumping in her chest. No, not Jace Rankin, she thought feverishly. She didn't want to dream about him, or any man. How could she?

Why did he, of all people, invade her sleep and give her such strong feelings of both sanctuary and yearning?

She didn't know. But she admitted to herself that lately, whenever she wasn't thinking about the ranch, or her revenge, or the past, Jace materialized in her mind. And last night, when he'd told her about his stepfather, he seemed more human to her, less invincible, and therefore infinitely more dangerous to her—

A sudden soft rap on the door jerked her out of her thoughts. She froze, then grabbed for her revolver which hung in its holster on the bedpost.

Creeping to the door, she stood with her shoulder pressed to the wall next to it, her gun at chest level.

"Who is it?" she demanded in Kyle's surliest voice.

"*Kyle*, it's me."

Rolling her eyes with an exasperated, relieved sigh, she reached down and unlocked the door. "Why are you prowling around out there in the hall?" she asked irritably and pulled open the door. Fright put an edge on her voice.

Jace looked at the gun she still clutched. "I wasn't prowling—I came straight up here." He closed the door behind him. He carried a large package wrapped with brown paper and tied with twine.

Kyla holstered the gun and moved closer to the window. He seemed to fill the little room with his presence. How odd that she should be unnerved by that, when they'd already spent so much time alone together, both on the road and in Misfortune. She lowered her eyes, as if he might see the evidence of her dream written there. "D-did you talk to McGuire?"

He tossed the package on the bed and sat on the edge of the mattress. He would have to sit *there*, she thought. Taking off his hat, he raked his fingers through his hair. It really was such beautiful hair, long and thick, Kyla thought, distracted by the urge to touch it. She wished he'd cover it again. Crossing her arms over her chest, she leaned against the window frame.

"Yeah, I found him. He was glad to know what happened in Silver City. Even though he was released from prison almost two years ago, I guess he didn't really feel like a free man until today." A pensive expression crossed his face.

"Did you tell him about me?"

He nodded. "A little. I told him where we're going next. We can leave tomorrow morning and head to Blakely. Tonight, though, we've been invited to dinner with Travis and Chloe. I told him we'd wait until nightfall just in case any of Hardesty's people are around."

"Dinner! Oh no, I wouldn't be comf—I mean I don't—" Self-consciously, she glanced down at her shirt and jeans and touched her damp hair. She thought again of the green dress in the store window and her chest grew tight. "No, they're your friends, you should go."

His gaze swept over her, making her even more uncomfortable. Rising from the mattress, he put his hand on the package. "This might make you change your mind."

Kyla surveyed the parcel warily. "What is it?"

He smiled. She wished he wouldn't smile like that, as if he knew what she was thinking. "Come and open it. Unless you're chicken."

Instinctively, she rose to the taunt. "I'm not chicken! I'm not afraid of you, Jace Rankin, or anyone else."

"Prove it, then, and see what's in here," he said. He was teasing her, she knew, but something else lurked in the blue depths of his eyes.

She edged one step closer and craned her neck with brows raised, as if the package held a bundle of snakes.

"Tell you what," he continued and plucked his hat from the mattress, "I'll go get washed up, and you open this. I'll be back here in an hour or so to take you to dinner."

"But—"

He sighed, and when he spoke the teasing was gone from his softly uttered words. "It'll be all right, Kyla. I didn't buy this to make you feel bad." His expression was solemn, unguarded. Then he opened the door and walked out.

Kyla left the window and went to close the door behind him. Leaning against the smooth wood panel, she heard his footsteps move down the hall and finally fade away.

She pressed her fist to her mouth. Oh, she didn't want him to look at her like that! It wasn't just desire she saw there, it was a glimpse of his soul and a man who was perhaps even lonelier than she was. She didn't want to think about any of that—the promise of seeing Tom Hardesty finally pay had brought her back from the edge of death. That was the only thing she wanted to focus on.

She glanced at the brown-paper package. She couldn't remember the last time she'd opened a gift—well, this wasn't a gift, she was sure, but it seemed like one. What had prompted him? She edged closer to the bed.

With a tentative hand she reached out and pulled the loose end of the slip knot tied in the string. Her hesitation fell away with it and she hurried to open the paper.

Kyla felt her jaw drop, and the breath left her lungs. Tucked within the wrapping she found a dress, a beautiful butter yellow dress, much lovelier than the one she'd seen in the dry-goods window. Almost reverently, she lifted it by its shoulders to look at its full length. The big leg-o'-mutton sleeves tapered to a slim fit from elbow to wrist. Its wide, ruffled yoke was trimmed with narrow lace and the bottom edge of the bodice was gathered at the waist where it had been stitched to the skirt with a V-shaped waistband.

Just holding the dress against herself made her heart feel lighter. It had been so long since she'd had anything really nice like this. Rushing to the small mirror over the washstand, she tried to see how it might look on her. She stood on tiptoe and ducked down, getting only a partial view.

But in the reflection she caught a glimpse of the bed behind her, and saw that there was more in the package. Laying the dress out on the mattress, she plowed through layers of tissue and found shoes and stockings, a beautiful underskirt trimmed with an embroidered ruffle, a white cambric chemise with a pair of matching drawers, even a lacy shawl and a velvet ribbon for her hair. A whole ensemble, and an expensive one. Her face felt as hot as a flatiron at the idea of a man buying underwear for her. In fact, the dress alone was a highly improper gift. She might have lived most of her life as a tomboy, but Kyla knew that much about what was acceptable between a man and a woman.

And as much as she wanted to, the idea of wearing a dress, of stepping out from behind Kyle and revealing her femininity, made her feel very vulnerable. Being herself, a female, had rarely been safe for her.

She knew she couldn't accept any of this.

Disappointment mingled with anger and she flopped on the bed and scowled at the lovely garments around her. Jace didn't seem like a man who could divine the secrets a woman held close. But that's what he had done, she thought as she fingered the fine embroidered edge of the underskirt. In her heart she yearned to be Kyla again, as much as she craved revenge on Tom Hardesty. Jace was giving her the chance to do just that, to be feminine.

But there had to be a catch—why else had he

bought all these things? She thought of the graze of his mouth on hers, the kiss that wasn't quite a kiss. But she wished that it had been . . .

Irritably, she batted the clouds of tissue paper; she'd just have to pack up all this stuff and give it back. He could return it to wherever he'd bought it and go to dinner without her. She reached for a sheet of tissue to wrap up the stockings, and the sparkle of gold caught her eye. Nearly lost within the depths of the wrapping was some piece of jewelry. A necklace? A bracelet? She pulled it out and discovered a heart-shaped locket engraved with intricate flowers and scrolls and suspended on a delicate chain.

"Oh," she breathed, feeling a sob fight its way up her throat.

I didn't buy this to make you feel bad.

For some reason, this one thing—a heart on a chain—made her believe him. Why it made a difference, she didn't know. Perhaps a man who bought a woman jeans and shirt one day, and then could think enough of her feelings to get her a locket the next—well, she supposed she ought to accept this. Touching the dress again, she knew it was too hard to refuse.

But it wasn't a gift. It was a loan, and she intended to tell him that. She'd pay him back. She swore she would, just as soon as she could get to her strongbox at the ranch.

All that stood between her and that money was Tom Hardesty.

Dusk was purpling the sky over Baker City when Jace pulled the window shades in his room and kicked off his boots and clothes. Striking a match, he held it to the wick of the lamp on the dresser. Harsh kerosene light threw tall shadows on the walls.

From the bottle he carried in his saddlebag, he poured a healthy measure of whiskey into the glass on the washstand and drank half of it down in one gulp. Then he looked at the man staring back at him in his shaving mirror and called him a fool.

"What the hell are you playing at?" he muttered aloud to the reflection. "What are you telling Kyla with your fancy presents?" He got no response. Because he had no answer to give.

Over the course of his years, he had faced bullies who wanted only to beat him to a pulp. He had been drawn on by men who would have shot him in the heart or the head or the balls without a moment's hesitation. But buying that female rigging was, without a doubt, the most fearsome thing he had ever done in his life. He hadn't known what to get; he'd simply told the shopkeeper's wife that he needed a dress and everything that went with it, from the skin out. The locket, though, he had chosen himself. It seemed to suit Kyla.

But his purpose?

He told himself that he just wanted her to have something decent to wear to dinner. But that was too simple.

He told himself that maybe he'd felt sorry for her when he saw the yearning in her face through the window at the dry-goods store. That buying those clothes was like giving a kid the candy she'd been hankering for. But it was more than that. And a hell of a lot different.

In Misfortune he had been tense with worry and fear for her life while he bathed her fevered body in cool water. Now, when he remembered it, he thought of her hot, silky skin.

With the memory of her smoothness, his imagination worked overtime to show him a picture of Kyla as a woman, fully curved, warm to his touch. In his daydream her soft, white shoulders bore no burdens and carried no chip. This image came to him at night, while he tried vainly to get comfortable sleeping on rock-hard ground. It drifted through his mind during the monotonous miles of the journey they had undertaken.

It aroused him, hot and hard, and made him yearn to hold Kyla in his arms. To honor and protect with his own the body that Hardesty had ravaged . . .

Goddamn, there he went again, thinking more of that mushy hogwash, he groused to himself. Maybe the old man hadn't beaten all of it out of him, after all. He plucked his shaving brush from the washstand and jammed it into the shaving mug, whipping up a fierce lather. Bolting the other half of his whiskey, he plied the brush with impatience and watched the scruff of his beard turn white with foam.

He just needed to visit the upstairs rooms at some saloon—that's what he'd always done when he wanted a woman. It was easy and uncomplicated, with no entanglements of feelings or questions about the future.

Yup, that's what he needed to do.

He picked up his razor to scrape off the lather, then halted in midstroke. The kerosene light cut harsh shadows across his face, making him look as old as he often felt. He stared at the man in the glass, and at the scar on his shoulder.

Maybe what he needed and what he wanted weren't the same anymore.

An hour later, Jace paced in the hall in front of Kyla's door. What would she look like? Hell, would she even answer when he knocked? The anticipation had tied his stomach in knots. He had never courted a woman in his life, and he wasn't courting one now. But he felt as if he should have brought flowers or some damn thing, so he wouldn't have to stand there, empty-handed.

Groping around in his shirt pocket, he brought out a cheroot and lit it. Finally he lifted his hand and knocked. Then remembering what had happened earlier, he called, "Kyle, are you ready?" It would be just his luck that she'd shoot him through the door.

There was an agonizing moment of silence.

"Yes," she finally answered with that smoky voice.

He heard the key rattle in the lock and the doorknob turn. When the door opened, Kyla appeared in the opening and Jace froze, the cheroot in his hand paused on its path to his mouth.

After weeks of seeing her in grubby boy's clothes, of watching her spit, wipe her nose on her sleeve and her hands on her pants, he could only gape at the completely feminine woman who stood before him now.

She'd managed to tie back her red hair with a

ribbon, concealing its blunt ends, and revealing her long, slim neck. The locket hung on its chain and rested at a spot just above her heart.

The rich swell of breast and hip that had been hidden by a shirt and baggy dungarees now showed themselves in a way that his daydreams had fallen far short of. And in between those curves was a long, slim waist that begged to be encircled by a man's hands.

His original impression of a woman dressed as a farm boy was utterly destroyed. Blood pumped into every part of him. He fought hard to resist the overwhelming urge to take her into his arms, to inhale the scent of her hair, to taste her mouth again with a kiss.

Her turquoise eyes sparkled and color filled her cheeks. She offered him a shy smile that shot another hole in his attempted indifference. He swallowed.

"Damn," Jace mumbled appreciatively, "you clean up pretty good."

"Thank you," Kyla replied. Her blush deepened. "You look nice, too."

He looked down the front of his own shirt. "Hell, this isn't nice. Not like you." He felt suddenly too rough and saddle-worn to escort her.

"About these clothes—" She plucked at the skirt and held it wide between her hands.

"What about them?"

"Well, they're lovely, and I appreciate you buying them. But I'll pay you for them as soon as we get to the ranch."

Jace felt a twinge of disappointment. "I don't want you to pay me back."

She pulled back a bit. "Dressing me up isn't part of

our agreement. After all, we have a business deal. So you should tack on the cost to the money I already owe you."

Yes, a business deal. And for the first time, he was sorry that it was not more than that. He nodded and sighed. "Okay, you pay me. Later. Right now, though, the McGuires are waiting for us."

She stepped out into the hall and closed the door behind her. Jace waved her ahead of him.

He saw her hips sway lightly under the soft fabric and heard the swish of her skirts. It was going to be a long evening.

Chapter Nine

Travis McGuire stood at the head of his table, cutting pieces of the apple pie in front of him. "We came to Baker City last spring. Misfortune was like a ghost town, and then after Doc Sherwood died there was no one left to deliver the baby." He grinned and winked at his very pregnant wife opposite him. "Chloe wasn't very enthusiastic about the idea of me doing it."

"Better you than Mildred DeGroot," Jace replied, stirring sugar into his coffee. "She'd be in your kitchen putting the water on to boil whether you wanted her help or not."

Chloe laughed and accepted a big wedge of pie from Travis. "I can't say that I miss any of the people we left back there." Her smile dimmed a little. "The ones I loved are gone now anyway." Looking at the portion he'd given her, she handed it back. "Oh, Travis—about *half* that much please, or I won't be able to wear any of my old clothes after the baby is born."

"I keep telling her that she's eating for two now, but

she won't go along with it," he said, cutting a narrow sliver off the piece.

Chloe pantomimed a cutting motion with her hand, and he took off a little more. "I miss being able to wear nice clothes, and that's something I'm looking forward to in a couple of months. *Your* dress is so pretty, Kyla."

Kyla caught Jace's ice blue gaze drifting over her, intimate and forthright, and she felt a flush creep up her neck. In fact, she'd sensed him watching her all evening. She dragged her eyes back to Chloe. "Oh, well, thank you. I—it's new."

Even shaved and combed and sitting here in this quiet dining room, Jace retained an aura of danger and strength that Kyla knew could inspire fear. But she wasn't afraid, exactly. In fact, with him she lost her worry about dressing up—Jace made her feel safe to be a woman. No, some other sensation rippled through her body—one that drew her and pushed her away at the same time.

Obviously catching the look that had passed between them, Chloe smiled like a cat with bowl of cream and quirked a brow as she passed pie to each of them.

Conversation flowed as dessert and coffee were consumed, and Kyla felt it was the nicest evening she had spent in recent years. No one asked awkward questions about the reason she had hired a bounty hunter, and spirits here seemed especially bright, even to Kyla, an outsider. She had expected to feel a bit awkward and out of place, but the McGuires' happiness filled this pleasant house and overflowed on their guests. Even Jace smiled and laughed more than she would have guessed he was capable of.

They were a very handsome couple—Travis with his dark hair and gray eyes, and Chloe with red-gold curls—and it was plain to her that they were very much in love. Beneath the laughter and casual banter a strong current ran between them, one of passion and respect.

Kyla felt a twinge of envy for what they shared. She had wished for such a love at one time, to be accepted for herself, without having to constantly seek approval. Hank had offered her that, she supposed. Perhaps given enough time, she might have come to care for him, as well. But Tom Hardesty had taken that possibility from her, too.

The shuffling of chairs and clinking silver brought her back to the present. Chloe stood and moved around the table with her ducklike gait, clearing dishes.

"Let me help you," Kyla said. She rose from the table to follow the woman back into her kitchen, carrying dirty plates as she went.

"Chloe, honey," Travis cautioned, starting to push his chair back, "you'd better sit down for a while longer."

"Now, stop fretting so much," Chloe called back from the hallway. "We can handle this. You and Jace go sit on the porch and catch up. I'm sure there are things you have to talk about."

After the women left the room, Travis went to the sideboard and brought out two whiskey glasses and a bottle. "Come on," he said.

Jace followed him through the parlor to the front porch and they settled into two chairs. The pale yellow glow from a parlor lamp fell in a long rectangle across the plank flooring. The evening was mild and stars twinkled in the night sky. On the western horizon, the very faintest last glow of sunset hinted at a daylight view of an expansive valley below the house.

"This is a nice place you've got here," Jace said, holding his glass while Travis poured a drink for him.

Travis poured his own shot and set the bottle down. "I had five years of trying to see the sky through a barred window. I wanted to live where I could see for miles. We found this bluff out here at the end of town and built the house."

"Marriage must be good for you—new house, new business. You've come a long way." Jace slouched down to rest on his spine and cradled the glass on his stomach.

"Yeah, we were pretty busy watching over the building of this place and the shop at the same time. Chloe took care of most of the details here. We finally moved in last month."

Jace could smell the still-fresh paint. "With the money you made from that gold strike, I thought you might retire," he said with a chuckle.

"Naw—a man has to have something to do, some purpose in the world besides making love to his wife. I admit I could try getting by on that, though." Travis leaned back and crossed his ankle over his knee. Silence fell between them for a moment, and when he spoke again, Jace heard a pale ghost of regret in his quiet words. "It took me a long time to get over Celia. I was crazy in love with her, you know."

Jace knew. He had always known, although Lyle had been able to convince him otherwise when Celia was found murdered. And while it was hard to admit to himself, he also knew that his sister had been a spoiled, faithless tease. Supremely confident of her doll-like beauty and charm, she had done exactly as she pleased and stopped at nothing to get her own way. In the end, her willfulness had cost her her life, and took five years of her husband's, too.

He nodded. "I know you loved her."

"Did—" Travis took a sip of whiskey and kept his gaze trained on the sunset. "Why did Clark kill her?"

Jace took a swallow of whiskey before he answered. "He said she laughed at him."

Travis said nothing, then shook his head and raised his glass slightly, as if in silent salute to the love of his youth. "It's all in the past now."

"You've got a good life," Jace added, feeling another twinge of envy. "Chloe is one hell of a woman."

His friend smiled. "Yeah, she is. Speaking of women, did I hear you right this afternoon when you said that Kyla is a little rough around the edges? Which edges would those be, Jace?"

Jace could hear the grin in Travis's words. Kyla had been a chief distraction since he'd laid eyes on her in the hotel hall. He couldn't even recall with any certainty what they had eaten for dinner. He found it almost impossible to believe that the smart-mouthed farm boy he'd saved from the miners in Silver City was the shy, beautiful woman with him here tonight.

He shifted in his chair and took a drink of whiskey.

"Yeah, well, you should have seen what she looked like when I found her. She said her name was *Kyle* and based on what I saw, I had no reason to doubt her. She fooled almost everyone with that disguise. But she only hired me to do a job—there's nothing more to it. I'll be moving on after that."

"Where to?"

"I don't know. Maybe California or Arizona. Someplace where the winters aren't so hard."

"Have you ever thought about settling down?"

"Nope," Jace lied, and downed another swallow of liquor. "That's for other men. Not me."

Travis tipped his chair back against the wall and looked up at the blue-black sky. "I don't know . . . there's a lot to be said for waking up under the same roof every morning. Having a woman to share your life with."

The very same thought had crossed Jace's mind more than once lately. He'd even pictured the woman. And each time he wrote off the notion almost as quickly as he did now. Almost.

"It always sounds like a good idea when winter is closing in," Jace said lightly. "Come springtime everything looks different again."

Travis let his chair come to rest on its four legs, and reached for the whiskey bottle next to him. "But there are just a certain number of springs in a man's years. You only need to lose a few of them to realize that. And you can never get them back."

The dishes were washed, and Chloe and Kyla sat at the kitchen table. Chloe poured coffee for them from a flowered pot. Her hands, Kyla noticed, were smooth and white, much smoother than her own. She had probably always lived a genteel life—if she'd worked, it sure hadn't been at rough jobs that created rough hands.

"It's good to sit down." Chloe sighed with pleasure. "I do get tired more easily now, but I still like to do some things myself. If Travis had his way I'd be sitting on a goosedown cushion all day."

"Are you hoping for a boy or a girl?"

Chloe waved her hand dismissively. "Women don't usually worry about that sort of thing. Either will be welcome. I don't think Travis even cares." Then she asked, "Do you have children, Kyla?" Jace had introduced her as a widow.

"No, my husband and I never—we didn't—we weren't married very long before he died." Kyla thought of the nights she'd spent pacing through the ranch house, terrified that a lasting consequence had come of Hardesty's assault.

"Oh, dear . . . well, maybe someday you'll meet a good man and have a family of your own. You can never tell what's waiting around the next turn in the road. Life is like that. It isn't just trouble and hard times that lie in our futures. There are good things, too. Believe me, I know."

Kyla couldn't imagine enduring a man's touch. Not after everything she had been through, including her brush with death. At that thought a pair of ice blue eyes rose in her mind, and she remembered Jace at her side during her illness, his hands on her face feeling for fever, tending to her, feeding her. No, that couldn't have been the real man, the one whose worried, exhausted face she had seen whenever she had awakened. Deliberately, she forced herself to think of the blood-chilling look on his face when she'd seen him confront Sawyer Clark in Silver City.

She shook her head. "I don't want to marry again. I can survive on my own."

Chloe gave her a kind, probing look, but she asked no questions. "I'm sure you can. But life can become almost meaningless when you're alone in the world." She laughed. "I never would have imagined myself married to Travis. When I met him, I believed he'd escaped from prison. He was bad-tempered, rude, dangerous—certainly not the kind of man I had pictured as my husband."

Kyla stirred a drizzle of cream into her cup, intrigued by this description. Travis McGuire seemed to be the ideal example of devoted husband and father-to-be. "What changed your mind? Did you find out that you were wrong about him? That he was none of those things you thought?"

Chloe laughed again and her green eyes sparkled. "Oh, my, no—he was! But beneath all that I found his true soul. He didn't make it easy for me, I must admit."

"You two seem very happy together," Kyla said, feeling that pang of envy again and the sudden wish that her life had been different.

"We're good for each other, I think." Chloe glanced at the table top and Kyla thought a faint frown crossed her brow. "I was having trouble of my own when Travis walked into my backyard to answer an advertisement

I'd placed for a blacksmith. My father had died leaving a mortgage on our house, and even though I took in washing, I couldn't earn enough to make the payment. If not for Travis, I would've lost the home place." She placed a tender hand on the life growing under her heart. "And missed out on a lot more.

"Trusting anyone came hard for him, and he had drifted so long, I didn't think he'd be able to settle down. Funny, that was what he'd craved all his life—a home, a place to belong to. That, and to be cared about. I think that's what Jace probably wants, too."

Kyla snapped up straight in her chair. "Jace!"

The older woman sat back and considered her with a strangely knowing look. Finally, she put a hand on Kyla's wrist. "Love can heal a lot of wounds, the ones that show and the ones that don't."

"Did you have a good time?" Jace asked Kyla as they walked back toward the hotel an hour later. Overhead, the stars rolled past, the constellations moving and changing like the hands on a clock.

"Oh, yes, I did! It was nice to spend time talking to another woman. I haven't had a chance to do much of that. I'm so glad I got to meet your friends," she answered. Alert to every noise and movement around them, he walked beside her with one hand jammed into his pants pocket, the other clamped around his rifle. Occasionally, his arm brushed hers, or her shoulder lightly bumped him. She almost wished she could tuck her hand in the crook of his arm. Instead she wrapped her shawl more tightly around her shoulders. "They seem so happy together, like they *really* love each other. Just the way I used to imagine married couples."

"I guess," he mumbled. Then abruptly shifting subjects, he said, "I want to get an early start in the morning. I figure it's about three days to Blakely. Does that sound about right to you?"

As they approached a noisy saloon, he put his hand on the small of her back to steer her across the street. It lingered there, a warm, tentative touch that made her draw a deep breath.

She could not wholly account for the restless tension between them. He wouldn't look at her, and when she glanced at his cleanly chiseled profile against the lighted windows they passed, he seemed preoccupied. Now and then, his scent would drift to her, blended with a hint of whiskey, and she thought about what Chloe McGuire had said.

"Jace?"

"Yeah?"

"Have you ever been in love?"

Even to her own ears, the question cracked through the darkness with the jarring impact of a gunshot. His hand fell away and he turned his head sharply to look at her. "What does that have to do with going to Blakely?"

She stared straight ahead. She was glad that he couldn't see the heat that filled her face. "Nothing. I just wondered."

He kept walking. The place where his hand had rested on her waist felt cold now and she shivered a bit.

"Well, have you? Been in love, I mean?"

A gulf of silence opened between them before he finally spoke.

"No." In the darkness, he sounded suddenly like an old man.

Jace heard a lifetime of regret in his answer, and it shook him to his bones. He'd never cared about that stuff before. He couldn't very well tell her that he wasn't capable of loving someone—that Lyle had beaten it out of him.

Until now, he hadn't cared.

Until he met this woman, he had been comfortable with his solitude and the dead spot in himself that took the place of feelings. Lately, though, that solitude had begun to seem like loneliness with a different name. And the dead spot, it wasn't exactly dead after all; it was really just empty.

He heard the rustle of her skirts as she walked next to him. "I think maybe love could save your soul."

An alarm bell went off in Jace's head, and he gave her a sour look. Where the hell had that remark come from? Did the change of dress change her personality, too? "Save my soul—for what? Look, I've heard a trainload of salvation speeches over the years. I don't have any interest in being 'saved.' "

"Oh, I'm not talking about saving your soul for God, although there's nothing wrong with that. I'm talking about saving it for yourself."

He could think of no response to that. What *would* it be like, he wondered again, to come home at night to a warm kitchen, mellow with lamplight and the aroma of a hot meal? To find his wife, soft and smiling, there to welcome him? To burrow beneath warm quilts with her on snow-laden winter nights, her skin bare and smooth against his? He could only daydream about it, and that, he'd begun to realize, wasn't a smart thing to do. That kind of daydreaming could tie a man up in knots and make him do something dumb.

They reached the hotel and Jace couldn't say that it made him happy. Despite the questions that she churned up in his mind, he had enjoyed walking next to Kyla, listening to the sound of her smoky voice and the whisper of her skirts.

"Let me go first," he said in a low voice, and his eyes touched on her red hair. "Better cover your head with your shawl, too."

She cringed and pulled up the shawl with a sudden, jerky movement. "Do you think—?" she whispered.

"I don't know, but it's best to be safe."

Jace led them inside, but the main floor was empty except for a cadaverous-looking clerk who sat at a roll-top desk behind the counter. Dozing with his feet on the desk, he didn't wake as they crossed the short lobby to the stairs, but snored on.

They stepped lightly in the uncarpeted second-floor hall to reach Kyla's room. Jace heard low voices behind a couple of doors, but the building was quiet for the most part.

Taking the key from her, he turned it in the lock. "I want to have a look in there before you go inside." He glanced around the empty room, then pulled a match from his pocket and flicked it with his thumbnail. Kyla took it from him and lit the lamp mounted on the wall.

Now he stood in the hall again, looking at her in the open doorway. He felt awkward, not wanting to go to his own room, but reluctant to stay. She gazed at him with those turquoise eyes and lowered her shawl to her shoulders. Her slim, white throat came into view again. What would it feel like to press a kiss there?

"Are we leaving at daybreak?" she asked, as if she felt the tension, too, and tried to cover it with small talk.

"A little later, maybe. We want to get there, but we can let the chill burn off the morning a bit. You should probably get another coat before we set out, anyway. The days aren't going to turn warmer now."

She shook her head. "I don't have the money for a coat."

"I'll get it. You can add it to the list of the other stuff you want to pay for," he said. "But I think this was money well spent." Carefully, he touched the lacy edge of the wide flounce that trimmed her gown's neckline. He stood close enough to smell the faint, clean scent of her skin. He looked up at her again—just gazing at her roused his desire. "You're beautiful." Voicing the thought came hard to him—he was unaccustomed to expressing such sentiments.

"I am?" she asked in barely more than a whisper. Her eyes were riveted on his face and he felt her breath fan his hand.

Yes, she was. The delicate planes of her face offered him a dozen places he wanted to kiss. Her long lashes, dark and lush, framed her eyes and made them offer promises he knew she could not keep. He wanted to skim his hands along her breasts and feel their fullness against his palms. He longed to sleep with her tucked in his arms and his bed.

But he could say none of those things. And those desires were only a daydream.

"More beautiful than I can tell you." He let his fingertips rise from the flounce to graze her flushed cheek and run along the edge of her jaw. He knew it was folly, that suffocating frustration was sure to be the result. But he just wanted to touch something soft in a life marked with coarseness. Dropping his gaze to her sensitive mouth, the mouth that never seemed to fit when she posed as a boy, he ached to caress it with his own lips.

The feel of Jace's hand on Kyla's cheek raised goose bumps on her scalp and arms. The moment felt so close, so intimate. Her heart picked up its tempo, beating in a way that made her breath come a little faster.

"Kyla." He pressed his forehead against hers. "Kyla, may I kiss you?" His voice was low, intense.

"Please don't ask," she said, surprised that he would seek permission.

His hand dropped from her jaw and he backed up a pace. He drew his mouth into a tight line, and he looked as if she had slapped him.

"You don't *need* to ask," she whispered again, hardly believing her own voice. Just a few days ago she'd promised herself that nothing like this would happen again. Now that promise evaporated like morning mist. She started to reach for his hand, but then thought better of it. "Just—just kiss me."

She heard his swift intake of air. Stepping closer again, he put his fingertips to her cheek.

At that moment, a door opened down the hall. Kyla flinched as though she'd been jabbed with a fork.

"Goddamn it to hell," Jace muttered at the intrusion. Quickly, he nudged her into the room and closed her door behind them. He leaned his rifle against the wall.

Turning to her, he took her face between his hands lightly, with his thumbs resting under her chin, as if she were a bowl from which he might drink. He gazed at her like a man who was searching for his last hope. His ice blue eyes, which could be so cold, now seemed as if they would melt her own frozen heart.

When his mouth touched hers, she was unprepared for the sweetness that coursed through her like drizzles of thick, warm honey. His lips moved over hers with a tender, aching hunger that excited rather than repelled her. She inhaled the smell of him—his shaving soap, a faint scent of whiskey, the essence that was his alone. He surrounded her.

Kyla's heart pounded inside her chest, born of a feeling she'd never known. Not fear, not revulsion. It was much too thrilling for either of those.

She was aware of all the sensations within and on her body: Jace's hot touch, her heartbeat, her breath, her stockings silky on her legs, the smoothness of her chemise.

He leaned against the wall behind him and his hands moved from her face to her hair as he deepened the kiss. Pulling her to him, he enfolded her in the strength of his embrace. She lost her balance and fell against his hard-muscled, lean body. He groaned deep in his throat—it was an anguished sound—and his arms around her tightened. Reaching to encircle his lean waist, her shawl fell from her shoulders. Through the fabric of his shirt he felt vital and warm.

Jace broke the kiss and pressed his lips to her throat, just as he'd imagined doing earlier. Her pulse throbbed swiftly under his mouth. All the desire he felt for this woman, the yearning that had slumbered uneasily inside him, awakened now with a fierce need. She was beautiful, like a butterfly emerged from her chrysalis, and more tempting than any woman he'd ever known.

He sought her lips again, this time teasing them with the tip of his tongue. She moaned softly, and his arousal burned hotter and higher. Without thinking, he dropped his hands to her buttocks and pulled her to him, gently, rhythmically thrusting his hardness against her softness.

Immediately, she stiffened and drew back, struggling to regain her feet. *No, no, don't pull away*, he wanted to beg her. He didn't want to let go of her, the only good thing left in a world gone so wrong.

"Jace, *don't*," she demanded. She pushed hard at his chest, and he heard the alarm in her voice.

The spell broken, he released her, his breath coming fast. He caught a glimpse of her fear. Somehow, the ribbon that held her hair back had come loose and hung over her shoulder. Her shawl lay in a puddle at her feet. Her mouth was red and slightly puffy. Had he done all that?

He could have kicked himself. Was his memory so damned short that he'd forgotten what Hardesty had done to her? Or how easy it would be to lose the trust he'd won from her? He wasn't even sure why that mattered, but he found that it did. Very much.

"Kyla, wait—" He tried to put his hand on her arm, but she backed up.

"It's time for you to be goin'," she said. Kyle's hard-edged speech contrasted wildly with the delicate, yellow-gowned woman who stood before him. She crossed her arms over her chest, withdrawing into herself, into Kyle.

"Kyla—God, I'm sorry. I didn't mean to—"

"You prob'ly didn't. But you go on now." She stepped to the door and opened it.

"In the morning—"

"I'll be ready to go."

Jace sighed and gazed at her set face. She didn't look mad, exactly, but he couldn't be sure what she was thinking. He was accustomed to being in control of most situations; now he felt stupid and guilty as he picked up the Henry and backed into the hallway.

"Well, I—aw, hell." He turned on his heel and strode toward his room and didn't look back. Behind him, the door closed and the key turned, distinct and unmistakable.

Locking her in. Locking him out.

It was the loneliest sound he'd ever heard.

Kyla lay in the darkness, the sheets cold against her legs where her drawers ended on her thighs. In fact, she was acutely aware of all her senses. The feel of her chemise on her nipples, the loud tick of the walls in the quiet night, the taste of a kiss—

Yes, Jace had scared her. When he put his hands on

her backside and pulled her to him, she felt the hard length of him against her abdomen. A confusion of fears had collided in her mind: a fleeting, cruel image of that night in the barn, the strength she felt in Jace's grip. But most of all, she was frightened by her own response, the sweet yearning that had grown inside her under his hands and his mouth.

The stone in her heart, the one upon which she had carved her bitter vow to exist alone, was shaken to its very foundation. So was her opinion of Jace Rankin.

He was hard and tough and merciless . . . wasn't he? At a place called the Bluebird Saloon, he had failed as a man in some way that he wouldn't talk about. In a way that had even surprised Hank.

But there was more to Jace than any of that. And layer by layer he was revealing another side to her, one that she would never have guessed lurked beneath that flinty veneer he showed to the world. She laid her palm over the locket, where it rested on her chest. A gold heart, the metal warmed with her body heat.

She thought of what Chloe McGuire had said about him, that perhaps what he really wanted was a home and place to belong. Might he be the man who would accept her strengths and her failings, and build the kind of life at the ranch she had once envisioned?

No, he was not. Where in the world did she get such an idea about the bounty hunter? Rolling to her side, she wadded up her pillow with annoyance. She would make it on her own—Tom Hardesty was the only obstacle in her way, and she'd *hired* Jace to help her with that. Why did she keep forgetting it?

Kyla wasn't certain she wanted to know. But as she

gazed at a square of faint moonlight on the wall from under heavy lids, she made no more promises to herself about Jace.

She didn't think she would keep them.

Jace knew it was all different now. It had been one thing to take care of Kyla while she was sick, to wash her hair, to sneak half a kiss in a kitchen. At that, he'd thought those were all torture. But, they were nothing compared to tonight. Until tonight, he'd only guessed at how she might look dressed as a female.

Now he'd seen it. Felt it. And she was more womanly than he had imagined, more poignantly innocent that he had dreamed.

He lay naked in the cold bed and tried to sleep, one arm thrown over his eyes. But his mind tormented him with the memory of her softness. He envisioned her tender mouth, he pictured running his hands over the bare curve and plane of her, suckling at her soft breast, reaching for the heat between her thighs, where completion and fulfillment waited. And afterward, sleeping in her arms—

His arousal was swift and heavy, pulling him to the mattress. He felt edgy and restless, and drawn as tight as a fiddle string. Oh, hell, sleep would be hours away now.

Aggravated, he dragged himself up to his elbow and reached for his shirt where it hung on the bedpost under his gun belt. He rummaged through the pockets till he found a cheroot and a match.

The room flared briefly with light when he struck a match on the iron bedpost. Pulling deeply on the cheroot, he cursed himself again. How was he going to get her out of his head? Even tomorrow, when she dressed like Kyle for their trip to Blakely, he wouldn't see her as the tough-talking female who masqueraded as a farm boy. For him, those boys' clothes would no longer screen her beauty.

He flopped over on his back and sighed. No, maybe they wouldn't, but Jace knew he had to conquer the images drifting through his mind. He had nothing to offer her, and he wouldn't fit into her life.

After Blakely, he and Kyla Springer Bailey would be parting company. And not a moment too soon.

Chapter Ten

"Mr. Hardesty! This just come for you."

Tom Hardesty stopped, his hand outstretched toward the swinging doors of the Pine Cone Saloon. He turned around to see Edner Pomeroy hurry out of his telegraph office holding a piece of paper high like a white flag. He was a short, heavy man, and the sprint just about undid him.

"Transcribed it myself," Edner panted, catching up to Tom. He perspired with his effort and squinted against the hard-edged morning sun. He was a nervous, servile toady, the kind who begged to serve, the kind who pleased Tom enormously. Edner *respected* him.

He plucked the telegram from Edner's pudgy hand and unfolded it. He permitted a wide grin to spread across his face as he read the short message. A surge of victory raced through his veins. Well, maybe not victory just yet, but it was pretty damned close. At least it might satisfy Jory for the time being.

"Good news, Mr. Hardesty?" the telegrapher asked, hovering eagerly.

"You might say so." Feeling magnanimous with his near triumph, Tom flipped a dime to the man. "Buy yourself a beer."

Edner stared at the dime in his hand as if it were a double eagle. "Thank *you*, Mr. Hardesty!" He looked ready to hug himself with joy. Tom laughed at the fool—if only Edner knew what he really thought of him. "Wait'll I tell the wife!" He turned then and hurried back toward the office, and Tom dropped his gaze to the telegram again.

TRACKED RANKIN AND WOMAN TO BAKER
CITY STOP
WILL WIRE AGAIN TOMORROW WHEN JOB IS
FINISHED STOP
SIGNED McINTYRE

Hobie McIntyre had proved to be worth more than a manure pile, after all. Grinning again, Tom jammed the paper into his jacket pocket and pushed through the saloon doors. Luke Jory would probably frown on his right-hand man indulging so early in the day. But by God, if this didn't call for a drink to celebrate, he didn't know what did.

"Whiskey over here, Pete," he called to the bartender. He slouched against the bar and surveyed the room. There were a couple of people in the saloon and they eyed him warily as did the silent bartender, who poured the drink and backed away.

He noticed their cautious regard, and he knew satisfaction. Yessir, now folks jumped when they saw Tom Hardesty, they were careful with their words when they spoke to him. After a lifetime of being written off as a lazy good-for-nothing by the people in this town, he'd given them something to chew on. By aligning himself with the Vigilance Union, he finally had everyone's respect or fear. In his mind, the two were equal.

He considered the amber liquid in the glass on the counter as a dark cloud dimmed his elation: only Kyla didn't fear or respect him, even after he had put it to her last fall in the barn. He knew if she were standing here right now she would still have the sass to spit in his face. And that fact tied a cold, angry knot in his gut. He knocked back the whiskey in one gulp.

So she was still with Rankin. Grimly, he wondered if Miss-Touch-Me-Not was giving it to the bounty hunter. Huh, Jace Rankin had nothing on Tom. He knew the man's reputation—unflinching, utterly without fear, he could make a man cower like a whipped dog just by looking at him.

But Tom had a reputation of his own, and he'd see Rankin out of his way and Kyla on her knees before the month was over.

"We need to cross these mountains as soon as we can. I think it's going to snow up here," Jace called back to Kyla. Stopped in the road, he let his blue gaze linger on her a moment, as if he could see through her clothes right down to her skin. Right into her heart.

He had been critical and distant all day, as though everything she did suddenly displeased him. Maybe he was angry with her for making him leave her room last night. Or maybe he was disgusted to discover her lack of experience when he'd kissed her. Kyla knew very little about such matters, despite Tom Hardesty and her marriage to Hank.

Whatever the reason, this morning Jace had been curt and impatient, speaking to her in one- and two-word sentences. Yet he had delayed their start until late morning, telling her she should rest up for the trip.

"Will we make it out by dark?" she asked, nudging Juniper closer.

He glanced at the lowering sky. "We'd better," he muttered, then swung his horse around to take the lead.

Not heartened by his answer, Kyla pulled her hat down tight and burrowed into the folds of her new coat, grateful for its warmth. Icy winds howled down from the northeast, spreading a blanket of ominous clouds over the late-afternoon sky.

Although she and Jace had left Baker City long after sunup, the chill had not burned off, as he'd suggested it might. The day had been long and cold, and as they climbed higher into the Blue Mountains, it only grew worse. Her healing arm had begun to ache as soon as they reached the foothills, and now it felt heavy with dull pain. Beside the road, dead bunchgrass and sage snapped and tumbled along, too brittle to bend in the dry, cold wind. A sharp, bitter gust came up, bringing tears to her eyes, and Juniper danced sideways, complaining with a whinny.

Kyla considered Jace as he rode ahead of her. He looked much the same as she supposed she did: hat pulled low on his head, coat collar turned up.

Her butter yellow dress and all its trappings were carefully repacked in their brown paper and tied behind her saddle with the rest of her gear. God knew when, or if, she'd be able to wear them. She was Kyle the farm boy again, now more reluctantly than ever.

As she studied Jace's straight back, she guessed that the chief distinction in their appearance was their size. Jace had shoulders much broader than hers. His arms were more muscled and far stronger. She had felt that when he held her against his hard body last night. Her skirts between them had done nothing to conceal it. Any of it. The memory sent a rush of heat up her neck that crept to her hairline.

Things were not the same between them. She caught herself watching his profile, the way his hands flexed on the reins, the lines etched around his eyes. The powerful sensation of his kiss was branded on her memory. To her chagrin, everything about him that was male beckoned her. In the deepest part of her he'd roused an ancient, instinctive urge—far different from the fear and revulsion she had come to associate with the physical contact between a man and a woman.

That urge meant nothing, she argued with herself. Those rhythms were present in every living creature on earth. She brushed at the tears that sprang to her irritated, wind-burned eyes. Simply because she had succumbed to a heated, indiscreet moment last night did not change her relationship with Jace, or make it into something it was not. Every time she let her imagination gallop loose to picture him sharing a life with her at the ranch, her logical side stepped in to squash the image. Jace Rankin was not a rancher. He was a bounty hunter.

But that didn't mean he couldn't learn if he wanted to, her heart whispered.

Right now, though, Jace wasn't thinking of ranching *or* bounty hunting. Right now, he was worried about getting them out of the mountains and down to lower ground. He'd spent a lot of years out in the weather, and he would bet that a good-size storm was coming—one that he and Kyla were not equipped for. On the flatlands, it might not be so bad. In fact, it might not hit down there at all. Up here, though, snow could fall so fast and thick they might either lose their way amid these treacherous slopes, or become trapped.

Keeping watch on the lead gray sky, he pushed his gelding over the narrow mountain path. They had left Baker City too late in the day and Jace cursed himself for letting thoughts of Kyla interfere with his better judgment. That had never happened to him before. He'd meant to make things easier for her, to let her spend a little time in the comfort of the hotel before they set out to travel this rough country again. The urge to treat her more like a lady and less like a boy had been a mistake.

Other men got distracted by women. They made fools of themselves, or let a female lead them around by the nose like a steer. Other men allowed lust or love to tangle up their thinking and make them all moony. Not him.

But now a powerful need pulled at him, a swift current that flowed through his soul, and he resisted it. It was *not* love; he knew that it couldn't be. But lust—he didn't like the sound of that either. It seemed, well, too raw and coarse when he applied it to Kyla.

He glanced over his shoulder and saw her back there, plodding along on the dun. The lower half of her face was hidden by her turned-up collar. But her beautiful features were etched in his mind—her slim nose, the roundness of her cheekbones, her mouth that felt even softer and more lush than it looked.

That round softness belied her courage, though. Whenever he stopped to think about what she had dared just to find him, he shook his head in amazement. It had taken more than plain stubbornness and a craving for revenge. Beautiful, smart, strong, with a tender heart lurking beneath—a man couldn't ask for more in a mate.

If he was looking for one—

Another fierce gust of wind wailed down the pass, cutting through his duster down to his bones, and yanking his mind back to their immediate problem. It was then that he saw sleet swirling against the darker backdrop of blue-gray granite. The frozen ice pellets were as small as bird shot. Driven by the wind, the sleet peppered his face like grains of fire. And he knew that snow would follow shortly. He could smell it, taste it. It was coming. He and Kyla would need at least two more hours to work their way down to flat ground, and it would be close to dark by then.

He turned to check on Kyla again, and saw her falling farther behind. Her head was down and for a moment he thought she was asleep. Then she lifted a hand to rub her wounded arm through her sleeve.

Yeah, he thought, this cold would make it ache. He knew the feeling.

"Stay close," he called to her. She glanced up and nodded, urging Juniper on, but the horse balked whenever a wind blast crossed his path or stung him with sleet. Jace could see she was struggling with him. Although he was a fairly steady mount, every animal had its quirks and in this weather it probably wouldn't take much to make him bolt. Jace surveyed the possibilities in that event, and they were not promising. On each side of the narrow road, sheer drop offs plunged to deep crevasses studded with spindly pines and sharp-edged rocks.

They moved onward, their progress gradually slowing as the snowfall began. Time became an enemy with the weather. Without the sun, marking the hour became impossible. Knowing the time, though, wouldn't tell him a lot beyond how much trouble they were in, and he'd already grasped that. They had to win the race against nightfall to the foothills on the other side of the ridge that still lay ahead, and that was his primary goal. He could see no farther than two or three feet ahead, and most landmarks vanished behind shrouds of white.

Every couple of minutes, he sought Kyla behind him, but she and her horse formed a vague, bulky shadow that faded in and out of his line of sight. Then she disappeared completely.

"Kyla! Are you there?" he yelled, turning in his saddle. The wind and snow smothered his words and threw them back at him. God, could she hear him? Was she there? He reined his horse and swung it around, listening, peering through the whiteness. Dread sat in his chest like a stone, heavy and suffocating. "Kyla, answer me, damn it!"

"I'm here!" she called back, but her voice sounded far away. Finally she emerged from the wall of flakes. Her face was red with cold, and snow clung to her hair and collected in the folds of her coat. Silvery rivulets marked her cheeks where her tears had frozen. She looked like a lost waif.

With a heavy exhale, Jace released the breath that he'd been holding. "Goddamn it to hell, woman! Try a little harder to stay with me, will you? And keep that horse on the road!" he barked. He had to shout at her to be heard over the gale, adding to the sharp edge that worry put in his tone.

"I'm doing the best I can!" she snapped back, scrubbing impatiently at her frozen tears. "If that's not good enough for you, then go on without me. I don't want to be responsible for holding you back. We can find our own way. Juniper doesn't like this weather any better than we do."

He could see that. The horse's eyes rolled with wild panic and its fright was evident in every jerky movement. Jace sighed. "I'm sor—I didn't mean—Look, I think we're close to the ridge. Once we get there we'll be on the downhill side. Just try to hold him in check a little longer. If you slip off the road in this snow I won't know it."

"I've already thought of that, thank you," she retorted.

Feeling guilty, he nodded and turned his horse to resume the slow climb uphill. The storm continued to howl, gathering greater strength with each passing moment. Again and again, Jace glanced over his shoulder to see if Kyla was behind him, only to see her struggle with Juniper. He thought of suggesting that she dismount and lead the horse blindfolded, but that would slow their progress even more.

Snow crusted on his own horse's coat, and inside his boots, Jace's feet were numb with cold. Knowing she was no better off, he wished he could offer more shelter to Kyla. But the best thing he could do right now was lead them down to safety.

The ridge he sought seemed to keep moving out of their reach, and time lost all meaning. He had no means to judge the time of day, but he suspected that several hours had passed in this frozen hell.

He shrugged deeper into his coat, trying to cover his face without blocking what little vision he had in the white wind. His thoughts turned morose. Damn it, he should have gone south to California as he'd originally planned. Living was easier there, he'd heard. Good weather, a big, wide-open state. A man could start over and leave his past behind. Jace could begin a new life in a place where no one knew who he was. Where people wouldn't automatically fear him or challenge him.

When this was all over, he'd go. Maybe he would find something there to fill the empty place in his soul that would remain when he and Kyla parted. . . .

Another razor-sharp gust blasted him, forcing him to tighten his knees on his gelding's ribs. At that moment he heard his name shrieked over the rocks and around the brush, high and thin, as though the wind mocked him and his thoughts. Spinning around, he turned just in time to see Juniper rearing wildly on his hind legs. Kyla scrambled to keep her seat but the angle was too sharp. She fell backward out of the saddle and tumbled to the edge of the narrow road, taking her gear along with her. It flew over the side of a deep ravine. Juniper, blowing great clouds of vapor, landed on all fours again and fled past Jace. Skidding on a curve, the dun vanished into the road ahead and probably into an abyss.

His heart thundering in his throat, Jace jumped down and ran to Kyla, pulling his own horse along none too gently. She lay unmoving in the snow, looking like a heap of discarded clothes.

Wrapping the reins around his gloved fist, he dropped to a crouch next to her and hurriedly brushed the snow out of her face. Her eyes were closed.

"Kyla! Are you all right?" he asked.

She moaned, then mumbled a few words he couldn't understand.

"Are you hurt?" he demanded again. He pulled off his glove and touched a hand to her forehead. It wouldn't tell him a thing about her condition, but right now he couldn't think of something better to do. He didn't want to move her until he knew if she'd broken any bones. He'd once seen a man with busted ribs get his lung punctured that way.

Kyla's eyes fluttered open, and she saw Jace leaning over her. He looked like she felt—pale and scared. Behind him, his horse waited restively.

She tried to speak but the fall had knocked the wind

out of her. "My dress . . ." she uttered in a breathless whisper. She'd seen her pack sail past her face, end over end. She groped the front of her shirt, searching for her locket under the fabric. She felt the warm, hard metal trapped against her breastbone.

Jace shook his head as if she were talking nonsense. "Can you move?" he asked.

"Yes, I guess so," she said and struggled to sit up. A rock pressed into her back. Jace gripped her arm to help her.

"Do you hurt anywhere?"

Her entire being shook as though she had palsy, and she was bruised, but nothing felt broken or sprained. "No. Where's Juniper?"

"He took off up that way," he said, pointing toward the ridge. "You'll have to ride with me, and we need to get going."

"But what about my horse? I can't just leave him."

He shook his head and the concern in his expression solidified to grim resolve. "There's nothing we can do about finding him, and you know it. We'll be buried in snow if we don't keep moving."

Yes, she knew he was right, but she was heartsick. She'd raised Juniper from a colt. It seemed that one by one, everything that mattered in her life was slipping away—the ranch, her horse, her identity, even her courage. She might get them back, but they might be gone forever. Or irrevocably changed.

"My horse is gone. I lost my dress, and my gear."

He frowned impatiently. "Hell, I'll get you another dress, if that'll make you feel better," he said, waving an arm at their surroundings. "But right now it's not the most important thing we have to worry about."

She glanced up at Jace's strained white face, then dropped her gaze to her snow-dusted lap. No, of course it wasn't the most important thing, but her sense of loss grew heavier, like a burden she could no longer carry. Her shoulders slumped and she suddenly felt too cold and tired to go on. How much could one person take?

As if sensing her looming resignation, Jace gripped her shoulders in his strong hands. "Come on, Kyla, don't you quit on me," he ordered. "We've come too far to give up now."

"M-my arm hurts," she fretted wearily. Hot tears sprang to her eyes, this time from utter despair. She hated to cry in front of anyone, especially Jace. He'd think she was just a weak, puling female. But in her misery she couldn't stop herself, and she began sobbing in earnest. "And—and I'm so cold."

He studied her for a moment, his gaze touching her mouth, her eyes. Then he did the most astounding thing. He opened his duster and took her into his embrace, closing the edges of the coat around her. Pressing her cheek to the wall of his chest, he murmured, "I know you're cold, honey, but we have to get out of here or we'll freeze to death."

As if she had no will or strength left, she leaned against him, comforted by the feel of his arms around her. This was not Jace Rankin, she thought with hazy surprise. Not the man with a reputation known throughout the territory. This was that other man, a handsome, warm-blooded stranger who smelled of soap and leather and horses, who offered reassurance and murmured a homey endearment. The one who had saved her life and had even washed her hair, and made her blood rush through her veins, hot and sweet, when he kissed her. A man to whom she could entrust her safekeeping—for a little while, anyway.

"Can you travel?" he asked at length.

She nodded against his chest, where her tears had dampened his shirt. "All right," she agreed, loath to leave the security and warmth of his arms.

Jace helped her stand and boosted her into his saddle. Then he climbed up behind her and wrapped her in his duster again. "Hold it closed around you," he said and turned his horse toward the ridge. The animal shifted a bit under the extra weight, but he made the adjustment and moved forward to wade through the deepening drifts.

Kyla's feet were numb with cold, and she'd lost a glove somewhere during this debacle. She knew that they were in far more serious danger than she'd originally thought.

But if anyone could save them, she knew Jace could.

"Oh, I think it's starting to rain!" Kyla sat forward in the saddle, her hat askew from leaning against Jace.

They were down to the last daylight. As twilight settled over the mountains, the snow began to change to rain. Jace felt the tight muscles in his shoulders relax a bit—they had crossed the ridge and now were near the bottom of the downward trail. Rain meant that they were out of immediate danger. But unlike snow, the rain fell in a heavy, cold torrent that soaked everything, including Kyla and him.

"Yeah, but we need to find a place to stop for the night. And it doesn't look like there's a dry spot left in the whole section."

An incongruous bright band of sunlight opened on the western horizon, just where the sun was setting. Jace scanned the terrain in the remaining light, searching for a likely place to make camp. But he saw no rocky overhangs, no dry, sheltering copses. He found only straggling scrub and drenched ground. If they had to camp in the open, they probably wouldn't even be able to get a fire going.

Being wet and cold, though, didn't quite distract him from the soft female resting against him inside his coat. Oh, sure, she had dressed as Kyle again, but just as he'd anticipated, he no longer noticed her disguise. He only remembered the woman behind it who tantalized him more than he wished, who made him think that he *might* be able to begin his life again. Maybe here, maybe somewhere else. Kyla might even decide to leave the Vigilance Union to heaven and come with him.

Now and then he got a glimpse of her profile when she turned her head. Her complexion looked like rich cream in the sunset light. It didn't tax his imagination to envision her in his arms, soft and yielding, her warm, soft flesh surrounding him. With every day that passed, the picture became more intimate, more boldly urgent. He realized that even if he were to visit the upstairs rooms over some saloon, it would do no good. Only Kyla could extinguish the fire that burned in him.

Only by losing himself in the sharing of their bodies would the ache be soothed, the wanting be satisfied.

And the hell of it was, he knew that the chance of such an event was less than none. After Tom Hardesty, Kyla's spirit had some healing to do before she'd invite the attentions of a man. Maybe Hardesty wasn't the whole story, either. Someone else had hurt her, he suspected, long before that.

"Hey, what's that?" she asked then, mercifully interrupting his thoughts. She pointed at a rough structure ahead.

"I don't know," he said, "but if it has walls and no one shoots at us from the door, we're staying there tonight."

Riding closer, they discovered an abandoned cabin. It loomed in black silence in the rain, lonesome and forsaken.

"Do you think it belongs to anyone?" Kyla almost whispered.

"Not anymore it doesn't. There are lots of deserted mining shacks like this scattered around these parts."

He pulled the Henry out of its scabbard and climbed down to investigate the place to make sure no animals, wild or human, had taken up residence. With the rifle braced diagonally across his torso, he kicked open the door, then jumped aside and waited for a reaction from within. But only the screech of rusted hinges cut through the rain.

Inside the tiny cabin, he struck a match and held it high. He found a couple of pieces of rough, home-made furniture, an oil lamp, a stove, and some firewood. A veil of gray dust rested on everything, and even a few dry leaves lay in the corners, probably blown in under the door.

Plainly, no one had lived here for quite a while, although not so long that the wood had begun to rot. At least the roof didn't leak, and it had a puncheon floor instead of dirt, an extravagant luxury in a cabin like this.

"All right, come on," he said, and walked back to unload his own gear. "It's not fancy, but it's better than sleeping in the wet."

Stiffly, Kyla swung a leg over the saddle and followed Jace into the shack. She hadn't done any serious damage in her fall, but some of her muscles were beginning to creak.

Jace laid the Henry across the table and touched a match to the oil lamp. She gazed over the top of the flame and encountered his ice blue eyes that held her without touching her, called her to him without words. Every detail of his appearance sprang to her notice: the length of his dark lashes, the mahogany and ebony stubble in his beard, the curve of his mouth. Heat and energy ricocheted between them in that instant, making her draw a deep breath.

Had it been only last night that he'd taken her into his arms and kissed her? Suddenly the rough, one-room cabin seemed even smaller.

He broke the contact first, tossing his rig into the corner. He unrolled his blankets, pointedly reminding Kyla that her own bedding now lay at the bottom of a ravine.

"Where will I sleep?" she asked, fearing the answer.

"Well, since your things are lost, unless you've got a better idea I guess it's going to be right here with me."

Being weary and cold hadn't robbed Kyla of her ability to blush, and she felt her face flame with heat. She knew Jace had slept next to her at least once back in Misfortune, but she'd been sick then, and he'd been nearly dead with exhaustion. That was not the case now.

Stripping off his soaked duster and hat, he gestured at the stove. "I'll see if I can fire up that old thing so we can warm up and dry our gear." He eyed the pipe doubtfully. "I hope that chimney will draw."

Kyla noticed that his shirt was wet, too, and clung damply to his skin, sculpting every detail of muscle and tendon beneath. Protected by his coat and the shelter of his body, she had fared much better in the rain.

Forcing her attention away from the flex of his shoulders as he collected the firewood, she threw her hat and coat on the table and glanced around the dark room. It had just one small window, and its glass was broken. A narrow rope-strung bed stood against one wall, and a single shelf that still held a couple of tin cans with faded labels served as a kitchen. A little table upon which the lamp rested stood on the opposite wall.

"Someone must have had a hard life here," she said, running her fingers over the battered tabletop. "This place isn't much bigger than a closet. And it would be so lonely."

Jace crouched in front of the open stove, feeding the dry wood into its belly. "These shacks were built by men who chased some addled, moonstruck dream about striking it rich on gold in the hills. I guess they didn't realize how rarely that happens."

She looked at him over her shoulder. "Did you ever have a dream? Something you longed for?" Despite what he had revealed about his past, he didn't talk much about himself.

His back was turned to her, but she thought she heard him sigh. "Yeah—I got over it."

She gazed at the open range through the broken window. "That's too bad. Everyone needs hope."

"Yeah? What are you hoping for?" he asked. She faced him again. Tall, bright flames that leapt in the stove cut his silhouette.

"You know what I want—to get the ranch back, to get even with Hardesty."

"And what did you want before that?" Shutting the stove door, he pivoted on his knee to look at her.

Somehow he had become the questioner, and she the one on the spot. She shrugged uncomfortably. "Oh, I don't remember now."

He stood and took off his wet shirt, draping it over the back of a chair that he turned toward the fire. "I think you remember just fine."

She backed up a step, confounded by the length and breadth of his bare upper torso, and his long dark hair that brushed his shoulders. Undone by his assertion, her gaze dropped to the waist of his jeans hanging low on his hipbones. "Well, maybe I do remember. But it ain't none of your business."

Much to her relief and vague disappointment, he reached into his gear and brought out another shirt, threading his arms into the sleeves. Not bothering with the buttons, he moved one step closer and reached for her hand. His fingers, warm and strong, closed around hers, and her heart fluttered in her chest. She thought she ought to pull away, but had no will to do so.

"Come on, Kyla, we've seen a lot together. Come out from behind that disguise and tell me about it," he murmured.

Her breath caught in her throat at his nearness. He smelled of clean rain and cold mountain air. "Why?"

"Because I think someone besides Hardesty let you down, someone you believed in. I want to know who."

She lowered her eyes to avoid his intense blue gaze. He had the unnerving ability to see into her thoughts, and she felt a great disadvantage. Don't ask this of me, she thought. But when she looked up again, the walls she'd erected around her heart shifted under the weight of the empathy she saw in his face. His hand tightened slightly on hers, and he drew her to the chair to sit. Keeping her fingers in his, he sat cross-legged on the blankets at her feet.

"What did you hope for?" he prompted gently.

Perched tightly on the edge of the seat, Kyla sighed and looked at her lap. Threatening tears made her voice a shaky whisper. "That my father would love me."

A moment passed before he spoke. "You think he didn't?"

"I know he didn't. My mother did, but she died when I was little." She cleared her throat. "After that, nothing I did pleased him. I felt like I didn't exist."

"Maybe he just missed your mother."

"No, it was more than that." Once she began speaking, the hurt she'd kept locked up for so many years poured out in a torrent. Finally, someone wanted to listen to her. How odd that it should be the man she'd hired to kill Tom Hardesty, that a cold-blooded bounty hunter should have more compassion than her own family. "Pa wanted a son, an heir to take over at the ranch—he told me that straight-out. A daughter was useless to him. But I learned to ride and rope, I branded cattle, mended fences, pulled calves—I worked as hard as the hands. Then Aggie and Tom came along." Tears streamed down her cheeks and she wiped them on her coat sleeve. "Pa married Aggie and thought Tom was the answer to his prayers. He spoiled him rotten. But Tom didn't care about the land the way I did, and he didn't want to work. He just wanted to chase girls and get drunk behind the springhouse. I saw the disappointment in Pa's eyes every time he let him down, so I kept doing my work, and Tom's, too. I don't think Pa ever gave up hope that Tom would come around—he refused to see or hear anything bad about him. And he refused to see or hear me at all. Tom knew he could get away with whatever he wanted. Even murder."

"So you dressed like a boy, not just to avoid Hardesty. You were trying to be the son you thought your old man wanted."

His voice was low and he sounded angry. She nodded mutely, unable to look him in the face. Her story seemed pathetic to her own ears. What must he think of it? His youth had been much worse. His stepfather had beaten him just because of his size, and he wasn't whining over it.

But Jace recognized the pain in Kyla's face and voice, and wondered how so many fools could visit two lives.

His own stepfather, who had never given him a chance to be a son ... Kyla's father, who ignored his own child to embrace a worthless stepson ... Tom Hardesty, whose day of reckoning for his years as a black-hearted prodigal was fast approaching ...

Kyla had received so little love—he wished he had it to offer.

Before, he had been satisfied with living day to day—the future and its possibilities never entered his head. But that afternoon at the Magnolia Saloon had changed everything. Sometimes he was almost sorry that he'd found Sawyer Clark. The search for him had kept Jace fixed on one goal, and gave him a purpose that asked no questions. It hadn't watched him with turquoise eyes that touched the place in him that had once felt dead.

Had he ever had a dream? Kyla had asked. No, not until he'd met her. And he knew it could not be fulfilled. All he could do was comfort a brave woman who deserved more than what life had dealt her so far.

But when he looked up into her face again, their eyes locked, just as they had over the lamp flame. Desire surged through his veins, so hot and sudden and thick, it scared him. His gaze darted over her coral lips that parted softly, her small hands, her flame-colored hair. He wanted her, to touch her smooth, bare curves, to feel her softness under his lips and hands. That was no surprise to him.

He had to be hallucinating, though, because he thought he saw the same yearning in her blue-green eyes.

Slowly he rose to his knees before her. "Kyla," he whispered, trying to keep the anguish out of his voice, "I don't think I can love anyone. I don't—it just isn't in me anymore."

"Yes it is." Lightly, she gripped the lapels of his shirt, her voice sounding as strangled as his own, her expression intense. "I don't want much from you—I know you have enough in your heart to love me for now, today."

"Don't do this, honey," Jace warned, and it was the hardest thing he'd ever done, turning her down. "You deserve more than what you're asking for, and a hell of a lot more than me. You'll hate us both for it later. You're not thinking straight right now."

"Jace, please . . . don't tell me no. I just want to feel close to you for a little while." Her voice was as small as a child's.

His heart clenched in his chest, and a familiar ache, heavy and low, throbbed in his groin. He had spent his adult years cultivating a reputation that made him seem larger than life to most people, to show the world he was not a man to be crossed. That he was a presence to be reckoned with.

But in reality, Jace Rankin was only a mortal man. And that which Kyla asked of him now, after weeks of craving her touch, of dreaming about her, was more than he could refuse. She beseeched him, but he was the one brought to his knees. Right now, at this moment, she had complete power over him.

He rested his head against her leg, his throat tight. He couldn't speak the words to tell her that she had humbled him with her request.

He didn't know how to say that he hoped he'd find his own soul again in her arms.

Chapter Eleven

Firelight from the stove window cast tall shadows on the rough-planked walls, mute witness to the struggles of heart and conscience being played out in its dull glow. Rain pelted the thin roof overhead, and outside the wind howled under the eaves. But in the tiny foothills cabin heat radiated from the stove, warming two people who circled each other warily, both waiting for cues from the other.

Kyla sat cross-legged on the blanket opposite Jace, her knees touching his. In the low light his eyes glimmered with a flame of their own, and the powerful need she saw in them made her hesitate.

Her devastating ordeal in the barn a year earlier was her only knowledge of men, and she had no idea what this night might bring. Fear battled with her desire for Jace. The joining of man and woman was rough and violent, but she hoped that it would be better with him.

So he surprised her when he simply reached for her hand and took it into his own. He turned her palm up and ran his fingertip lightly over its perimeter. Exquisite chills flew over her arms and spine, making her shiver. She pulled away.

"Do you want to stop?" he asked, his voice sounding like warmed honey, low and throaty, as if he already knew her answer. Her gaze fell to his chest and flat belly, revealed in the gap of his unbuttoned shirt. A dusting of dark hair that began just below his collarbones narrowed and disappeared into the waist of his jeans.

"N-no, I just don't know how—is this what—"

He pressed a finger to her mouth. "Shh. *I* know. I promise I won't force you and it won't hurt."

That sounded impossible, she thought. When he pushed her down and crushed her with his demanding body, how could it not hurt and bruise? Her skepticism must have been mirrored in her face.

Rising to his knees, he gripped her elbow and pulled her up, too, then closed his arms around her. "I *promise.*"

Hip to hip, thigh to thigh, their bodies matched so well. It felt good to be held like that, to be touched without being squeezed or groped, or made to feel dirty. His embrace was solid, the wall of his chest, strong and unyielding. With a soft cry she flung her arms around his narrow waist. He cradled the back of her head with a gentle hand and stroked her hair. He made it seem less important that her curls were gone.

Murmuring comforting sounds against her ear, he chanted her name, vowing to make this right. Before she realized it, she was lying on the blankets with his cast-off clean shirt rolled up under her head.

He lay on his side next to her, braced on one elbow, and let his eyes roam the length of her. Sinew and cord swelled with his movements, and slats of rib and lean muscle were defined in light and shadow. The low firelight gleamed red on his bare shoulders and arms. At that moment, she thought he was everything a man ought to be, compassionate, strong, unbearably attractive. She put out a tentative hand to sweep his hair behind his shoulder.

"God, you *are* beautiful, even dressed like this," he said, wonder in his voice. "I never wanted to kiss a woman"—he lowered his head to her lips—"so much."

The moment their lips met, Kyla moaned. His mouth on hers was hot and slick and insistent, and his tongue probed the soft recesses of her mouth. Her heart pounded with the spark he kindled, not with fear. He pulled back to look at her with a hungry, feral gaze, but still she was not afraid.

His free hand roamed her shoulder and arm, and it seemed as if he left a trail of fire behind. Finally she felt his warm palm slide up her ribs to her unbound breast. Her breath caught, and he sealed it in her throat with another kiss, this one more fevered than the last.

"Kyla, God, honey," he groaned low in his throat, sounding like a man who was trying to save his own life. With proficient dexterity, he worked open the buttons of her shirt to find her bare skin.

Jace heard her formless whimper as she timidly let her hands glide over his chest. Never had he known a need so fierce. But the woman responsible for the grinding ache in his groin required that he go slowly, carefully. The full weight of his responsibility to her was not lost on him, and he bore it gravely. But oh, goddamn, how would he hold on when even now, so early in their lovemaking, the throbbing low in his belly was nearly unbearable? Weeks of denial and unsatisfied temptation had reached a flash point. It was the sweetest torture he'd ever experienced.

Her eyes were cobalt and heavy-lidded with arousal. Just one shirt button remained and he reached for it as if it were the lock on a treasure house. When he opened it, he saw a metallic glimmer on her creamy skin. Looking closer, he realized it was the gold locket he'd given her.

"You kept your necklace on."

She gazed up at him, innocent desire suffusing her features. She took his hand and placed it over the heart-shaped pendant, and covered it with her own. "It's the nicest thing anyone ever gave me."

That she'd left it on, wearing it close to her heart, touched him in a way he would not have expected. He had chosen that necklace just for her, and although the rest of her things had been lost, the locket remained. He lifted her hand and kissed her palm.

Opening her shirt then, he folded back one side at a time to uncover the smooth, ripe breasts he had first glimpsed the day she was shot. He had felt like a low-down weasel for looking at her then, and in the days that had followed while she was sick. Now, though, she was healthy and yielding, and he gazed upon her like a starving man at a banquet table.

"May I take off your shirt?" he asked.

She lifted her hand and gripped her sleeve where he knew her arm bore the scar of her gunshot wound. "Oh, do you have to?" Her voice sounded small and self-conscious. "I mean, my arm looks . . ." The sentence hung unfinished.

Damn it, he swore to himself, so much had been taken from her. He lifted her hand away and pressed a kiss on her knuckles, then carried it higher to the scar on his own shoulder.

"Hell, sweetheart, you're in good company." He chuckled, trying to keep his tone light. Then he added more seriously, "I won't see anything but you."

For several moments, Kyla lay motionless, her eyes on his shoulder. Finally, she sat up and pulled her arms from her sleeves, baring a curved alabaster torso that made Jace swallow hard. The fullness of her breasts was accentuated by the curve of her waist and gentle flare of her hips.

"Just as I remember," he admitted, fighting the urge to hide his face against her breast and inhale the scent of her fragrant flesh.

The shiny red wound on her arm was an outrage, a senseless defilement of perfection. But it was also a mark of courage and honor, and she wore it well. "Beautiful Kyla," he murmured, his gaze touching here and there. She smiled shyly, and his heart lightened.

Gently pressing her back to the bedroll, he ran his hand over her flesh and felt her erect nipple graze his palm. At last giving into his craving, he dipped his head and closed his lips on one firm coral peak.

Kyla gasped and arched against his mouth, her spine curving away from the blankets. The light tug

on her nipple sent arrows of pleasure shooting down
to her abdomen where a pulse began to throb, hot and
liquid.

This ... was this how it was supposed to be
between a man and a woman? The endearments, the
caresses? This tender fire that sent flames licking
through every part of her body?

But when Jace rocked his pelvis against her leg, and
she felt his arousal, hard and full, her fear took over.
Whether or not she wanted them, dark, fearsome
memories crowded into her heart to steal the pleasure
Jace was giving her.

Obviously sensing her anxiety, he backed away so
that their bodies didn't touch. His face reflected a
blend of need and concern. "Have you changed your
mind?" he asked quietly.

She shook her head. "No, I just—that night—" She
turned her head away. "Oh, it's hard to explain."

"But not so hard to understand. *You* have to realize
how big a difference there is between then and now."
He propped his head on his hand and stared down at
her, while he stroked her cheek with the back of his
finger. "A year ago, you had no say, no choice.
Tonight you're the one in charge. We're here because
you asked to do this. It's all up to you."

"Really?"

His soothing touch moved to her hair. "It was that
way from the minute we started this. If you want to
stop right now, then we will."

"I don't want to stop, but—" She cast a quick,
embarrassed glance down his torso to his very evident
hardness straining his fly buttons.

Catching the path of her gaze, he said, "Remember, I promised it won't hurt."

She nodded, not completely convinced.

"Trust me," he whispered and crowded close again. "I'll do everything I can to make it right for you." With one arm under her shoulders, he kissed her while his other hand roamed more freely on her body, over her denim-clad legs and up the insides of her thighs. Finally he reached the heat at their apex and pressed his hand against it, hard.

Kyla moaned, forgetting to be frightened or self-conscious. A need much more primitive and demanding took over then, and she lifted her hips to press back. He continued this sweet agony for several moments, until finally he sat up and pulled off her boots, and then his own.

With a dreamy languor, she lay against the blankets, watching him unbuckle his belt and rip open his fly buttons with one sharp tug. Impatiently he shed his jeans and kicked them away, revealing his lean, fully erect body. Would he do the same to her?

As if reading her thoughts, he laid his hand on her belt buckle. He didn't speak, but he sought her permission with his eyes. She let her hands rest at her sides, giving it to him.

And in a moment, she lay beside him, bare skin against bare skin. He was lean and long and beautiful to look at. Perhaps he wasn't tall, but his torso was finely wrought with sinew and bone, and led to tight, lean hips and legs that were hard with saddle muscles.

Jace gazed at her nakedness with ravenous eyes, as if he would devour her, but not hurt her. He dropped his head to tease her nipple again, then blazed a path of warm, moist kisses that began at her throat and wandered feverishly over her breasts and stomach. His hair trailed softly behind the kisses, like the brush of feathers on her skin.

No, this was nothing like what she had expected, this tender assault on her senses. She could not have anticipated the sensation that she felt between her legs and in her womb, a feeling that was both thrilling and frustrating, as if even more awaited her.

Her frustration climbed to a new level when Jace's fingertips drifted down her abdomen, lower, lower until they caressed the wet, aching want of her.

"Jace," she gasped, writhing under his ministrations. Hot and slick, like tongues of fire he stroked her deftly while he muttered a stream of endearments in her ear. She lay beneath his hand in sweet, helpless torment, inflamed by his touch. "Oh, God, Jace, please—"

"Do you want me to stop?" he asked again. His own breathing had grown labored and his voice sounded hoarse, but she thought she heard a smile in his question.

"Yes—no, don't—" Kyla didn't know how long she could endure this. Every nerve in her body sizzled and her heart thundered as if she had been running with all her strength. Nearing a state of delirium, she heard a woman's voice begging her lover to help end the agony.

"This is what you need, the way it should be," Jace whispered roughly.

Then he leaned over and kissed her again, and the

strokes on her sensitive flesh came faster and harder, doubling in their intensity, pushing her closer to a dark chasm that would surely consume her in a white-hot fire.

Suddenly, the heaviness gripped her in a tight knot and silence fell, as if the world held its breath. Then waves of spasms wracked Kyla, hot and fierce and deep, as her body triumphed in its struggle to surrender to Jace. She turned her face into his shoulder, muffling her sobs.

Kyla's intense release had pushed Jace to a fever-pitch. He pulled her beneath him, hoping he wouldn't frighten her, but she tensed as soon as she felt his weight on her. And when he tried to part her legs, she grew rigid and gripped the blanket beneath her in both fists. Maybe asking her to help him was the best way to quiet her apprehension.

"I won't hurt you," he said softly. Bracketing her face between his hands, he dropped swift kisses on her cheeks and temples. "I swear I won't. This is going to be so different. This is going to be your *first* time, and it's going to be with me. Your first time making love. Do you believe me?" He gazed down at her, his face just a couple of inches from hers.

She lifted her eyes to his. He saw fear there, but he saw trust too. "I believe you."

"I need your help, honey," he said, and her tension eased. He pressed his forehead to hers. "Will you open your legs to me?"

"Yes," she sighed and shifted her legs to accommodate him.

With an incoherent groan, Jace gently entered her

with a long, slow stroke. She drew a sharp breath and tilted her hips upward to take him into herself. Her sweet warmth surrounded him, clasping him in a liquid glove. By joining himself to her, he thought he'd never felt so whole, so complete, or so distant from his solitary existence.

But the demands of his body had reached an urgent level and he began moving in her, working toward the release that he'd held in tight check in order to give her pleasure first. He lifted himself to the full length of his arms, and his thrusts grew hard and short.

Kyla lay beneath Jace, filled with him, awed by him, overwhelmed with the sensation of fulfillment. She watched the long column of his throat, surprised to feel restless, knife-edged passion rebuilding with each stroke. He was beautiful, every part of him. The muscles in his arms flexed as he strained against her body, advancing and ebbing. Faster and faster he thrust into her. Sweat bathed him and his breathing matched his movements. He pulled her toward a vortex that would either deliver her, or send her spinning into a dark oblivion.

When she was certain that she could bear no more of this renewed torment, with a hard thrust he pushed her over the edge to release. Her muscles clamped down around him in a surge of pleasure that made her call his name in a high, thin wail, and stole her heart away, surely, completely, irretrievably.

He dropped his head to hers, covering her mouth with a desperate kiss. Then with what seemed like the last of his strength, he plunged forward, and a sobbing groan rose from his chest while his body convulsed with swift, hot pulsations that poured into Kyla.

He rested with his face turned into her neck and she wrapped her arms around him, waiting for their breathing to slow. His heart thudded against her own, powerful and steady.

"Are you okay?" he asked finally, his head still resting against her shoulder. He shifted his weight to avoid crushing her, but they remained joined.

She nodded, feeling amazed and honored. "You were right, Jace. It *was* completely different."

"The way it's supposed to be," he said and kissed her eyelids and temples.

The way it was supposed to be, she echoed in her mind. Giving and receiving. Yes, it was frantic and turbulent and urgent. But not humiliating, not violent or painful.

He was hers now, even if she were never to see him again after this moment. And she was his, branded by his touch. Ripening love that she had kept hidden from herself, that she had compelled to remain in darkness, now bloomed. Germinating in the days of her convalescence in Misfortune, it had waited for this moment of heat and passion to spring forth, and would no longer be denied. The wound on her spirit caused by Hardesty's cruelty was not erased, but it had begun healing when she met Jace, and now was closed. A confusion of emotions clashed within her, joy, acceptance, despair.

Jace rolled over with a low, sated groan, taking Kyla with him to nestle against his side. He drew the blanket to her chin. His arms and legs were as heavy as lead, completely relaxed, and despite the hard floor beneath them, he knew that he would sleep well for the first time in months.

He refused to think about what tomorrow or next week would bring. Life provided plenty of opportunities to worry and brood; he wouldn't miss anything by passing on the chance now.

Tonight, he would sleep with Kyla in his arms, and pretend that the world beyond these rough walls didn't exist.

Chapter Twelve

Jace woke with a start, the sound of heavy steps nearby breaking into his sleep. Chilled and disoriented, he wondered what weight anchored him to the earth. Then he detected the smell of sage and realized that Kyla slept with her head on his shoulder. Her bare softness kept one side of him warm.

Briefly, he lifted the blanket to study her creamy nakedness. Her breast was flattened against his ribs and she lay with her arm looped around his middle. He smiled.

In the gray-blue dawn, he scanned his surroundings and remembered where they were. Overhead, the rain had slowed to an occasional drip. That would give them a break. Yesterday had been a wild, exhausting day for them both, fighting the weather, surviving their narrow escape from the mountains, and his gut-twisting fear when he'd seen Kyla fall.

But this morning, Jace felt completely rested, almost renewed. Her legs tangled with his, Kyla stirred in her sleep, and he knew the reason for his sense of well-being. Last night . . .

Something had happened to him that went far beyond any experience he'd had with a saloon girl. Certainly he'd met a few with skills so amazing they'd left him exhausted and drained dry. But then he'd gotten up from their well-worn beds and ridden away without a backward glance. Money paid, service received. Not much different from buying a haircut or a meal.

Last night had been a sharing of souls and bodies, basic and honest, having little to do with expertise. He'd made love for the first time in his life. And he felt humbled by it.

Life, and the work he had chosen, had forced Jace into a loner's existence. He'd grown accustomed to that, to the isolation. Sometimes he'd hated the fact that his only company were his thoughts, but it was all he knew and he was used to it.

A few hours ago, though, the woman lying next to him had breached that solitude. He had thought only to comfort her. He hadn't realized that he would lose part of himself, and regain much more.

That empty space in him was stirring to life, making him look beyond today and next week to wonder, what then? What would happen after Blakely?

Impatiently, he pushed off the blanket. Nothing would happen, he reminded himself, pulling his mind away from the hazy, half-formed images there. He would go his way, because there was nothing else he could do. And Kyla would withdraw to a corner of his heart to become a bittersweet memory that he would

take out to savor in the years of rainy nights yet
to come.

Now, though, he had to see this through, the thing
with Hardesty, to give Kyla a safe future after he was
gone. And it wasn't going to be easy. He kissed her
forehead, and allowed himself the luxury of running
his hand down her silky back and buttocks just once
before disentangling from her embrace. She made a
soft little complaint in her sleep and rolled over,
pulling the blanket tight around her.

Those heavy footsteps—there they were again, this
time accompanied by the jingle of bridle and bit, just
on the other side of the thin wall. Jace paused with his
head down to listen—damn, someone was out there.
Plucking his gun belt from his gear, silently he crept to
the window with a cool, detached calm, his revolver
firmly in his grip. Nakedness might be his disadvantage, but his deliberate control and the ability to focus
on survival made up for it.

What he saw, though, only made him laugh and he
let the gun drop to his side. "Damn, son, we thought
you were dead," he called to Juniper, Kyla's dun
gelding. The horse looked fit and uninjured, and still
wore his saddle, although it was pretty soaked.

Turning to the stove, he stoked it to get the fire
going again, then pulled on his pants and boots to go
outside to dip water from an old rain barrel he spotted
near the window. A noisy search of the few items left
behind in the cabin turned up a cast-iron pot. Kyla
slept through the racket.

"Come on, sweetheart, wake up," he said, and his
face grew warm. The endearment slipped out too

readily, too comfortably. He gestured at the stove. "I've got some water heating for you here if you want to, you know, um, wash." Jesus, he was stumbling around like a tongue-tied schoolboy.

Kyla stirred unwillingly, and opened her eyes to find Jace towering over her. From her place on the floor, she looked straight up one long, denim-covered leg, past the swell behind his fly buttons and beyond his flat belly to his ice blue eyes. He dropped to a crouch beside her and rested his arms on his knees. He was so handsome, especially now, tousled and shirt-less from sleep.

"Are you hungry?" he asked and reached for his dry shirt where it hung on the back of the chair.

She nodded and dragged up the blanket. "Starving. We didn't have much time to eat yesterday." In fact, she felt wonderful—hungry, rested, and energized, as if the shackle on her spirit had been broken.

She even looked forward to the long miles of travel they still faced. Before, the days had been arduous and long, made even harder by the pressure she'd put on herself to prove her ability to Jace. Now she knew she had nothing to prove.

"All right, then," he said, and stood to tuck his shirt tails in. "You hurry and get dressed, and we'll eat. Then we need to get started—oh, and someone is waiting for you outside."

"Who?" she asked, immediately suspicious.

Grinning, he reached out and took her chin between his thumb and forefinger. "You'll have to get up and look. But I think you'll be happy about it." He dropped his hand. "I'll go see about my horse while you dress."

Wrapping a blanket around herself, Kyla padded to the window and peeked out. Juniper, wet and muddy but seeming otherwise unharmed, paced near Jace's horse.

"Juniper!" She turned to Jace. "How did he get here?"

He shrugged. "I don't know, but it's a real stroke of luck. It would probably take awhile to find you another horse out here."

While Jace went outside to saddle his horse, she washed in the water warming on the stove and recalled moments from the night before.

Kyla never would have imagined that an act she had learned to think of as degrading and vulgar could be so moving, so emotionally uplifting. How far she had come since that day in Silver City. Then, she would have shot anyone who tried to touch her, especially intimately. But Jace had gradually changed all of that, leading her back one step at a time to the ability to enjoy his kiss, his caress. She thought of the feelings he had summoned from her, the way he had responded to her with a hot, dark passion, and the intensely personal communion they had shared. It had been the most satisfying experience of her adult life, and one that she would hold dear. . . .

Just as she finished dressing, she heard the unmistakable sound of gunshots. Jace—Kyla froze, a boot in her hand, and her heart pounding behind her breastbone. A moment of silence ensued, followed by more shots. They were carried on the wind, and she couldn't tell from which direction they came, but instinct made her duck. Dropping to her hands and knees, she scrambled for her gunbelt in the corner, and began to strap it on with hands that shook.

Jace was out there.

The door crashed open then and Jace dove toward the table to grab the Henry.

"Oh, thank God you're safe! What is that?" she asked uneasily. "Is someone shooting at you?"

He nodded. "I think so," he said, peering around the edge of the window. The long muscles in his forearms swelled as he gripped the rifle. "But I'm going to find out for sure." He glanced at her. "You stay here, and stay down. No one has seen you so they won't know you're here. I'll be back as soon as I can." He grabbed his duster and his hat.

"Why do you have to go out there?" she asked, trying to keep the quiver out of her voice. "Can't we just wait and see if they go away?"

"Kyla, if they're looking for me, they aren't going to go away. They've already seen me."

"But you don't have to rush out there to meet them!"

"I'm not going to meet them," he said, his eyes wearing that cold, flat expression she'd first seen through the window at the Magnolia Saloon, when he stood over Sawyer Clark. "I'm going to run them off."

"Jace, don't go. Please," she implored. "It's too dangerous."

He smiled, and glanced away almost self-consciously. Maybe no one had ever bothered to worry about him before. "Hell, I'll be all right," he said, returning his gaze to her.

When had she ever seen eyes that color? she wondered irrelevantly. Like ice, like a hot blue summer sky.

He crossed the tiny floor to the corner where she still knelt, and gave her a long, searching look. Then, shooting out his free hand, he gripped her by the back of the neck to press his mouth to hers in a hard, brief kiss. "Stay safe, and stay down. I won't be away long." He winked at her and gestured at her revolver where it rested against her thigh. "Just don't shoot me when I come back."

With gnawing apprehension, Kyla watched him walk to the door, his boots reverberating on the floorboards.

And then he was gone.

Kyla paced the length and width of the small, dark cabin, a task that was accomplished in very few steps. The shooting continued, although more sporadically now, and it seemed to be coming from farther away. She had no way of knowing if any of the shots fired were from Jace's guns.

Although she had held him in her arms last night, and had seen him at his most vulnerable moment, that didn't change who he was. He was Jace Rankin, the most famous bounty hunter in the region, smart, dangerous, and utterly fearless. He could take care of himself—he'd been doing it, and very well, for years. But her mind showed her pictures of a bullet, white-hot and deadly, finding its mark. And it only took *one* shot with the right aim to strike a heart or a head or a belly.

The thought made her throat tight with terror and anguish.

She sank to the rickety chair next to the stove and propped her feet on the fender. She hadn't expected to fall in love with him. In fact, falling in love with anyone was the last thing she wanted. It was a pretty ideal that had nothing to do with her goal. But in the most secret corner of her heart, she recognized that loving him was an inevitability, a path upon which she had unwittingly set her feet the day she sought him out. To make matters worse, her feelings for Jace were one-sided. Oh, she supposed he liked her well enough, and she had earned his respect. He didn't love her though, and she wished she could shut off the emotion flooding her heart.

Time and again he had proven his honor, and had revealed so many good and decent facets of his complex personality. She touched her locket where it hung suspended above her heart. Maybe given the chance, and enough love to make up for all that he'd been denied as a youngster, Jace might find his own heart again—

Suddenly, the door flew open. Kyla jumped to her feet to face five men she didn't recognize, and five guns all pointed at her. Panic engulfed her and made her heart give a tremendous lurch in her chest. But as they advanced on her, she found Kyle's toughest voice, and whipped out her own gun.

The men were coarse and rough, reminding her of some buffalo hunters she'd seen once when she was a girl. One of them, a short, wiry redhead, studied her with small, rabbity eyes. The cabin filled with their rank, unwashed stench.

"All right, you come along now," one of them ordered. "Mr. Hardesty's waitin' on you."

"You stinkin' sheep turds stay back, or I'll shoot your balls off, if you got any!" She swung the revolver in a wide arc, threatening all of them.

"Shee-it, ain't she a sassy one?" another remarked, faintly amused, as if he were merely a spectator.

"She won't talk so sassy once she realizes it ain't no use," the apparent leader said, laughing as well. Aghast, Kyla recognized the speaker as Hobie McIntyre. He was the low-down saddle tramp who had shot her. "Lem, see to that," he added, inclining his head at her revolver.

The man answering to the name Lem was big and stupid-looking, and missing most of his front teeth. He took a step forward, and Kyla flashed the gun at him.

"Best you *don't* see to it, Lem," she challenged with false bravado. She cocked the hammer but she silently cursed her hand for shaking nearly as much as her voice.

In the confusion of being threatened by so many, it wasn't difficult for one of them to distract her. Lem grabbed her arm and twisted it so hard she thought it would snap. She suppressed the cry that crawled up her throat, but the revolver fell from her nerveless hand like a ripe apple from a tree.

"Mr. Hardesty sent us to find you and bring you back to Blakely," McIntyre said, gazing at her with his pale, bulging eyes. "And that's what we aim to do. It can be easylike, or we can do it the hard way, if you've a mind to." He looked her up and down with distaste, while he sucked some food particle from his ocher-colored teeth. "Like I told him, I don't know what he wants with a wildcat like you. I seen the scar you left on his face. Oh, he didn't say where he got it, but everyone knows. I don't fancy that you're even worth gettin' hard for, but he's got a hankerin' for you. After we take you to Blakely, he can do with you what he will. I 'spect he's got some big welcome-home planned for you." He grinned suddenly.

"I dunno . . ." the fifth one said, appraising Kyla speculatively, rubbing his chin. "I done some bronc bustin' in my time. It might be fun with a filly like her. She'd prob'ly give a man a good ride."

Kyla swallowed hard, trying to unstick the sides of her dry throat. Oh, dear God, no—

"Just forgit it, Sims. If she comes back to Hardesty with even one hair out of place, there'll be the devil to pay and she ain't worth it," McIntyre said.

Although she continued to search for an opening, a single opportunity to escape or divert these men, she knew circumstances were against her. "I ain't goin' anywhere with you. Hardesty and the rest of you can go to hell!" she shot back with brave venom, but inside she trembled.

"Now you shut up, or I'll shoot you again," McIntyre snapped, his smile gone. "We stood here yappin' long enough. Boys, get her and let's go."

She suddenly found herself being hustled toward the door—there might not be much she could do, but she refused to be herded along like a lamb to the slaughter. She fought and kicked, struggling against the hands that gripped her. Being shorter than the rest of them, she couldn't see much beyond a confusion of sweat-stained buckskins, grimy denim, and greasy, beard-shadowed faces. Her heart nearly bursting with fear and rage, she squirmed and thrashed around, hoping desperately that she might break free. Once, her boot connected hard with a nearby shin and she heard someone swear. She screamed blue murder, then sank her teeth into the dirty, foul-smelling hand that covered her mouth and nostrils to silence her. She spit out the taste, and screamed again. Maybe Jace would hear her . . .

"Goddamn it, shut her up!" McIntyre ordered as they struggled out the door as a unit. "I can't hear myself think."

"I'm tryin'!" Dirty Hand yelped indignantly, clamping his injured hand between his knees. "She bit me, the bitch!"

"Well, tie her up and gag her so's she can't bite you," McIntyre said, "then get to ridin'. Rankin ain't no fool—it won't take him long to figure out he's been lured away. We want to be ready."

Despite her bucking and wriggling, Kyla couldn't prevent them from lashing a rope around her wrists and ankles. Dirty Hand grabbed Jace's bandana from the table and gagged her, and her screams were silenced. Carried outside like a sack of grain, she was flung across a horse's back and the wet ground was her only view from then on. The sound of horses' hooves, creaking saddle leather, and rough voices were all she could hear.

"All right, you two take her off to those trees," she heard McIntyre say. "We'll meet you there after Rankin is dead."

Jace rode far from the cabin to a distant tree line. He wove in and out of the dark firs, staying away from open rangeland. The morning sky was heavily overcast, working to his advantage to provide cover. But it also gave the gunman the same edge. Intermittent shots continued to ring out, occasionally striking just close enough to acknowledge his presence, but not to necessarily hit him. All right, goddamn it, they had his attention, whoever they were, he thought with cold fury. And he was going to find out what the hell this was all about. The situation was too risky to ignore. If he turned back and tried to ride out with Kyla, she would be in danger, too. He'd have to confront the person on the other end of that gun.

Finally, Jace determined the location from which the shots were coming. Whoever the bastard was, he made no effort to hide evidence of himself: a small fire, obviously built with wet wood, sent up a tall plume of smoke over the trees ahead of him.

Something about this felt wrong; Jace rechecked the rounds in the Henry and broadened his sweeping inspection of the woods near him. He never lost sight of the fact that there was always someone who wanted to make his own reputation by challenging Jace Rankin. That could be the case here, too.

As he drew closer to the smoldering fire, a horse and rider burst from the trees and galloped off in the opposite direction, away from Jace.

"Hey, wait up!" he barked, and took off after him, spurring his horse into a flat run. But the rider was already far ahead, as if his true purpose was to lure him out and farther away. What the hell was going on? Then he realized the answer.

God—Kyla! A shiver plunged down Jace's back like a bolt of ice-cold lightning. He sawed at the reins, pulling his horse to a skidding halt, then swung around toward the cabin, cursing himself for a damned fool every step of the way. How could he have been so stupid, so careless?

If he hadn't been wary and alert every moment for the last twenty-two years, he wouldn't have lived to see thirty. Why had he chosen this point in time, when he was responsible for someone else, to let his judgment falter?

He hadn't forgotten about Hardesty's men, but thus far they had proved to be so bumbling and lazy, that despite the episode in Cord, in his mind he had reduced the extent of their threat. Could they be behind this?

His heart hammering against his ribs, he pulled his hat on tighter and bent low over the pommel. He urged the horse on, pushing it to a thundering speed over the rain-soaked range that tore up muddy sod with every fall of its hooves.

To Jace it felt as though they were wading through fields of molasses, slow and frustrating and terrifying. The cabin, a faraway speck at the mist-gray base of the mountains, seemed to get no closer, even though the horse's sides heaved with effort. It all had a nightmare quality, except Jace knew that he wouldn't wake up to find Kyla asleep next to him. There was no waking up from this, and he wouldn't relax until he saw her again, in the flesh and safe.

But even as watery sunlight began to emerge from the slate-colored clouds, Jace saw a group of riders in the distance. Cantering away from the general direction of the cabin, there were three of them, although the one on that dun looked pretty small. More like a kid than a man.

A kid . . .

Oh, Jesus. Hoping his horse survived to forgive him, he pushed on, and tried hard to ignore the sickening clenching in his stomach. He strained to see the details of their appearance, but he was too far away. He needed to get close enough to see better, to see if his eyes were playing tricks on him, or if that kid really did have red hair.

"Hooo-eee, look at that bounty hunter ride! I never seen such slick ridin'," Lem remarked from behind the remains of his tobacco-stained teeth. "Guess he'll be surprised when he catches up with those boys. Hobie will fix him up just fine." His laughter was free and hearty. It made Kyla's blood freeze in her veins.

Terrified, outraged, helpless, from their hiding place in the dark trees she saw Jace gallop past on the open rangeland, lashing his horse toward certain disaster. But bound hand and foot, and gagged with his bandana, she could do nothing but watch. And listen to Lem and Dirty Hand congratulate themselves on their cleverness.

"Yeah, Hobie's real smart, comin' up with that idea.

Where'd he find that red-haired kid?" Dirty Hand asked. Since Kyla hadn't heard the man's name, based on her own experience, she thought of him thus. He had tied a filthy rag around his fist to cover the wound that her bite had inflicted.

"I dunno—it sure beats all, don't it? But it was *my* idea to give the kid the wildcat's coat to wear and put him on her dun. Rankin won't know the truth of it until they've got him locked up in that box canyon."

"Yup, that'll be the end of him," Lem pronounced, then turned to Kyla. "I hope you said good-bye real nice to your hee-ro before he left. You won't be seein' him again."

Kyla gave him a murderous look, then turned her gaze to Jace's diminishing figure and followed it until it was gone. Slumped against a ponderosa pine on the wet ground, she shivered as much from fear as from the cold. Tears kept trying to work their way up from her chest, and she persistently choked them back. Jace pursued McIntyre, the Bronc Buster, and the Redhead across the open range, undoubtedly believing, as he was intended to, that he was rescuing her.

Questions and possibilities pelted her frantic mind like hail, and bounced against her remorse.

Could he prevail in a fight of three against one? Yes, perhaps, if he discovered the trap in time.

Was there some way they could have avoided being discovered by McIntyre? If they had pressed on last evening instead of stopping? Who knew how fate might have been altered if they had?

And, oh God, if he were killed—she lowered her head. It would be her fault, as surely as if she had pulled the trigger herself. Would she be able to escape the confinement of five men? And then where would she go?

Suddenly, a barrage of distant shots penetrated the mist of her thoughts, jerking her upright and causing her to bump her head against the tree. It was like hearing the report of a firing squad, tearing at her own heart.

A long interval of silence followed, punctuated only by a the twitter of a sparrow.

"Well, I guess that's that, and goddamn good riddance to him, too," Lem said finally. "Bounty hunters are lower'n snakes, and Rankin was the worst. He tracked down my little brother for a bank robbery in Yakima. Weren't no call for that—that teller Billy shot didn't die." He shot a stream of tobacco juice at the ground and pushed his bulk away from the tree trunk he leaned against, using his shotgun for a cane. "Now Billy's sittin' in prison, givin' my ma more gray hair. If I had the chance, I'd spit on Rankin's stinkin' carcass and leave it for the buzzards to pick at."

"Amen to that," Dirty Hand concurred. "Well, Hobie'll be back in a few minutes, and we can be on our way."

Lem turned his gaze on Kyla, studying her with a look she had seen before and didn't like. "If this hellcat here wasn't intended for Mr. Hardesty, I might like a taste of her myself. There's somethin' about a killin' that always gets my blood up."

The other man shook his head and clutched his injured hand. "Not me—that gal spits and bites like a viper." He paused a moment, then added with a greasy smile, "'Course, if she was tied up proper and still gagged, she couldn't kick, spit *or* bite. All she could do is buck."

"I'll bet she ain't quite so horny-hided under them clothes as she lets on, either," Lem added with an infuriating cackle, scratching his privates with no regard for Kyla's presence.

Kyla suppressed a shudder. Showing fear of any kind right now could be her undoing, but her heart pounded so hard she felt it nudging her stomach.

"Just think—Hobie McIntyre, the man who finally brung down the famous Jace Rankin. And we was here for it. This story ought to be good for a few free drinks in any saloon in the territory," Dirty Hand predicted.

Beyond mere disgust, she averted her head and stared dully at the vista of mountains against the gray sky, while the two chatted amiably about Jace's death and the money and fame this job would bring them. Every reference to Jace lacerated her heart with excruciating pain.

Their annoying voices faded to a drone; her fierce struggle to escape, combined with her grief and anxiety, left her drained and listless. Her hands and feet were becoming numb from the tight ropes tied around her ankles and wrists.

Jace couldn't die—he was larger than life, she told herself. He'd survived a hundred dangerous situations, a thousand. He couldn't die when she had only just found him and had had a glimpse of his heart. Fate and five evil men couldn't take him without giving them a chance to heal each other's souls.

She tried to blank out the pictures trooping through her mind, but she was too tired to fight them. She remembered her own childhood, always seeking her father's approval and never winning it, no matter how she tried.

And there was Jace, just a youngster, facing a step-father whose notion of manhood was so twisted he had extinguished Jace's ability to love anyone, including Kyla. . . .

That night a year ago—oh, God, was that what waited for her now? Becoming a prisoner of Tom Hardesty, trapped in a place where no one would help her, perhaps even being forced to marry him?

No, she wouldn't do it. Especially after the tenderness that she and Jace had shared. *The way it's supposed to be*, he'd said. And she knew he was right. If she couldn't escape, she'd kill herself or Hardesty before she'd become his victim again. She swore she would.

Kyla's grim thoughts were interrupted by an uneasy tone she heard in Dirty Hand's voice. Keeping her gaze fixed on the landscape, she turned her attention back to the conversation.

"—oughtta be back by now? It's been a long time and that canyon ain't but a couple of miles from here."

Lem stepped out of the trees and craned his neck toward the canyon, then walked back, squirting another stream of tobacco juice. "It could be there was *a little* trouble. But just a little."

"What should we do?"

"We'll wait," Lem decided firmly. "Hobie said to wait, and so we will."

It *had* been a long time since those shots were fired,

Kyla realized. If Jace were—if he had been—she had trouble even thinking the word. If he'd been killed, surely he would have taken a man or two with him. And without a leader, Lem and Dirty Hand were lost, or so she believed until more time passed and Lem had an inspiration.

"Maybe they're all dead," he suggested, giving voice to everyone's thoughts. "But if Hobie and the others don't come back, and we take the woman to Hardesty . . . won't that be worth a big reward?" He spoke in hushed tones, as if the spirits of the departed might hear him and strike him down. "Hell, we could even say it was us who killed Rankin after he got Hobie."

The more Lem and Dirty Hand discussed this idea, the more eager they became.

"We could hole up a day," Lem went on. "You know, spend it at that cabin over yonder. Restin' up and takin' our ease with the woman." He spoke as if Kyla were a horse or a wagon wheel, with no ability to comprehend them. But she stared back at them with the coldest look she could muster, one that she thought would make Jace proud.

"That's right, take our ease," Dirty Hand said, repeating the phrase with a certain relish. "Who's left to say we can't?"

"I am."

Lem and Dirty Hand swung their guns around to an intruder. Kyla's head swiveled to see Jace standing at the edge of the trees, his Henry rifle trained on the two men. She uttered a shapeless cry, muffled by the gag.

He spared her the briefest of glances, then approached slowly, deliberately.

He seemed ten feet tall to her. A day's growth of dark beard shadowed his face, making him seem even more sinister, and he moved with an easy but controlled grace. He looked as frightening as she'd ever seen him, and as welcome as the cavalry. Waves of emotion sluiced through her: love, joy, overwhelming relief, and the sense that now the situation had become really perilous.

"I'll see to it that you won't have an easy moment for the rest of your lives," Jace added, his eyes flat and cold, nearly colorless. "You'd better drop your weapons."

"Like hell I will," Lem said, holding fast to his shotgun. His gaze darted around, as if he were searching for one of his own group to appear behind Jace. It didn't happen. "Where's Hobie and the others?"

Jace lifted the Henry a notch. "Dead." His voice had a dry, papery sound, like October leaves tumbling over a grave in the wind.

"You're a liar, mister. No one by himself could outgun three armed men. Not even you," Dirty Hand said. Any crude amiability he'd shown earlier was gone.

Without taking his eyes or his aim off the two men, Jace reached into his coat pocket and produced a leather thong strung with bear teeth. "Recognize this?"

Lem started. "It belongs to Hobie, everybody knows that. He cut it off'n a Indian he killed. Where'd you get it?" he demanded.

Jace smiled slightly, cool and deadly. "I cut if off Hobie."

The blood drained out of the two men's faces, as if the true danger of their situation had begun to dawn upon them.

"Only a no-count snake would rob a dead man," Lem charged with shaky indignation.

"I wonder what that makes a bunch of cowards who would lure another man into a trap to kill him." Jace stuffed the thong back into his pocket. "Drop your guns, or I'll shoot you where you stand."

A taut moment passed when neither Lem nor Dirty Hand spoke or moved. Jace watched them, unblinking like a blue-eyed cat. The air crackled with tension, and Kyla scarcely breathed.

Suddenly, Lem lunged at Kyla where she sat against the tree and jammed the shotgun barrel against her jaw. He crowded his face next to hers and gripped her neck with his free hand. "You decide, Rankin—is she gonna live through this? Let us go or the hellcat dies."

Kyla froze, and her eyes grew wide with terror as she stared at Jace. But he kept his gaze on the man next to her and never looked at her once. Lem's breath against her neck was moist and sour, and the smell of fear oozing from his pores compounded his rank odor. "Don't you think we make a pretty—"

A rifle blast exploded in the forest morning, and Lem was blown backward and away from Kyla, with a neat dime-size hole just above the bridge of his nose. She screamed behind her gag at the horror of it all. The bullet had come so close, she'd felt its heat. She swallowed and swallowed, but her mouth and throat were bone-dry. God, what was Jace thinking? Was he crazy? Events were whizzing by so quickly she struggled to grasp them as they occurred.

Dirty Hand stared at Lem's inert form uncomprehendingly, then turned his angry, malevolent glare on Jace. "You killed my partner!" Instead of putting down his gun, to Kyla's utter amazement, he lifted his revolver and extended it the full length of his hamlike arm to point it at Jace. Another shot rang out and Dirty Hand fell like a sack of meal into the pine needles, facedown. The smell of burning sulphur was thick.

Jace approached slowly, then rolled him over with his foot. A bright red stain bloomed in the center of his chest. Prying the gun from the dead man's hand, he threw it into the woods with what looked like his full strength. Then he turned to Kyla. His face was pale and blank, and his eyes narrowed, as if against the gunsmoke hanging over them

"Are you hurt?" he asked, worry overlaying his voice. He yanked down the bandana that served as her gag. "Did they hurt you?"

She shook loose of the scarf. Now that the emergency had passed, she felt the remains of her courage ebbing away, leaving her shaky and rubber-limbed. "No, I'm not hurt. Oh, God, Jace," she said in a low, quivering voice, "I didn't think I'd ever see you again. I thought . . . I thought you were dead." Tears edged her eyes and she lowered her gaze to hide them.

He drew his long hunting knife from the scabbard at his waist and cut the ropes tying her wrists and ankles with two swift strokes. Pulling her into a tight embrace, he murmured against her ear. "It's all right now, it's all right. You're safe."

Kyla tried to stop her tears, but the longer he held her and reassured her, the harder her sobs came, and she poured them out on his shoulder. He stroked the back of her hair and she clung to him, feeling as if she could be safe only in his arms. Her face pressed against the canvas of his duster, she smelled the familiar and comforting scents of him—horses, leather, fresh air—so much different from those of unwashed, sweat-stale bodies and rotting teeth.

"How—how did you get away?"

He backed up and took her face between his gloved hands. "Hell, honey, I'm a lot smarter than they bargained for. I know what kind of track your horse leaves when you ride him. The man they put on Juniper weighed a lot more than you. I figured out what they were up to."

Was there anything that this man didn't know? Couldn't do? Hadn't seen? Kyla knew that Hobie McIntyre would have easily killed a man less capable than Jace.

His gaze drifted over her face and shoulders, down her torso to her legs and feet. "You're sure you aren't hurt?"

She shook her head. "Just a little bruised from being pushed around and thrown over a horse's back. And cold—they took my coat." She stole a glance at the bodies sharing the small clearing. "If you hadn't come back when you did, though—well, I guess you heard their plans." She sighed tiredly. "Are the others really dead?"

He looked at her straight on. "Yeah. It was them or me." His voice reflected the weary sound of a man who had seen too much in his years. Perhaps that was why, when the light was just right, lines emerged in his young face, the ones around his eyes. He pulled off his glove and rubbed the back of his neck. "This is a hard life, you know. And it doesn't get easier."

She wasn't sure if he referred to life in general, or his own. "Jace, please—take me away from here."

Nodding, he stood and pulled her to her feet. Pins and needles shot through her legs, and her backside was soaked from sitting on the wet forest floor.

"I've got the horses tied up on the other side of those trees," he said, gesturing in a westerly direction.

"Oh, did you bring Juniper back? Is he all right?" she asked, hope giving her new energy.

"Yeah, he's a sturdy mount, even if he doesn't like snow. Can you walk?" he asked, lifting his hat and resetting it.

"I think so—" But her knee buckled and he swung her up into his arms. His muscles flexed under her, strong and capable, and she hid her face against his neck to shut out the gruesome scene.

"We'll go back to the cabin so you can dry off," Jace said. "Then we've got to get you another coat somewhere." He laughed humorlessly. "Damn, Kyla, you need to hang on to your horse and stop losing your gear."

Chapter Thirteen

In his life Jace had learned that there were a number of ways to insult a man. They included questioning his heritage, his courage, and the size of his privates. In his opinion, the person doing the insulting usually revealed more about his own shortcomings than anyone else's.

And to his way of thinking, no affront was worse than to willingly leave a dead man unburied.

So while he was inclined to abandon Hobie McIntyre's worthless carcass and those of his men to the coyotes, decency would not let him. He had discovered a spade outside the abandoned cabin, and after taking Kyla back to rest and warm up, he returned to begin the backbreaking job. As he rode away from the graves he had dug for them, his shoulders ached but he was satisfied that he had done the right thing.

Kyla had said nothing about his decision, but he could tell she was baffled. Hell, maybe no one would understand it. But he didn't have anyone to answer to but himself. The one thing he would not do, though, was mark the graves. Burying those bastards was enough—certainly more than they would have done for him.

This day never should have happened, he thought grimly. He realized now how obvious the trick had been to lure him out. It was a clever-enough scheme for a man of Hobie McIntyre's limited intelligence. But Jace had years of experience—he had outmaneuvered men like McIntyre a dozen times or more.

The plain truth of it was that Jace had gotten sloppy, careless. And it was because he'd let himself fall into the arms of Kyla's comfort. For a brief moment, he'd permitted himself the luxury of needing someone and filling the emptiness that he'd begun to feel lately.

Crossing the open range, silent and autumn gold beneath the clear, late-day sky, he gazed at the cabin ahead. The weather had finally broken, and the landscape was serene and peaceful, giving no hint of the blood spilled here today. If he blocked the day's events out of his mind, he could almost picture that scene again, the one that had him riding home to a warm kitchen and a hot meal. Lying with Kyla last night had made the image sharper, brighter. There she was in the open doorway, flame-haired and welcoming, waiting for him.

Trouble was, he couldn't block out today, or any of the days that had gone before. And she had to be told that.

"It's done?" Kyla asked, watching him unsaddle his horse. The low sun filled her hair with fiery glints and turned her turquoise eyes translucent. Jesus Christ, but she was beautiful, with a faint roundness to her cheeks that he knew would reach full bloom if she ate three meals a day and wasn't living on the run.

"Yeah, it's done. I guess it might be hard for someone else to understand." He hobbled his own horse next to Juniper, then glanced up at her. "I suppose I hope that when my time comes, someone will do the same for me, and not leave me out for the buzzards to pick at."

"Oh, Jace," she said, her voice dropping to barely more than a whisper, "please don't talk like that. I was so worried today, so scared. Not just for me, but you . . . for you."

His head came up sharply. Strange—even though no woman had ever told him she cared about him, he knew that was the emotion hovering behind her words. It was more than her reluctance to lose the man she'd hired to do a job for her, or a woman's fear of losing her protector. A lot more.

No, Kyla, don't say it, he willed her silently. Don't even think it. She stood aside to let him pass into the cabin, and he paused to lightly grip her shoulders.

"Listen, now, don't start worrying about me."

"How can I not, after all that's happened? Jace, maybe after this is over, after Hardesty is taken care of, maybe then we—maybe together—" She left the sentence unfinished but her meaning was plain enough, the possibilities she implied as bright as a new morning. She gazed up at him, trusting, vulnerable, her moist pink mouth just inches from his own.

She was right—they had been through a lot, and today he'd almost been killed. A kiss, he could permit himself that, a small celebration of his own survival and hers. Her eyes drifted closed and her clean fragrance, of sage and new-mowed grass, floated to him from her body heat. And beneath the rough shirt and jeans he knew she was smooth and lush. A familiar heavy tightness gathered in his groin. He lowered his head to her upturned lips, his mouth just grazing their warmth—

No, he couldn't let it happen. He pulled back suddenly and turned from her, avoiding her puzzled expression. Where she was concerned, he couldn't afford to let himself be an ordinary man with ordinary desires. He needed to be stronger. Pacing over the flooring, he pulled off the duster and flung it on the table.

"Come here and sit down." He pulled the flimsy chair forward with the toe of his boot. "I need to make you understand something."

Kyla edged toward the chair and perched on its rough seat. Her posture, rigid and taut, spoke of her apprehension.

"You could have been killed today," he began. "If that had happened I'd have had no one to blame but myself."

He would have thought it impossible, but she snapped up even straighter in the chair. "How can you say that?"

He resumed his pacing in narrow circles around the cabin floor. Every muscle in his body was tight. "If I'd been paying attention, McIntyre and his men never could have lured me away from here. But I wasn't on my guard—I was busy thinking about how it felt to make love with you."

She glanced down at the floor, but not before he caught a glimpse of the blush that stained her face. "Well, I'm sorry . . ." she murmured. Her hands were folded into a tight knot on her lap.

He dropped to one knee in front of her. "Jesus, Kyla, don't think I'm blaming *you* for what happened." He put his hand on top of hers, but then withdrew it. "It was my fault—"

"Why does it have to be anyone's fault, yours or mine?" she demanded then, trapping him in an angry turquoise glare. "There's nothing wrong with wanting a normal life, to be close to someone."

"No, there isn't, and you should have that. But don't expect to have it with me. I don't have a normal life and I can't. There will always be a Hobie McIntyre out there someplace." He felt as if he were on his knees before her, begging her to understand his situation, one that she stubbornly refused to see.

"But he was looking for me, not you," she pointed out, pressing her hand to her chest. "It wouldn't have mattered if they found me with you or by myself. Hardesty sent them."

"Do you think it should have taken five men and a big plan to steal you? They were hunting for you, yes, but McIntyre had a bone to pick with me, probably just because of the kind of work I do. He *wanted* to kill me. Even if Hardesty ordered him to do it, I knew from the first time I saw him that the idea had him drooling to get at me. Kyla, there's a territory full of men out there bearing grudges like that, or kids who want to face off with me in the street to see of they can outdraw me. I'm just one man—I have to watch my back all the time and I'm the only one doing it. I can't let anything distract me that could get me killed." He paused and added in a lower voice, "I'm not afraid of death, but I'm not rushing to meet it, either. And you might get caught in the crossfire."

"You could quit—do something else like—"

"Like what? Ranching? Farming?" he asked, lacing the words with sarcastic edge. He stood up impatiently and began pacing again. "I can't quit. I don't want to quit!" he lied.

"You're scared!" she charged, jumping to her feet.

"The hell I am!" he said, taken aback. No one could accuse him of being a coward, and no one had since Lyle died. "I'm not scared of anything or anybody."

"Oh, yes, you are. It isn't that you can't care about anyone. You're just afraid to. It would mean admitting that you need someone besides yourself. To you, facing men with loaded guns is safer." They stood almost chest to chest, breath coming hard, the rising tension like sparks between them.

Jace felt a flush creep up his neck and over his face. "You're treading on dangerous ground, Kyla," he warned in a low voice. "You'd better leave it alone."

Unflinching, she lifted her chin, stubborn and challenging. "No. After last night and today, I think we should talk about it," she dared him. "Tell me the truth."

"We're not going to talk about it," he stressed in a tone that had made mule skinners back down in saloon

fights. But this tough female—damn, she only swallowed and kept her eyes fixed on his.

Unable to withstand the piercing, soul-searching look she directed at him, he turned away and changed the subject. "We're leaving tomorrow so you'd better get something to eat and turn in. You take my blankets."

"No, thank you."

He turned back to her and stabbed an index finger in her direction. "I still get the last word here, and you agreed to do as you're told. So take my blankets and don't argue. We'll get you a coat and a bedroll tomorrow."

"I'll pay—"

"Yeah, yeah, I know, you'll pay me back when we get to Blakely." He gestured in the general direction of her breasts. "And you'd better start wrapping yourself up again. I don't want to be out on the road and run the risk of having someone discover that you're actually a woman. It's a lot less dangerous traveling with a farm boy named Kyle."

Her eyes glittered like hard, blue-green agates. "Yeah, well, Kyle is the one who took that bullet for you in Cord." She dragged her sleeve across her nose. "So I guess it's less dangerous only for you."

Kyla lay awake in the musty, dark cabin, the dead of night surrounding her. On the other side of the small room she could hear Jace's even, quiet breathing. Whether he slept she didn't know, but it sounded like it. Obviously he was untroubled by the same turmoil churning inside of her. He'd settled down on the floor

with his head propped against his saddle and his
ankles crossed. Tonight the Henry lay beside him.
He'd once told her that he thought more of that rifle
than he did most humans, and she was beginning to
believe him.

A return of the hostile, unfriendly mood of their
early days together made their dismal meal of biscuits
and hot coffee silent and awkward. Jace withdrew into
the solitary figure that he presented to the world, and
she wore Kyle's sullenness to hide her double pain.
Not only did she suffer keenly from him shutting her
out—he either didn't realize or didn't care how much
it hurt to be consigned again to the prison of Kyle
Springer.

Barring her experiences with Hardesty, she couldn't
remember the last time she'd been so miserable and
lonely. She wished she could roll over and weep into
Jace's blanket, but he would hear her. And when she
thought of the night before, she felt even worse. The
heat and passion that had blazed between them only
twenty-four hours earlier now burned as anger.

Better that she had kept her attention focused on her
original goal of vengeance instead of straying into this
matter of two hearts. But that goal was not as clear
now as it had once been. Oh, she was still determined
to prevail, to see Tom Hardesty pay. Only ... She
shifted on the hard floor, seeking a comfortable position that continued to elude her. Only, after she'd
nearly died in Misfortune, she'd doggedly believed
that her craving for revenge had saved her. That the
powerful presence dragging her back into her body

during that odd dream with Many Braids had been grim determination to see justice done.

Now she realized that it had been love, and she felt trapped by the emotion. She had no outlet for it, because the man she wanted to give it to would not receive it or return it. The glimpse he'd permitted her of the true man behind his reputation had disappeared again. She let her fingers drift over her locket.

Though she lay wrapped in his blankets just a couple of feet from him, Kyla missed Jace.

"Sorry, Mr. Hardesty, I still haven't seen a wire for you."

Tom Hardesty swore audibly under his breath, a single, malignant vituperation. On his side of the counter Edner Pomeroy blanched, his expression one of cringing regret.

"I know you're expecting something important, so I'm ready and waiting for that message to come through. Just as soon as I see it, I'll drop everything else to bring it along personally."

Today, Tom found the man's fawning to be irritating. "See that you do, Edner." Without another word, he slammed out of the telegraph office and looked at the pale blue autumn sky. Brown leaves scudded over the dry street and gathered against the edges of the sidewalks, and the wind had a decided bite. That, and the business with McIntyre was enough to make him turn toward the Pine Cone Saloon. It was almost four o'clock—that was late enough for a little elbow-bending at the bar.

Three days, three long, silent days, and no word

from Hobie McIntyre or any of his men. Goddamn it, if he had let Kyla and Rankin slip away from him once more Tom would—Well, there wasn't much Tom could do; he didn't expect to see McIntyre again if he failed. But Luke Jory would have plenty to say about it. His kettle was already boiling over this situation, and he was not a patient man.

As Tom passed the shops on his way to the Pine Cone, he made deliberate eye contact with a clerk here, a proprietor there. It was a useful tactic he'd learned from Jory to keep people around town aware of the Vigilance Union. Not much happened in Blakely that he and Jory didn't know about.

Tom's own anger, which he rarely bothered to curb, was on the rise over gossip he'd heard: people seemed to know that Rankin was on his way. *How* they'd heard was a mystery to him since no telegrams came in or went out without his knowledge. It was as if the man's reputation had a power of its own, carried on the wind and whispered in men's minds.

Although he'd never seen the bounty hunter, he'd begun dreaming of an eight-foot-tall, rifle-toting angel of death, mowing down rows of adversaries with a single shot that felled men like wheat in a hailstorm. He shook off the image. Jesus, this was no time to get jittery.

But he'd rather face the phantom from his dreams than Luke Jory if he were to get wind of the rumor. Since his last message from McIntyre, Tom had visited the telegraph office more and more often every day, looking for word that the bounty hunter was dead and Kyla captured. But there was no such news.

He paused in front of the saloon as he pictured Rankin's image again. Tom had to solve this problem. No goddamned bounty hunter was going to make him look like a horse's rump.

Or steal his woman.

Perversely, now that Jace had decided he must distance himself from Kyla, he wanted her more than ever. Their last night in the cabin he told himself that he didn't sleep because the episode with McIntyre had made him leery of intruders. But that didn't explain why he was alert to every breath Kyla took, every restless movement she made during the night. Or why he wished to God that he could lie down with her again, even if only to hold her in his arms and taste her kiss. But he had pushed her away and now he had to live with the decision.

Riding ahead most of the time, Jace felt her eyes burning into his back. She remained watchful but she had stopped speaking, for the most part. When she did talk it was with a farm boy's bad grammar, and she had taken up Kyle's personal habits again. His memory of a soft, yellow-gowned, beribboned woman was a sore contrast to this belching, hostile female. In fact, she seemed to go out of her way to be obnoxious. He had himself to blame, he knew; he'd told her to resume the disguise, secretly hoping that it would distract him from the beauty that he knew lay underneath. Originally he'd been amused by Kyle Springer. Now the boy was downright irritating.

In Dayville, they stopped at a general store to get Kyla another coat and a bedroll. Since Jace felt pretty certain that no one was following them, he took advantage of the freedom to buy them a decent meal in a chop house. Amid the busy clatter of dishes and silver, no one had seemed to recognize him so they placed their order with the stout woman waiting tables. Jace asked for a beer as well, but when Kyla tried to follow suit he sent the woman on her way.

When she returned a few minutes later with their supper, Jace watched with brows lifted, as Kyla wolfed her food with a fork she held like a shovel. At least she'd tucked her blue-checkered napkin into her shirt collar. "Hungry?" he inquired dryly.

She gave him a sullen look, then put both elbows on the table and mopped up the gravy on her plate with a piece of biscuit that she shoved into her mouth.

He scowled back, unable to stop himself. By God, if she had been a boy, he'd turn her over his knee and give her a smart paddling to teach her some respect. She'd been a snotty pain in the ass ever since the scene in the cabin last evening.

"We're about two days outside of Blakely," he went on, doing his best to ignore her conduct. He took a long drink of beer, then added, "I think it's time to let Hardesty know we're coming."

She looked up. "Let him know—what for? We ought to sneak up and surprise him."

"Oh, he'll be surprised. But a little mental advantage"—he tapped his temple—"won't hurt, either. I have something in mind for him."

She shrugged, and poking another biscuit half into her mouth, chewed noisily.

Short of a spanking he couldn't deliver to a woman,

he reached over and lightly tugged her ear in repri-
mand. "You mind your manners, *Kyle*, or you'll be
eating in the livery stable with the horses."

Kyla sat back in her chair and glanced at her lap, as
embarrassed as if he'd slapped her hands, and her face
grew hot with shame. She knew she'd behaved ter-
ribly, but she was so angry and hurt that she couldn't
make herself be civil.

She looked at the meal she pretended to enjoy, and
wished she could, but it sat in her stomach like a rock.
It was her own fault for gobbling it up like a hog. At
least that was part of the reason.

"I know how to handle Hardesty," he continued
quietly. "I'm going to make him sweat a little before I
call him out. So we'll need a place to hide for a couple
of days after we get to Blakely. Is there anyone you
trust who can put us up?"

She nodded. "Jim Porter would probably do it. He's
one of the Moonlighters and his ranch is near town."

Jace threw a couple of silver dollars on the table and
pushed back his chair. "All right, then. I've got one
stop to make at the post office, then we'll ride for
Blakely."

Riding for Blakely, Kyla thought as she followed
him out to the street. And he was one day closer to
riding out of her life.

After two days of traveling, Jace and Kyla reached
the Painted Hills and embarked on the final leg of
their trip into Blakely. The landscape began to look
familiar to her, and she stopped to consider how long

she'd been away from here and everything that had happened since she left.

She had been shot, she'd nearly lost her life, she had been kidnapped, Juniper had been lost twice before coming back to her. And her heart—that she feared was gone for good, lost to the man riding ahead of her.

That night, their last on the road before they reached town, they sat around the campfire she had built. Although their hostility had cooled, Kyla still had not achieved the sense of dull resignation she hoped for, and she stared at the fire, alone in her reflections. Even Jace, who usually gave no indication of his thoughts, was uncommonly quiet and pensive. A rim of sunset lit the darkening blue sky with brilliant fire, and on the opposite side of the sky a full autumn moon, heavy and golden, began its ascent on the eastern horizon. It was a beautiful night, full of stars and longing.

When Jace broke the silence, his question amazed her. "Do you have much regret for things past? I mean, do you wish you could go back and live some things over again?" He didn't meet her eyes, but twiddled with a stick at the edge of the fire.

"Well, sure," she replied a bit warily. Oh, please, God, she thought—she couldn't bear to hear that he regretted making love with her, or that he was sorry he'd agreed to help her. She didn't think she deserved that punishment. "I can think of a few things I'd do differently, if I had the chance."

He nodded and remained silent for a moment. The firelight leaped across his handsome features and deepened his eyes to cobalt. Then in a low voice he admitted, "Sometimes I wish I *had* learned to be a rancher instead of a bounty hunter." He looked up at her, a rueful, unguarded smile on his face.

Kyla swallowed hard but she couldn't dispel the sudden lump compressing her voice. "It's not—" She cleared her throat and tried again. "It's not too late, you know. Hank gave up bounty hunting and settled down."

"Yeah, well, Hank had someplace to go, something to do. This is the only job I've ever had, that and being a deputy sheriff. I don't know how to do anything else."

"You were a deputy?"

He tossed the stick into the flames. "Yeah, in Salem. It was just for a few months, and I wasn't much more than a kid. Then I saw a wanted poster on the sheriff's desk for a man who'd robbed a bank in Hood River. Five hundred dollars, dead or alive. It was more money than I could earn in two years, and I thought if I captured him it would really show Lyle and the rest that I was tougher than they thought. I brought in the robber, alive—there's no trick in bringing in a dead man. After that, there was another robber, and after that a murderer. One year rolled into the next, and I liked the respect I got."

"Well, going into ranching now might be too big a change," she agreed. "But you could be a sheriff or a marshal. You have a lot of experience now to draw on."

His eyes gleamed briefly as if he were considering the idea, then he shook his head. "Sometimes there's no going back. I worked so hard to make people fear me, no one would want me in their town. I trapped myself in my own reputation, and there's no escape from it. I'm an outsider now." A huff of humorless laughter left him, and he looked at her. "Anyway, I'm glad to have Kyla to talk with again, instead of that snot-nosed brat Kyle."

On another night, she might have taken issue with his remark and reminded him that it was he who had resurrected her disguise. But in the years to come, she did not want to add this last night to her own list of regrets. She felt like crying for them, for the lack of love that had pushed Jace into the life he had now, and for all that could never be between them.

"When this is over, Kyle will disappear forever. Maybe I'll wear pants to rope and ride, because I don't want to give that up. But I'll do it as a female."

Up in the hills a coyote howled at the moon, lonesome and far away.

He considered her with an amused, assessing gaze, and the corners of his eyes crinkled with his light smile. "That day I found out that you weren't a boy— Jesus, I was mad."

"I remember. You acted as though I'd stolen your horse," she retorted, glad for the easing of the tension between them. They had been through a lot together; she would rather that some goodwill remain between them if there could be nothing more. Nothing more. Her heart contracted in her chest.

"But then I wondered how I could have been so blind," he added, and the tone of his voice became huskier, more intimate.

Kyla's breath caught and her pulse raced on. His

blue gaze drifted across her flattened breasts and hips and brushed over her lap before it rose again to her face. Reaching over, he took her hand in his warm grip and examined it in the low light, opening her fingers to reveal her palm. The stars seemed to stop twinkling as if waiting to see what he would do next.

"I remember thinking that even though you fooled me into believing you as Kyle, there were so many things about you that could only belong to a girl." He flattened out her fingers with his own. "The smooth hands, your mouth, tender and soft, the way you smelled, like sage on an August morning."

His words were like simple, beautiful poetry, not empty flattery. But if possible, they were even more dangerous for their frankness. Kyla closed her eyes, wishing he would hold her hand forever, and yet afraid to let him touch her for another second.

Then as if he felt the danger, too, he released her. "You're one hell of a woman, Kyla. When you told me that you'd been married to Hank, I couldn't picture a tough-hided loner like him settling down with you. Now I know what he saw that drew him. And I'm betting that the kindness of his heart had nothing to do with it." He sounded like a man who had seen the fate of his own future and was powerless to change it. "If I were a different man—" He sighed and let the sentence hang unfinished.

"You wouldn't need to be a different man, Jace," she said over the ache in her throat. "You just need to take a different path."

He shook his head and his smile was shadowed with regret. "Nope. It *is* too late for me to do that,

Kyla. This is the path I chose and there's no changing it now. Anyway I still have a job to do for you so that you can get on with your life." He rolled himself into his blankets then and turned his back to her.

Kyla glanced at the stars again and wondered why that life he referred to didn't seem as clear as it once had.

Chapter Fourteen

Tom Hardesty sat at a corner table in the Pine Cone Saloon, nursing his fourth shot of whiskey. The morning sun threw a bright slash of light across the plank flooring and up the wall next to him. Saloons always looked a lot different in the morning than they did at night—almost as somber as funeral parlors. Shit, what a comparison, he thought.

Business wasn't as good in this place as it had been, he noticed. Ever since he started coming in on a regular basis, for some reason customer traffic had fallen off. More often than not, Pete, the bartender, stood behind the counter looking glum and polishing glasses, for lack of anything better to do. That was fine with Tom; he wasn't in any mood for company.

He sat here every day now, fidgety and short-tempered, waiting for word from Hobie McIntyre. The few men who came in eyed him with furtive glances and sidled to the bar, or to far tables. No one had the nerve to actually look him in the face. That was fine with Tom, too.

Even Mayella Cathcart had lost her allure for him. Before she had been a little on the docile side, but now she looked as dull-eyed as a cow and had no fight at all. Damn, who wanted to poke a limp dishrag who stared at the ceiling the whole time and whispered to Jesus to save her? At least he knew he could count on the redhead to fight back and make it interesting.

He took another drink of whiskey, and the flames on his anger climbed higher. Where the hell was Kyla, anyway? Maybe McIntyre hadn't bothered to send a wire and was simply on his way back to Blakely. If that was the case, he'd throttle the saddle bum for not reporting in. Throttle him. He poured another shot and knocked it back in one gulp, and another after that. Presently, the frames around the windows grew blurry, and the grooves between the floor planks began to blend.

Goddamned Rankin.

Lousy red-haired bitch.

"Mr. Hardesty, sir?"

Tom's head snapped up and he found the general store's young delivery boy standing a few feet from his table. He was blurry, too.

"Whatcha want, kid? Cantcha see I'm m-b-busy?"

The boy extended a package the full length of his arm and leaned forward, as if his boots were nailed to the floor just beyond Tom's easy reach. "The stage brought this in the mail pouch for you. My pa said to bring it to you right away."

Tom made a couple of lunging passes at the brown-paper package before catching it. "I s'pose you think I should pay you for your trouble and—"

"Nossir," the boy said, turning tail. He ducked under the swinging doors and ran out to the street before Tom realized he was gone.

"Hmm, damned kid," he groused and looked down at the package. It sure as hell wasn't the telegram he'd been waiting for, goddamn it. He tried to focus on the writing in the address but it was too dark in this corner to see much. He recognized his name, anyway. Cutting through the twine with his pocket knife, he tore at the paper impatiently.

"Jesus Christ!" he yelped, jumping back with his chair. Nestled in its folds he found something that made him drop the package on the table as if it contained a scorpion. Both unnerved and infuriated, gingerly he pulled out a leather thong strung with bear's teeth.

The same one that Hobie McIntyre had worn around his neck until someone had cut it off.

So the rumors were true, Tom thought, shaken from his boozy contemplations by everything this message implied.

Jace Rankin was coming.

After waiting for the shelter of darkness, Jace and Kyla circled Blakely and stole onto Jim Porter's property just outside of town.

From the road, Kyla saw that the ranch-house windows were dark, but a single lantern glowed on the porch railing. "That means the Moonlighters are meeting in Jim's barn," she whispered. "He took over after Hank was killed. He's the only one who knows I went looking for someone to help me."

She heard Jace breathe a long-suffering sigh. "He probably isn't anymore. It's my experience that most people can't keep secrets. It sure as hell would explain why Hobie McIntyre knew to find you in Silver City."

She frowned at him, but they climbed out of their saddles and edged closer to the barn, leading the horses. Along the corral fence other horses were tied up. Although she couldn't see it in the darkness, she heard Jace pull the Henry from its scabbard.

"Just in case they have someone jittery on watch," he murmured.

This meeting was a lucky break, she thought. If Jace met these people and heard what the Vigilance Union had done to them, maybe he'd change his mind about helping them.

Motioning him to drop back, she crept to the door and listened. Inside, she heard the low hum of male tones. They spoke quietly—she could distinguish no words, identify no individual voices. Using the code Hank had taught her, she tapped four times, two short knocks, and two long. All conversation from within ceased and a tense pause followed. She glanced back at Jace and he waved her to the side, away from a direct line of fire in the event that someone decided to shoot through the door.

After what seemed like an eternity, her taps were answered with two short knocks, the response she expected, and the door opened. Jim Porter held a lantern high and searched her face, plainly not recognizing her. Through the narrow opening, she saw a few men behind him sitting on hay bales and crates.

"Jim, it's me, Kyla Springer." she whispered. "I'm back."

"Kyla?" Finally a big grin flashed across the weathered old rancher's face, and he gripped her hand and pumped it until she thought her arm might loosen in its socket. Then he clapped her hard on the back. "By God, honey, we didn't know if we'd ever see you again!" he said in a loud whisper. He turned to the gathering. "Kyla's here. She made it back."

A surge of emotion coursed through her. These were her neighbors, her friends, people she'd known all of her life. It was good to be among them again and united in a common cause.

"I'm sorry to barge in during the meeting, but we need to talk to you for a minute," she said.

He pulled the door closed behind him and stepped outside into the darkness. Putting the lantern on top of a barrel, he asked, "What can I do for you?"

She glanced over her shoulder at Jace, who lingered in the shadows. "I've brought someone with me, a friend." That was an understatement, she thought, still yearning for the protection of Jace's arms around her, the feel of his fingertips tracing her mouth, the soft scratch of his beard under her hands. She motioned him closer. He came, but with obvious reluctance. "Jim, this is Jace Rankin."

The older man stiffened noticeably. It was true, she thought, what Jace had said about people fearing him, even people who should feel no threat from him. But Jim recovered almost immediately, and put out his hand. "Mr. Rankin. You're welcome here."

Jace shook the hand offered to him and nodded in

acknowledgement. "I'm not 'Mr. Rankin' to anyone, so Jace is just fine."

"We have some business to take care of, Jim, and if Tom is still at the ranch, you know we can't go there," Kyla whispered. No one alive but Jace knew what Hardesty had done to her, but it was no secret that he had killed Hank.

"He's still there," Jim said grimly, hate hardening his creased face.

"I was wondering if we could stay in your barn without anyone else knowing." Automatically, she glanced around the yard. "We need to keep it quiet."

Jim shrugged. "Sure, you can stay. I'm going out on the range for a few days with the hands, but you're welcome to use the place. You should know, though, there are rumors floating around town about Mr.— Jace. People have been talking about him, expecting him, but I don't know why."

Briefly, Jace explained what had happened with McIntyre and his men, from the afternoon in Cord to the miner's cabin. "McIntyre might have been keeping Hardesty informed of our whereabouts. Word could have leaked out and the story took its own turn."

Jim Porter shook his gray head. "I'll tell you, between Luke Jory, Tom Hardesty, and the rest of the Vigilance Union, life in Blakely has been more like hell on earth." He jerked a thumb over his shoulder. "We've been inside tonight, trying to come up with a plan to get rid of those sons of bitches. So far we've gotten nowhere. When Hank died, he took a lot our spirit with him. I think we might have had a chance with him." He eyed Jace speculatively. "You two may as well come in—we were about to break up for tonight anyway."

Jace groaned inside, trying to figure out a way to avoid it but he felt stuck. Despite the name he'd made for himself, he hated being the center of attention. But when they followed Jim into the barn, the situation became even worse than he'd anticipated.

A moment of gaping, awkward silence opened following his introduction to the men. Then a man in the back wearing farmer's overalls filled the void. "By God, maybe that's what we need to do—*hire* someone from the outside to wipe 'em all out. Every last stinkin' one of 'em."

"That's right! Fight fire with fire!"

"They should have a taste of their own."

"Someone needs to teach them a lesson they'll never forget. Someone like Rankin here, who isn't afraid of them."

To Jace's horror, this idea was picked up and carried from man to man like a torch, and it burned hotter with each passing minute. Pretty soon, the men were on their feet, their eyes lit with the fire of revenge and hope. Kyla did nothing to intervene, and he sent her a sour look, which she chose to ignore.

"Now wait a minute," he said, trying to interrupt the wave of bitter zeal that rolled over them. "I don't do this kind of—" He turned to Kyla and bent a stern look on her. "You'd better tell them to forget it."

"Jace, you're the only one who can help with this," she said, talking as crazy as the rest of them. Her turquoise eyes gleamed with the same fire.

"*What?*" He was astounded. I didn't come to

Blakely to take on those vigilantes! I told you I wouldn't do that. I told you from the beginning."

"They've stolen my cattle in broad daylight, put their brand on them, and told me it was their payment for keeping the peace," one rancher complained.

"Luke Jory is charging me now so that 'rustlers' won't steal my stock in the middle of the night. Rustlers, my Aunt Sophie!"

The farmer in the overalls, the one who had begun this, held out his hands, appealing to the group to hear his story. "Tom Hardesty forced himself on my Mayella after he made me let her go cook for him. It was after he moved into your house, Kyla. Now . . . now she don't even talk anymore. If it wasn't for the Vigilance Union, he never would have been able to do that to my little girl." His voice quivered when he added, "She's only fifteen years old."

Silence fell again for a moment, and Kyla's eyes grew as wide as dollars. She turned to look at Jace. She said nothing, but her expression revealed every word of her thoughts.

"I'll take care of Hardesty," he assured her in a voice that carried only to her ears. "That's why I'm here."

"But it's like I told you in Silver City," she said. "What good will that do when Jory finds another Tom? And you know he will—the world has more than its share of people like him. Evil, greedy, always watching for someone weaker to take advantage of."

Jace felt his conscience stirring, a sensation that he did not like. "Well, Jesus, I can't save the whole world!"

"No one is asking you to do that." Then she gave him a knowing look, the gaze that seemed to examine his very soul. "But maybe this is a good chance to make up for what happened at the Bluebird Saloon."

He felt as if she'd punched him in the stomach, as if she had been saving this one vague fact she knew about him to hold over his head. All the air seemed to leave his lungs and he couldn't get a breath. "God-damn it, Kyla—"

"I propose we hire Jace Rankin to wipe out the Vigilance Union," someone then suggested. The proposal was met with unanimous approval.

"Wait a minute!" Jace said, appalled, his voice rising to a roar above their conversation. Grabbing a crate, he stepped up to try and gain their attention, but only the horses in the stalls appeared to heed him. "Listen to me!" he thundered again. "I'm no crusader, saving ranchers and farmers from vigilantes! I'm a bounty hunter."

They rallied closer, as if at a leader's feet, and finally quieted long enough to let him speak. He looked down at the upturned faces. It was a new experience to have people hanging on his every word. "I'm a bounty hunter," he went on in a lower voice. "And I'm just one man, I can't take on this group alone." He glanced down at Kyla and drew a deep breath. God, he couldn't believe he was going to say this—"If you want my help, you have to help me. You can't just hire someone to do your dirty work for you, and then sit back and wait for things to get better, like you've been doing. You have to take action and fight for what's yours."

The men shuffled uncomfortably under the bluntness of his words, but from his place leaning against a stall, Jim Porter smiled at him, as if Jace had said exactly what he wanted him to.

"Well, you men heard him," he said. "And it's the same thing Hank Bailey told you, too. Are you ready to fight?"

Murmurs of agreement swept through the group.

"Hell, yes, I'm ready. I can't afford to lose one more head of cattle to those thieves."

"I'm tired of payin' 'em for the privilege of grazin' stock on my own land."

"I want to see Luke Jory fall from that throne he put himself on."

"All right, then," Jace said, catching a glimpse of Kyla's face, beatific as she gazed up at him. This was almost worth it to see her look at him like that. "But I've got business to take care of first. We'll meet here again in a week, and in the meantime don't talk about this with anyone. *Not anyone.*"

The meeting broke up then, and while most of the men didn't go so far as to shake Jace's hand as if he were one of them, there was a lot of smiling and hat-tipping.

As he watched the last of them go, he shook his head in disbelief. He'd never been part of a group in his entire life and long ago had grown accustomed to his solitude, and the sound of his own thoughts for conversation. Now, with absolutely no intention of doing so, he had agreed to lead these people in a battle against the Vigilance Union.

"Shit."

* * *

"Jace?"

"What."

"Will you tell me what happened at the Bluebird Saloon?"

Kyla waited in the darkness for his answer. They had bedded down in the only empty stall in Jim Porter's barn, she on one end, and he on the other. They had done the same thing many times out on the open prairie, fully dressed as they were now. But somehow the shelter of the barn made it seem all the more intimate to her, and she was keenly aware of Jace wrapped in his blankets a few feet away. Moonlight cut through the hayloft window and threw a bright square of light between them.

"Aw, damn it, Kyla." He sighed, more with weary resignation than irritation.

"Was it really bad?"

She heard the straw rustle on the other side of the box, and he sat up and leaned against the wall. A gray-white slice of moonlight fell over him, accentuating the shadows of his cheekbones and his mantle of dark hair.

When he began speaking, chills flew over Kyla's arms and scalp. It was as if she were listening to some other man, a stranger whose voice she didn't recognize. "I'd been trailing a cattle rustler and it was turning out to be more work than the reward was worth. Losing propositions have never much interested me, so I stopped in Paradise Creek to think over my next move and get a meal and a beer." Kyla saw him cross his ankles in the low light. "I was halfway through a steak supper when a women walked up to my table. She had a little kid with her, a girl with big blue eyes and gold hair. They were both dressed like they'd gotten their clothes from a charity barrel. I don't think I'd ever seen two people who looked so tired. And the woman, she kept glancing around her, like she thought she might be followed. The little girl—I think she was about five years old—she just stared at me with those big blue eyes."

"What did they want?" Kyla whispered.

"The woman asked me to take her and her daughter to Pendleton so they could catch the train. The stage wouldn't be in Paradise Creek for a week, and she was in a panic to get away before her husband found out she'd gone."

"Why?"

He shrugged. "She said she was afraid he'd kill her. She pulled out a lace handkerchief with some gold coins tied in it to prove she could pay. Oh, I sure as hell didn't want any part of that. She asked me two more times—practically begged me. It wasn't like I didn't notice the bruises on both of them. But I wasn't about to get involved in some mess between a husband and wife. Anyway, that wasn't the kind of work I did, nursemaiding women and kids. I chased bank robbers and horse thieves. I thought Hank was somewhere in town, so I told her to go to find him. Maybe he'd help her." He wrapped a blanket around his shoulders, as if taken with a sudden chill.

Kyla knew he could see her in the moonlight, but he didn't look at her. "Did Hank help her?"

He shook his head. "She never talked to him. When

I saw him late that night at the Bluebird, I found out he'd been gone most of the day, seeing about a horse he wanted to buy. It was pretty quiet in there at that hour, quiet enough to hear a gunshot that came from a house at the end of the street."

"Oh, no . . ." Kyla moaned, horrified, and pressed her hand to the base of her throat.

"Well, we all ran down there to have a look." His voice grew suddenly rough and he paused. "There she was, and her little girl, too. But her husband hadn't shot them. He'd shot himself after he slashed their throats with a skinning knife. I'd never seen so much blood."

"Oh, God, Jace—" she whispered, completely unprepared for what he'd told her.

"I dreamed about that night for three or four years. It was the worst thing I've ever seen . . . ever. I lost count of how many times I wished I could live that day over. I should have taken them to Pendleton. If I had they'd still be alive, and maybe living a new life away from that man."

Kyla gaped at his shadowed form. He must have condemned himself countless times for the death of that woman and her child. And Kyla had unwittingly dredged up the event and used it as a means to gain her own ends. She waded through the straw to his side of the stall and sat beside him. The Henry lay between them.

"Jace, I'm sorry. When I mentioned it—I didn't know—"

She saw the careless lift of his shoulders in the dim light, and her heart ached with love for him.

"Hank knew. You were in danger, and he knew I wouldn't make the same mistake twice. That's why he sent you to me for help."

She felt guilty for dragging the story out of him. With a little hesitation, she covered his hand with her own, where it rested on his knee. "And you've done that more than once. You took care of me when I was sick, you saved me from those men, you brought me back to Blakely."

Jace gazed down at the small hand on his. Yeah, and somewhere along the trail between Silver City and Blakely, this scrappy, red-haired woman, with a cast-iron will and beauty as delicate as a butterfly's wings, had roused his heart, stirring it in its emptiness. He didn't want to think of it as anything more, because there could be nothing between them. As soon as he finished here, he reminded himself, he would be gone. It didn't matter how tempting the image was that he carried in his mind, of riding home—*home*—to this woman, of crystal cold nights, wrapped in thick quilts with her, warming his heart on hers. He gave up any chance for that the day he picked up that wanted poster on the sheriff's desk.

"I think you're a very good man," she added softly. "The finest I've ever known."

Her words shook him to his soul. He felt her next to him, soft and vital, her thigh brushing his. The denim between them didn't hinder his memory of that night in the cabin, and her body under his hands and lips, fragrant, smooth, lush.

She edged closer, and her hand on his tightened. Unbelievably, she leaned forward and laid a trail of timid kisses that began at his temple and touched the corner of his eye, his cheek, the edge of his upper lip.

He put an arm around her to enclose her within the blanket. When he turned his head toward her lips, she surprised him by claiming his mouth in a moist kiss. He couldn't suppress the groan that rose in his throat. Her touch was silky, healing as she slid her fingertips along his jaw. When she broke the kiss, she sat back and unbuttoned her shirt, holding his eyes with her gaze. The binding, bright in the moonlight, came away as if by magic. Her breasts, pale and full, called for his caress but he didn't move. Jace swallowed, uncertain for the first time in his adult life. If he obeyed the demands of his body, they would have this moment but it wouldn't change their future. And perhaps after, she might think less of him than she did now for bedding her in a stable because he could offer nothing more. He couldn't bear to lose her respect.

"Kyla, I don't think—"

"I don't want you to think," she whispered. "This is something I want to give you, and take from you."

Her innocent seduction roused a familiar aching heat in his groin, the urge to proclaim and reaffirm his life within her. To surrender himself to her in a dark conflagration and rise from his own ashes, reborn. A different Jace Rankin.

But when still he made no move to touch her, she reached for his hand and cradled it under her breast. Her taut nipple pressed against his thumb.

With an oath, Jace flung away the remains of his shredded resistance. Pulling her to him, he buried his mouth against her flesh, muttering her name even as he

closed his lips over it to suckle her. His heart pounded
in his chest, thundering between his deep breaths.

Two spirits brimming with emotion and lifetimes of
hurt, they fell to his blanket on the sweet straw, desperate and twisting, pulling clothes and boots away as
they fought to get closer. She lay naked beside him,
beautiful, unafraid, the scar on her arm forgotten. He
sank his hands into her hair and held her while he
kissed her greedily, his tongue seeking the slick
warmth inside her mouth. Her hands moved restlessly
up and down his bare back. Feverishly he traced the
indent of her waist, the swell of her hip. Her breast,
full and heavy, fit perfectly in his hand. Each moan he
summoned from her, every sigh fueled his own
arousal until he thought he would explode.

Jace enfolded Kyla in his arms and rolled her over
so that she lay on top of him. With his hands gripping
her buttocks he pulled her hips flush to his own in a
rhythm that was as primal as the course of the tides.
Boldly, she pushed against him, feeling his erection
that lay between them.

She dropped to his side and let her fingers roam the
naked length of him, over the soft hair on his chest
and down his flat belly to his hard fullness.

"You're in charge, Kyla," he told her as he had the
first time, his voice gritty and low. He lay on his back,
arms open, unguarded. "You make love to *me*."

"I don't know what to do . . ."

"Then I'll show you," he said, and whispered brief,
urgent instructions to her. Suddenly Kyla found herself
lifted up to lie on him again, her breasts flattened
against his chest. His hands and her own instinct carried

her the rest of the way. He entered her, completed her, filling the emptiness that was meant to hold only him. But as she began to move with him, she found what he had meant when he gave her power over their bodies. She thrust along the length of him, spiraling the intense waves of tightly coiled pressure that grew tighter in her abdomen. No self-consciousness or fear hindered her. There were just the two of them in the world tonight, making love in the shaft of a moonbeam.

She heard him murmuring to her as he lay beneath her, while he let her seek her pleasure with his body. The pressure continued to build, winding tighter and tighter, until with a final stroke he pushed her into a dark oblivion of excruciating sensation. Spasms of pleasure wracked her with the swiftness of wing beats.

Unable to delay his own release another moment, Jace rolled her onto her back again. Cradling her head in his hands, he plunged into her with fast, pounding thrusts as he sought to relieve the heavy ache in his belly and groin.

Seeking her mouth, he took her with a fierce kiss that equaled his need. "Kyla," he ground out. Her name was ripped from him as she became a part of the rapid, white-hot pulsations that convulsed him as his climax tore through his body.

After, they lay entwined, their bodies cooling while a peaceful languor stole over Jace. Making love to Kyla on the floor of a shack or in a stable wasn't ideal—she deserved far better. But if his luck held, if he lived long enough to be able to reflect back on his life, these two nights would be the sweetest he had ever known.

Chapter Fifteen

After weeks on the road, the captivity of Jim Porter's barn made Kyla edgy. She cooked and helped out with chores close to the yard, but there weren't enough things to do to keep her busy for long. She would have liked to ride the range, but Jace wouldn't permit her to wander too far in case one of the Vigilance Union should spot her. It was a good bet that any one of them would see through her disguise now.

Jim's wife had died several years earlier and his daughters were married and gone, so there were no other women for her to talk to.

Jace, on the other hand, seemed unaffected by the inactivity. He filled his hours polishing the Henry and cleaning his guns, or tending the horses.

She wasn't used to so much free time. Although she'd always yearned for the trappings of her gender, she'd never wanted to sit for hours and sew a fine seam. She was accustomed to working. Her restlessness stemmed not only from boredom, but also from the anticipation of events to come. They'd reached Blakely, but she wasn't home yet.

Even worse, though, sitting around left her with nothing to do but think. After all of this was over, she would go back to the ranch, to the same life she'd had before Hardesty returned. The problem was she was a different person from the one who had stolen away under the cover of night with a dead man's instructions to find a bounty hunter. She had fallen in love with her rescuer, and now when she pictured her life at the ranch, she had trouble envisioning it alone.

But Jace was right: he wouldn't make a rancher. His skills lay in his talent for reading men's hearts, not the land and weather. He was different from Hank in that respect, and there were not a lot of occupations that called for such an ability. Her own heart ached whenever she thought of seeing him ride away for the last time. And since she had little to do, she thought of it often enough, adding to her sense of impending doom.

On the third afternoon of idleness, Kyla found Jace at the corral. She paced back and forth in front of him as he held Juniper's hoof in his hands and searched for rocks. The sun cast a halo of red and gold on the crown of his dark, downturned head, and made the fine hair on his lean forearms sparkle. His faded blue shirt stretched across his shoulders, hinting at the muscle she knew lay underneath. He was beautiful to look at, even performing such a mundane task.

She kicked a rock into the fence post, making the horse twitch. Then sighing heavily, she paced some more.

Finally Jace glanced up. "Jesus, Kyla, go find something to do. You're scaring the horse."

"There isn't anything left to do around here," she crabbed impatiently. "How long are we going to wait before we go after Hardesty?"

Dropping Juniper's hoof, he shook his head and chuckled. "You would have been a lousy bounty hunter. Waiting and watching have a lot to do with capturing outlaws."

She frowned. "But if we wait too long, he's bound to find out that we're in town. We'll lose the advantage of surprise."

"Yeah, I want him to know." He said this as if it were the most obvious course of action.

She stopped pacing and stared at him. "God, why? He'll just lie in wait for us."

"At first he will. But how long can a man keep that up without going crazy? He'll never know exactly when I'll be there. Will it be at sunrise or sometime in the afternoon? Will I face him in the street or sneak into the house in the middle of the night and shove a gun barrel up his nose?" Idly he patted Juniper's neck. "I'll have the advantage, all right. He'll just get more and more hotheaded. And hotheads make mistakes."

"Well, what *are* we going to do?" she asked.

"Kyla, there isn't any 'we' about this. When I decide the time is right to confront Tom Hardesty, you'll wait here."

"No!" she protested. She never once thought that she would be left behind. "You have to take me with you."

His blue gaze turned flinty. "The hell I do. I work alone. Anyway, I don't want to have to worry about watching your back and mine, too. This isn't a church picnic we're planning, you know."

Hot blood suffused her face. "Don't you talk down to me now, Jace Rankin. I didn't travel all those miles to find you, and get shot and kidnapped just to sit back at the end and miss seeing Hardesty get what he deserves!"

He shrugged and picked up Juniper's other foreleg. "You'll just have to trust me to do the job you hired me to do," he said, effectively ending the debate and the conversation.

Unable to answer him, Kyla lapsed into hurt, angry silence. He had pointedly reminded her that, first and foremost, theirs was a business deal, and that whatever else had taken place between them did not affect him. Well, so be it, then, she thought. She had the right to see what her money was paying for.

And if it meant watching Jace as closely as Hardesty was watching him, that was what she'd do.

Jace watched Kyla stalk to the barn in the afternoon sun. Her nose was up so high he wondered how she could see where she was going. And her hips swayed slightly under her jeans, although he supposed she didn't realize that.

Picking up a horse brush, he stroked Juniper's coat. The reason he gave her for stalling Tom Hardesty was a legitimate one. But not the only one. The longer he delayed, the more time he would have with Kyla before he had to tell her good-bye. When the day came that he had to ride away from her, it would be the hardest thing he ever did.

He pulled the brush through Juniper's mane with long, smooth strokes while his thoughts strayed to Kyla.

He had told her that he didn't think he was capable of caring for anyone, and he'd believed his own words at the time. The old man had seen to that, somehow honing in on the part of Jace's boyhood heart that felt compassion, affection, and love, and beating it until it was wiped clean of all emotion.

But Kyla—he shook his head, stunned when he thought about it. She had revived him with a touch, with respect that was not earned through fear, and with love. And like a drought-dry plant waiting for rain, his heart had responded.

What would he do with these newfound feelings, though? Too bad he couldn't stick around to see what might have been. He leaned both arms on Juniper's back and gazed at the mountains in the distance.

Too bad he couldn't tell her he loved her.

Tom Hardesty sat at the kitchen table, checking the rounds in his Colt and his shotgun with quick, jerky movements. He'd done it earlier today. Twice. He would soon be doing it again.

After that, he would go to each window in the house to check the yard for any sign of trespassers. He would spend a half hour at each one, staring at the yard with gritty eyes. He'd done that many times today, too. And last night. Yesterday. Waiting. Watching.

He'd given up on sleeping, but hell, he didn't want to be caught napping when Jace Rankin decided to come. That would be rude, wouldn't it? A high little laugh escaped him at the thought. Anyway, if he slept he'd just have those dreams again, the ones about an eight-foot-tall bounty hunter, an angel of death who had reached Blakely, despite all the men Tom had sent to defeat him.

So far Tom had managed to elude Luke Jory, but he knew that he must have heard the news: Jace Rankin was on his way. Although it wouldn't matter after Tom killed the bounty hunter. Jory would be satisfied with that. And Tom knew he could do it—he was the *only* man who could do it. He just had to be ready.

He brought out the Colt again to check it.

Jace Rankin was coming.

Pouring himself another drink, Tom pushed a dirty dish out of his way to make room on the tabletop. The place was a mess—that worthless Mayella had stopped coming by almost a week ago, just after he had received that string of teeth in the mail. She must have known that Rankin was on his way, too.

The hell with her. The angel of death was coming, but he was bringing the woman with him, red-haired and high-hipped. He touched the scar on his face with a hand that shook ever so slightly. He'd even the score then.

When he got the woman.

Jace sat on the edge of an empty water trough, stitching his stirrup. The late October sun felt good on his shoulders, especially the one that bore the year-old scar. He knew that Kyla was watching him. He almost laughed; she was smart and strong, but not nearly subtle enough to fool him. And since she didn't have enough to do to keep her busy, her scrutiny was even more noticeable.

She trailed him to the corral and sat outside when

he sat outside. Whenever he went near the horse, she sidled over and made small talk. He was on the verge of asking if she'd like to come to the outhouse with him.

But the time was upon him—he would have to act. He had strung Hardesty along for several days. Based on what Kyla had told him about the man, he ought to have achieved just the right measure of jumpy anxiety by now. Enough to be sloppy, and maybe dangerous, too. No matter. He forced the heavy, curved needle through the leather.

Everything he'd heard about Tom Hardesty told him that the man was a blue-ribbon bastard. But it didn't matter. He'd faced sons of bitches of all stripes and types. And taking on this one would give him grim pleasure—this was for Kyla.

The sun was a yellow-white ball on the horizon when Kyla finished slapping together a meal of biscuits and gravy. Since Jim Porter hadn't returned yet, she set just two plates at the table and dished up the supper. It wasn't fancy, but it beat some of the things she and Jace had eaten on the trail all those days.

She paused at the kitchen window with the silverware clutched in her hand. The evening at the McGuires' in Baker City seemed like a lifetime ago now. The butter yellow gown and all of its matching accessories lay at the bottom of a mountain ravine, probably buried under snow and ice. She touched her locket, grateful that she had been wearing it that day. Memories sometimes faded; her mother's image was dim and indistinct now after so many years. But when

Jace was gone, she would have the locket to remember him by. Whether he thought of her after they parted, she would never know.

Turning away from the window with a sigh, she went to the door to call him to supper. Beyond the screen door, the yard was quiet and lonesome in the autumn sunset—with Jim and his crew gone, she felt as if she were the only one here.

"Jace!" she called. "Supper!"

She went back to the stove and lifted a stove lid to throw in another stick of wood. It was nearly November, and even in this warm ranch kitchen, she could feel a chill gathering.

She walked to the door again. "Jace!"

In the empty yard, not even a bird twittered in the silence, no horse nickered, no chicken clucked. And Kyla's heart froze. She pushed open the screen door and raced outside to the barn.

There she found Juniper and Jim Porter's wagon horses. But Jace's gelding was gone.

"Damn you, Jace!" she cursed, her voice quivering with tears that gathered in her throat. He'd left her behind, he'd really done it.

Saddling Juniper took twice as long as it should have; anger and haste made her clumsy. When she had finally accomplished the job, she mounted the horse and hunching low over the pommel, galloped out of the barn. Oddly, there was no question about which direction she would take. Jace could have decided to track Hardesty anywhere, but like a pin on a compass, she turned the horse toward her home.

That was the place where they would face off. She sensed it—she could envision it.

Tom Hardesty was about to meet Jace Rankin and a Henry rifle.

Jace crept up to the Springer ranch house, sliding behind the sunset shadows for concealment. Glancing at the sky, he imagined that Kyla was just now discovering that he had gone. After watching her habits for a day or so, he realized that he would be able to slip away right before any meal. It had been so simple he almost felt sorry for tricking her. But it was for her own good as well as his. If she were here, he would have to worry about her safety. She would just be a distraction, and if things were to go wrong, Hardesty could use her as a hostage.

Finding the ranch hadn't been difficult; Kyla had spoken of it often enough to give him sufficient clues as to its location. It was just as she had described it, two miles outside of town, a beautiful spot that was part rolling green hills, part rangeland scrub, situated on a low rise next to a creek.

He stood behind a big oak and studied the house. It had a forsaken feel about it, as if the character of its latest occupant had spread a pall of gloom over the place. He was certain that Hardesty was inside.

"Okay," he said under his breath, "let's find out where you are." From his pocket Jace withdrew a few pebbles, and emerged just long enough to pitch one at the window in the kitchen door before ducking behind the tree again. Almost immediately, an answering shot was fired from the house. Jace smiled.

He let a moment pass, then he tossed another pebble, this time at a metal washtub that stood next to the back door. The stone made a sharp pinging noise when it struck. This was followed by two more shots, each recklessly fired, each hitting nothing. They were coming from behind a curtained window on the first floor, which was opened a crack to allow the width of a gun barrel.

Jace tossed pebbles at a washboard, at the side of the house, at a box of canning jars that stood on the porch. In response, wild, unaimed shots hit the fence, the windmill, a wagon. Jesus, the man acted as if he were blind. Or struck with consuming, judgment-robbing anxiety. This was going to be easier than he thought. As long as he stayed out of the path of one of his reckless shots.

Remaining behind the tree, Jace tightened his grip on the Henry. "All right, come on, Hardesty, it's time to show your face," he yelled at the house. "We've got business to discuss, you and me."

Still more shots. Then a long moment of silence fell. Finally from within Jace heard, "The only business I've got with you, Rankin, is the red-haired woman. Where is she?" The voice was demanding, vicious.

After everything he'd done to her, the son of a bitch still wouldn't let up on her, Jace thought. "I've got her, but you'll have to come out to the porch if you want to talk about her."

"You must think I'm pretty goddamned stupid if you believe I'm going to fall for that."

"No, Hardesty," Jace called in a light, sarcastic tone. "I just think you're a goddamned coward."

There was a crash from within the house, as if chairs or some other furniture had been tipped over. Suddenly, the back door flew open and Tom Hardesty appeared in the frame, carrying a shotgun and wearing a two-gun rig. His eyes were red-rimmed and bloodshot, his dark hair greasy, and down one side of his beard-shadowed face a long, purple scar, newly healed, cleaved his jawline. Just as Jace had guessed, a white-hot temper was one of Hardesty's chief failings. It impaired his judgment and made him act foolishly, and brutally. Apparently no one, not even Luke Jory, had curbed him. That was over now.

"I'm not afraid of you," Hardesty growled, reminding Jace of a stupid, vicious dog—untrained, snapping at anything, everything. The notable difference, however, was that this dog was a raping murderer.

Jace stepped from behind the tree, then as if it were a formal proclamation, he stated, "I'm calling you out, Hardesty, for two people. For my friend Hank Bailey, the man you killed. And for his widow, Kyla Springer Bailey, *one* of the women you raped. I'm sure there are other people, dead or alive with grievances against you, but these two are my business."

Hardesty hooted, "You can't prove a thing, Rankin. No one is going to listen to you. The Vigilance Union is even bigger than you are. They'll get rid of you, and Kyla will be on her knees begging to give me whatever I want."

God, the man was crazy, Jace thought. He might as well have held a target between his own eyes for Jace to shoot at. He felt a slow, hot flame ignite in his belly, a hate so profound he wished he could step away from it. He'd faced a lot of desperate, big-talking men in his career, men who when cornered had boasted of ridiculous things or had pelted him with insults. He had been able to ignore them. This time, he felt his control slipping away from him.

"Don't press me, Hardesty," he warned, and took three deliberate steps toward the porch. "I have no reason to see you live another minute."

Hardesty squinted at him. "You know, close up, you don't look like such a big man. You just look like a runt." Then, without warning, he pulled out his revolver and pointed it at Jace.

Jace took one step back and raised the Henry to pull the trigger and to his horror, the weapon jammed.

Extending the revolver, Hardesty laughed, sounding jubilant and relieved. "You blinked, Rankin! I out-stared the angel of death," he laughed and cocked the pistol. "You blinked and I won!"

Jace worked the Henry's trigger, but it wouldn't budge. He hadn't bothered to bring his revolver—he had depended on this rifle that had never let him down. Events did not slow, but instead seemed to speed up, moving too quickly for him to act upon. For the first time in the last ten years, he knew without a doubt that he was going to die. His heart pounded like a hammer in his chest. Images of his life darted through his mind . . . Lyle Upton reaching for his belt . . . a woman and a little girl in the Bluebird Saloon . . . Travis McGuire and his wife Chloe . . . a scared kid hiding under a soap crate, crying . . . and there was a red-haired female who talked tough but had the power to heal his soul. . . .

"Good-bye, little man."

Hardesty fired—it might have been a wild shot. In the back of his head, behind the sound of his pulse rushing past his ears, he thought he heard a scream. Another shot rang out and he tried to figure out where he was hit. Time and events flickered past as quickly as his memories, as fast as the blades turned on a windmill. He felt nothing but he knew that wouldn't last. He looked for blood . . . where was the blood? But then he glanced up at Hardesty just in time to see the hole in his forehead before he tumbled facedown off the porch.

Whirling around, Jace saw Kyla emerge from behind the wagon across the yard, her pistol extended with both hands, her turquoise eyes huge in her blank, white face.

"Kyla!" He ran to her on legs that felt numb, but she stood rigid and paralyzed, with the gun still pointed at Hardesty. "Honey, put the gun down," he said, but he didn't touch her.

"Is he dead?" she asked. Her voice sounded flat and emotionless.

"Yeah, he's dead." He put his hands on her stiff arms to lower the revolver. "Kyla, come on, give me the gun."

She gazed at him uncomprehendingly, then finally allowed him to pry the weapon out of her hands. "He would have killed you," she said and looked from Jace to Hardesty's lifeless form, and back again. Twilight began to come on but it was easy to see her chalky pallor in sharp contrast with her hair. "He was going to kill you. It all happened so fast. I had to shoot him!"

And it was one hell of a shot, Jace thought grimly. "I know you had to, Kyla. You did exactly what I would have done in your place. And you saved my life." But now she would have to live with the deed, and it might not be easy.

She began to tremble then, with shivers so violent she could no longer stand. She fell against him. Dropping his useless rifle, he swept her up into his arms and carried her to the front porch, away from the grisly scene. They huddled there, clinging fiercely to each other for several moments; Jace wasn't sure how long. The silence was broken only by Kyla's gasping sobs. She gripped his coat in her clenched fists and he rocked her, even as he took comfort from her warmth.

Finally Kyla lifted her head and gazed into Jace's blue eyes. He looked haggard and bloodless, so different from earlier that afternoon. She didn't bother to stem the tears streaming down her own face, and her words came out in jerky snips. "I-I'm not sorry that he's dead. And I'm so glad that you're alive. All those nights I dreamed of pointing a gun at Tom Hardesty and pulling the trigger. I pictured that nasty smirk wiped off his face forever. But it's not—it isn't the way I thought it would be. I don't . . ." She let the sentence trail away unfinished, not sure how to phrase what she meant. She was confused, disappointed.

"You don't feel satisfaction," he said, his voice low and reflective. "Not like you expected."

She shook her head and dragged her sleeve over her cheeks.

He took her icy hands in his and pressed them to his lips. Then, as if searching for the right words, he glanced at the first stars of the evening where they hovered above the distant hills. "I tried to tell you about this early on but the truth is, I guess no one can understand it until they've been through it. Anytime you take another person's life, no matter what the reason, you lose a little of your own life, too, a little of yourself. Some people like Hardesty are so empty and dark-hearted to begin with, they don't notice what killing does to them. And even if they knew, they wouldn't care. But the rest of us"—he shrugged—"we have trouble sleeping afterward. It's like I said before. Nothing will be different just because Hardesty is dead. You still have to live your life, and shooting him didn't bring back Hank, or change what he did to you."

She shuddered again. "I'll have to bury him, I suppose."

He kissed her knuckles again, and then took her into his arms. "No, we'll put him on his horse and take him to the undertaker's. There's no point in hiding out any longer. If Luke Jory didn't know I was in town before, he will now. His right-hand man is dead."

Yes, and she was responsible. She could not shake the hollow feeling. "At least I stopped Hardesty from killing *you*."

"You did, honey, and I'm not sorry about that. That makes us even now."

Even. And over with. A torrent of emotions sluiced through Kyla, including shame. Not for what she had done, because in that, she'd had no choice. But she had believed Jace to be a cold-blooded killer, and in fact, had sought him out because of that. She had supposed it was easy for him, and that issues of conscience or morality never came up to haunt him.

Searching his handsome face, she gripped his lapels again and desperately hoped that he would listen. "Jace, please give—give this up. Give up bounty hunting and stay in Blakely. You're not a killer, and you have nothing left to prove. No one would dream of questioning your courage."

He gave her a wobbly smile and shook his head. "We talked about this before, Kyla. I can't quit now. I'm not trying to prove anything, but it's way too late. I don't fit in anywhere."

She released his coat and sat back. "It's never too late. Not if you're still alive. Not if someone loves you the way I do!"

His blue eyes fixed on her, and it seemed that suddenly and briefly he looked five years younger. She felt a dull flush creep into her own cheeks. God, she hadn't meant to blurt it out like that. After everything they had been through and had done together, after all the sides she had revealed to him, she shouldn't feel self-conscious about baring her heart. But she did—it was the most risky thing she had done yet. And oddly, the most freeing.

Though he had been a good man, when she could not love Hank, she'd worried that, like Jace, her life had robbed her of the ability to give and feel love. Thank God, neither her disapproving father, nor Tom Hardesty, alive or dead, had done that to her.

"*I* love you, Jace," she repeated, this time more emphatically. "Stay in Blakely."

He held up his hand. "Kyla, I don't want you to love—"

"Or take me with you," she said, hurrying on before he could stop her, terrified of his rejection. "We could go some place and start a new life where nobody knows you."

He shook his head and waved his hand in the general direction of the range. "You're happy here. This is handsome land . . . really handsome." His expression turned pensive as he scanned the quiet, rolling plains. "This is where you belong. Since I've promised to help you with the vigilantes, I'll do it, but then I'll be leaving. You and I had a deal and it's finished."

"A deal," she repeated dully, feeling a wave of anger and pain roll over her. That was all it had ever been to him, she supposed, all he would let it be. "Yes, we had a business deal. Of course, you'll want to be paid."

He gripped her upper arms. "Kyla, that's not what I meant."

"I know what you meant," she replied, trying to keep her tears in check. She batted away his hands and stood up on legs that felt like lead. Trudging to a back corner of the porch, she yanked up two loose boards and peered down to the darkness beneath. Good, there it was—Hardesty hadn't found it. She detected the vague shadow of her strongbox and dropping to a crouch, she closed her hands around it to bring it up. It was small but heavy, and she struggled with it.

"Let me give you a hand." She heard Jace's quiet

voice, felt his boot steps vibrate through the boards under his feet.

"I don't need your help, I can do it," she snapped from behind gritted teeth, and turned her back to him. "I learned to do for myself long before I met you."

Jace backed up as she hauled the box to the porch floor. Her cold anger was as sharp as a newly stropped razor, and it sliced through him, a clean, swift stroke. He was almost surprised to see the box under the floorboards. So she really did have money. She had talked about it often enough, but he'd doubted its existence from the outset. Besides, he had long ago decided against accepting any pay from her. He gazed down at the top of her russet head and had to stop himself from caressing her hair.

She lifted the lid on the strongbox and withdrew a sack of coins, testing its weight in her hand. She poured the gold out into her hand, counted it, and then replaced it in the pouch. "Two hundred and fifty dollars for Hardesty. What about the clothes? How much did you spend?"

Her face was set and hard—he'd seen eyes as cold staring at him above a revolver in a shoot-out. He knew they masked the hurt he had caused her. How had things come to this point between them? He wished he could tell her that he longed to stay here more than anything he had ever wanted in his life. But that would give a voice to the dream he had envisioned so many times. As long as he kept it as a wistful image tucked in the back of his heart, it wouldn't hurt so much when the time came to ride away. At least he hoped it wouldn't.

"I don't remember," he said truthfully. He had never intended that she pay him back. The things he'd bought her had been gifts.

She glared up at him and shook her head. Crouching there, she looked ready to spring at him like a frightened, wounded cat on the defensive. "Then I'll pay you what I think they were worth." She began ticking off items on her fingers. "A pair of jeans, a shirt, two coats"—her voice trembled and she cleared her throat—"a-a dress and—and the other things." Briefly, she lifted her hand and pressed it against her shirt where he knew the locket lay beneath. She cleared her throat again. "I figure another thirty dollars."

He dropped to one knee next to her. "Goddamn it, Kyla, I don't want your mon—" She threw the sack of heavy coins at him and it hit him square in the chest before tumbling to the porch floor.

She gave him a cold smile. "Jace, it's just like I said—every man has his price. There's three hundred dollars in that pouch. Take it."

Offended, he picked up the pouch and put it back in her hand. "I didn't agree to help you because of money. It was never about money between you and me!"

"Just what was it between us, then?" she demanded. He saw a glint behind her eyes, as if she were waiting for a specific answer.

Jace shifted from one foot to the other, unable to give it to her. "If I were just interested in the money, I would have asked for *five* hundred dollars or a thousand."

"It doesn't matter anymore, though, does it?" she said, and pushed the coins toward him. "Take it or not. It's up to you." She stood then with the box in her arms, and gazed down at him with a long turquoise look that seared his heart. Her chin quivered slightly, and her voice was not much more than an anguished whisper. "Good-bye, Jace." She turned to open the front door.

"What do you mean, good-bye? Where are you going?" he asked, lurching up to grab her elbow.

She pulled away from him. "That's plain enough, I think," she said, sounding so weary he wished he could take her into his arms again. But he felt as if sometime in the last few minutes he'd lost that right. "I'm home now."

He stared at her. "You can't stay here alone. This isn't over yet, you know."

"It is for me. I'm tired of fighting, of sleeping in the open, or in barns and cabins."

"Kyla—"

"I hope you find hap—good-bye, Jace," she said. Turning, she fled into the house and slammed the door behind her.

He stood there for a moment, his throat tight and eyes stinging. Gazing at the door, suddenly he felt twelve years old again, friendless, scared, and crying, hiding under a soap crate on a hot July afternoon. He took a deep breath. He had never expected to feel like that again.

But he did now.

Chapter Sixteen

"I want a bath, and a steak dinner in my room in twenty minutes."

The hotel clerk eyed Jace askance until he spun the register around to read the name his demanding guest had written there. The bony little man practically saluted him. "Yes*sir*, Mr. Rankin. The bath is at the end of the hall upstairs, and I'll send someone to order your steak over at Connor's. They have the best food in—"

"Twenty minutes," Jace reiterated and plucked his room key from the counter. Then he turned and trudged up the stairs to the second floor.

"Yes*sir*, Mr. Rank—"

Jesus Christ, Jace thought, disgusted with all the toadying his reputation had earned him. More and more often these days, he wished for anonymity. He wondered what it would be like to walk through a town without being called out by an unknown enemy, or having men pull their wives and children aside when they saw him on the street, or fawned over by some cringing bootlicker.

After a boy brought up buckets of water, Jace sank into the wooden tub in a closet at the end of the hall. The hot water closed over him, and he scrubbed with a bar of white soap and a brush. He wished he could wash off everything that had happened to him today.

He had taken Tom Hardesty's body to the undertaker, and had instructed the man to personally deliver the bill to Luke Jory. That would definitely bring matters to a head. Jory wouldn't be able to ignore such an insulting challenge, and Jace had no idea when or where the response might come.

His revolver lay on a stool within easy reach. The most vulnerable moments of a man's life were when he took a bath, sat in the outhouse, or made love.

Making love. Even now, despite everything that had happened, Jace had only to envision Kyla, beautiful, delicate, finely spun steel, and his body responded instantly. He lay back and closed his eyes. His mind took him on a journey over her ripe smoothness, stopping briefly at her breasts, then moved along to her hips and her legs, and the slick moist heat that lay between them.

Jace groaned and sat up impatiently, splashing water over the edge of the tub. He loved her, he wanted her, but fate had decreed that he could not have her. A deep sigh escaped him, and he felt as if a stone sat on his chest.

His regrets were mounting up.

Kyla slept very little that night. She had never minded her own company, but she felt miserably

alone at the ranch house. She was almost sorry she
had insisted upon staying here.

Although no ghost rose to haunt her conscience,
Tom Hardesty seemed to have left his mark on everything in her house. Feeling as if there were no clean
place to lie down, at first she tried sleeping on the
floor in the parlor. But when that didn't work, she
gave up and began cleaning.

Late into the night she scrubbed and mopped and
washed. The man had lived like a pig, and the kitchen
alone took her hours to finish.

But the work didn't take her mind off Jace. All the
while, her heart ached for him, as much as her anger at
him simmered. Ultimately, she blamed herself for ever
falling in love with him. He was right, she told herself—what kind of life could she have with him? Who
would want a man who was smart and capable, and
so handsome that women on the street cast subtle,
sidelong glances at him? Why should she yearn for a
man who summoned such intense pleasure from her
body that he could make her forget she had ever felt
otherwise? And lastly, what woman would desire a
man whose heart was an empty jar, just waiting to be
filled with love, if only he would allow it? But he
wouldn't allow it and she had to decide how to go on
with her life.

She continued working through the night, her back
and hands aching with the task.

Scrubbing Tom Hardesty out of her house.

Hoping to scrub Jace Rankin out of her heart.

Finally, just before sunup, with only a crescent
moon and blue stars for company, Kyla stood in the

yard, soaking the heap of Hardesty's belongings with kerosene. Lighting a match, she tossed it onto the pile and watched with grim satisfaction as flames engulfed every trace the man had left behind.

Jace would not be so easily banished.

"Mr. Jory?" Harvey Sewell approached Luke Jory's table in the Pine Cone Saloon.

"Harvey," Jory returned over the top of his paper. It gave him the creeps to have an undertaker around. He continued to sip his coffee and hoped that the man would go away.

Jory did not make a habit of frequenting saloons before noon, but he was looking for Tom Hardesty, and he knew the man was inclined to drop by here as soon as the doors opened. Tom's drinking and immoderate habits were becoming a serious liability to the Vigilance Union. He had his value, just as a vicious, snapping dog could discourage trespassers. And as with a wild dog allowed to run loose, accidents were bound to occur. The rape of that Cathcart girl was a good example. Tom had handled the emergency with the bounty hunter and the Bailey woman well enough, but he'd created the problem to begin with, and Jory believed it might be time to rein Tom in.

"Mr. Jory, um, Mr. Rankin said that you would probably like to know about this."

Jory's head came up sharply, and he lowered the newspaper, crumpling it beneath his hands. "Jace Rankin?"

Harvey held out a document. "Yes."

All conversation in the saloon ceased.

Jory snapped the paper out of Harvey's damp grip.
It was a bill for five dollars. "What is this, Sewell?"

Harvey laced his hands in a show of deferential
respect for the dead. "Well, Tom Hardesty is deceased,
Mr. Jory. Shot in the forehead. Jace Rankin brought
him in last night." He brightened then. "But don't you
worry—he'll look all right for the funeral."

Jory felt the blood leave his face. Rankin in Blakely.
He was not supposed to have gotten this far. Hardesty
had assured him that everything was under control,
and now he was laid out in Harvey Sewell's back
room. He shoved his chair away from the table and
stood.

"What time would you like to begin Mr. Hardesty's
funeral?" Harvey inquired.

"Goddamn it, man!" Jory whirled on the cringing
undertaker, fury boiling in him. "I don't give a damn
what you do with Hardesty, or what time you do it!"

Clenching his fists, Jory stormed through the
swinging doors. He jerked his horse's reins from the
hitching post, and climbing into the saddle, he
wheeled the animal about.

By God, he would not let this pass unanswered.
One way or another, Rankin would answer for this.

Shortly after sundown that night, Jace sat on a hay
bale in Jim Porter's barn. He had called for a meeting
with some of the Midnighters to let them know about
Hardesty. He didn't tell them that Kyla had shot him.
If she wanted them to know, he figured it was her
business.

"How many men does Jory have?"

"About twenny-five or thirty, I guess," Ivan Kluss offered glumly. "And they'll be on us like ants on a sugar loaf now that Hardesty is dead."

"And how many Midnighters are there?"

"About the same," Jim Porter said, absently twirling a straw between his fingers. "Maybe a few less."

This wasn't good news, Jace thought. Most of these men were farmers and ranchers, not hired killers with nothing better to do all day than target practice.

"We need to raise more men, even ten or fifteen more. Can we do that?"

"Well, I dunno," Jim said. "Everyone's so scared of the Vigilance Union it's been hard to get most of 'em to help out. They're afraid of rilin' up Luke Jory."

A sense of futility washed over Jace. Damn, why had he let himself get talked into this? If these people wouldn't even help themselves—In order to succeed, he had to think of a way to rouse these people, to make them see beyond their fear to an ultimate goal. They were counting on him to make everything right, as if he could fell ten men with each bullet he fired and they need do nothing. Yet for all that they seemed to expect of him, he sensed their lack of trust.

He sighed with mounting impatience. "If you people want to get rid of Jory and his thieves, you're going to have to—"

Just then a loud banging sounded on the barn door. Although it was in code, two short and two long, it reverberated through the cavernous building, and brought everyone to their feet and their weapons.

Jim opened the door and on the other side, Ivan Kluss's young son panted, "Everyone ... come quick . . . the—the Springer place . . . is on fire! I saw the flames . . . from our kitchen window!"

Jace felt as if his heart had stopped. He took two deep breaths but didn't seem to be getting any air. "God . . . Kyla." He turned to them. "Kyla is out there by herself!" He charged through the group and ran for his horse, fear gripping his chest with a cruel fist. The crescent moon provided little light, but a lurid glow lit the southern sky and he cut across Porter's field and rode toward it.

As he spurred his horse, he cursed himself from there to Sunday and back. He never should have walked away from her and left her at that ranch alone. She was stubborn and willful, but he should have gone back after he delivered Hardesty and stayed with her, whether she wanted him there or not. Now, Jory and the vigilantes could have stolen her again or set fire to the house, too.

The smell of smoke drifted to him on the breeze. Pushing his horse faster than he should in the darkness, he splashed through a creek, hoping that the animal wouldn't step in a chuckhole and snap a leg. Behind him, he became aware of hooves thundering after him, and he turned to see some of the Midnighters drawing close.

By the time they had galloped into Kyla's bright yard, the barn was a yellow-white skeleton, engulfed in flames that seemed to brush the belly of heaven. Waves of heat carried on the wind, and cinders floated on the hot drafts. There was nothing that anyone could do but watch the fire consume the building. At least the ranch house had been spared.

Jace circled the house twice looking for Kyla before dismounting to search inside. He bounded up the front steps and grasped the knob to turn it. "Kyla!" he called, walking through the parlor. Fear licked through him like the fire outside. No lamp was lit, but the barn provided plenty of illumination.

Just when he began to fear the worst, that she had been taken, he heard her voice, thin and scared, coming from a darkened corner of the kitchen.

"Jace?"

"I'm here, honey," he said and groped for a match inside his pocket. When he lit it, he found her huddled beside the stove, white and scared, with her revolver in her lap. Their eyes connected, and with a cry she sprang from the corner into his arms. She felt so small and fragile, especially now that she dressed in women's clothes.

"Oh, Jace—they came just after sunset. I saw them," she said, her voice muffled against his neck. "It was Jory and some of his men. I was so scared they'd take me again, I hid by the stove." He heard the disgust in her words, as if she had failed somehow. God, she had more courage than the twenty grown men who met in Jim Porter's barn.

"Was there any shooting?" he asked.

She shook her head. "But I was afraid they would fire the house, too. I don't know if Jory ever saw me, but he yelled up this way, saying that the Vigilance Union would destroy the Midnighters. And that no one, not even Jace Rankin, could do anything about it."

"Yeah, well, we'll see about that. But for now, we're going to the hotel. We can't stay here."

Grateful for his strength and protection, Kyla didn't argue. It had been foolish, she realized now, to stay out here alone. She had assumed that her only threat had been Hardesty and that Luke Jory would have no interest in her.

He gave her a moment to get some clothes together. Then with an escort of Jace and the Midnighters, Kyla set out for town.

Among the men who rode with them through the dark night, she detected a new energy, an anger that had not been there before.

"Damnation, if those bastards are goin' to start burnin' houses and barns, we won't have nothin' left!"

"It's time they was stopped."

"Don't you worry, Kyla," Jim Porter assured her. "When this is over, we'll build you a new barn." To Jace he added, "This is somethin' that affects everyone—I'm thinkin' you won't have much trouble getting people to help you now. Barn burnin' is as bad as horse theft in these parts."

Kyla was also assured that some of the boys from the neighboring ranches would see to her cattle until this trouble was behind them.

The streets were quiet when they reached town, but there was a vague feeling hanging over Blakely, as if everyone held a collective breath, waiting to see what might happen next.

Staring down the disapproving glare from the desk clerk, Jace took Kyla directly upstairs to his room. Though more concealing, her soft shirt and blouse did not offer as much camouflage as had the jeans and work shirt he had expected her to wear.

"I'm not going to put you in another room and then spend my time worrying about someone breaking in," he said, opening the door. "Your safety is a hell of a lot more important than a desk clerk's opinion of your reputation."

Strange that the bed loomed so large in here, she thought, and glanced away from it. She had spent weeks alone with him, in circumstances even more intimate than this, so her own shyness baffled her. As if reading her thoughts, his eyes connected with hers, deepening to blue smoke before he broke the contact.

"It's late, so you, um, you take the bed and I'll just, uh, bunk here," he said, gesturing at a settee against the wall.

It was on the tip of her tongue to tell him he should sleep here on the bed next to her, as he had in Misfortune. But that would probably be a mistake, given the sudden awkward desire that had vibrated between them. He waited in the hallway while she stripped down to her camisole and drawers, and climbed beneath the covers. When he came back in, she had already turned down the lamp. Then she lay stiffly in the darkness, listening as he searched for a comfortable place on the settee.

Kyla had not expected to see Jace again. She knew she was safe from harm now. But her heart was once more in critical danger.

When Kyla awoke the next morning, Jace was already gone. She found a heavily laden breakfast tray and a note from him telling her that he might be gone for hours, but to admit no one except him. She would find her revolver on the bureau, cleaned, oiled, and loaded. And under no circumstances was she to leave this room.

She went to the window and looked at the street below. Saturdays were always busy in Blakely, particularly around harvest time. But on this Saturday morning the streets were empty. Still, a sense of expectation lingered, just as it had the night before. Some of the shades on the shop windows were pulled, although the clock in the bank's window read nine-forty. Even the Pine Cone Saloon was closed. At least it wasn't serving the general public, although she saw members of the Vigilance Union straggle into the saloon and not come out again.

She gripped the windowsill. Something was coming—it was as vague yet as tangible as an approaching thunderstorm.

As the hours wore on and Jace did not return, Kyla felt her nerves being stretched to their limit. Was he safe? What was happening? She knew she could not defy his instructions and leave this room, but she began pacing.

At dusk, she was dozing on the settee by the open window when the sound of horses' hooves and the jingle of bit and bridle stirred her from her nap. She sat up straight and looked out the window, and her jaw dropped.

Below in the street she saw scores of mounted riders approaching. They rode calmly but fully armed down the main street of the dusty little cow town. Each man carried a lighted pine knot torch and the street was lit as bright as day.

"What in the world . . ." Kyla began, and then she saw him. There was Jace Rankin at the head of the procession of what looked to be about eighty men. Eighty Midnighters! She recognized original members, but also saw many men who had previously hung back out of fear of reprisal. With her throat as dry as chalk and her heart pounding in her chest, she craned her neck to see. The riders halted across the street and amassed in the semicircle outside the Pine Cone Saloon.

"Jory, you murdering barn burner!" Jace's voice ricocheted off the buildings like rolling thunder. "Bring out your cattle rustlers and fight! The Midnighters are calling you out!"

A breathless thrill rippled through Kyla—she had never been so proud of anyone as she was of Jace at that moment. Even though she watched from the second floor, he sat his horse as if he were ten feet tall. And with his strong leadership, the others had finally been galvanized into taking action.

No sound came from the saloon, although she saw a window shade move aside, as if the coward within were peeking at his conquerors.

"Come out, Jory!" Jace called again, and now the rest began to take up the chant. "Jory! Jory! Jory!"

Still no one emerged from the Pine Cone Saloon. After an hour, Kyla watched with a knot in her throat as Jace climbed down from his horse and mounted the steps in front of the saloon. He faced the men he had brought here, his eyes gleaming like fire and ice.

"See what cowards the vigilantes are?" He gestured at the closed doors behind him. "Are you men ready to take back your town from these egg-sucking weasels, and make it a decent place to live again?"

A cheer rolled through them, heartfelt and plainspoken.

He nodded and turned toward the saloon. "The Vigilance Union is dead!"

Then from the back, someone yelled, "They're gettin' away! They snuck out the back of the Pine Cone!" A few of the group broke ranks to chase after them.

"Let 'em go!" Jim Porter called, standing in his stirrup. "Let 'em go! There's no place in this county where those men will be able to show their faces again. Blakely will never let them come back."

Kyla's eyes welled up with tears as she watched from the window. The tyranny that had gripped this town for so long had at last been defeated.

And they had a bounty hunter with a killer's reputation to thank for it.

It was decided that Kyla would linger awhile at Jim Porter's place until she could hire hands to return to her ranch with her. Although Jory and many of his men were seen riding out of town between sunrise and morning, there was no point in putting herself in danger again.

At the hotel the next morning, Jace took Kyla's hand in his. "Well, I guess this is good-bye," he said.

The sun cast a copper halo on the top of her hair. It had grown longer, he realized. He wished he could be around to see how it looked when it reached the length she yearned for.

She nodded but said nothing more about him staying in Blakely. Secretly he supposed he was disappointed, but he had asked for it. How many times did he think he could push her away and tell her no before she finally gave up? It made their good-bye all the more poignant as he gazed into her turquoise eyes.

She nodded. "I know. You did a wonderful thing for this town, Jace," she said. Her voice trembled but she remained dry-eyed.

"If you ever need anything—" He let the sentence hang unfinished. The truth was even if she needed something, with the life he lived she would have no way to reach him. Every feeling that Lyle Upton had silenced in those early years chose this moment to come to life, and the pain of leaving her was as fierce as a raw nerve. The weight of his regrets was growing heavier by the moment.

He took her into his arms and gave her a long, soft kiss, one that expressed more love than any words he could tell her. One that he would remember on those endless nights when he had only the sound of rain and his own heartbeat for company.

As she pressed her lips to his, Kyla knew she could not be mad at Jace—he had done everything he had promised to do and more. If he could not love her, well, there was nothing she could do about that. She couldn't force him to it. Her throat grew tight with longing.

Stepping away from her, he pulled his horse's reins from the hitching post and climbed into his saddle. He gave her one long, final look, his ice blue eyes riveted on her face, then pulled the horse around and kicked him into a trot.

"Good-bye, Jace," she choked.

Chapter Seventeen

Jace trotted slowly down Blakely's main street, steadfastly resisting the urge to look back over his shoulder. Kyla might be back there watching him from the sidewalk, and he didn't want to know. He already felt sick and empty inside. So he kept his gaze pointed forward and away from the thin November sun that warmed his back.

He passed the shops and restaurant, the church and homes. It was a pretty little town, a nice place that would be better now that Luke Jory and his thieves had been dealt with. It might even be a good place to settle down, if a man was so inclined. And if he was able to follow his inclinations.

But Jace was hoping to make it to California before hard winter set in. He wondered just how far away it was. No matter, he supposed. There was nothing to hold him here any longer. He'd done the job he had taken on back in Silver City when a young boy with one hell of a sassy attitude and a lot of grit had come looking for him.

He shifted in his saddle and gazed at the hills beyond town. It all seemed like a lifetime ago, the things he and Kyla had lived through. Now he could look back and almost chuckle over Mildred DeGroot walking in while he kissed Kyla and believing that he was kissing "the boy." But he still shuddered when he thought of sitting next to Kyla while she lay delirious with fever, more dead than alive from Hobie McIntyre's gunshot wound. And when he remembered her in a yellow gown with ribbons in her hair, he had to force himself to keep the horse aimed west.

But perhaps by coming here he had atoned for the Bluebird Saloon. Maybe the woman and her little girl were watching him from some peaceful place where no harm could come to them, and they approved of what he had done for Kyla and Blakely. He hoped so. He'd asked for their forgiveness often enough. Perhaps he had it now.

"Hey, Rankin."

Oh God, no, he thought. He knew the tone of that phrase. Instantly, a dozen noonday scenes flashed through his memory; a dozen hotheaded men with axes to grind or coup to count had approached him with those very words.

"Mr. Rankin, wait."

But when Jace looked up, he recognized not only the speaker on the sidewalk, but the group of men he was with. Most of them he had met yesterday. He nudged his horse to their side of the street.

"Something I can do for you?" he asked, curious but on guard.

"There might be something we can do for each other."

"Yeah?"

"We have a proposition to discuss with you, if you're interested."

Sure, why not, he thought. That was the mixed blessing of having nowhere to go and nothing to do. He had all the time in the world.

Kyla went back to Jim Porter's place that afternoon with a heart as heavy as lead. Although she had believed she could take it, watching Jace ride away for the last time was the hardest thing she had done since they had set out together.

Now dressed as Kyle again, she dragged around Jim's muddy corral, currying the horses for lack of anything else to do. Although she knew better, her mind insisted upon reviewing what she might have said or done differently to make Jace want to stay in Blakely.

But the bald fact of the matter was that he was his own man, and he had done exactly as he had wanted. If only she didn't feel so bereft. She had her ranch back, and Hardesty—well, maybe she wouldn't get over being the one who had ended his life. Jace had been right—there was no joy in revenge. But she wasn't sorry that he couldn't torment her any longer. The Vigilance Union had been taken care of; everything had turned out better than she could have hoped when she first went looking for Jace back in September.

For a moment she pressed her hand flat against her locket. The hardest thing of all, she fretted, would be forgetting his strong, attractive features. The clean, sculpted lines of his face, the pattern of his beard, the mouth that was neither thin nor full, but in a kiss was infinitely soothing and arousing, those piercing eyes that saw down to her soul. And he wore his handsomeness in complete ignorance—in her limited experience she had found that good-looking men tended to be a bit vain. Jace was anything but.

She rested her head against a fence rail for a moment. How would she forget? In what part of her heart and mind did Jace dwell so that she might erase him? But even as she wished for it, she clung to the image she carried, hoping that it would never fade. The love of a lifetime should not be so easily banished.

She lifted her head then, as if she had heard someone call her name. There was no one around—Jim was in town and his cowboys were off working on the other side of the creek. Scanning the open rangeland, she saw no other person. Maybe the events of the last few days had made her a little jumpy. It might even have been the wind sighing through the cottonwoods that grew along the creek bottom. She shrugged and went back to her task.

"I see you are well now, Winter Moon."

Kyla jumped and spun around. She saw Many Braids on the other side of the corral fence. He seemed to have materialized out of thin air—no one had been anywhere near the ranch house and corral when she had looked just a moment earlier.

The medicine man appeared exactly as she remembered: tall and straight as a yew, ageless, and dignified in his hodgepodge of buckskin pants and army coat.

She had thought of him from time to time since her fever dream of him in Misfortune.

"Many Braids!" She hurried to the fence to talk to him. "Yes, I'm well now. My arm still aches but Jace said it will improve with time."

He nodded and considered her with his black, unwavering eyes. "When last I saw you, you stood with one foot in each world, this one and the next. I am pleased to see that you chose to remain with this world."

Hearing his words, a rash of goose bumps rose all over Kyla. In her dream he had told her the very same thing, that she had a foot in each world. "Y-you mean when you came to our fire that night?"

"Jace Rankin was very worried about you," he said, not really answering her question. "You are the one who fills the empty place he has borne in his weary heart. He learned to trust you more than he did his rifle."

Kyla shifted. It was disconcerting to hear her feelings and Jace's so frankly discussed by a man she had met only once. How he knew these things, she couldn't imagine. But Jace had been right. Many Braids was not an ordinary man. "Well, I—he doesn't—"

"Now Jace Rankin must choose which world *he* will stand in. He must decide if he will stand with you, Winter Moon, or remain forever alone in his."

"Many Braids," she began, her voice low with regret, "he has already decided. He and I said good-bye this morning."

"And your heart is heavy. But things are not as they seemed then."

She put both hands on the fence rail and leaned forward eagerly. "Have you seen him? Talked to him?"

"No, but Jace Rankin is a good man. He will make the right decision." He took a step backward then and looked at the sky. "The white owl will be flying soon. It is time for me to return to the People for the winter."

"Wait, Many Braids—will I see you again?"

He gave her an inscrutable smile. "I have found you three times now, Winter Moon. I will find you again." Then he turned and strode across the field on his long legs that carried him out of her sight. She didn't see or hear a horse; he must have walked. But to where? From where?

I have found you three times. . . .

Three times? She had talked with him only twice, the night she met him, and now. Unless—Jace had sworn Many Braids never came to Misfortune, but she had seen him . . . heard him. . . .

Kyla shook her head. It was a puzzle that only the medicine man could clear up, but he just made it more mysterious. And Jace—did he really care for her, as Many Braids hinted?

She sat on the bottom fence rail and idly picked up the curry comb. It wouldn't matter, even if he did. He was on his way to California, or somewhere else. For several moments she lingered there, her eyes closed against the pale afternoon sun. She didn't realize she had dozed until a shadow fell between her and the warm sun. Perhaps Many Braids had returned—

"Kyla?"

Her eyes snapped open, and she found Jace standing before her, looking handsome and very pleased, as if some good fortune had befallen him.

"Jace—I didn't expect to see you again."

He shrugged a shoulder. "I didn't know I would be staying in Blakely."

Her eyes grew wider. "Staying? You mean for a few days? For a week?"

He smiled at her and pulled back the lapel of his duster to show her the sheriff's badge pinned to his vest. "No, it looks more permanent than that."

Kyla's thoughts tumbled over each other in the face of this stunning news. "What happened?"

He dropped to a crouch in front of her. "Well, I was on my way out of town and doing my damnedest not to turn and look over my shoulder for you. Jim Porter and the group of men called to me from the street corner and invited me to a meeting at the Pine Cone. They were so pleased with the way things worked out yesterday with the Vigilance Committee, they asked if I thought I'd like a lawman's job, full time."

Kyla raised her brows. "When I suggested that, you weren't very interested in the idea."

He took her hand between his own. "I know this is hard for you to understand, but . . ." He paused, as if searching for the right words. "Remember when you told me how much you envied my being feared on sight?"

She nodded.

"Well, that's all I've known for years. I admit it was my own doing, but I couldn't go anywhere and be accepted for who I was. I dragged that goddamned reputation around with me like a mangy venison haunch. I just didn't fit in anywhere because people tend to not like a man they fear. But now, this town has gotten to know me, at least well enough to offer me this job. I finally can stop drifting."

Kyla put on a face of indifference and dropped her gaze to the curry comb in her lap. "So what does this mean to me?"

Jace put his finger under her chin and lifted her face to his. "It means that I'm in Blakely to stay."

She nodded. "I hope you enjoy the town. It's a nice place to live."

He frowned slightly. "Damn it, Kyla—"

"What do you want me to say, Jace?" she asked.

"Nothing. I mean I want to tell you that I—well—"

Her heart began beating faster. "Yes? Tell me what?"

He held her with his gaze. "I know I said that I couldn't love anyone, that it was too late for me to make a new start, but—I was wrong. You gave me back my heart, honey." He peered into her face, his expression naked and open. "I lived for years with a dead place inside me. Except I found out it wasn't really dead, but just empty. You showed me that. The thing is, the only person who can fill that emptiness is you. I *need* to love you, as much as I need you to love me."

"Jace," she whispered, because that was all her tight throat would let her do. "I need to love you, too."

He gave her a crooked smile and pressed kisses to her knuckles. "So will you marry the first sheriff of Blakely?"

She laughed, so happy she didn't know if her heart could contain her joy. "Yes, I will! What's your first order of business?"

He grinned at her. "To hire a deputy so that we can have a honeymoon." He held open his arms to her and she fell into them, thanking God and Many Braids' spirits for letting Jace find his heart in her.

"Maybe I should make Kyle Springer a deputy," he teased.

"Nope, I don't think Kyle will be around anymore. There's just me."

He smiled. "Mmm, with a head full of long red hair, and a yellow dress to wear to dinner."

"That's right," she said, "you promised to buy me another dress to replace the one that got lost in the mountains."

"Kyla, for the chance to see that smile for the rest of my life, I'll buy you all the dresses you want." He leaned in and kissed her, that wonderful soft, healing kiss of his.

"No," she said and laid her palm against his cheek. "I just want you."

He gazed at her with his whole heart in his eyes. "It's a deal, Kyla. It's a deal."

WE NEED YOUR HELP
To continue to bring you quality romance
that meets your personal expectations,
we at TOPAZ books want to hear from you.
Help us by filling out this questionnaire, and in exchange
we will give you a **free gift** as a token of our gratitude.

- Is this the first TOPAZ book you've purchased? (circle one)

    YES   NO

    The title and author of this book is: _____

- If this was not the first TOPAZ book you've purchased, how many have you bought in the past year?

    a: 0 - 5   b: 6 - 10   c: more than 10   d: more than 20

- How many romances in total did you buy in the past year?

    a: 0 - 5   b: 6 - 10   c: more than 10   d: more than 20 ____

- How would you rate your overall satisfaction with this book?

    a: Excellent   b: Good   c: Fair   d: Poor

- What was the main reason you bought this book?

    a: It is a TOPAZ novel, and I know that TOPAZ stands
       for quality romance fiction
    b: I liked the cover
    c: The story-line intrigued me
    d: I love this author
    e: I really liked the setting
    f: I love the cover models
    g: Other: _____

- Where did you buy this TOPAZ novel?

    a: Bookstore   b: Airport   c: Warehouse Club
    d: Department Store   e: Supermarket   f: Drugstore
    g: Other: _____

- Did you pay the full cover price for this TOPAZ novel? (circle one)

    YES   NO

    If you did not, what price did you pay? _____

- Who are your favorite TOPAZ authors? (Please list)

- How did you first hear about TOPAZ books?

    a: I saw the books in a bookstore
    b: I saw the TOPAZ Man on TV or at a signing
    c: A friend told me about TOPAZ
    d: I saw an advertisement in_____magazine
    e: Other: _____

- What type of romance do you generally prefer?

    a: Historical   b: Contemporary
    c: Romantic Suspense   d: Paranormal (time travel,
       futuristic, vampires, ghosts, warlocks, etc.)
    d: Regency   e: Other: _____

- What historical settings do you prefer?

    a: England   b: Regency England   c: Scotland
    e: Ireland   f: America   g: Western Americana
    h: American Indian   i: Other: _____

- What type of story do you prefer?
  - a: Very sexy
  - b: Sweet, less explicit
  - c: Light and humorous
  - d: More emotionally intense
  - e: Dealing with darker issues
  - f: Other

- What kind of covers do you prefer?
  - a: Illustrating both hero and heroine
  - b: Hero alone
  - c: No people (art only)
  - d: Other_____

- What other genres do you like to read (circle all that apply)

  Mystery   Medical Thrillers   Science Fiction
  Suspense   Fantasy   Self-help
  Classics   General Fiction   Legal Thrillers
  Historical Fiction

- Who is your favorite author, and why?_____
  _____

- What magazines do you like to read? (circle all that apply)
  - a: *People*
  - b: *Time/Newsweek*
  - c: *Entertainment Weekly*
  - d: *Romantic Times*
  - e: *Star*
  - f: *National Enquirer*
  - g: *Cosmopolitan*
  - h: *Woman's Day*
  - i: *Ladies' Home Journal*
  - j: *Redbook*
  - k: Other:_____

- In which region of the United States do you reside?
  - a: Northeast
  - b: Midatlantic
  - c: South
  - d: Midwest
  - e: Mountain
  - f: Southwest
  - g: Pacific Coast

- What is your age group/sex?   a: Female   b: Male
  - a: under 18
  - b: 19-25
  - c: 26-30
  - d: 31-35
  - e: 36-40
  - f: 41-45
  - g: 46-50
  - h: 51-55
  - i: 56-60
  - j: Over 60

- What is your marital status?
  - a: Married
  - b: Single
  - c: No longer married

- What is your current level of education?
  - a: High school
  - b: College Degree
  - c: Graduate Degree
  - d: Other:_____

- Do you receive the TOPAZ *Romantic Liaisons* newsletter, a quarterly newsletter with the latest information on Topaz books and authors?

  YES   NO

  If not, would you like to?   YES   NO

  Fill in the address where you would like your free gift to be sent:

  Name: _____

  Address: _____

  City: _____ Zip Code: _____

  You should receive your free gift in 6 to 8 weeks.
  Please send the completed survey to:

  Penguin USA•Mass Market
  Dept. TS
  375 Hudson St.
  New York, NY 10014